Samuel Boyse, William Cooke

The New Pantheon

Or Fabulous History of the Heathen Gods, Goddesses, Heroes, etc

Samuel Boyse, William Cooke

The New Pantheon
Or Fabulous History of the Heathen Gods, Goddesses, Heroes, etc

ISBN/EAN: 9783337202224

Printed in Europe, USA, Canada, Australia, Japan

Cover: Foto ©Andreas Hilbeck / pixelio.de

More available books at **www.hansebooks.com**

The Pantheon was built by M. AGRIPPA Son in law to Augustus
Cæsar & according to y.e Signification of its name dedicated to
y.e Honour of all y.e Gods every of whose Images were plac'd in
severall Niches round y.e same The Building w.th some diminution
continues to this day only Pope BONIFACE IV reconsecrated it to
y.e worship of y.e Virgin Mary & all y.e S.ts Male & Female it is
now called y.e Church of S. Maria Rotonda

THE NEW

PANTHEON:

OR,

FABULOUS HISTORY

OF THE

HEATHEN GODS,

GODDESSES, HEROES, &c.

Explained in a Manner entirely New;

And rendered much more useful than any hitherto published.

ADORNED WITH

Figures from ancient Paintings, Medals and Gems, for the Use of those who would understand History, Poetry, Painting, Statuary, Coins, Medals, &c.

WITH

An Explanation of the Mythology of the Ancients from the Writings of Moses; the Egyptian, Grecian, Roman, and Eastern Historians, Philosophers, Poets, &c.

BY SAMUEL BOYSE, A. M.

THE SIXTH EDITION,

Revised and Corrected, with large Additions, and a Dissertation on the Theology of the Heathens.

By WILLIAM COOKE, M. A.

Rector of Oldbury and Didmarton in Gloucestershire, Vicar of Enford in Wiltshire, and Chaplain to the Right Honourable the Earl of Suffolk.

To which is subjoined,

AN APPENDIX,

Treating of their Astrology, Prodigies, Auguries, Auspices, Oracles, &c. in which the Origin of each is pointed out: And an Historical Account of the Rise of Altars, Sacred Groves, Priests and Temples.

WATERFORD:

Printed by H. and J. RAMSEY, Printers and Booksellers on the Quay.

M,DCC,LXXII.

H E N R Y
D U K E of B E A U F O R T.

May it Pleaſe your GRACE,

IT has been long objected to the modern Method of Education, that ſo great and valuable a part of Youth is ſpent amidſt the Ruins of Idolatry; whence an early Taint and Corruption (hard to be got over) both in Principles and Morals has ſometimes enſued. Indeed the Heathen Theology is ſo interwoven with the Writings of the Ancients, and makes ſo large a Part of Claſſical Learning eſpecially, as to be utterly inſeparable from it. He therefore, who ſhall effectually diveſt it of the Marvellous, leaving it rational and accountable and at the ſame Time make the Whole ſubſervient to the Cauſe of Virtue and true Religion, will be allowed to have rendered an acceptable Service to Mankind.

Such was the Attempt of the ingenious Author of this Work. It muſt be admitted that he has in great Part ſucceeded. Had he lived to reviſe it carefully, and to prepare it for another Edition, all foreign Aſſiſtance had probably been needleſs. As it is, what ſeemed wanting, or the Effect of Inadver

a

tency

tency and Error, I have endeavoured to supply and amend.

Having thus done what I could for this a-
dopted Offspring; it is time that I recom-
mend it to a better and more able Benefactor
whofe further fupport may be of ufe towards
its fettlement in the World.

Your GRACE's Name will bring it to the
public Teft; and if it fhall appear in fome
fort to anfwer the Intent, and be poffeffed of
intrinfic Worth enough to fave it, I fhall find
my great and leading Expectation anfwered
in the fame Degree; which was, that it might
be improved into fomething agreeable
and ufeful to your GRACE; an End, which
will ever principally command the Attention
of

May it pleafe your GRACE,

Your GRACE's *moft dutiful*

And devoted humble Servant,

WILLIAM COOKE.

THE

THE
PREFACE.

WE have here no Design to raise the Reputation of this Work, by depreciating the many others that have already been published on this subject; it is sufficient for us to say, that we have followed a Plan entirely new, and at the same time such an one as appeared to us much more useful, more rational, and less dry than any that has gone before it.

As all works of this kind must necessarily consist of Materials collected from other Authors, no expence, no labour has been spared the most celebrated Works on this subject have been consulted and compared with each other, and it has frequently happened that scattered hints, widely dispersed, have served to clear up the most difficult and intricate meanings, to a degree of demonstration; but amongst all the Authors to which we have had Recourse, we must here particularly acknowledge the great advantage we have received from that ingenious Gentleman the Abbe Pluche, in his History of the Heavens. But as that learned and valuable Writer seems now and then to have carried matters a little too far; the Reader will find less use made of him, than in the former E-

dition.-

dition. We have been careful to allow all
things to evidence and reason; but as little
as might be to conjecture. We have also received some useful hints from the Abbe Banier's Mythology. But it behoves us especially, to acknowledge the great service which
we have received from the Writings of the
learned Bochart, Pignorius, Casalius, Kircher, Lipsius, Montfaucon and others, who
have professed to treat of the Phænician, E-
gyptian, Greek and Roman Antiquities.

Some acquaintance with the Heathen Gods
and the ancient Fables, is a necessary Branch
of polite Learning, as without this it is impossible to obtain a competent knowledge of
the classics, impossible to form a Judgment
of Antique Medals, Statues or Paintings or e-
ven to understand the Performances of the
Moderns in these polite Arts.

Hence these Studies have been generally
esteemed necessary for the improvement of
Youth; but in works of this kind, sufficient
care has not been taken, to unfold the Origin of the Heathen Gods, which has generally been mistaken. Some imagining that they
had been Kings and Princes; others, that
they were the various parts of Nature. And
others that they were the Patriarchs and
Heroes of the Jewish Nation. But each of
these have been found equally contrary to
Truth, when applied to the Pagan Theology, tho' some of their Fables have been
embellished with many Circumstances related

ted in the Mosaic History.   In Works of this kind, no care has hitherto been taken to give the least intimation of Abundance of Circumstances necessary to be known ; and a person reads the History of the Gods without finding any thing added, that can help him to unravel the Mysteries he meets with in every Page, or to entertain the least Idea of the Religion of their Worshippers.

The Greeks were enitrely ignorant as to the Origin of their Gods, and incapable of transmitting their History to Posterity. Herodotus informs us, that the Gods of the Greeks were originally brought from Egypt and Phænicia, where they had been the Objects of religious Worship before any Colonies from these Countries settled in Greece. We ought then to search in Egypt and Phænicia for the Origin of the Gods ; for the Gods whose Worship was chiefly promoted by the Egyptians, and carried by the Phœnicians over all the Coasts of the World then known.   The first Egyptians, unacquainted with Letters, gave all the Informations to the People, all the Rules of their conduct, by erecting Figures, easily understood, and which served as Rules and Orders necessary to regulate their Behaviour, and as Advertisements to provide for their own safety.   A very few Figures diversified by what they held in their Hands, or carried on their Heads, were sufficient for this purpose.   These were ingenious Contrivances,

and

and such as were absolutely neceſſary in a Country where the leaſt miſtake in Point of Time was ſufficient to ruin all their affairs.

But theſe Egyptian Symbols, giving Way to the eaſy method of reaping Inſtruction from the uſe of Letters, which were afterwards introduced, ſoon became obſolete, and the Memory of ſome particular Virtues ſtill remaining, they were revered as the Images or Repreſentations of ſuperior and friendly Beings, who had frequently delivered them from impending Dangers, and ſoon were worſhipped as the Gods of their Fathers.— Their Hiſtories were wrote in Verſe and embelliſhed with Fictions founded on ancient Traditions. The Prieſts of different Countries increaſed the Deluſion; they had read the Moſaic Hiſtory, or at leaſt had heard that the Sons of God had converſation with the daughters of men; and from hence, influenced by Luſt or Avarice, cloaked their own Debaucheries, and ſometimes thoſe of Princes and great men under thoſe of a God, and the Poets, whenever a Princeſs failed in point of Modeſty, had recourſe to the ſame method, in order to ſhelter her Reptutationfrom vulgar Cenſure. By this means the Deities in after times were ſaid to live in various Countries, and even in far diſtant Ages. Thus there became three hundred Jupiters, an opinion derived from there being a number of places in which, in different ages, Jupiter was ſaid to have lived, reigned, and performed ſome extraordinary actions, which antient

ent Fables, the fictions of the Poets, and the artifices of Priests had rendered famous.— But notwithstanding all these Fables, Jupiter was always acknowledged by the wisest Heathens to be impeccable, immortal, the Author of life, the universal Creator, and the Fountain of Goodness.

This scheme is here carried on and explained with respect to each Heathen Deity, and added to the common Histories and Fables of the Gods and Goddesses.

In the short Dissertation on the Theology of the Antients, we have shewn the Rise of Idolatry, and its Connection with the antient Symbols. We have there exhibited the Sentiments of the Pagans with regard to the Unity of the Deity, and the Perfections they ascribe to him, from the concurrent Testimony of the Philosophers in various Ages, amongst the Egyptians, Greeks and Romans. And the whole is concluded with a short account of the Progress of Idolatry.

In the Dissertation on the Mythology of the Antients, we have endeavoured to account for the Rise of a variety of Fables from the Licence of Poetry, imbellishing the common Incidents of Life by personating inanimate Beings, introducing fictitious Characters, and supernatural Agents. We have given the History of the creation of the world, the state of innocence, the fall of man, the universal Deluge, &c. according to the Traditions of different Nations, and the Opini-

ons

ons of the Poets and moſt eminent Philoſophers, and compared them with the account given by Moſes. In ſhort, we have here given a view of their religious, as well as moral ſentiments.

To the Whole is added, by Way of Appendix, a rational Account of the various ſuperſtitious Obſervances of Aſtrology, and the Manner by which influences and Powers became aſcribed to the ſigns and planets; of Prodigies, Auguries, the Auruſpices and Oracles, of Altars, ſacred Groves and Sacrifices; of Prieſts and Temples, &c. In which the Origin of each is pointed out, and the whole interſperſed with ſuch moral Reflections, as have a Tendency to preſerve the minds of Youth from the Infection of ſuperſtitious Follies, and to give them ſuch fundamental Principles, as may be of the greateſt ſervice in helping them to form juſt Ideas of the Manners, Principles, and Conduct of the Heathen Nations.

THE LARES
PAMONA
VIRTUES & VICES
RURAL DEITIES

ORA

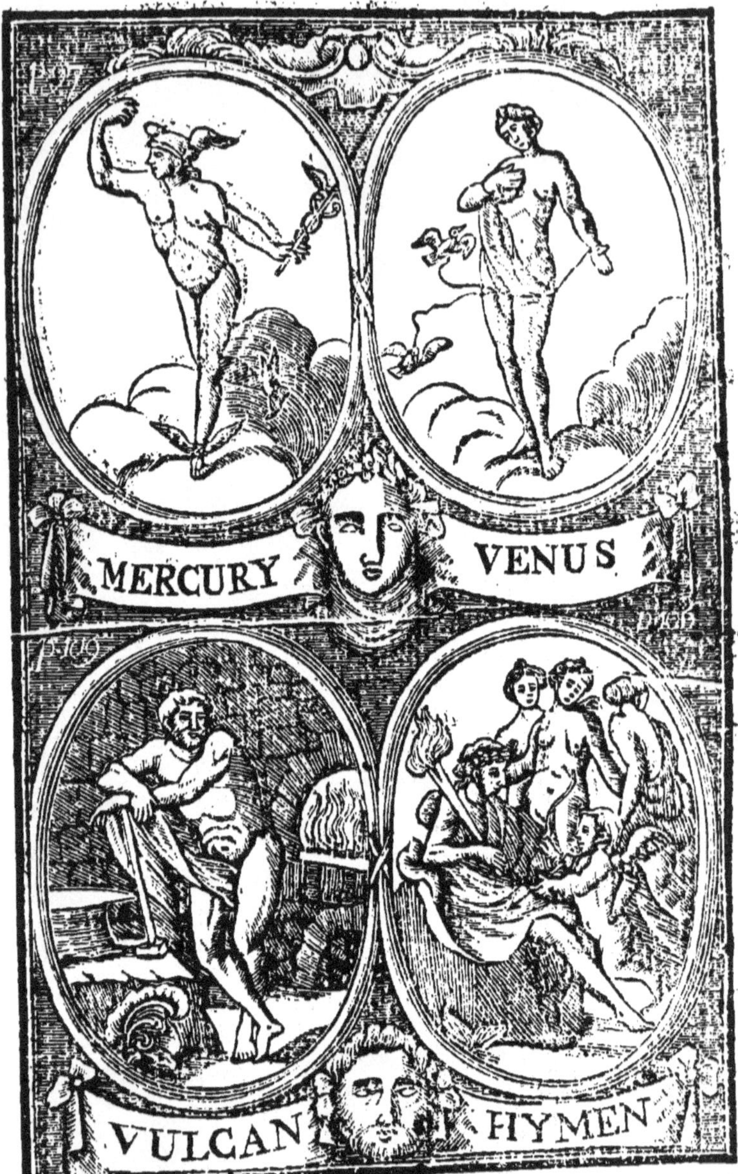

MERCURY
VENUS
VULCAN
HYMEN

IUSTICE
HERCULES
THE FURIES
THE FATES

MINERVA
APOLLO
CERES
MARS

FORTUNE
BACCHUS
DIANA
MUSES. &

PERSEUS
CASTOR & POLLUX
ACHILLES
JASON

JASON
ACHILLES

P. 46
NEPTUNE
IUNO
PROSERPINE
PLUTO

AURORA
OCEANUS
DEUCALION
ATLAS

ÆOLUS
CADMUS
ORION
MOMUS

IANUS
SATURN
IUPITER
CYBELE

ELYSIUM
NIGHT.
CHARON
HARPYES

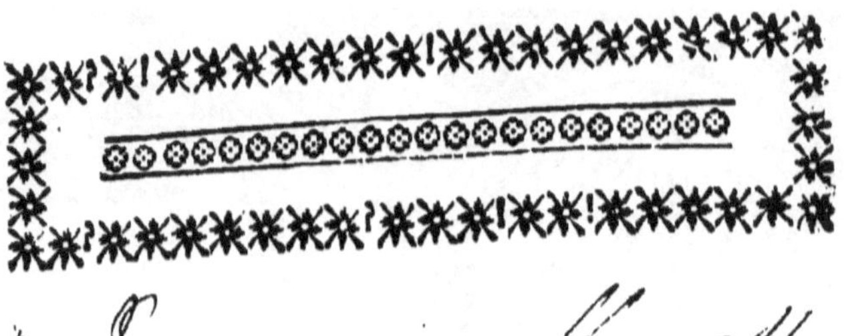

THE

THEOLOGY and HISTORY,

OF THE

HEATHENS,

Explained and Illuftrated.

CHAP. I. Of Chaos.

HESIOD, the firft Author of the fabulous Syftem of the Creation, begins his Genealogy of
the Gods with Chaos. Incapable of conceiving
how fomething could be produced from nothing,
he afferted the Eternity of Matter, and imagined
to himfelf a confufed Mafs lying in the Womb of Nature, which contained the Principles of all Beings,
and which afterwards rifing by degrees into order and
Harmony, at length produced the Univerfe. Thus
the Heathen Poets endeavoured to account for the
Origin of the World; of which they knew fo little,
that it is no wonder they difguifed rather than illu-
ftrated the Subject in their Writings. We find Virgil
reprefenting Chaos as one of the infernal Deities, and
Ovid, at his firft fetting out in the Metamorphofis, or
Transformation of the Gods, giving a very poetical
Picture of that diforderly State in which all the Ele-

                    ments

ments lay blended without Order or Diſtinction. It is eaſy to ſee, under all this Confuſion and Perplexity the Remains of Truth: The ancient Tradition of the Creation being obſcured with a multiplicity of Images and Allegories became an inexhauſtible Fund for Fiction to iprove upon, and ſwelled the Heathen Theology into an unmeaſurable Compaſs; ſo that in this Senſe Chaos may indeed be properly ſtyled the Father of the Gods.

- Though it does not ſeem eaſy to give a Picture, or graphical repreſentation of Chaos, a modern Painter (a) has been ſo bold to attempt it. Beyond the clouds which compoſe the Body of his Piece, he has repreſented an immenſe Abyſs of Darkneſs, and in the Clouds an odd Medley of Water, Earth, Fire, Smoke, Winds, &c. But he has unluckily thrown the Signs of the Zodiack into his Work, and thereby ſpoiled his whole deſign.

Our great Milton in a noble and maſterly Manner has painted the State in which Matter lay before the Creation.

> On heavenly Ground they ſtood, and from the ſhore
> They view'd the vaſt unmeaſurable Abyſs
> Outrageous as a Sea, dark, waſteful, wild:
> Up from the Bottom turn'd by furious Winds
> And ſurging Waves, as Mountains, to aſſault
> Heav'ns Height, and with the Centre mix the Pole.
> Book VII. l. 215.

CHAP. II.   Of Cælus and Terra:

CÆLUS, or Uranus, as he was called by the Greeks, is ſaid to be the Offspring of Gaia or

(a) The Painter's Name was Abraham Diepenbeke. He was born at Bois le Duc, and for ſome Time ſtudied under Peter-Paul Rubens. M. Meyſſens in his Book entitled Des Images des Peintres, gives him the Character of a great Artiſt, eſpecially in painting on Glaſs. The Piece above-mentioned has been conſidered by moſt People as a very ingenious Jumble, and 'tis plain the Painter himſelf was fond of it; for he wrote his Name in the Maſs to complete the Confuſion.

Terra

Terra. This Goddefs had given him Birth, that fhe might be furrounded and covered by him, and that he might afford a Manfion for the Gods. She next bore Ourea, or the Mountains, the Refidence of the Wood Nymphs; and laftly, fhe became the Mother of Pelagus or the Ocean. After this fhe married her Son Uranus, and had by him a numerous Offspring, among whom were Oceanus, Cæus, Creus, Hyperion, Japhet, Theia, Rhea Themis, Mnemofyne, Phæbe, Tethys, Saturn, the three Cyclops, viz. Brontes, Steropes, and Arges; and the Giants, Cottus, Gyges, and Briareus. Terra, however, was not ftrictly bound by her conjugal Vow, for by Tartarus fhe had Typhæus, or Typhon, the great Enemy of Jupiter. Cælus, having for fome Offence imprifoned the Cyclops, his wife, to revenge herfelf, incited her Son Saturn, who by her affiftance took the Opportunity to caftrate his Father with an inftrument fhe furnifhed him with. The Blood of the Wound produced the three Furies, the Giants, and the Wood Nymphs. The Genital Parts, which fell into the Sea, impregnating the Waters, formed Venus, the moft potent and charming of the Goddeffes.

According to Lactantius, Cælus was an ambitious and mighty Prince, who affecting Grandeur called himfelf the Son of the Sky, which Title his Son Saturn alfo affumed in his turn. But Diodorus makes Uranus the firft Monarch of the Atlantides, a Nation inhabiting the Weftern Coaft of Africa, and famous for Commerce and Hofpitality. From his Skill in Aftronomy, the ftarry Heavens were called by his Name, and for his Equity and Beneficence he was denominated King of the Univerfe. Nor was his Queen Titea lefs efteemed for her Wifdom and Goodnefs, which after her Death procured her the Honour of being deified by the Name of Terra. She is reprefented in the fame Manner as Vefta, of whom we fhall have occafion to fpeak more particularly.

CHAP. III. Of Hyperion and Theia.

THEIA, or Bafilea, fucceeded her Parents Cælus and Terra, in the Throne; fhe was remarkable for her Modefty and Chaftity; but being defirous of Heirs, fhe married Hyperion her Brother, to whom fhe bore Helios and Selene (the Sun and Moon,) as alfo a fecond Daughter, called Aurora (or the Morning) but the Brothers of Theia, confpiring againft her Hufband caufed him to be affaffinated and drowned her Son Helios in the River Eridanus. (a) Selene, who was extremely fond of her Brother, on hearing his fate precipitated herfelf from a high tower. They were both raifed to the Skies, and Theia after wandering diftracted, at laft difappeared in a ftorm of Thunder and Lightning.   After her death the confpirators divided the Kingdom.

Hiftorians fay, that Hyperion was a famous Aftronomer, who, on Account of his difcovering the Motions of the celeftial Bodies, and particularly the two great Luminaries of Heaven, was called the Father of thofe Planets.

CHAP. IV. Of Oceanus and Tethys.

OCEANUS was one of the eldeft Sons of Cælus and Terra, and married his Sifter Tethys; befides whom he had feveral other Wives. Each of them poffeffed a hundred Woods, and as many Rivers. By Tethys he had Ephyre, who was matched to Epimetheus, and Pleione the wife of Atlas. He had feveral other Daughters and Sons, whofe Names it would be endlefs to enumerate, and indeed they are only thofe of the principal Rivers of the World.

Two of the Wives of Oceanus were Pamphyloge and Parthenope. By the firft he had two Daughters, Afia and Lybia; and by the laft, two more, called

Europa and Thracia, who gave their Names to the Countries so denominated. He had also a Daughter, called Cephyra who educated Neptune and three Sons, viz. Triptolemus, the Favourite of Ceres, Nereus, who presided over Salt-Waters, and Achelous, the Deity of Fountains and Rivers.

The Ancients regarded Oceanus as the Father of Gods and Men, on Account of the Ocean's encompassing the Earth with his Waves, and because he was the Principle of that radical Moisture diffused through universal Matter, without which, according to Thales, nothing could either be produced or subsist.

Homer makes Juno visit him at the remotest Limits of the Earth, and acknowledge him and Tethys as the Parents of the Gods, adding that she herself had been brought up under their Tuition.

Oceanus was depicted with a Bull's-Head, to represent the Rage and Bellowing of the Ocean when agitated by Storms.

CHAP. V. Of AURORA and TITHONUS.

WE have already observed, that this Goddess was the youngest Daughter of Hyperian and Theia. By the Greeks she was styled Eos; and by the Latins Aurora, on account of her bright or golden Colour, and the Dew which attends her. Orpheus calls her the Harbinger of Titan, because the Dawn bespeaks the Approach of the Sun; others make her the Daughter of Titan and the Earth. She fell in Love with a beautiful Youth named Cephalus (whom some suppose to be the same with the Sun,) by whom she had Phaeton. She had also an Amour with Orion, whom she first saw a Hunting in the Woods, and carried him with her to Delos. By Astroeus her husband, one of the Titans, she had the Stars, and the four Winds, Argestes, Zephyrus, Boreas, and Notus. But her greatest Favourite was Tithonus, to whom she bore Æmathion and Memnon. This young Prince she transported to

Delos,

Delos, thence to Æthiopia, and laft into Heaven where fhe obtained for him from the Deftinies, the Gift of Immortality ; but at the fame Time forgot to add Youth, which alone could render the Prefent valuable. Tithonus grew old, and fo decrepid as to be rocked to fleep like an infant. His Miftrefs not being able to procure Death, to end his Mifery, changed him into a Grafshopper ; an Infect which by cafting its fkin renews its Youth, and in its chirping ftill retains the Loquacity of old Age.

The Hiftorians fay that Tithonus was a great Improver of Aftronomy, and ufed to rife before morning to make his Obfervations. They add, that his Vigilance and Temperance were rewarded with a long Life ; but when the Infirmities of old Age came on at laft Aurora by the help of oriential Drugs, reftored him to Health and Vigour. Thus have they done Juftice to the Salubrity of the Morning. This Prince is faid to have reigned in Media, where he founded the City of Sufa on the River Choafpes, which became afterwards the Seat of the Perfian Empire.

The Story of Cephalus is related differently. He was the Nephew of Æleus, and had married Procris Daughter of Erichtheus King of Athens. Aurora feeing him often early in the Woods, intent on his fport, conceived a violent Paffion for him, and carried him with her to Heaven, where fhe in vain ufed all her Arts to engage him to violate his conjugal Vow. The Prince, as fond of his Wife as the Goddefs was of him, remained inexorably faithful. Aurora, therefore, to undeceive him, fent him to Procris in the Difguife of a Merchent, to tempt her conftancy by large Prefents: This Artifice fucceeded, and juft when his Spoufe was on the point of yielding, the unhappy Hufband difcovered himfelf, and Procris fled to the Woods to hide her fhame. But being afterwards reconciled, fhe made Cephalus a prefent of an unnerring Dart. A Prefent like this increafed his Inclination to Hunting, and proved doubly fatal to the Donor. It happened the young Prince one day wearied with his Toil, fat down in the Woods and called for Aurora,

or

or the gentle Breeze to cool him (e); this being over-heard was carried to Procris, who though inconftant, was Woman enough to be jealous; influenced by this Paffion fhe followed her Hufband, and concealed her-felf in a Thicket, where fhe could obferve his Moti-ons. Unluckily the Noife fhe made alarmed her Hufband, who thinking fome wild Beaft lay conceal-ed, difcharged the the unerring Arrow, and pierced her to the Heart.

Mr. Pope in fome Lines upon a Lady's Fan of his own Defign, painted with this Story, has with his wonted Delicacy and Judgment applied it.

> Come gentle Air! th' Æolian Shepherd faid,
> While Procris painted in the fecret fhade;
> Come, gentle Air, the fairer Delia cries,
> While at her feet her Swain expiring lies.
> Lo the glad Gales o'er all her Beauties ftray,
> Breath on her Lips, and in her Bofom play!
> In Delia's Hand this Toy is fatal found,
> Nor cou'd that fabled Dart more furely Wound.
> Both Gifts deftructive to the Givers prove;
> Alike both Lovers fall by thofe they love.
> Yet guiltlefs too this bright Deftroyer lives,
> At random wounds, nor knows the Wounds fhe
>   gives.
> She views the Story with attentive Eyes.
> And pities Procris while her Lover dies.

There is no Goddefs of whom we have fo many beautiful defcriptions in the Poets as Aurora. Indeed it is no Wonder they are luxuriant on this Subject, as there is perhaps no Thame in Nature, which affords fuch an extenfive Field for Poetry or Painting as the varied Beauties of the Morning, whofe approach feems to exhilarate and enliven the whole inanimate Creation.

(e) In a capital Picture near the Hague, the Goddefs is reprefented in a golden Chariot drawn by white Horfes winged; on her Head is the Morning Star, and fhe is attended by Phœbus and the Dawn.

CHAP.

CHAP. VI. Of ATLAS.

ATLAS was the fon of Japetus and Clymene, and the Brother of Prometheus. In the Divifion of his Father's Dominions, Mauritania fell to his fhare, where he gave his own Name to that Mountain, which ftill bears it. As he was greatly fkilled in Aftronomy, he became the firft Inventer of the Sphere which gave Rife to the Fable, of his fupporting the Heavens on his Shoulders. He had many Children. Of his fons the moft famous was Hefperus. Tooke calls him his Brother, p. 325, who reigned fome time in Italy, which from him was called Hefperia. It is faid, this Prince being on Mount Atlas to obferve the motion of the Stars, was carried away by a Tempeft, and in Honour to his Memory the Morning Star was afterwards called by his Name. He left three Daughters, Ægle, Arethufa, and Hefperithufa, who went by the general Appellation of Hefperides, and were poffeffed of thofe famous Gardens which bore golden Fruit, and were guarded by the Vigilance of a formidable Dragon.

Atlas had feven daughters, called after his own Name Atlantides, viz. Maia, Electra, Taygete, Afterope, Merope, Halcyone and Celæno. All thefe were matched either to Gods or Heroes, by whom they left a numerous Pofterity. Thefe from their Mother Fleione, were alfo ftiled Pleiades. (a) Bufiris King of Egypt carried them off by violence, but Hercules travelling thro' Africa conquered him, and delivering the Princeffes reftored them to their Father, who to requite his kindnefs taught him Aftronomy, whence arofe the Fable of that Heroes fupporting the Heavens for a Day to eafe Atlas of his Toil. The Pleiades, however, endured a new Perfecution from Orion, who purfued them five Years, till Jove prevailed on by their Prayers took them up into the Hea-

---

(a) So called from a Greek Word, which fignifies Sailing: becaufe they were reckoned favourable to Navigation.

vens

vens, where they form the Conftellation, which bears their Name.

By Æthra, Atlas was the Father of feven Daughters, called Ambrofia, Eudora, Pafithoe, Coronis, Plexaris, Pytho, and Tyche, who bore one common Appellation of the Hyades (b)   Thefe Virgins grieved fo immoderately for the Death of their Brother Hyas, devoured by a Lion, that Jupiter, out of Compaffion, changed them into Stars, and placed them in the Head of Taurus, where they ftill retain their Grief, their Rifing and Setting being attended with extraordinary Ruin.   Others make thefe laft the Daughter of Lycurgus, born in the Ifle of Naxas and tranflated to the Skies, for their care in the Education of Bacchus, probably becaufe thefe fhowers are of great benefit in forwarding the Vintage.

According to Hyginus, Atlas having affifted the Giants in their War againft Jupiter, was by the victorious God doomed as a punifhment, to fuftain the Weight of the Heavens.

Ovid gives a very different account of Atlas, who, as he fays, was the Son of Japetus, and Afia.   He reprefents him as a powerful and wealthy Monarch, Proprietor of the Gardens which bore golden Fruit; but te.ls us, that being warned by the Oracle of Themis, that he fhould fuffer fome great Injury from a Son of Jupiter, he ftrictly forbad all Foreigners Accefs to his Court or prefence.   Perfeus, however, had the courage to appear before him but was ordered to retire with ftrong Menaces in cafe of difobedience. But the Hero prefenting his Shield with the dreadful Head of Medufa to him, turned him into the Mountain which ftill Bears his Name.

The Abbe La Pluche has given a very clear and ingenious Explication of this Fable.   Of all Nations the Egyptians had with the greateft Affiduity cultivated Aftronomy.   To point out the Difficulties which at-

---

(b) From the Greek Verb to Rain, the Latins called them Suculæ, from the Greek Word HUES, or Swine, becaufe they feemed to delight in wet and dirty Weather.

tend the Study of this Science, they reprefented it by an Image, bearing a Globe or Sphere on its Back, and which they called Atlas, a Word fignifying (c) great Toil or Labour. But the Word alfo fignifying fupport (d), the Phænicians, led by the Reprefentation, took it in this laft Senfe ; and in their Voyages to Mauritania, feeing the high Mountains of that Country covered with fnow, and loofing their Tops in the Clouds, gave them the Name of Atlas, and fo produced the Fable, by which the Symbol of Aftronomy ufed among the Egyptians became a Mauritanian King, transformed into a Mountain, whofe Head fupports the Heavens.

'The reft of the Fable is equally eafy to account for. The annual Inundations of the Nile obliged that People, to be very exact in obferving the Motions of the heavenly Bodies. The Hyades or Huades, took their Name from the figure V which they form in the Head of Taurus. The Pleiades were a remarkable Conftellation, and of great Ufe to the Egyptians in regulating the Seafons. Hence they became the Daughters of Atlas : And Orion, who rifes juft as they fet, was called their Lover. By the golden Apples which grew in the Gardens of the Hefperides, the Phænicians expreffed the rich and beneficial Commerce they had in the Mediterranean ; which being carried on during three Months of the year only, gave Rife to the Fable of the Hefperian Sifters (e).

(c) From Thelaah, to ftrive, comes Atlah Toil; whence the Greeks derived their AETLOS, or Labour, and the Romans exantlo to furmount great Difficulties.

(d) From Telah, to fufpend, is derived, Atlah, [Support whence the Greek Word EIEL for Column or Pillar.

(e) From Efper, the good Share, or the beft Lot.

CHAP. VII. Of JAPETUS, and his Sons EPIME-
THEUS and PROMETHEUS: of PANDORA's Box,
and the Story of DEUCALION and PYRRHA.

JAPETUS was the Offspring of Cœlus and Terra,
and one of the Giants who revolted against Jupiter. He was a powerful and haughty Prince, who
lived so long, that his age became a Proverb. Before
the War he had a Daughter, called Anchiale, who
founded a City of her own Name in Cilicia. He had
several Sons; the chief of whom were Atlas, (mentioned in the preceding Chapter) Buphagus, Prometheus,
(f) and Epimetheus. Of these Prometheus became
remarkable, by being the object of Jupiter's Resentment. The Occasion is related thus; Having sacrificed two Bulls to that Deity, he put all the Flesh of
both in one skin, and the Bones in the other, and
gave the God his choice, whose wisdom for once
failed him so that he pitched upon the worst Lot.
Jupiter incensed at the Trick put upon him, took
away Fire from the Earth, 'till Prometheus, by the
Assistance of Minerva, stole into Heaven, and light-
ing a stick at the Chariot of the Sun, recovered the
Blessing and brought it down again to Mankind.
Others say the cause of Jupiter's Anger was different,
Prometheus being a great Artist, had formed a man of
Clay of such exquisite Workmanship, that Pallas,
charmed with his ingenuity, offered him whatever in
Heaven could contribute to finish his Design; For this
End she took him up with her to the celestial Mansi-
ons, where, in a Ferula, he hid some of the Fire of
the Sun's Chariot Wheel, and used it to animate his
Image (g). Jupiter, either to revenge his Theft, or
the former Affront, commanded Vulcan to make a
Woman, which, when he had done, she was introduced into the Assembly of the Gods, each of whom

[f] So called from Tes Prometheas or Providence, that is, his
Skill in Divination

[g] Some say his Crime was not the enlivening a Man o
Clay; but the Formation of a Woman.

B

bestowed

beftowed on her fome Additional Charm or Perfection.
Venus gave her Beauty, Pallas Wifdom, Juno Riches,
Mercury taught her Eloquence and Apollo Mufick:
From all thefe Accomplifhments, fhe was ftyled Pandora [h], and was the firft of her Sex. Jupiter, to
complete his defigns, prefented her a Box, in which
he had enclofed Age, Difeafes, War, Famine, Peftilence, Difcord, Envy, Calumny, and in fhort, all the
Evils and Vices which he intended to afflict the World
with. Thus equipped, fhe was fent down to Prometheus, who wifely was on his Guard againft the Mifchief defigned him. Epimetheus his Brother, though
forewarned of the danger, had lefs Refolution ; for
enamoured with the Beauty of Pandora [i], he married her and opened the fatal Box, the Contents of
which foon overfpread the World. Hope alone refted
at the Bottom. But Jupiter, not yet fatisfied, difpatched Mercury and Vulcan to feize Prometheus,
whom they carried to Mount Caucafus, where they
chained him to a Rock, and an Eagle or Vulture was
commiffioned to prey on his Liver, which every Night
was renewed in proportion as it was confumed by
Day. But Hercules foon after killed the Vulture and
delivered him. Others fay, Jupiter reftored his
Freedom for difcovering his Father Saturn's Confpiracy, [k] and diffuading his intended marriage with
Thetis. Nicander to this Fable of Prometheus, lends
an additional Circumftance. He tells us fome un-
grateful Men difcovered the Theft of Promotheus firft
to Jupiter, who rewarded them with perpetual youth:
This prefent they loaded on the back of an Afs, who
ftopping at a Fountain to quench his thirft, was hindered by a Water Snake, who would not let him

[h] So called from Pan Doron i. e. loaded with Gifts, or
Accomplifhments. Hefiod has given a fine Defcription of her in
his Theology, Cooke, p 770
[i] Others fay Pandora only gave the Box to the Wife of
Epimetheus, who opened it from a Curiofity natural to her Sex.
[k] Lucian has a very fine Dialogue between Prometheus
and Jupiter on this Subject.

drink

drink 'till he gave him the Burthen he carried. Hence the Serpent renews his Youth upon changing his Skin.

Prometheus had an Altar in the Academy at Athens in common with Vulcan and Pallas. His Statues are reprefented with a Sceptre in the Hand.

There is a very ingenious Explanation of this Fable; it is faid Prometheus was a wife Prince, who reclaiming his Subjects from a favage to a focial Life, was faid to have animated Men out of clay : He firft inftituted Sacrifices (according to (a) Pliny) which gave Rife to the Story of the two Oxen. Being expelled his Dominions by Jupiter, he fled to Scythia, where he retired to Mount Caucafus, either to make Aftronomical Obfervations, or to indulge his Melancholy for the lofs of his Dominions. This occafioned the Fable of the Vulture feeding upon his Liver. As he was alfo the firft Inventor of forging Metals by Fire, he was faid to have ftole the Element from Heaven. In fhort as the firft Knowledge of Agriculture, and even Navigation, is afcribed to him, it is no wonder if he was celebrated for forming a living man from an inanimated Subftance.

Some Authors imagine Prometheus to be the fame with Noah. The learned Bochart imagines him to be Magog. Each opinion is fupported by Arguments which do not want a Shew of Probability.

The Story of Pandora affords very diftinct Traces of the Tradition of the fall of our firft Parents, and the Seduction of Adam by his Wife Eve.

CHAP. VIII. Of DEUCALION and PYRRHA.

DEUCALION was the Son of Prometheus, and had married his Coufin German Pyrrha the daughter of Epimetheus, who bore him a Son, called Helenes, who gave his Name to Greece. Deucalion reigned in Theffaly (e) which he governed with Equi-

(a) Pliny, Book 7. cap. 56.
(e) By the Arundelian Marbles, Deucalion ruled at Lyceres, in the Neighbourhood of Parnaffus, about the Beginning of the Reign of Cecrops King of Athens.

ty

ty and Juftice; but his Country, for the Wickednefs of the Inhabitants, being deftroyed by a Flood, he and his Queen only efcaped by faving themfelves on Mount Parnaffus. After the Decreafe of the Waters, this illuftrious Pair confulted the Oracle of Themis in their Diftrefs The Anfwer was in thefe Terms, ' De-' part the Temple, veil your Hands and Faces, unloofe ' your Girdles, and throw behind your Backs the ' Bones of your Grandmother.' Pyrrha was fhocked at an advice, which her Piety made her regard with Horror. But Deucalion penetrating the myftical fenfe revived her, by telling her the Earth was their Grand-mother, and that the Bones were only Stones. They immediately obey the Oracle, and behold its Effect. The ftones which Deucalion threw, became living Men : Thofe caft by Pyrrha rofe into Women. With thefe, returning into Theffaly, that Prince repeopled his Kingdom, and was honoured as the R ftorer of Mankind.

To explain this Fable it is neceffary to obferve, there were five Deluges, of which the one in Quef-tion was the Fourth, in order of Time, and lafted, according to Ariftotle's Account the whole Winter. It is therefore needlefs to wafte Time in drawing a Parallel between this ftory and the Mofaic Flood. The Circumftance of the Stones [1] feems occafioned by the fame Word bearing two fignifications ; fo that thefe myfterious ftones are only the Children of fuch as efcaped the general Inundation.

CHAP. IX. Of SATURN.

SATURN was the younger Son of Cœlus and Ter-ra, and married his fifter Vefta. Under the Ar-ticle of Cœlus, we have taken Notice how he treated his Father. We find a new proof of his Ambition in his endeavouring, by the Affiftance of his Mother, to

[i] The Phœnician Word Abon or Eben, fignifies both a Stone and a Child ; and the Laos Greek Word, denotes either a Stone or a People.

exclude

exclude his elder Brother Titan from the Throne, in which he so far succeeded, that this Prince was obliged to resign his Birthright, on these Terms, that Saturn should not bring up any Male Children, so that the succession might devolve to the right Male Line again.

Saturn, it is said, observed these Conditions so faithfully, that he devoured all the sons he had by his wife, as soon as born. But his Exactness in this point was at last frustrated by the Artifice of Vesta. Having brought forth the Twins, Jupiter and Juno, she presented the latter to her husband, and concealing the Boy, sent him to be nursed on Mount Ida in Crete, committing the care of him to the Curetes and Corybantes. Saturn, however, getting some intelligence of the Affair, demanded the Child, in whose stead his Wife gave him a stone swaddled up, which he swallowed. This stone had the name of Ab-addir [or the potent Father] and received divine Honours.

This Fiction of Saturn's devouring his sons, according to Mr Le Clerc [o], was founded upon a Custom which he had of banishing or confining his Children, for fear they should one Day rebel against him. As to the stone which Saturn is said to swallow this is another Fiction founded on the double Meaning of the word Eben, which signifies both a stone and a child, and means no more than, that Saturn was deceived by Rhea's substituting another Child in the Room of Jupiter.

Titan finding the mutual compact made between him and his Brother thus violated, took Arms to revenge the Injury, and not only defeated Saturn, but made him and his Wife Vesta Prisoners, whom he confined in Tartarus, a place, so dark and dismal, that it afterwards became one of the Apellations of the infernal Regions. In the mean Time Jupiter being grown up, raised an Army in Crete for his Father's Deliverance. He also hired the Cecrops to aid him in this Expedition ; but on their Refusal to join him af-

[o] Remarks upon Hesiod.

ter

ter taking the Money, he turned them into Apes. After this he marched againſt the Titans, and obtained a
complete victory The Eagle which appeared before
the Engagement, as an auſpicious Omen, was ever after choſen to carry his Thunder. From the Blood of
the Titans ſlain in the Battle, proceeded ſerpents,
ſcorpions, and all venemous Reptiles. Having by
this ſucceſs freed his Parents, the young Prince cauſed all the Gods aſſembled to renew their Oath of Fidelity to Saturn, on an Altar, which on that account
has been raiſed to a Conſtellation in the Heavens. Jupiter after this married Metis Daughter of Oceanus,
who it is reported gave Saturn a Potion, which cauſed him to bring up Neptune and Pluto, with the reſt
of the Children he had formerly devoured [a].

The Merit of the ſon [as it often happens] only
ſerved to increaſe the Father's Iealouſy, which received new ſtrength from an antient Oracle or Tradition,
that he ſhould be dethroned by one of his ſons. Jupiter therefore, ſecretly informed of the Meaſures taken to deſtroy him, ſuffered his Ambition to get the
Aſcendant over his Duty, and taking up Arms, de-
poſed his Father, whom, by the advice of Prometheus, he bound in woollen Fetters, and threw into Tartarus with Japetus his Uncle. Here Saturn ſuffered the
ſame barbarous Puniſhment of Caſtration he had in-
flicted on his Father Cœlus.

Macrobius ſearches into the Reaſon why this God
was bound with Fetters of Wool, and adds from the
Teſtimony of Apollidorus, that he broke theſe Cords
once a year at the Celebration of the Saturnalia [b].
This he explains by ſaying that this Fable alluded to
the Corn, which being ſhut up in the Earth, and de-
tained by Chains, ſoft and eaſily broken, ſprung forth
and annually arrived at Maturity. The Abbe Banier
ſays [c], that the Greeks looked upon the places ſitu-
ated to the Eaſt, as higher than thoſe that lay weſtward; and from hence concludes, that by Tartarus or

[a] By this, Jupiter ſhould be the youngeſt Son of Saturn.
[b] Sat. Lib. 1. c. 8.   [c] Banier's Mythology, Vol. 2. 185.
Hell

Hell, they only meant Spain. As to the Castration of Saturn, Mr. Le Clerc conjectures [a], that it only means that Jupiter had corrupted his Father's Council, and prevailed upon the most considerable Persons of his Court to desert him.

The manner in which Saturn escaped from his Prison is not related. He fled to Italy, where he was kindly received by Janus then King of that Country, who associated him in the Government. From hence that Part of the World obtained the Name of Saturnia Tellus, as also that of Latium from Lateo to lie hid, because he found a Refuge here in his Distress. On this Account Money was coined with a Ship on one side to signify his Arrival, and a Janus with a double Head on the other, to denote his sharing the regal Authority.

The Reign of Saturn was so mild and happy, that the Poets have given it the Name of the GOLDEN AGE, and celebrated it with all the Pomp and Luxuriancy of Imagination [b]. According to Varro, this Deity from his instructing the People in Agriculture and Tillage, obtained his Name [c] of Saturn. The sickle which he used in reaping being cast into Sicily, gave that Island its antient Name of Drepanom, which in Greek signifies that Instrument.

The Historians give us a very different picture of Saturn. Diodorus represents him, as a tyrannical, covetous and cruel Prince, who reigned over Italy and Sicily, and enlarged his Dominions by Conquest: He adds, that he oppressed his subjects by severe taxes, and kept them in Awe by strong Garrisons. This Account agrees very well with those who make Saturn the first who instituted human sacrifices, which probably gave rise to the Fable of his devouring his own Children. Certain it is, that the Carthaginians [d]

offered

[a] Remarks upon Hesiod.

[b] The Reader will see more on this Head under the succeeding article.

[c] From Satus, that is, Sowing or Seed-Time.

[d] Mr. Selden in his Treatise of the Syrian Gods, speaking of Moloch, imagines from the Cruelty of his Sacrifices, he was the

same

offered young Children to this Deity; and amongst the Romans, his Priests were cloathed in Red, and at his Festivals, Gladiators were employed to kill each other.

The Feasts of this Deity were celebrated with great solemnity amongst the Romans about the Middle of December. They were first instituted by Tullus Hostilius, though Livy dates them from the Consulship of Manilius and Sempronius. They lasted but one Day till the time of Julius Cæsar, who ordered them to be protracted to three Days; and in Process of Time they were extended to five. During these, all public Business was stopped, the Senate never assembled, no war could be proclaimed, or offender executed. Mutual Presents of all kinds, (particularly Wax Lights) were sent and received, Servants wore the Pileus or Cap of Liberty, and were waited on by their Masters at Table. All which was designed to shew the Equality and Happiness of Mankind under the Golden Age.

The Romans kept in the Temple of Saturn, the Libri Elephantini, or Rolls, containing the Names of the Roman Citizens, as also the public Treasure. This Custom they borrowed from the Egyptians, who in the Temple of Sudec, or Chrone, deposited their Genealogies of Families and the public Money.

Saturn like the other Heathen Deities, had his Amours. He fell in Love with the Nymph Phyllyra, the Daughter of Oceanus, and was by his Wife Rhea so near being surprized in her Company, that he was forced to assume the Form of a Horse. This sudden Transformation had such an effect on his Mistress, that she bore a Creature whose upper Part was like a Man, and the rest like a Horse. This son of Saturn became famous for his skill in Music and Surgery.

A modern Author, M. La Pluche, has very justly accounted for this fabulous History of Saturn, which

same as Saturn. In the Reign of Tiberius, that Prince crucifyed the Priests of Saturn for offering young Infants at his Altars.— This Idea of Saturn's Malignity is, perhaps, the Reason why the Planet, which bears this Name, was thought so inauspicious and unfriendly to Mankind.

certainly

certainly derived its Origin from Egypt. The annual Meeting of the Judges in that Country was notifyed by an Image with a long Beard, and a Scythe in his Hand. The firſt denoted the Age and Gravity of the Magiſtrates, and the latter pointed out the Seaſon of their aſſembling, juſt before the firſt Hay-making or Harveſt. This Figure they called by the Names of Sudec [a], Chrone [b], Chiun [c], and Saterin [d]; and in Company with it, always expoſed another ſtatue repreſenting Iſis, with ſeveral Breaſts and ſurrounded with the Heads of Animals, which they called Rhea [e], as theſe Images continued expoſed till the Beginning of the new Solar Year, or the Return of Oſiris [the Sun] ſo Saturn became regarded as the Father of Time. Upon other Occaſions the Egyptians depicted him with Eyes before and behind, ſome of them open, others aſleep; and with four Wings, two ſhut and two expanded [g]. The Greeks took theſe Pictures in the literal Senſe, and turned into fabulous Hiſtory, what was only allegorical.

Bochart, and ſome other learned Antiquaries, conceived Saturn to be the ſame with Noah, and drew a Parallel, in many Inſtances, which ſeem to favour their opinion.

Saturn was uſually repreſented as an old Man, bareheaded and bald, with all the Marks of Age and Infirmity in his Face. In his Right-Hand they ſometimes placed a ſickle or ſcythe, at others a Key and a Serpent biting its own Tail, and circumflexed in his Left. He ſometimes was pictured with ſix Wings, and Feet of Wool, to ſhew how inſenſibly and ſwiftly Time paſſes. The Scythe denoted his cutting down and impairing all Things, and the Serpent the Revolution of the Year : *Quod in ſeſe volvitur Annus.*

[a] From Tſadick, or Sudec, Juſtice, or the Juſt.
[b] From Keren, Splendor, the Name given to Moſes on his Decent from the Mount; hence the Greek CHRONOS.
[c] From Cahen, a Prieſt, is derived Keunah, or the ſacerdotal Office.
[d] From Seter, a Judge, is the Plural Seterim, or the Judges.
[e] From Rahah, to feed, comes Rehea, or Rhea, a Nurſe.
[g] This Figure ſeems borrowed from the Cherubim of the Hebrews.

CHAP. X.   Of the GOLDEN AGE.

DIFFICULT as it is, to reconcile the Inconfiftencies between the Poets and Hiftorians in the preceding Account of Saturn, yet the Concurrent Teftimony of the former in placing the Golden Age in his Time, feems to determine the Point in his Favour; and to prove that he was a Benefactor and Friend to Mankind, fince they enjoyed fuch Felicity under his Adminiftration. We can never fufficiently admire the mafterly Defcription given by Virgil of thefe Halcyon Days, when Peace and Innocence adorned the World, and fweetened all the Bleffings of untroubled Life. Ovid has yet heightened the Defcription with thofe Touches of Imagination peculiar to him. Amongft the Greek Poets, Hefiod has touched this Subject with that agreeable Simplicity which diftinguifhes all his Writings.

By the Golden Age might be figured out the Happinefs of the primeval State before the firft and univerfal Deluge, when the Earth remaining in the fame Pofition in which it was firft created, flourifhed with perpetual Spring, and the Air always temperate and ferene, was neither difcompofed by Storms, nor darkened by Clouds. The Reafon of affixing this Time to the Reign of Saturn, was probably this ; the Egyptians held the firft annual Affembly of their Judges in the Month of February, and as the Decifions of thefe Sages were always attended with the higheft Equity, fo the People regarded that Seafon as a Time of general Joy and Happinefs, rather as all nature with them was then in Bloom, and the whole Country looked like one enamelled Garden, or Carpet.

But after all it appears, that thefe Halcyon Times were but of a fhort Duration, fince the Character Plato, Pythagoras, and others give of this Age can only relate to that ftate of perfect Innocence which ended with the Fall.

CHAP. XI. Of the GIANTS

THE Giants were produced (as has been already observed) of the Blood which flowed from the Wound of Saturn, when castrated by his Son Jupiter. Proud of their own Strength, and fired with a daring Ambition, they entered into an Association to dethrone Jupiter, for which purpose they piled Rocks on Rocks, in order to scale the Skies. This engagement is differently related by Authors, both as to the place where it happened, and the Circumstances which attended it: some Writers laying the Scene in Italy [h], others in Greece [i]. It seems the Father of the Gods was apprized of the danger as there was a prophetical Rumour amongst the Deities, that the Giants should not be overcome, unless a Mortal assisted in the War. For this Reason Jove, by the Advice of Pallas, called up Hercules, and being assisted by the rest of the Gods gained a complete Victory over the Rebels, most of whom perished in the Conflict. Hercules first slew Alcyon with an Arrow, but he still survived and grew stronger, till Minerva drew him out of the Moon's Orb, when he expired. This Goddess also cut off the Heads of Enceladus and Pallantes, and afterwards encountering Alcyoneus at the Corinthian Isthmus, killed him in spite of his monstrous Bulk. Porphyris, about to ravish Juno, fell by the Hands of Jupiter and Hercules. Apollo and Hercules dispatched Ephialtes, and Hercules slew Eurytus, by darting an oak at him. Clytius was slain by Hecate, and Polybotes flying through the Sea, came to the Isle of Coos, where Neptune tearing off part of the Land, hurled it at him, and formed the Isle of Nisyros. Mercury slew Hypolitus, Gratian was vanquished by Diana, and the Parcæ claimed their share in the Victory, by the De-

---

[h] In the Phlegræan Plains, in Campania, near Mount Vesuvius, which abound with subterraneous Fire, and hot Mineral Springs.

[i] Where they set Mount Ossa on Pelion, in order to ascend the Skies.

struction

ftruction of Agryus and Thoan. Even Silenus his Afs by his opportune Braying, contributed to put the Giants in Confufion, and complete their Ruin. During this War, of which Ovid has left us a fhort Defcription, Pallas diftinguifhed herfelf by her Wifdom, Hercules by his Strength, Pan by his Trumpet, which ftruck a Terror in the Enemy, and Bacchus by his Activity and Courage. Indeed their Affiftance was no more than feafonable; for when the Giants firft made their audacious attempt, the Gods were fo aftonifhed, that they fled into Egypt, where they concealed themfelves in various fhapes.

But the moft dreadful of thefe Monfters, and the moft difficult to fubdue, was Typhon or Typhæus; whom, when he had almoft difcomfited all the Gods, Jupiter purfued to Mount Caucafus, where he wounded him with his Thunder; but Typhon turning upon him took him prifoner, and after cutting with his own Sickle the Nerves of his Hands and Feet, threw him on his back, carried him into Cilicia, and imprifoned him in a Cave, whence he was delivered by Mercury, who reftored him to his former Vigour. After this Jove had a fecond engagement with Typhon, who flying into Sicily, was overwhelmed by Mount Ætna.

The Giants are reprefented by the Poets as men of huge Stature and horrible Afpect, their lower parts being of a Serpentine Form. But above all, Typhon, or Typhæus, is defcribed in the moft fhocking Manner. Hefiod has given him an hundred Heads of Dragons uttering dreadful founds, and having Eyes that darted Fire. He makes him, by Echidna, the Father of the Dog Orthus, of Cerberus, Hydra, Chimæra, Sphinx the Nemæan Lion, the Hefperian Dragon, and of Storms and Tempefts.

Hiftorians fay Typhæus was the Brother of Ofiris, King of Egypt, who, in the Abfence of this Monarch, formed a Confpiracy to dethrone him at his Return, for which End he invited him to a Feaft, at the conclufion of which, a Cheft of exquifite Workmanfhip was brought in, and offered to him who lying down in it fhould be found to fit it beft. Ofiris

not diftrufting the Contrivance, had no fooner got in
but the Lid was cloſed upon him, and the unhappy
King thrown into the Nile. Iſis his Queen, to revenge
the Death of her beloved Huſband, raiſed an Army,
the Command of which ſhe gave to her Son Orus, who
after vanquiſhing the Uſurper, put him to Death.
Hence the Egyptians, who deteſted his Memory,
painted him in their Hieroglyphic Characters in ſo
frightful a Manner. The Length and Multiplicity of
his Arms denoted his power: The Serpents which
formed his Heads ſignified his Addreſs and Cunning:
The Crocodile Scales which covered his Body expreſſed his Cruelty and Diſſimulation: and the flight of
the Gods into Egypt, ſhewed the precautions taken
by the great Men to ſhelter themſelves from his Fury
and Reſentment.

It is eaſy in this Story of the Giants to trace the
Moſaic Hiſtory, which informs us how the Earth was
afflicted with Men of uncommon ſtature and great
wickedneſs. The Tradition of the Tower of Babel,
and the Defeat of that impious Deſign, might naturally
give Riſe to the Attempt of theſe Monſters, to inſult
the ſkies and make War on the Gods.

But there is another Explication of this Fable which
ſeems both more rational and curious. Amongſt the
Names of the Giants we find thoſe of Briareus [a],
Rœchus [b], Othus [c], Ephialtes [d], Porphyrion [e]
Enceladus [f], and Mimas [g]. Now the literal Sig-

[a] From Beri Serenity; and Harcus, loſt, to ſhew the Tem-
perature of the Air deſtroyed.

[b] From Reuach the Winds.

[c] From Ouitta, or Othus, the Times, to tipiˊy the Viciſſi-
tude of Seaſons.

[d] From Evi, or Ephi, Clouds; and Altah, Darkneſs, i. c,
dark gloomy Clouds.

[e] From Phaur, to break, comes Pharpher, to ſeparate mi-
nutely: To denote the general Diſſolution of the Principal Syſtem.

[f] From Enctlod, Violent Springs or Torrents.

[g] From Maim, great and heavy Rains. Now all theſe were
Phænomenons new and unknown before the Flood, See La Plu-
chets Hiſtory of the Heavens, Vol. I, p. 6o.

C

nifica-

nification of these leads us to the sense of the Allegory, which was designed to point out the fatal consequences of the Flood and the considerable changes it introduced with Regard to the Face of Nature. This is further confirmed by their Tradition, that their Osiris vanquished the Giants, and that Orus his Son, in particular, stopped the pursuit of Rœchus, by appearing before him in the Form of a Lion. By which they meant, that, that industrious people had no Way of securing themselves against the bad effects of the vernal Winds, which brought on their annual inundation, but by exactly observing the Sun's Entrance into Leo, and then retiring to the high Grounds, to wait the going off of the Waters.

It may not be improper to add, that from the Blood of the Giants defeated by Jupiter, were produced Serpents and all kinds of venemous Creatures.

CHAP. XII. Of JANUS

THE Connection between Saturn and Janus, renders the Account of the Latter a proper supplement to the History of the Former. Writers vary as to the birth of this Deity, some making him the Son of Cœlus and Hecate; others the offspring of Apollo, by Creusa Daughter of Erictheus, King of Athens. Hesiod is silent about him in his Theogony, and indeed Janus was a God little known to the Greeks. According to Cato, he was a Scythian Prince, who at the Head of a victorious Army, subdued and depopulated Italy. But the most probable opinion is, that he was an Etrurian King, and one of the earliest Monarchs of that Country, which he governed with great Wisdom, according to the Testimony of Plutarch, who says, ' whatever he was, whether a King or a God, he was ' a great Politician, who tempered the manners of his ' subjects, and taught them Civility, on which Account he was regarded as the God of Peace, and ' never invoked during the Time of War.' The Romans held him in peculiar Veneration.

From

From Fabius Pictor, one of the old Roman Histo-
rians, we learn, that the ancient Tuscans were first
taught by this good King to improve the Vine, to fow
Corn, and to make Bread, and that he first raifed
Temples and Altars to the Gods, who were before
worfhipped in Groves. We have already mentioned
Saturn, as the Introducer of thefe Arts into Italy,
where Janus admitted him into a fhare of his power.
Some fay he was married to the youngeft Vefta, the
Goddefs of Fire: others make his Wife the Goddefs
Carna, or Carma [h].

It is certain that he early obtained divine Honours at
Rome, where Numa Pompilius inftituted an annual
Feftival to him in January, which was celebrated with
manly Exercifes. Romulus and Tatius had before e-
rected him a Temple upon Occafion of the Union of
the Romans with the Sabines. Numa ordained it fhould
be opened in time of War, and fhut in time of Peace
[i], which happened but thrice for feveral Centuries.
1. In the Reign of Numa, 2. In the confulate of Attilius Balbus, and Manlius Torquatus: and 3. By
Auguftus Cæfar, after the Death of Antony, and Re-
duction of Egypt.

Janus was the God who prefided over all new Undertakings. Hence in all facrifices the firft Libations of
Wine and Wheat were offered to him, as likewife all
prayers were prefaced with a fhort Addrefs to him.
The peculiar offerings at his Feftival were cakes of new
Meal and falt, with new Wine and Frankincenfe [k].
Then all Artificers and Tradefmen began their Works,
and the Roman Confuls for the New Year folemnly
entered on their Office. All Quarrels were laid afide
mutual prefents were made, and the Day concluded
with Joy and Mirth.

[h] Carna, or Carma, was a Goddefs who prefided over the
vital Parts, and occafioned a healthy Conftitution of Body.

[i] Hence Janus took the Names of Patuleius and Clufius.

[k] Tooke contradicts Ovid, and fuppofes Pliny to prove, that
the Ancients did not ufe this Gum in their Sacrifice, but the Paffage of that Author, only fay it was not ufed in the Time of the
Trojan War.

Janus

Janus was reprefented with two Faces, and called Bi-frons, Biceps, and Dicymaus; as forming another Image of himfelf on the Difk of the Moon, and look-ing to the paft and approaching year; with Keys, as opening and fhutting up the Day [a]. He is faid to have regulated the Months, the firft of which is dif-tinguifhed by his Name, as the firft Day of every Month was alfo facred to him. He was therefore fea-ted in the Center of twelve Altars: and had on his Hands Figures to the amount of days in a year.——Sometimes his Image had four faces, to exprefs the four Seafons of the year over which he prefided.

Though Janus be properly a Roman Deity, yet it is amongft the Egyptians we muft feek for the true Ex-planation of his Hiftory. That Nation reprefented the Opening of their Solar year by an Image, with a Key in its hand, and two Faces, one old and another young, to tipify or mark the old and new year. King Picus with a Hawk's Head, who is ufually drawn near Ja-nus, leaves no doubt but that the Symbol of this Dei-ty was borrowed from that People. The Reader af-ter putting all this together, will reafonably conclude, that by this Figure could only be intended the Sun, the great Ruler of the Year.

CHAP. XIII. Of the Elder Vesta or Cybele the Wife of Saturn.

IT is highly neceffary, in claffing the Heathen Divi-nities, to diftinguifh between this Goddefs, who is alfo called Rhea and Ops, from another Vefta their Daughter, becaufe the Poets have been faulty in con-founding them, and afcribing the Attributes and Acti-ons of the one to the other.

The elder Vefta, commonly called Eftia by the Greeks, was the Daughter of Coelus and Terra, and married to her brother Saturn, to whom fhe bore a

[a] Quafi utriufque januæ cœleftis potentem; qui exoriens a-pellat diem, occidens claudat. Macrob. l. 1, c. 9.

numerous

numerous offspring. She had a Multiplicity of names besides, of which the principal were Cybele, Magna Mater, or the great Mother of the Gods: and Bona Dea, or the good Goddess, &c.   Under different Characters she had different Representations, and different Sacrifices.

Vesta is generally represented upon ancient Coins sitting, though sometimes standing with a lighted Torch in one Hand and a Sphere in the other.

Under the Character of Cybele she makes a more magnificent Appearance, being seated on a lofty chariot drawn by Lions, crowned with Towers, and having a key extended in her Hand.

Some indeed make the Phrygian Cybele a different Person from Vesta: They say she was the Daughter of Mœones an antient King of Phrygia and Dyndima, and that her Mother, for some Reasons, exposed her on Mount Cybelus, where she was nourished by Lions. Her Parents afterwards owned her, and she fell in love with Atys, by whom conceiving, her Father caused her Lover to be slain, and his Body thrown to the wild Beasts; Cybele upon this ran mad, and filled the Woods with her Lamentations. Soon after a Plague and Famine laying waste the Country, the Oracle was consulted, who advised them to bury Atys with great Pomp, and to worship Cybele as a Goddess. Accordingly they erected a Temple to her Honour at Pessinus, and placed Lions at her Feet, to denote her being educated by these Animals.

Ovid relates the Story a little more in the marvellous Way; Atys was a Boy so called by Cybele, whom she appointed but to preside in her Rites, enjoining him inviolate Chastity; but the Youth happening to forget his Vow, in Resentment the Goddess deprived him of his senses: But at last pitying his Misery, she turned him into a Pine-Tree, which, as well as the Boy, was held sacred to her. The Animal commonly sacrificed to Cybele, was the Sow on Account of its Fæcundity.

The Priests of this Deity were the Corybantes, Curetes, Idæi, Dactyli and Telchines, who in their myl-

tica

tical Rites made great ufe of Cymbals and other Inftruments of Brafs, attended with extravagant Cries
and Howlings. They facrificed fitting on the Earth,
and offered only the Hearts of the Victims.

The Goddefs Cybele was unknown to the Romans
till the Time of Hannibal, when confulting the Sybil-
ine Oracles, they found that formidable Enemy could
not be expelled till they fent for the Idæ Mother to
Rome.   Attalus then King of Phrygia, at the Requeft
of their Ambaffadors, fent her ftatue which was of
ftone.   But the Veffel which carried it arriving in the
Tyber, was miraculoufly ftopped, till Claudia, one of
the Veftal-Virgins, drew it afhore with her Girdle.

This Veftal, to whom the living Flame was facred,
is the fame with the Egyptian Ifis, and reprefented the
pure Æther, inclofing, containing and pervading all
Things.   Their Expreffions and Attributes are alike.
She was confidered as the caufe of Generation and
Motion ; The Parent of all the Luminaries, and is
confounded with Nature and the World.   She obtained the Name of Eftia, as being the Life or Effence
of all things [a].

As to the Priefts of Cybele, the Corybantes, Cure-
tes, &c. they are of the fame Original.   Crete was a
colony of the Egyptians, confifting of three claffes of
People,   1. The Corybantes or Priefts [b]. 2. The
Curetes, [c] or Hufbandmen, and Inhabitants of
Towns. 3. The Dactyli [d], or Artificers and labouring
Poor.   All which names are of Egyptian Derivation.

Cybele was honoured at Rome by the Title of Eo-
na Dea, or good Goddefs But this Devotion was only
paid her by the Matrons, and the Rites were celebrated fo fecret a manner, that it was no lefs than

[a] Plato in Cratylo.
[b] From Corban, a Sacrifice or Oblation.
[c] From Keret, a City or Town, comes the Plural Keretim,
to fignify the Inhabitants.
[d] From dac, poor ; and tul erty, a Migration : Hence our
ultima Thule. The Greeks for the fame Reafon call the Fingers
Dactyli, becaufe they are the Inftruments of Labour.

Death

Death for any Man to be prefent at the Affembly [a]
whence they were called Opertoria.

The Roman Farmers and Shepherds worfhipped
Cybele or Vefta, by the Title of Magna Pales, or the
Goddefs of Cattle and Paftures. Her Feftival was in
April at which time they purified their Flocks and
Herds with the Fumes of Rofemary, Laurel, and Sul-
phur, offered facrifices of Milk and Millet Cakes,
and concluded the ceremony by dancing round ftraw-
fires. Thefe annual Feafts were called Pulilia, and
were the fame with the Thefmophoria of the Greeks,
and probably of Phænician or Egyptian Original.

The great Feftival of Cybele called Megalefia, was
always celebrated in April, and lafted eight Days at
Rome.

CHAP. XIV: Of VESTA, the younger.

COLLECTED Fire is the Offspring of Æther.
Hence we have another Vefta, faid to be the
Daughter of the other, by Saturn, or Time, and the
fifter of Cerus, Juno, Pluto, Neptune, and Jupiter;
fhe was fo fond of a fingle Life, that when her Brother Jupiter afcended the Throne, and offered to
grant whatever fhe afked, fhe defired only the Prefervation of her Virginity, and that fhe might have the
firft Oblation in all Sacrifices [b], which fhe obtained.
According to Lactantius, the Chaftity of Vefta is
meant to exprefs the Nature of Fire, which is incapable of mixture, producing nothing, but converting all
Things into itfelf.

Numa Pompilius, the great Founder of Religion
among the Romans, is faid firft to have reftored the
antient Rites and Worfhip of this Goddefs, to whom
he erected a circular Temple, which in fucceeding

[a] So we learn from Tibullus, Eclogue VI.
     Sacra Bonæ maribus non adeunda Deæ.
[b] It is a Queftion if this Privilege did not rather belong to
the Elder Vefta, in common with Janus.

Ages

Ages, was much embellished. He also appointed four
Priestesses to be chosen out of the noblest Families in
Rome, and of spotless Character, whose Office was to
attend the sacred Fire kept continually burning near
her Altar. These Vestal Virgins continued in their
charge for thirty Years, and had very great Privileges
annexed to their Dignity. This Fire was annally renewed, with great Ceremony, from the Rays of the
Sun, on the Kalends of March. It was preserved in
Earthen Pots suspended in the air, and esteemed so sacred, that if by any misfortune it became extinguish-
ed, (as happened once) a Cessation ensued from all business, till they had expiated the Prodigy. If this Accident appeared owing to the neglect of the Vestals
they were severely punished; and if they violated their
Vow of Chastity, they were interred alive.

As Vesta was the Goddess of Fire, the Romans had
no Images in her Temple to represent her, the Reason
of which we learn in Ovid [a]. Yet as she was the
Guardian of Houses or Hearths, her Image was u-
sually placed in the porch or Entry, and a daily Sacrifice offered her [b].

It is certain nothing could be a stronger or more
lively Symbol of the Supreme Being, than Fire. Accordingly we find this Emblem in early Use throughout all the East. The Persians held it in Veneration
long before Zoroaster, who in the Reign of Darius
Histaspes reduced the Worship of it to a certain plan.
The Prytanei of the Greeks were perpetual and holy
Fires. We find Æneas bringing with him to Italy his
Penates (or houshold Gods) the Palladium and the sacred Fire. The Vesta of the Etrurians, Sabines, and
Romans, was the same.

[a] His Words are these.

   Effigiem nullam Vesta nec Ignis habet. Fasti, Lib. VI.

   No Image Vesta's Semblance can express,
   Fire is too subtile to admit of Dress.

[b] Hence the Word Vestibulum, for a Porch or Entry; and
the Romans called their round Tables Vestæ, as the Greeks used
the common Word Estia to signify Chimneys and Altars.

CHAP. XV. Of JUPITER.

WE come now to the great King, or Master of the Gods. This Deity was the son of Saturn and Rhea, or Vesta, at least this is that Jupiter, to whom the Actions of all the others were chiefly ascribed. For there were so many Princes called by his Name, that it seems to have been a common Appellation in early Times for a powerful or victorious Prince [a]. The most considerable of these was certainly the Cretan Jove above-mentioned, of whose Education we have very various Accounts, as well as the Place of his Birth. The Messenians pretended to show in the Neighbourhood of their City a Fountain called Clepsydra, where Jupiter was educated by the Nymphs Ithome and Nedo; others say he was born at Thebes in Bœotia: but the most general and received Opinion is, that he was brought up near Mount Ida in Crete. Virgil tells us he was fed by the Bees, out of Gratitude for which he changed them from an Iron to a golden colour. Some say his Nurses were Amalthœa and Melissa, Daughters of Melissus King of Crete, who gave his Goats Milk and Honey; others that Amalthœa was the Name of the goat that nursed him, whose Horn he presented to those Princesses with this Privilege annexed, that whoever possessed it should immediately have whatever they desired; whence it came to be called the Horn of Plenty. After this the Goat dying, Jupiter placed her amongst the Stars, and by the Advice of Themis covered his Shield with her skin to strike Terror in the Giants, whence it obtained the Name of Ægis. According to others, he and his Sister Juno sucked the Breasts of Fortune. Some alledge his Mother Vesta suckled him; some, that he was fed by wild Pigeons, who brought him Ambrosia from Oceanus, and by an Eagle, who carried Nectar in his Beak from a steep Rock; in recompense of

____

[a] Varro reckoned up 300 Jupiters, and each Nation seems to have had one peculiar to itself.

which

which Services, he made the Former the Fore-tellers of Winter and Summer, and gave the Latter the Reward of Immortality, and the office of bearing his 'Thunder. In short, the Nymphs and the Bears claim a fhare in the Honour of his Education, nor is it yet decided which has the beft 'Title to it.

Let us now come to the Actions of Jupiter. The firft, and indeed the moft memorable of his Exploits, was his Expedition againft the Titans for his Father's Deliverance and Reftoration, of which we have already fpoken under the Article of Saturn. After this he dethroned his Father, and having poffeffed himfelf of his Throne, was acknowledged by all the Gods in Quality of their fupreme Apollo, himfelf crowned with Laurel, and robed with Purple, condefcended to fing his Praifes to his Lyre. Hercules, in order to perpetuate the Memory of his Triumphs, inftituted the Olympic Games, where it is faid that Phœbus carried off the firft prize by overcoming Mercury at the Race. After this, Jupiter being fully fettled, divided his Dominions with his Brothers Neptune and Pluto, as will be fhewn in the Sequel.

Jupiter, however, is thought to ufe his power in a little too tyrannical a Manner, for which we find Juno, Neptune and Pallas confpired againft, and actually feized, his Perfon. But the Giants Cottys, Gyges and Briareus, who were then his Guards, and whom Thetis called to his Affiftance, fet him at Liberty. How thefe Giants with others of their Race, afterwards revolted againft him, and were overthrown, has been already mentioned in its place.

The Story of Lycaon is not the leaft diftinguifhing of his Actions. Hearing of the prevailing Wickednefs of Mankind, Jove defcended to Earth, and arriving at the Palace of this Monarch, King of Arcadia, declared who he was; on which the People prepared Sacrifices, and the other Honours due to him. But Lycaon, both impious and incredulous, killed one of his Domefticks, and ferved up the Flefh dreffed at the Entertainment he gave the God, who detefting fuch horrid Inhumanity, immediately confumed the Palace with Lightening

ing and turned the Barbarian into a Wolf.   Ovid has related this Story with his usual art.

But as Ambition, when arrived at the Height of its Wishes, seldom strictly adheres to the Rules of Moderation, so the Air of a Court is always in a peculiar Manner fatal to Virtue. If any Monarch deserved the Character of encouraging Gallantry by his Example, it was certainly Jupiter, whose Amours are as numberless as the Metamorphoses he assumed to accomplish them, and have afforded an extensive Field of Description to the Poets and Painters, both antient and modern.

Jupiter had several Wives. Metis, or Prudence, his first, he is said to nave devoured, when big with child, by which himself becoming pregnant, Minerva issued out of his Head adult and completely armed. His second was Themis, or Justice, by whom he had the Hours, meaning the Regulation of Time, Eunomia or Good Order, Diche or Law, Eirene or Peace and the Destinies He also married Juno, his Sister, whom it is reported he deceived under the Form of a Cuckoo, who to shun the violence of a Storm, fled for Shelter to her Lap [a]. She bore to him Hebe, Mars, Lucina, and Vulcan. By Eurynome he had the three Graces; by Cerus, Proserpine; by Mnemosyne, the nine Muses; by Latona, Apollo and Diana; by Maia, Mercury.

Of his Intrigues we have a pretty curious Detail. One of his first Mistresses was Califto the Daughter of Lycaon, one of the Nymphs of Diana.   To Deceive her he assumed the Form of the Goddess of Chastity, and succeeded so far as to make the Virgin violate her Vow But her disgrace being revealed as she was bathing with her patroness, the incensed Deity not only disgraced her, [b] but turned her into a Bear. Jove, in compassion to her Punishment and Sufferings, raised her to a Constellation in the Heavens [c]. Califto, however, left a son called Arcas, who having instruc-

<hr>

[a] At a Mountain near Corinth, thence called Coceyx.
[b] Some say it was Juno turned her into that Animal.
[c] Called Ursa Major by the Latins, and Helice by the Greeks

ted

ted the Pelasgians in Tillage and the Social Arts, they from him took the Name of Arcadians, and after his Death he was by his Divine Father, allotted also [a] a seat in the Skies.

There is scarce any Form which Jupiter did not at some time or other assume to gratify his Desires. Under the Figure of a Satyr he violated Antiope the wife of Lycus King of Thebes, by whom he had two Sons, Zethus and Amphion. In the Resemblance of a Swan he corrupted Leda, the sponse of Tyndarus, King of Laconia. Under the Appearance of a white Bull he carried off Europa, Daughter of Agenor King of Phænicia, into Crete, where he enjoyed her. In the Shape of an Eagle he surprised Asteria the Daughter of Cæus and bore her away in his Talons in spite of her Modesty. Aided by the same Disguise, he seized the beauteous Ganymede Son of Tros, as he was hunting on Mount Ida, and raised him to the joint Functions of his Cup bearer and Catamite.

It was indeed difficult to escape the pursuits of a God, who by his unlimited power made all Nature subservient to his purposes. Of this we have a remarkable Instance in Danae, whose Father, Acrisius, jealous of her Conduct, had secured her in a Brazen Tower; but Jupiter descending in a golden Shower, found means to elude all the Vigilance of her Keepers. He found Means to inflame Ægina the Daughter of Æsopus, King of Bœotia, in the similitude of a lambent Fire, and then carried her from Epidaurius to a desert Isle called OEnope, to which she gave her own Name [b]. Clytoris, a fair Virgin of Thessally, he debauched in the Shape of an Ant; but to corrupt Alcmena, the Wife of Amphytrion, he was obliged to assume the Form of her Husband, under which the fair one being deceived, innocently yielded to his desires. By Thalia he had two Sons, called the Pallaci; and two by Protegena, viz. Æthlius the Father of Endymion, and Epaphus the Founder of Memphis in E:

[a] The Ursa Minor of the Latins, and Cynosura of the Greeks
[b] The Isle of Ægina in the Archipelago.

gypt, and Father of Libya, who gave her Name to the Continent of Africk. Electra bore him Dardanus, Laodamia, Sarpedon, and Argus, Jodama Deucalion, with many others too tedious to enumerate, tho' mentioned by the Poets.

It is very evident that moſt, if not all the Stories relating to the Amours of the Gods, were invented by their reſpective Prieſts to cover their Corruption or Debauchery. Of which this of Danae ſeems at leaſt a palpable Inſtance, and may ſerve to give ſome Idea of the reſt : Acriſius was informed by an Oracle that his Grandſon would one Day deprive him of his Crown and Life ; on which he ſhut up his Daughter Danae in a Brazen Tower of the Temple of Apollo at Delphos, the Prieſts of which Oracle probably gave him this information with no other view but to forward their Scheme, which tended to gratify the Luſt of Præteus the King's brother, who being let through the Roof pretending to be Jupiter, and throwing large Quantities of Gold amongſt her Domeſticks, obtained his Wiſhes.

Two particular Adventures of his are too remarkable to be paſſed in Silence. He had deluded by his Arts, Semele daughter of Cadmus, King of Thebes, who proved with Child. Juno hearing of it, and intent on Revenge, under the diſguiſe of Beroe, Nurſe to the Princeſs, was admitted to her preſence, and artfully inſinuating to her that ſhe might not be deceived in her Lover, ſhe adviſed her the next time he viſited her, to requeſt as a Proof of his Love, that ſhe might ſee him in the ſame Majeſty with which he embraced Juno. Jupiter granted, not without Reluctance a Favour he knew would be ſo fatal to his Miſtreſs. The unhappy fair one unable to bear the dazzling Effulgence, periſhed in the Flames, and with her, her Offspring muſt have done ſo too, if the God had not taken it out and incloſed it in his Thigh, where it lay the full time, when he came into the World and was named Bacchus.

Jupiter next became enamoured of Io, the Daughter of Inachus, and, as ſome ſay, the Prieſteſs of Ju-

no,

Io : having one Day met the Virgin returning from
her Father's Grotto, he endeavoured to seduce her
to an adjacent Forest ; but the Nymph flying his embraces, he involved her in so thick a mist, that she lost
her way, so that he easily undertook and enjoyed
her. Juno, whose Jealousy always kept her watchful,
missing her husband, and perceiving a thick Darkness
on the Earth descended, dispelled the Cloud, and had
certainly discovered the Intrigue, had not Jupiter sudden'y transformed Io into a white Heifer. Juno pleased
with the Beauty of the Animal begged her, and to allay her Jealousy, he was obliged to yield her up. The
Goddess immediately gave her in charge to Argus, who
had a hundred Eyes, two of which only slept at a time.
Her Lover pitying the Misery of Io in so strict a Con-
finement, sent Mercury down disguised like a Shepherd, who with his Flute charmed Argus to sleep,
sealed his Eyes with his Caduceus or Rod, and then
cut off his Head. Juno, in regard to his Memory, placed his Eyes in the Tail of the Peacock, a Bird sacred
to her, and then turning her Rage against Io, sent the
Furies to pursue her wherever she went [a] ; so that
the wretched Fugitive weary of Life implored Jove
to end her Misery. Accordingly the God intreats his
Spouse to shew her Compassion, swearing by Styx never to give her further Cause of Jealousy. Juno on
this becomes appeased, and Io being restored to her
former Shape, is worshipped in Egypt by the name of
Isis.

The Fable of Io and Argus is certainly of Egyptian Birth, and the true Mythology is this : The Art of
weaving first invented in Egypt, was by the Colonies
of that Nation carried to Greece and Cholcis where it
was practised with this Difference, that the Seasons for
working were varied in each Country according to the

[a] Dr. King relates this Story a little differently. Io pursue
by Tisiphone, (one of the Furies) fell into the Sea, and was carried first to the Thracian Bosphorus, and thence into Egypt, where
the Monster still pursuing her was repelled by the Nile. After
this she was Deified by Jupiter, and appointed to preside over
Winds and Navigation. It is easy to see this agrees better with
the Egyptian Mythology

Nature of the Climate. The Months of February, March, April and May they employed in Egypt in cultivating their Lands, whereas thefe being Winter Months with the Grecians, they kept the Looms bufy. Now the Ifis, which pointed out the Neomeniæ or Monthly Feftivals in Egypt, was always attended with an Horus or Figure expreffive of the Labour peculiar to the Seafon. Thus the Horus of the weaving-Months was a little Figure ftuck over with Eyes, to denote the many Lights neceffary for working by Night. This Image was called Argus [b], to fignify his intention. Now the vernal Ifis being depicted with the Head of a Heifer, to exemplify the Fertility and Pleafantnefs of Egypt on the Sun's Entrance into Taurus, at the Approach of Winter fhe quitted this form, and fo was faid to be taken into Cuftody of Argus, from whom fhe was next Seafon delivered, by the Horus reprefenting Anibus, (or Mercury) that is the rifing of the Dog Star. The taking thefe Symbolical Reprefentations, in a literal fenfe, gave Rife to the Fable.

It is no Wonder if the Number of Jupiter's Gallantries made him the Subject of Deteftation among the primitive Chriftians. as well as the Ridicule of the wifer amongft the Heathens. Tertullian obferves with Judgment, " That it was no way ftrange to fee all " Ranks fo debauched, when they were encouraged in " the moft infamous Crimes by the Example of thofe " they worfhipped, and from whom they were to expect " Rewards and Punifhments." Lucian in his Dialogues introduces Momus pleafantly rallying Jove with regard to his amorous Metamorphofes. I have often trembled for you fays he, " Left when you ap- " peared like a Bull, they fhould have carried you to " the Shambles, or clapped you in the Plough : had " a Goldfmith met you when you vifited Danae, he " would have melted down your Godfhip in his Cru-

[b] From Argoth, or Argos, Weaver's Work ; whence the Greeks borrowed their Ergon, Opus, or a Work. Hence the Ifle of Amorgos, one of the Ægean Ifles, derives its Name from Am, Mother ; and Orgin, Weavers, or the Mother or Colony of Weavers being firft planted from Egypt.

" cible

" cible. Or when you courted Leda like a Swan,
what if her Father had put you on the spit?"

Jupiter had a multiplicity of Names, either from the
Places where he was worshipped, or the Attributes a-
scribed to him. He had the Epithets of Xenius, or the
Hospitable ; Elicius on account of his Goodness and
Clemency ; and Dodonæus on Account of the oracular
Grove or Dodona, consecrated to him, and famous
thro' all Greece.

Amongst the Romans he had the Appellations of Op-
timus Maximus, on Account of his Beneficence and
Power: Almus, from his cherishing all Things ; Stabi-
litor from his supporting the world· Opitulator from his
helping the distressed : Stator from his suspending the
Flight of the Romans at the Prayer of Romulus ; and
Prædator on account of the part of the Plunder being
sacred to him in all Victories From his Temple at
the Capitol, on the Turpeian Rock he was called Ca-
pitolinus and Tarpeius. When a Roman King or General slew an Enemy of the same Quality, the Spoils
were offered to him by the Name of Feretrius.

The Reign of Jupiter having not been so agreeable
to his Subjects as that of Saturn, gave occasion to the
Notion of thr SILVER AGE ; by which is meant an
Age inferior in Happiness to that which preceded, tho'
superior to those which followed.

This Father of Gods and Men is commonly figured
as a Majestic Man with a Beard, enthron'd. In his left
Hand he holds a Victory, and his Right-Hand grasps
the Thunder. At his feet an Eagle with his Wings
displayed. The Greeks called him Zena and Dia as the
Cause of Life [c]. the Romans, Jupiter, i. e. juvans
pater, the assisting Father.

The Heathens had amongst their Deities different
Representatives of the same Thing. What Vesta, or
the Idean Mother, was to the Phrygians, and Isis to
the Egyptians ; the same was Jupiter to the Greeks
and Romans, the great Symbol of Æther. So the Author of the Life of Homer, supposed to be the Elder

Dionyſius of Halicarnaſſus, and the Poet himſelf [a].
So Ennius, as quoted by Cicero [b],

Lo, the bright Heav'n, which all invoke as Jove!
and Euripides [b].

——See the ſublime Expanſe,
The boundleſs Æther, which enfolds this Ball,
That hold for Jove, the God ſupreme o'er All

To conclude with the Words of Orpheus; " Jove
" is omnipotent, he is the Firſt and the Laſt; the
" Head and the Middle, the Giver of all Things; the
" Foundation of the Earth and Starry Heavens: He
" is both Male and Female, and immortal. Jupiter
" is the Source of enlivening Fire, and the Spirit of
" all Things."

CHAP. XVI. Of JUNO.

JUNO the Siſter and Conſort of Jupiter, was on
that Account ſtyled the Queen of Heaven, and
indeed we find her in the Poets ſupporting that Dignity with an Ambition and Pride ſuitable to the Rank
ſhe bore,
Though the Poetical Hiſtorians agree ſhe came into
the World at a Birth with her Huſband, yet they differ as to the Place, ſome placing her Nativity at Argos,
others at Samos near the River Imbraſus. Some ſay
ſhe was nurſed by Eubæa, Porſymna, and Aræa,
Daughters of the River Aſterion, others by the Nymphs
of the Ocean. Otes, an antient Poet, tells us ſhe was

---

[a] Zeus de o aither, touteſtin e purodes kai endermos ouſia;
　　Zeus d'elach, ouram non eurum en aitheri kai nepheleſin.
　　　　　　　　　　　Opuſc. Mytholog. p. 326 & 327.
[b] Aſpice hoc ſublime candens, quem invocant omnes Jovem.
[c] Vides ſublime, fuſum, immoderatum æthera,
　　Qui tenero terram circumjectu amplectitur,
　　Hunc ſummum habeto divum; hunc per hibeto Jovem.
　　　　　　　　　　　Cibero de Nat Deorum, l. 2.

educated by the Horæ or Hours: and Homer assigns this Pest to Oceanus and Tethys themselves.

It is said that this Goddess, by bathing annually in the Fountain of Canatho near Argos, renewed her Virginity. The places where she was principally honoured were Sparta, Mycene, and Argos. At this Place the Sacrifice offered to her consisted of 100 Oxen

Juno in a peculiar Manner presided over Marriage and Child birth; on the first occasion, in sacrificing to her, the Gall of the Victim was always thrown behind the Altar, to denote no Spleen should subsist between married Persons. Women were peculiarly thought to be under her protection, of whom every one had her Juno, as every man had his Guardian Genius. Numa ordered, that if any unchaste Woman should approach her Temple, she should offer a female Lamb to expiate her offence.

The Lacedemonians styled her Ægophaga, from the Goat which Hercules sacrificed to her. At Elis she was called Hoplosmia, her Statue being completely armed. At Corinth, she was termed Bunœa, from Buno, who erected a Temple to her there. She had another at Eubœa, to which the Emperor Adrian presented a magnificient Offering, consisting of a Crown of Gold, and a purple Mantle embroidered with the Marriage of Hercules and Hebe in Silver and a large Peacock whose body was Gold, and his Tail composed of precious Stones resembling the natural colours.

Amongst the Romans, who held her in high Veneration, she had a Multiplicity of Names. The Chief were Lucina, from her first shewing the Light to Infants; Pronuba, because no Marriage was lawful without previously invoking her; Socigena and Juga from her introducing the conjugal Yoke, and promoting matrimonial Union. Domiduca on account of her bringing home the Bride; Unxia from the anointing the Door Posts at that Ceremony. Cinxia from her unloosing the Virgin-Zone, or Girdle; Perfecta, because Marriage completes the Sexes; Opigena and Obstetrix from her assisting Women in Labour; Populosa, because Procreation peoples the World: and

Sospita

Sospita from her preserving the Female Sex. She was also named Quiritis or Curitis, from a Spear represented in her Statues and Medals; Kalendaris, because of the Sacrifices offered her the first Day of every Month; and Moneta from her being regarded as the Goddess of Riches and Wealth.

It is said when the Gods fled into Egypt, Juno disguised herself in the Form of a white Cow, which Animal was, on that account, thought to be acceptable to her in her Sacrifices.

Juno as the Queen of Heaven, preserved a good deal of State. Her usual Attendants were Terror and Boldness, Castor and Pollux, and fourteen Nymphs; but her most faithful and inseparable Companion was Iris the Daughter of Thaumas, who for her surprizing Beauty was represented with Wings borne upon her own Rainbow to denote her Swiftness. She was the Messenger of Juno, as Mercury was of Jove; and at Death separated the Souls of Women from their corporeal Chains.

This Goddess was not the most complaisant of Wives. We find in Homer, that Jupiter was sometimes obliged to make use of all his Authority to keep her in due subjection. When she entered into that famous conspiracy against him the same Author relates that by way of Punishment, she had two Anvils tied to her Feet, golden Manacles fastened to her Hands, and so was suspended in the Air or Sky, where she hovered on account of her Levity, while all the Deities looked on without a possibility of helping her. By this the Mythologists say is meant the Harmony and Connexion of the Air with the Earth, and the Inablity of the Gods to relieve her signifies that no Force human or divine, can dissolve the Frame or Texture of the Universe. According to Pausanias, the Temple of Juno at Athens had neither Doors nor Roof, to denote that Juno being the Air in which we breathe can be inclosed in no certain Bounds.

The implacable and arrogant Temper of Juno once made her abandon her Throne in Heaven and fly into Eubœa. Jupiter in vain sought a Reconciliation, till

he

he confulted Citheron King of the Platæans, then accounted the wifeft of Men. By his Advice the God dreffed up a magnificent Image, feated it in a Chariot, and gave out it was Platæa the Daughter of Æfopus; whom he defigned to make his Queen. Juno upon this refuming her antient Jealoufy, attacked the mock Bride, and by tearing off its Ornaments found the Deceit, quieted her ill Humour, and was glad to make up the Matter with her Hufband.

Though none ever felt her Refentment more fenfibly than Hercules, he was indebted to her for his immortality; for Pallas brought him to Jupiter while an Infant, who, while Juno was afleep, put him to her breaft. But the Goddefs waking haftily, fome of her Milk falling upon Heaven formed the Milky way. The reft dropped on the earth, where it made the Lillies white, which before were of a faffron colour.

Juno is reprefented by Homer as drawn in a Chariot adorned with precious Stones, the Wheels of Ebony nailed with filver, and drawn by Horfes with Reins of Gold; but moft commonly her Car is drawn by Peacocks, her favourite Bird. At Corinth fhe was depicted in her Temples as feated on a Throne, crowned with a Pomegranate in one hand, and in the other a fceptre with a Cuckoo at top. This ftatue was of Gold and Ivory. That at Hierapolis was fupported by Lions, and fo contrived as to participate of Minerva, Venus, Luna, Rhea, Diana, Nemefis, and the Deftinies, according to the different Points in View. She held in one Hand a fceptre, in the other a Diftaff. Her Head was crowned with Rays and a Tower; and fhe was girt with the Ceftus of Venus.

As Jupiter is the Æther, Juno is the Atmofphere, fhe is Female on Account of its foftnefs, and is called the wife and fifter of the other, to import the intimate Conjunction between thefe two [a].

---

[a] Aer autem, ut Stoici difputant, inter mare & cœlum, Junonis nomine confecratur, quæ eft foror & conjux Jovis, quod & fimilitudo eft ætheris & cum eo fumma conjunctio. Effeminarunt autem eum, Junonique tribuerunt, quod nihil eft eo mollius. Cicero de Nat. Deor. l. 2.

CHAP.

C H A P. XVII. Of Neptune.

THIS remarkable Deity was the Son of Saturn and Vesta, or Ops and the Brother of Jupiter. Some say he was devoured by his Father. Others alledge his Mother gave him to some Shepherds to be brought up amongst the Lambs, and pretending to be delivered of a Foal, gave it instead of him to Saturn. Some say his Nurse's Name was Arno: others that he was brought up by his Sister Juno.

His most remarkable Exploit was his assisting his Brother Jupiter in his Expeditions, for which that God when he arrived at the supreme Power, assigned him the Sea and the Islands for his Empire. Others imagine he was Admiral of Saturn's Fleet, or rather, according to Pamphus, Generalissimo of his Forces by Sea and Land.

The favourite Wife of Neptune was Amphitrite, whom he courted a long Time to no purpose, till he sent the Dolphin to intercede for him, who succeeding, the God in Acknowledgement placed him amidst the Stars. By her he had Triton. Neptune had two other Wives, the one called Salacia, from the Salt-Water, the other Venilia, from the Ebbing and Flowing of the Tides.

Neptune is said to be the first inventor of Horsemanship and Chariot-racing. Hence Mithridates King of Pontus threw Chariots drawn by four Horses into the Sea in Honour of him, and the Romans instituted Horse-races in the Circus during his Festival, at which Time all Horses left working, and the Mules were adorned with Wreaths of Flowers. Probably this Idea of Neptune arose from the famous controversy between him and Minerva, when they disputed who should give Name to Cecropia. The God by striking the Earth with his Trident, produced a Horse. Pallas raised an Olive-Tree, by which she gained the Victory, and the New City was from her called Athens. But the true meaning of this Fable is a Ship, not a Horse; for the Question really was, whether the Athenians

should

ſhould apply themſelves to Navigation or Agriculture, and as they naturally inclined to the firſt, it was neceſſary to ſhew them their Miſtake, by convincing them that Huſbandry was preferable to Sailing. However, it is certain Neptune had ſome ſkill in the Management of Horſes ; for we find in Pamphus, the moſt ancient Writer of Divine Hymns, this Encomium of him, ' That he was the Benefactor of Mankind in beſtow-' ing on them Horſes, and Ships with Decks reſem-' bling Towers.'

When Neptune was expelled Heaven for his Conſpiracy againſt Jupiter, he fled with Apollo to Laomedon King of Troy ; but he treated them differently, For having employed them in raiſing Walls round this City in which the Lyre of Apollo was highly ſerviceable, he paid that Deity divine honours, whereas he diſmiſſed Neptune unrewarded, who in Revenge, ſent a vaſt Sea Monſter to lay waſte the Country, to appeaſe which Laomedon was forced to expoſe his Daughter Heſione.

On another Occaſion this Deity had a Conteſt with Vulcan and Minerva in regard to their ſkill. The Goddeſs as a proof of her's made a Houſe, Vulcan erected a Man, and Neptune a Bull ; whence that Animal was uſed in the Sacrifices paid him, but it is probable, that as the Victim was to be black, the Deſign was to point out the raging Quality and Fury of the Sea, over which he preſided.

Neptune fell little ſhort o his Brother Jupiter in point of Gallantry. Ovid in his Epiſtles has given a Catalogue of his Miſtreſſes: By Venus he had a Son called Eryx. Nor did he aſſume leſs different ſhapes to ſucceed in his Amours. Ceres fled from him in the form of a Mare, he purſued in that of a Horſe ; but it is uncertain whether this Union produced the Centaur, called Orion, or a Daughter. Under the Reſemblance of the River Enipeus, he debauched Tyro the Daughter of Salmoneus, who bore him Pelius and Neleus. In the ſame Diſguiſe he begot Othus and Ephialtes, by Ephimedia, wife of the Giant Aloëus. Melantho Daughter of Proteus often diverting herſelf by riding on a Dolphin, Neptune in that Figure ſurpriſed and enjoyed her. He

changed

changed Theophane, a beautiful Virgin, into an Ewe, and affuming the Form of a Ram, begot the Golden fleeced Ram, which carried Phryxus to Cholcis. In the Likeneſs of a Bird he had Pegafus by Medufa.

He was not only fond of his Power of transforming himſelf, but he took a pleafure in beſtowing it on his Favourites; Proteus his Son poſſeſſed it in a high degree. He conferred it on Periclimenus the Brother of Neſtor, who was at laſt killed by Hercules, as he watched him in the form of a Fly. He even obliged his Miſtreſſes with it. We find an Inſtance of this in Metra the Daughter of Eriſichton. Her Father for cutting down an Oak-Grove confecrated to Ceres, was puniſhed with fuch an infatiable Hunger, that to fupply it he was forced to fell all he had. His Daughter upon this entreated of her Lover the Power of changing her form at Pleafure; fo that becoming fometimes a Mare, a Cow, or a Sheep, her Father fold her to relieve his wants, while the Buyers were ſtill cheated in their Purchafe. Having raviſhed Cænis, to appeafe her he promiſed her any fatisfaction, on which ſhe defired to be turned into a Man, that ſhe might no more fuffer the like Injury. Her Requeſt was granted, and by the name of Cæneus ſhe became a famous warrior.

Neptune was a confiderable Deity amongſt the Greeks. He had a Temple in Arcadia by the Name Proclyſtius; or, the Over flower; becaufe at Juno's Requeſt he delivered the Country from an Inundation. He was called Hippius, Hippocourius, and Taraxippus, from his regulation of Horfemanſhip. The places moſt celebrated for his Worſhip were Tanarus, Corinth and Calabria, which laſt Country was peculiarly dedicated to him. He had alſo a celebrated Temple at Rome enriched with many naval Trophies; but he received a fignal Affront from Auguſtus Cæfar, who pulled down his Statue in Refentment for a Tempeſt, which had difperfed his Fleet and endangered his life. Some think Neptune the fame with the antient God Cenfus worſhipped at Rome, and fo called from his advifing Romulus to the Rape of the Sabines.

Le:

Let us now examine the mythological Senfe of the
Fable. The Egyptians to denote Navigation, and the
annual Return of the Phænician Fleet, which vifited
their coaft, ufed the Figure of an Ofiris carried on a
winged Horfe, or holding a three-forked Spear or
Harpoon in his Hand. To this Image they gave the
Names of Pofeidon [a] or Neptune [b] which the
Greeks and Romans afterwards adopted;—but which
fufficiently prove this Deity had his Birth here. Thus
the Maritime Ofiris of the Egyptians became a new
Deity with thofe who knew not the Meaning of the
fymbol. But Herodotus, lib. 2. is pofitive that the
Greeks received not their knowledge of Neptune from
the Egyptians, but from the Lybians. The former received him not till afterwards; and even then however they might apply the Figure to civil purpofes, paid
him no divine Honors. However, according to Plutarch, they called the maritime Coaft Nephthen Bochart thinks that he has found the Origin of this God
in the Perfon of Japhet: and has given Reafons which
render the Opinion very probable.

Neptune reprefented as God of the Sea, makes a
confiderable Figure. He is defcribed with black or
dark Hair, his Garment of an Azure or Sea-Green
Colour, feated in a large fhell drawn by Whales or fea-
horfes, with his Trident in his Hand [c], attended by
the Sea Gods Palæmon, Glaucus, and Phorcys; the
Sea Goddeffes, Thetis, Melita and Panopæa, and a
long Train of Tritons and Sea Nymphs. In fome antient Gems he appears on fhore; but always holding
in his hand the three-forked Trident, the Emblem of
his Power, as it is called by Homer and Virgil, who
have given us a fine Contraft with regard to its Ufe.

[a] From Pafh, Plenty, or Provifions, and Jedaim, the Sea-
coaft; or the Provifion of the maritime Countries.

[b] From Nouph to difturb or agitate; and Oni a Fleet, which
forms Neptoni, the Arrival of the Fleet.

[c] Some by a far-fetched Allufion, imagine the triple Forks
of the Trident reprefent the three-fold Power of Neptune in dif-
turbing, moderating or calming the Seas. Others, his Power
over falt Water, frefh Water; and that of Lakes or Pool

The

The antient Poets all make this Inftrument of Brafs; the modern Painters of filver.

CHHP. XVIII. Of PLUTO.

WE now come to the Third Brother of Jupiter, and not the leaft formidable, if we confider his Power and Dominion. He was alfo the fon of Saturn and Ops, and when his victorious Brother had eftablifhed himfelf in the Throne, he was rewarded with a fhare in his Father's Dominions, which as fome Authors fay, was the Eaftern Continent and lower Part of Afia. Others make his divifion lie in the Weft, and that he fixed his Refidence in Spain, which being a fertile Country, and abounding in Mines, he was efteemed the God of Wealth [a].

Some imagine that his being regarded as the Ruler of the Dead, and King of the infernal Regions, proceeded from his firft teaching Men to bury the Deceafed, and inventing Funeral Rites to their Honour. Others fay he was a King of the Moloffians in Epirus called Aidonius or Orcus, that he ftole Proferpina's Wife and kept a Dog called Cerberus, who devoured Pirithous, and would have ferved Thefeus in the fame Manner, if Hercules had not timely interpofed to fave him.

The Poets relate the Matter differently : They tell us that Pluto, chagrined to fee himfelf childlefs and unmarried, while his two Brothers had large Families, mounted his Chariot, to vifit the World, and arriving in Sicily, chanced to view Proferpine, with her Companions, gathering Flowers [b]. Urged by his Paffion he forced her into his Chariot, and drove her to the River Chemarus, thro' which he opened himfelf a Paffage back to the Realms of Night. Ceres difcon-

[a] Some Poets confound Pluto the God of Hell with Plutus the God of Riches; whereas they are two very diftinct Deities, and were always fo confidered by the Antients.
[b] In the Valley of AEnna near Mount AEtna.

E

folate

folate for the Lofs of her beloved Daughter lighted two Torches at the Flames of Mount Ætna, and wandered through the World in fearch of her; till hearing at laft where fhe was, fhe carried her Complaint to Jupiter, who on her repeated Sol'citations, promifed that Proferpine fhould be reftored to her provided fhe had not yet tafted any Thing in Hell. Ceres joyfully bore this Commiffion, and her Daughter was preparing to return, when Afcalaphus the Son of Acheron and Gorgyra gave Information, that he faw Proferpine eat fome Grains of a Pomegranate fhe had gathered in Pluto's Orchard, fo that her Return was immediately countermanded Afcalaphus was for this malicious intelligence transformed into a Toad. But Jupiter in order to mitigate the Grief of Ceres, for her difappointment, granted that her Daughter fhould half the Year refide with her, and the other Half continue in Hell with her Hufband. It is eafy to fee, that this Part of the Fable alludes to the Corn, which muft remain all the Winter hid in the Ground, in order to fprout forth in the Spring and produce the Harveft.

Pluto was extremely revered both amongft the Greeks and Romans. He had a magnificent Temple at Pylos near which was a Mountain, that derived its Name from the Nymph Menthe, whom Proferpine, out of jealoufy at Pluto's familiarity with her, changed into the Herb called Mint. Near the River Corellus in Bœotia this Deity had alfo an Altar in common with Pallas, for fome myftical Reafon. The Greeks called him Angeleftus, becaufe all Mirth and Laughter were banifhed his Dominions; as alfo Hades, on Account of the Gloominefs of his Dominions. Among the Romans he had the Name of Februus, from the Luftrations ufed at Funerals, and Summanus becaufe he was the chief of Ghofts, or rather the Prince of the infernal Deities. He was alfo called the Terreftrial or infernal Jupiter.

His chief Feftival was in February, and called Chariftia, becaufe then Oblations were made for the Dead, at which Relations affifted, and all Quarrels
were

were amicably adjusted. Black Bulls were the Victims offered up, and the Ceremonies were performed in the Night, it not being lawful to sacrifice to him in the Day time (a).

Pluto is usually represented in an Ebony Chariot, drawn by four Black Horses, whose Names the Poets have been careful to transmit (b) to us. Sometimes he holds a Sceptre to denote his Power, at others a wand with which he commands and drives the Ghosts. Homer speaks of his Helmet, as having the Quality of rendering the Wearer invisible; and tells us that Minerva borrowed it when she fought against the Trojans, to be concealed from Mars.

Let us now seek the Mythology of the Fable in that Country where it first sprung, and we shall find that the mysterious Symbols of Truth became, in the Sequel, through Abuse, the very Sources of Idolatry and Error. Pluto was indeed the Funeral Osiris of the Egyptians. These People (c) every Year, at an appointed Season, assembled to mourn over and offer Sacrifices for their Dead. The Image that was exposed to denote the Approach of this Solemnity, had the Name of Peloutah (d), or the Deliverance, because they regarded the Death of the Good, as a Deliverance from Evil. This Figure was represented with a radiant crown, his body being entwined with a serpent accompanied with the signs of the Zodiack, to signify the Duration of our Sun, or Solar Year.

CHAP. XIX. Of PROSERPINE.

THIS Goddess was the Daughter of Jupiter and Ceres, and educated in Sicily, from whence she was stolen by Pluto, as is related in the preceding

(a) On Account of his Aversion to the Light.
(b) Orpheus, Aëthon, Nycteus, and Alastor.
(c) The Jews retained this Custom, as we find by the annual Lamentations of the Virgins over Jeptha's Daughter.
(d) From Palat to free or deliver, comes Peloutah Deliverance, which is is easily by Corruption made Pluto.

Chapter. Some say she was brought up by Minerva and Diana, and being extremely beautiful was courted both by Mars and Apollo, who could neither of them obtain her Mother's Consent. Jupiter, it is said, was more fuccefsful, and ravished her in the Form of a Dragon. The Phœnicians on the other Hand affirm with more Reafon, that she was earlier known to them than to the Greeks or Romans; and that it was about 200 Years after the Time of Mofes, that she was carried off by by Aidoneus or Orcus King of the Moloffians.

Jupiter, on her Marriage with Pluto, gave her the Ifle of Sicily as a Dowry: but she had not been long in the infernal Regions, when the fame of her charms induced Thefeus and Pirithous, to form an Affociation to carry her off. They defcended by way of Tænarus, but fitting to reft themfelves on a Rock in the infernal Regions, they could not rife again, but continued fix'd, till Hercules delivered Thefeus, becaufe his Crime confifted only in affifting his Friend, as bound by Oath [a]; but Pirithous was left in durance becaufe he had endangered himfelf through his own Wilfulnefs and Rafhnefs.

Others made Proferpine the fame with Luna, Hecate, and Diana, the fame Goddefs being called Luna in Heaven, Diana on Earth, and Hecate in Hell, when she had the Name of Triformis or Tergemina. The Greeks called her Defpoina, or the Lady, on Account of her being Queen of the Dead. Dogs and barren Cows are the facrifices ufually offered to her.

She is reprefented under the Form of a beautiful Woman enthroned, having fomething ftern and melancholy in her Afpect.

The mytholigical fenfe of the Fable is this.—The Name of Proferpine or Profephone, amongft the Egyptians, was ufed to denote the Change produced in the Earth by the Deluge [b], which deftroyed its former

[a] They agreed to affift each other in gaining a Miftrefs, Pirithous had helped Thefeus to get Helena, who in return attended him in his Expedition.

[b] From Peri, Fruit, and Patat, to perifh, comes Perephtifh, or the Fruit loft: From Peri, Fruit, and Saphon, to hide comes Perfephoneh, or the Corn deftroyed or hid.

Fertility

Fertility, and rendered Tillage and Agriculture necessary to Mankind.

CHAP. XX. Of the INFERNAL REGIONS.

IT is evident that the Heathens had a Notion of future Punishments and Rewards, from the Descriptions their Poets have given of Tartarus and Elysium; though the whole is incumbered with Fiction.—According to Plato, Apollo and Ops brought certain brazen Tablets from the Hyperboreans to Delos, describing the Court of Pluto as little inferior to that of Jove; but that the Approach to it was exceeding difficult on Account of the Rivers Acheron, Cocytus, Styx and Phlegethon, which it was necessary to pass in order to reach these infernal Regions.

Acheron was, according to some, the son of Titan and Terra, or as others say, born of Cerus in a Cave; without a Father. The Reason assigned for his being sent to Hell is, that he furnished the Titans with Water, during their War with the Gods. This shews it was a River, not a Person; but the Place of it is not ascertained. Some fixing it amongst the Cimmerians near Mount Circe (a), and in the Neighbourhood of Cocytus; others making it that sulphureous and stinking Lake near Cape Misenum in the Bay of Naples (b) and not a few tracing its Rise from the Acherusian Fen in Epirus, near the City of Pandosia; from whence it flows till it falls into the Gulf of Ambracia.

The next River of the Plutonian Mansions is Styx; though whether the Daughter of Oceanus or Terra, is uncertain. She was married to Pallas or Piras, by whom she had Hydra. To Acheron she bore Victory, who having assisted Jupiter against the Giants, he rewarded her Mother (c) with this privilege, that the most solemn Oath amongst the Gods should be by her

(a) On the Coast of Naples.   (b) Near Cuma.
(c) Some say it was on her own Account, for discovering the Combination of the Giants against Jupiter.

                    Deity

Deity, viz. the River Styx ; so that when any of them
were suspected of Falshood, Iris was dispatched to
bring the Stygian Water in a golden Cup, by which
he swore; and if he afterwards proved perjured, he
was deprived for a Year of his Nectar aud Ambrosia,
and for nine Years more, separated from the celestial
Assembly. Some place Styx near the Lake of Avernus
in Italy, others make it a Fountain near Nonacris in
Arcadia, of so poisonous and cold a Nature, that it
would dissolve all Metals (a), and could be contained
in no Vessel.

Cocytus and Phlegethon are said to flow out of
Styx by contrary Ways, and reunite to increase the
vast Channel of Acheron. The Waters of Phlegethon
were represented as Streams of Fire. probably on account of their hot and sulphureous Nature.

CHAP. XXI. Of the PARCÆ or DESTINIES.

THESE infernal Deities, who presided over human Life, were in Number Three, and had
each their peculiar Province assigned, Clotho held the
Distaff, Lachesis drew or spun off the Thread, and
Atrapos stood ready with her Scissars to cut it asunder

These were three Sisters, the Daughters of Jupiter
and Themis, and Sisters to the Horæ or Hours; according to others, the Children of Erebus and Nox.——
They were Secretaries to the Gods, whose Decrees
they wrote.

We are indebted to a late ingenious Writer for the
true Mythology of these Characters. They were nothing more originally than the mystical Figures or
Symbols which represented the Months of January,
February and March amongst the Egyptians. They
depicted these in Female Dresses, with the Instruments of Spinning and Weaving, which was the great
Business carried on in that Season. These Images

(a) It is reported Alexander was poisoned with it at Babylon;
and that it was carried for this Purpose in an Ass's Hoof.

they

they call'd [a] Parc, which signifies Linen Cloth to
denote the Manufacture produced by this Industry.
The Greeks, who knew nothing of the true Sense of
these allegorical Figures gave them a turn suitable to
their Genius, fertile in Fiction.

The Parcæ were described or represented in Robes
of white, bordered with Purple, and seated on
Thrones, with Crowns on their Heads, composed of
the Flowers of the Narcissus:

CHAP. XXII.   Of the HARPYES.

THE next Group of Figures we meet in the
shadowy Realms are the Harpyes, who were
Three in Number, Celeno, Aello, and Ocypete, the
Daughters of Oceanus, and Terra. They lived in
Thrace, had the Faces of Virgins, the Ears of Bears,
the Bodies of Vultures, with human Arms and Feet,
and long Claws. Pheneus King of Arcadia, for re-
vealing the Mysteries of Jupiter, was so tormented by
them, that he was ready to perish for Hunger, they
devouring whatever was set before him, till the Sons
of Boreas, who attended Jason in his Expedition to
Colchis, delivered the good old King, and drove these
Monsters to the Islands called Echinades, compelling
them to swear to return no more.

This Fable is of the same Original with the former
one. During the Months of April, May, and June,
especially the two latter, Egypt was greatly subject to
stormy Winds, which laid waste their Olive Grounds,
and brought numerous swarms of Grashoppers and
other troublesome Insects from the shores of the Red
Sea, which did infinite Damage to the Country. The
Egyptians therefore gave Figures which proclaimed
these three Months, a Female Face, with the Bodies
and Claws of Birds, and called them Harop [b], a

---

[a] From Parc, or Paroket, a Cloth, Curtain or Sail.
[b] From Haroph, or Harop, a noxious Fly; or from Arbeh, a
Locust.

Name

Name which sufficiently denoted the true sense of the
Symbol.   All this the Greeks realized, and embellished in their Way.

CHAP. XXIII. Of CHARON and CERBERUS.

CHARON, according to Hesiod's Theology,
was the Son of Erebus and Nox, the Parents of
the greatest Part of the infernal Monsters.   His Post
was to ferry the Souls of the deceased over the Waters of Acheron.   His Fare was never under one Half-
penny, nor exceeding Three, which were put in the
Mouths of the Persons interred ; for as to such Bodies
who were denied Funeral Rites, their Ghosts were
forced to wander an hundred Years on the Banks of
the River, Virgil's Eneid VI. 330, before they could
be admitted to a Passage.   The Hermoniences alone
claimed a free Passage, because their Country lay so
near Hell.   Some mortal Heroes also, by the Favour
of the Gods, were allowed to visit the infernal Regions, and return to Light ; such as Hercules, Orpheus,
Ulysses,, Theseus and Æneas.

'This venerable Boatman of the lower World, is represented as a fat squalid old Man, with a bushy
grey Beard and rheumatick Eyes, his tattered Rags
scarce covering his Nakedness.   His Disposition is
mentioned as rough and morose, treating all his pas-
sengers with the same impartial Rudeness, without
Regard to Rank, Age, or Sex.   We shall in the Sequel see that Charon was indeed a Real Person and
justly merited this Character.

After crossing the Acheron, in a Den adjoining to
the Entrance of Pluto's Palace, was placed Cerberus,
or the three headed Dog, born of Typhon and Echidna, and the dreadful Mastiff, who guarded these
gloomy Abodes.   He fawned upon all who entered,
but devoured all who attempted to get back ; yet

Hercules once maftered him, and dragged him up to
Earth, where in ftruggling, a Foam dropped from his
Mouth, which produced the poifonous Herb, called
Aconite or Wolf Bane.

Hefiod gives Cerberus fifty, and fome a hundred
Heads; but he is more commonly reprefented with
Three. As to the reft he had the Tail of a Dragon,
and inftead of Hair, his Body was covered with Serpents of all kinds. The dreadfulnefs of his Bark or
Howl, Virgil's Eneid VI. 416, and the intolerable
Stench of his Breath, heightened the Deformity of
the Picture, which of itfelf was fufficiently difagrea-
ble.

CHAP. XXIV. Of Nox and her Progeny,
DEATH, SLEEP, &c.

NOX was the moft antient of the Deities, and
Orpheus afcribes to her the Generation of
Gods and Men. She was even reckoned older than
Chaos. She had a num-rous Offspring of imaginary
Children as Lyffa, or Madnefs, Erys, or Contention,
Death, Sleep, and Dreams, all which fhe bore without
a Father. From her Marriage with Erebus, pro-
ceeded Old Age, Labour, Love, Fear, Deceit, Emu-
lation, Mifery, Darknefs, Complaint, Obftinacy, and
Partiality, Want, Care, Difappointment, Difeafe, War
and Hunger. In fhort, all the Evils which attend
Life, and which wait round the Palace of Pluto receive his Commands.

Death brings down all Mortals to the infernal Fer-
ry. It is faid that her Mother, Nox, beftowed a pecu-
liar care in her Education, and that Death had a great
Affection for her Brother Somnus, or Sleep, of whofe
Palace Virgil has given us a fine Defcription, Æneid
VI. 894. Somnus had feveral Children, of whom
Morpheus was the moft remarkable, for his fatirical
Humour, and excellent Talent in mimicking the Ac-
tions of Mankind.

Amongft

Amongſt the Eleans, the Goddeſs Nox, or Night, was repreſented by a Woman holding in each Hand a Boy aſleep, with their Legs diſtorted; that in her Right was White, to ſignify Sleep, that in her Leſt Black, to figure or repreſent Death. The Sacrifice offered to her was a Cock, becauſe of its Enmity to Darkneſs, and rejoicing at the Light. Somnus was uſually repreſented with Wings to denote his univerſal Sway.

CHAP. XXV. Of the Infernal Judges, MINOS, RHADAMANTHUS, and ÆACUS.

AFTER entering the Infernal Regions, juſt at the Separation of the two Roads which lead to Tartarus and Elyſium, is placed the Tribunal of the three inexorable Judges, who examine the Dead, and paſs a final Sentence on departed Souls. The chief of theſe, was Minos the Son of Jupiter, by Europa, and Brother of Rhadamanthus and Sarpedon. After his Father's Death the Cretans would not admit him to ſucceed him in the Kingdom, till praying to Neptune to give him a Sign, that God cauſed a Horſe to riſe out of the Sea, on which he obtained the Kingdom. Some think that this alludes to his reducing theſe Iſlanders to Subjection, by Means of a powerful Fleet. It is added that Jove kept him nine Years concealed in a Cave, to teach him Laws, and the Art of Government.

Rhadamanthus his Brother was alſo a great Legiſlator. It is ſaid, that having killed his Brother, he fled to OEchalia in Bœotia, where he married Alcmena, Widow of Amphytrion His Province was to judge ſuch as died impenitent.

Æacus was the Son of Jupiter, by Ægina. When the Iſle of Ægina (ſo called from his Mother) was depopulated by a Plague, his Father, in Compaſſion to his Grief, changed all the Ants there into Men and Women. The Meaning of which Fable is, that when

when the Pyrates had depopulated the Country, and forced the People to fly to caves, Æacus encouraged them to come out, and by Commerce and Induftry recover what they had loft His Character for Juftice was fuch, that in a Time of univerfal Drought, he was nominated by the Delphic Oracle to intercede for Greece, and his Prayer was anfwered.

Rhadamanthus and Æacus were only inferior Judges, the firft of whom examined the Afiaticks, the latter the Europeans, and bore only Rods as a Mark of their Office. But all difficult Cafes were referred to Minos, who fat over them with a Sceptre of Gold. Their Court was held in a large Meadow, called the Field of Truth. Plato and Tully add Triptolimus to thefe as a Fourth Judge.

CHAP. XXVI. Of TARTARUS and the EUMENIDES OF FURIES.

IN the Receffes of the infernal Regions lay the feat or Abode of the wicked Souls, called Tartarus, reprefented by the Poets, as a vaft deep pit, furrounwith Walls and Gates of Brafs, and totally deprived of Light. This dreadful prifon is furrounded by the Waters of Phlegethon, which emit continual Flames. The Cuftody of the unfortunate Wretches doomed to this place of Punifhment, is given to the Eumenides or Furies. who are at once their Gaolers and Executioners.

The Names of thefe avengeful Sifters were Tifiphone, Alecto, and Megæra ; but they went by the general Appellation of the Furiæ, on account of the Rage and Diftraction attending a guilty Confcience; of Erynniæ or Erynnyes, becaufe of the Severity of their Punifhment ; and Eumenides, becaufe though cruel they were capable of Supplication, as Oreftes found by following the advice of Pallas. Their birth is fo differently related, that it is impoffible to fix their Genealogy or Parentage. Indeed the Theogony of the Greeks and Romans requires an uncommon Clue

to get out of the Labyrinth, which Fiction has contrived.

Though the Furies were implacable, they were fufceptible of Love. We find an Inftance of this in Tifiphone, who growing enamoured with Cythæron, an amiable Youth, and fearing to affright him by her Form, got a third Perfon to difclofe her Flame. He was fo unhappy as to reject her Suit, on which fhe threw one of her Snakes at him, which twining round his Body ftrangled him. All the Confolation he had in Death was to be changed into a Mountain, which ftill bears his Name.

Thefe Goddeffes were fo terrible, that it was in fome Degree facrilegious to invoke their name. Yet however the Objects of Terror, they had their Temples, as at Athens near the Areopagus, at Cafina in Arcadia, and at Carmia in the Peloponnefus. But their higheft folemnities were at Telphufia in Arcadia, where their Prieftefses went by the name of Hefychidæ, and the Sacrifices were performed at Midnight, amidft a profound filence, a black Ewe burnt whole being the Victim. No wine was ufed in the Libations, but only limpid Water, or a Liquor made of Honey; and the Wreaths ufed, were of the Flowers of the Narciffus and Crocus intermixed.

The Mythologifts have affigned each of thefe Tormentreffes their particular Department. Tifiphone is faid to punifh the fins arifing from Hatred and Anger: Megæra thofe occafioned by Envy; and Alecto the Crimes owing to Ambition and Luft. Some make but one Fury, called Adraftia, the daughter of Jupiter and Neceffity, and the Avenger of all Vice.

The Furies are depicted with Hair compofed of Snakes, and Eyes inflamed with Madnefs, carrying in one hand Whips and Iron Chains, and in the other flaming Torches, yielding a difmal Light. Their Robes are black, and their Feet of Brafs to fhew their purfuit, though flow, is fteady and certain.

Is it poffible to conceive, that after this folemn and horrid Reprefentation, the Eumenides, or Furies, fhould be harmlefs Beings? And the very Deformities,
afcribed

bed to them the Symbols of national Joy and Repole. The Egyptians used thefe Figures to denote the three Months of Autumn. The Serpent was with that People, the Hieroglyphic of Life, Light and Happinefs; the Torch was the public Indication of a Sacrifice, and they placed two Quails at the Feet of the Figure, to fignify that the general Security was owing to the plenty of the Seafon. All this is elucidated by the Names of thefe vifionary Beings, Tifiphone [a], Alecto [b], Megæra [c]; which are all derived from Circumftances relating to the Vintage.

CHAP. XXVII. Of the fabulous Perfons punifhed in TARTARUS.

THE Poets in order to people this difmal Region, have placed here the Giants or Titans, who rebelled againft Jupiter, and who are bound in everlafting Chains. They alfo mention feveral other notorious Criminals condemned to fuffer here, the chief of whom follow.

Tityus was the Son of Jupiter and Elara, Daughter of the River Orchomenius in Theffaly. His Father apprehenfive of Juno's Jealoufy, it is faid, concealed him in the Earth, where he grew to a monftrous Bulk. He refided in Panopœa, where he became formidable for Rapine and Cruelty till Apollo killed him for endeavouring to ravifh Latona, though others fay he was flain by Diana for an attempt on her Chaftity. He was next fent to Tartarus, and chained down on his Back, his Body taking up fuch a compafs as to cover nine Acres. In this Pofture a Vulture continually preyed on his Liver, which ftill grew again as faft as it was confumed.

[a] From Tfaphon, to inclofe or to hide, and Tfeponeh, the Time of putting the Wine into Pitchers.
[b] From Leket, to gather.
[c] From Migerah, the finking of the Dregs, or the clarifying the Wine.

Phlegya

Phlegyas was the Son of Mars, and King of the Lapithæ, a people of Theſſaly; Apollo having debauched his Daughter Coronis, to revenge the Injury he ſet fire to the Temple of Delphos, for which Sacrilege that God killed him with his Arrows, and thruſt him into Tartarus, where he is ſentenced to ſit under a huge Rock, which hanging over his Head threatens him with perpetual Deſtruction.

Ixion was the Son of Mars and Piſidice, or as others ſay of Æthon and Piſione. Having married Dia the Daughter of Dioneus, he promiſed very conſiderable preſents to her Father for his conſent; but to elude the performance, he invited him to a Feaſt, and murdered him. Stung with Remorſe for the Crime he ran mad, ſo that Jupiter in compaſſion not only forgave him, but took him into Heaven, where he had the Impiety to endeavour to corrupt Juno. Jupiter, to be the better aſſured of his Wickedneſs, formed a Cloud in the ſhape of his Wife, upon which Ixion begot the Centaurs. But boaſting of his happineſs, Jove hurled him down to Tartarus, where he lies fixed on a Wheel encompaſſed with Serpents, and which turns without ceaſing.

Syſiphus was a deſcendant of Æolus, and married Merope, one of the Pleiades, who bore him Glaucus. His Reſidence was at Epira in Peloponneſus, and he was a crafty Man. The Reaſons given for his puniſhment are various, though all the Poets agree as to its Nature, which was to roll a great ſtone to the Top of a hill, from whence it conſtantly fell down again, ſo that his Labour was inceſſantly renewed [d].

Tantalus a Phrygian Monarch, the Son of Jupiter and the Nymph Plota, had the impiety in an Entertainment he gave the Gods, to kill his Son Pelops and ſerve him up as one of the Diſhes. All the Deities perceived the Fraud but Ceres, who eat one of his ſhoulders, but in Compaſſion to his Fate, ſhe reſtored

---

[d] Some make Syſiphus a Trojan Secretary, who was puniſhed for diſcovering Secrets of State. Others ſay he was a notorious Robber killed by Theſeus

him

him to Life by boiling him in a Cauldron, and gave him an Ivory Arm to supply the defect.   The Crime of the Father did not pass unpunished.   He was placed in Tartarus, where he was afflicted with eternal Thirst and Hunger, having Water and the most delicious Fruits still within his Reach ; but not being able to taste either, because they vanquished before his touch. Ovid IV 445.

Salmoneus, King of Elis, Virgil. Æn. VI. 585, had the presumption to personate Jupiter, by driving a Chariot over a Bridge of Brass, and casting flaming Torches amongst the Spectators, to imitate Thunder and Lightening.   For this he was doomed to the Tortures of this infernal Dungeon.

The Belides complete this fabulous Catalogue.— They were the Daughters of Danaus the Son of Belus, who was cotemporary with Cecrops, King of Athens. This Prince, who came from Egypt into Greece, expelled Sthenelus King of the Argives out of his Kingdom, and by different Wives had these fifty Sisters. His Brother Egyptus, with whom he had some difference, proposed a Reconciliation, by marrying his fifty Sons with their fair Cousin Germans.   The Wedding was agreed, but Danaus perfidiously directed each of his Daughters to murder their Husbands on the Marriage Night.   Hypermnestra alone suffered Lynceus to escape to Lyrcea near Argos [e].   The Belides, for this unnatural Crime, were condemned to draw Water out of a Well with Sieves, and pour it into a certain Vessel so that their Labour was without End or Success.

CHAP. XXVIII.   Of the ELYSIAN FIELDS, and LETHE.

BY Way of Contrast to Tartarus, or the Prison of the Wicked, let us place the Elysian Fields, or the happy abodes of the Just and Good, of which

[e] He afterwards dethroned Danaus.

                Virgil

Virgil, of all the ancient Poets has given us the moſt agreeable Picture, Virgil's Æneid VI. 635. It were endleſs to give all the Variety of Deſcriptions, which a Subject of this Nature affords Room for. An eternal Spring of Flowers or Verdure, a Sky always ſerene, and fanned by ambroſial Breezes, an univerſal Harmony and uninterrupted Joy enbalmed theſe delightful Regions. But at the end of a certain Period, the Souls placed here returned to the World to re animate new Bodies, before which they were obliged to drink at the River Lethe [f], whoſe Waters had the Virtue to create an Oblivion of all that had paſſed in the former part of their Lives.

To illuſtrate all this complexed Chaos of Fable, let us once more have recourſe to the Egyptian Mythology, where we ſhall find the whole ſecret of Tartarus and the Elyſian Fields unravelled. There was near each of the Egyptian Towns a certain Ground appointed for a common Burial place. That at Memphis, as deſcribed by Diodorus, lay on the other ſide of the Lake Acheruſia [g] to the Shore of which the deceaſed perſon was brought, and ſet before a Tribunal of Judges appointed to examine into his Conduct. If he had not paid his Debts his Body was delivered to his Creditors, till his Relations releaſed it, by collecting the Sums Due. If he had not faithfully obſerved the Laws, his Body was left unburied, or probably thrown into a kind of common Shore called Tartarus [h]. The ſame Hiſtorian informs us, that near Memphis there was a leaking Veſſel into which they inceſſantly poured Nile Water, which Circumſtance gives ground to imagine, that the Place where unburied bodies were caſt out, was ſurrounded with Emblems expreſſive of Torture or Remorſe, ſuch as a Man tied on a Wheel always in Motion; another whoſe Heart was the Prey of a Vulture; and a Third

[f] Apo tes lethes, or Oblivion.
[g] From Acharei, after, and iſh, Man, comes Achariis, or the laſt State of Man, or Acheron, that is the ultimate Condition.
[h] From the Chaldaick Tarah, Admonition, doubled, comes Tartarah, or Tartarus, that is, an extraordinary Warning.

rolling

rolling a Stone up a Hill with fruitless Toil. Hence the Fables of Ixion, Prometheus and Syfiphus.

When no Accufer appeared againft the deceafed, or the accufer was convicted of Falfhood, they ceafed to lament him, and his Panegyrick was made; after which he was delivered to a certain fevere Ferryman, who by Order of the Judges, and never without it, received the Body into his Boat (a) and tranfported it acrofs the Lake, to a plain embellifhed with Groves, Brooks, and other rural Ornaments. This place was called Elizout, [b] or the Habitation of Joy. At the Entrance of it, was placed the Figure of a Dog with three pair of Jaws, which they called Cerberus [c]; and the Ceremony of Interment was ended by thrice [d] fprinkling Sand over the Aperture of the Vault, and thrice bidding the Deceafed Adieu. All thefe wife Symbols addreffed as fo many Inftructions to the People, became the Sources of endlefs Fiction, when tranfplanted to Greece and Rome. The Egyptians regarded Death as a Deliverance [e]. The Boat of Tranfportation they called Beris [f], or Tranquility: and the Waterman who was impartial in the juft execution of his Office, they ftiled Charon which fignifies Inflexibility or Wrath.

[a] Sometimes the Judges denied even their Kings Funeral Rites on Account of their Mif-government.

[b] From Elizout, full Satisfaction, or a Place of Repofe and Joy.

[c] They placed this Image on Account of that Animal's known Fidelity to Man. The three Heads denoted the three Funeral Cries over the Corpfe, which is the Meaning of the Name from Ceri, or Cri, an Exclamation; and from Ber the Grave or Vault, comes Cerber, or Cerberus, the Cries of the Grave.

[d] Injecto ter pulvere Horace, Book I. Ode 28.

[e] They call it Pelourah, Alleviation or Deliverance. Horace has the fame thought.

Levare functum pauperum Laboribus. Carm. l. 2. Od. 18.

[f] From Beri, Quiet, Serenity; whence Diodorus Siculus calls Charon's Bark Baris.

CHAP. XXIX.   Of Apollo.

THIS Deity makes one of the moſt conſpicuous Figures in the Heathen Theology, indeed not unjuſtly, from the glorious Attributes aſcribed to him of being the God of Light, Medicine, Verſe and Prophecy.   Tully mentions four of this Name, the moſt antient of whom was the Son of Vulcan, and tutelary God of the Athenians; the Second a Son of Corybas, and born in Crete; the Third an Arcadian, called Nomion, from his being a great Legiſlator; and the laſt, to whom the greateſt Honour is aſcribed, the Son of Jupiter and Latona [a], whoſe Beauty having gained the Affection of the King of the Gods, Juno, on diſcovering her pregnancy, drove her out of Heaven, and commanded the Serpent Python to deſtroy her, from whoſe purſuit Latona fled to the Iſle of Delos in the ſhape of a Quail [b], where ſhe was delivered of Twins, called Diana and Apollo, the latter of whom ſoon after his Birth, deſtroyed the Monſter Python with his Arrows [c], tho' ſome defer the time of this Victory till he came to riper Years.   But Latona's Troubles did not end here, for flying into Lycia with her Children, ſhe was denied the Water of the Fountain Mela, by the Shepherd Niocles and his Clowns, upon which ſhe turned them into Frogs. After ſettling her Son Appollo in Lycia, ſhe returned to Delos and Diana went to reſide in Crete.

The Adventures of Apollo are pretty numerous. The moſt remarkable, are his Quarrels with Jupiter, on account of the Death of his Son Æſculapius, killed by that Deity on the Complaint of Pluto, that he decreaſed the Number of the dead by the Cures he performed.   Apollo to revenge this Injury, killed the Cyclops, who forged Joves Thunderbolts, for which

[a] The Daughter of Cæus the Titan, and Phæbe.
[b] Whence the Iſle was called Ortygia, tho' ſome ſay that Neptune raiſed it out of the Sea to give her Refuge.
[c] Some aſſert that Diana aſſiſted him in this Flight.

he was banifhed Heaven, and endured great Sufferings
on earth, being forced to hire himfelf as a Shepherd to
[a] Admetus King of Theffaly, during his exerci-
fing which Office, he is faid to have invented the Lyre
or Lute, to footh his Trouble. In this Retirement
an odd incident happened to him: Mercury was born
in the Morning, by Noon he had learned Mufick,
and compofed the Teftudo; and in the Evening coming to Apollo he fo amufed him with this new Inftrument, that he found an Opportunity to Steal his Cattle. Apollo difcovering the Theft, and infifting on
Reftitution, the fly Deity ftole his Bow and Arrows;
fo that he was forced to change his Refentment into
Laughter [b].

From Theffaly,, Apollo removed to Sparta, and
fettled near the River Euroras where he fell in Love
with a fair Boy called Hyacinthus, with whom being
at play, Zephirus thro Envy blew Apollo's Quoit at
his Head, and killed him on the Spot. To preferve
his Memory, the God from his Blood raifed the Flower which bears his Name [c]. Though according to
others, he only tinged with it the Violet (which was
white before) into a Purple.

Cypariffus, a beautiful Boy, a Favourite of Apollo
being exceffively grieved for the Death of a Fawn or
Deer he loved, was changed by him to a Cyprefs Tree
which is fince facred to Funeral Rites.

Apollo next vifited Laomedon King of Troy, where
finding Neptune in the fame Condition with himfelf,
and exiled from Heaven, they agreed with that King
to furnifh Bricks to build the Walls of his Capital:
He alfo affifted Alcathous in building a Labyrynth, in

---

[a] Some give this Hiftory another Turn, and tell us that Apollo being King of the Arcadians, and depofed for his Tyranny, fled
to Admetus, who gave him the Command of the Country lying
near the River Amphryfas, inhabited by Shepherds.

    [b] Te boves olim, nifi reddidiffes
        Per dolum amotas, puerum minaci
        Voce dum terret, Viduus Pharetra
            Rifit Apollo.   Horat. Lib. I. Ode X. l. 10.
[c] The Hyacinth or Violet.

which

which was a ſtone whereon he uſed to depoſit his Lyre, and which admitted an harmonious ſound on the ſlighteſt Stroke.

Though Apollo was diſtinguiſhed for his Excellence in Muſick, yet he was extremely jealous of Rivalſhip on this Head. The Muſes were under his immediate Protection, and the Graſshopper was conſecrated to him by the Athenians on account of its Harmony [a]. We find Midas King of Phrygia being conſtituted Judge between him and Pan, who pretended to vie with him in Harmony, and giving Judgment for the Latter was rewarded with a Pair of Aſſes Ears, to point out his bad taſte [b]. Ovid has deſcribed this Story in an agreeable Manner. Linus, who excelled all-Mortals in Muſick, preſuming to ſing with Apollo, was puniſhed with Death; nor did Marſyas the Satyr eſcape much better, for having found a Flute or Pipe, which Minerva threw away [c] he had the Vanity to diſpute the Prize with Apollo, who being decreed Victor, hung up his Antagoniſt on the next Pine Tree, and flayed him alive; but afterwards changed him into a River, which falls into the Meander

This Deity was ſo ſkilled in the Bow, that his Arrows were always fatal. Python and the Cyclops experienced their Force. When the Giant Tityus endeavoured to raviſh Diana, he transfixed and threw him into Hell, where the Vultures preyed on his Liver. Niobe the daughter of Tantalus, and Wife of Amphion, being happy in ſeven Sons and as many Daughters, was ſo fooliſh as to prefer herſelf to Latona. This ſo enraged Apollo and Diana, that the former ſlew her Sons with his Darts, and the latter killed her daughters in the Embraces of their Mother, whom

[a] The Grecian Poets celebrate the Graſshopper as a very muſical Inſect, that ſings amongſt the higheſt Branches of the Trees; ſo that it muſt have been a very different Creature from the Graſshopper known to us. See the Notes in Cookes Heſiod.

[a] Ovid, Book XI. Fab. III. l. 90.

[c] Becauſe as ſhe blew it, ſeeing herſelf in a Fountain, ſhe found it deformed her Face.

Jupiter

Jupiter, in compaſſion to her inceſſant Grief turned into a Stone, which ſtill emits moiſture inſtead of Tears [a].

The true meaning of the Fable of Niobe is this; it ſignified the Annual Innundation of Egypt. The Affront ſhe offered to Latona was a Symbol, to denote the Neceſſity ſhe laid that People under of retreating to the higher Grounds. The fourteen Children of Niobe are the fourt en Cubits, that marked the encreaſe of the Nile [b]. Apollo and Diana killing them with their arrows, repreſent Labour and Induſtry, with the aſſiſtance of the Sun's warm Influence, overcoming theſe Difficulties after the Retreat of the Flood. Niobe's being turned to a Stone, was owing to an Equivocation. The Continuance of Niobe was the Preſervation of Egypt. But the word Selau, which ſignified Safety, by a ſmall Alteration (Selaw) expreſſed a Stone. Thus Niobe became a real Perſon metamorphoſed to a Rock.

Apollo reſembled his Father Jupiter, in his great Propenſity to love. He ſpent ſome 'Time with Veﬁnus in the iſle of Rhodes, and during their interview it is ſaid the Sky rained Gold and the Earth was covered with Lillies and Roſes. His moſt celebrated Amour was with Daphne (the Daughter of the River Peneus), a Virgin of Theſſaly, who was herſelf prepoſſeſſed in favour of Leucippus, a Youth of her own age. Apollo, to be revenged on his Rival, put it in his Head to diſguiſe himſelf amongſt the Virgins who went a Bathing, who diſcovering the Deceit, ſtabbed him. After this the God purſued Daphne, who flying to preſerve her Chaſtity, was, on her Intreaties to the Gods, changed into a Laurel [c], whoſe Leaves Apollo immediately conſecrated to bind his Temples, and made that Tree the Reward of Poetry.

[a] Ovid, Book VI. l. 310.

[b] The Statue of Nile in the Tuilleries at Paris, has fourteen Children placed by it, to denote theſe Cubits.

[c] Ovid, Book I. l. 556.
———graſping at empty Praiſe.
He ſnatch'd at Love, and filled his Arms with Bays. Waller.

The

The Nymph Bolina rather than yield to his Suit threw herself into the Sea for which he rendered her immortal: Nor was he more succefsful in his Court-ship of the Nymph Caftalia, who vanifhed from him in the form of a Fountain, which was afterwards sa-cred to the Mufes [a]. He debauched Leucothoe Daughter of Orchamus, King of Babylon, in the fhape of her Mother Eurynome. Clytia her Sifter, jealous of her Happinefs, difcovered the Amour to their Fa-ther, who ordered Leucothoe to be buried alive. Her Lover in Pity to her Fate, poured Nectar on her Grave, which turned the body into the Tree, which weeps the Gum called Frankincenfe. He then aban-doned Clytia, who pined away continually looking on the Sun, till fhe became the Heliotrope or Sun Flow-er [b].

Of the Children of Apollo, we fhall fpeak more at large in the following Section.

Apollo had a great Variety of Names, either taken from his principal Attributes, or the chief Places where he was worfhipped. He was called the Healer, from his enlivening Warmth and cheering Influence, and Pæan [c], from the Peftilential Heats: to fignify the Former, the Ancients placed the Graces in his Right Hand, and for the Latter a Bow and Arrows in his left: Nomius, or the Shepherd from his fertilizing the earth, and thence fuftaining the Animal Creation; Delius [c] from his rendering all Things manifeft; Pythius, from his Victory over Python, Lycius, Phœ-bus, and Phaneta, from his Purity and Splendor.

The principal places where he was worfhipped were Chryfus, Tenedos, Smyntha, Cylla, Cyrrha, Patræa, Claros, Cynthius, Abœa, a City in Lycia, at Miletus and amongft the Mæonians, from all which Places, he was denominated. He had an Oracle and Temple at Tegyra, near which were two remarkable Fountains,

[a] Thence called Caftalian Sifters.
[b] Ovid, Book IV. 205.

[c] Apo tou paiein tas anias.
[d] Apo tou dela panta poiein.

called

called the Palm and the Olave, on account of the
Sweetnefs and Tranfparency of the Water. He had
an oracle at Delos, for fix Months in the Summer
feafon, which for the Reft of the Year was removed
to Patara in Lycia, and thefe Removals were made
with great Solemnity. But his moft celebrated Temple was at Delphos, the Original of which was thus:
Apollo being inftructed in the Art of Divination by
Pan the Son of Jupiter, and the Nymph Thymbris,
went to this Oracle, where at that Time Themis gave
her Anfwers; but the Serpent Python hindering him
from approaching the Oracle, he flew it, and fo took
poffeffion of it. His Temple here, in Procefs of Time,
became fo frequented, that it was called the Oracle of
the Earth, and all the Nations and Princes in the
World vied with each other in their Munificence to
it. Craefus, King of Lydia, gave at one Time a thoufand Talents of Gold to make an Altar there, befides
Prefents of immenfe value at other Times. Phalaris,
the Tyrant of Agrigentum prefented it a brazen Bull,
a Mafter-piece of Art. The Refponfes here were delivered by a Virgin Prieftefs [a] called Pythia, or Phae-
bas, placed on a Tripos [b], or Stool with three Feet,
called alfo Cortina, from the Skin of the Python with
which it was covered. It is uncertain after what
Manner thefe Oracles were delivered, though Cicero
fuppofes the Pythonefs was infpired, or rather intoxi-
cated by certain Vapours which afcended from the
Cave. In Italy, Apollo had a celebrated Shrine at
Mount Soracte, where his Priefts were fo remarkable
for Sanctity that they could walk on burning coals unhurt. The Romans erected to him many Temples.
After the Battle of Actium, which decided the Fate
of the World, and fecured the Empire to Auguftus,
this Prince not only built him a Chapel on that Promontory, and renewed the folemn Games to him, but

[a] Some fay that the Pythonefs being once debauched, the O
racles were afterwards delivered by an old Woman in the Drefs
of a young Maid.

[b] Authors vary as to the Tripos, fome making it a Veffel in
which the Prieftefs bathed.

foon

foon after raifed a moft magnificient Temple to him on Mount Palatine in Rome, the whole of Parian Marble. The Gates were of Ivory exquifitely carved and over the Frontifpiece was the Solar Chariot and Horfes of maffy Gold. The Portico contained a noble Library of the Greek and Latin Authors. Within, the place was decorated with noble Paintings, and a Statue of the God by the famous Scopas, attended by a gigantic Figure in Brafs fifty Feet high. In the A-rea were four Brazen Cows, reprefenting the Daughters of Prœtus King of the Argives, who were chan-ged into that form for prefuming to rival Juno in Beauty. Thefe Statues were wrought by Myron.

The ufual Sacrifices to Apollo, were Lambs, Bulls, and Oxen. The Animals facred to him were the Wolf, from his Acutenefs of Sight; the Crow, from her Augury, or foretelling the Weather; the Swan, from its divining its own Death; the Hawk, from its boldnefs in Flight; and the Cock, from its foretelling his Rife. The Grafshopper, was alfo reckoned agree-able to him on account of his Mufick. Of Trees, the Laurel, Palm, Olive and Juniper were moft in efteem with him. All young Men when their Beards grew confecrated their Locks in his Temple, as the Virgins did theirs in the Temple of Diana.

The four great Attributes of Apollo were Divinati-tion, Healing, Mufick, and Archery; all which ma-nifeftly refer to the Sun. Light difpelling Darknefs is a ftrong Emblem of Truth diffipating Ignorance; what conduces more to Life and Health than the Solar Warmth, or can there be a jufter Symbol of the Plane-tary Harmony than Apollo's [a] Lyre? As his Darts are faid to have deftroyed the Monfter Python, fo his Rays dry up the noxious moifture, which is pernicious to Vegitation and Fruitfulnefs.

The Perfians, who had a high Veneration for this Planet, adored it, and the Light proceeding from it, by the Names of Mithra and Orafmanes; the Egyp-

[a] The feven Strings of which are faid to reprefent the feven Planets.

tians

tians by thofe of Ofiris and Orus: and from their Antiquities, let us now feek fome illuftration of the Birth and Adventures of Apollo.

The Ifis, which pointed out the Neomenia or monthly Feftival before their annual Inundation, was the fymbolical Figure of a Creature with the upper part of a Woman, and the hinder of a Lizard placed in a reclining Pofture. This they called Leto [d], and ufed it to fignify to the people the Neceffity of laying in the Provifions of Olives, parched Corn, and fuch other kinds of dry Food, for their fubfiftence, during the Flood. Now when the Waters of the Nile decreafed time enough to allow them a Month before the Entrance of the Sun into Sagittarius, the Egyptian Farmer was fure of Leifure enough to furvey and fow his Ground, and of remaining in abfolute fecurity till Harveft. This Conqueft of the Nile was reprefented by an Orus, or Image, and armed with Arrows, and fubduing the Monfter Python. This they called Ores [e], or Apollo [f]. The Figure of Ifis abovementioned, they alfo ftiled Deione, or Diana [g], and they put in her Hand the Quail, a Bird which with them was the Emblem of Security [h].

Thefe Emblems carried by the Phænicians into Greece, gave Rife to all the Fable of Latona perfecuted by the Python, and flying to Delos in the form of a Quail, where fhe bore Orus and Dione, or Apollo and Diana. Thus (as on former Occafions) the Hieroglyphicks only defigned to point out the regular Feftivals, and to inftruct the People in what they were to do, became in the End the Objects of a fenfelefs and grofs Idolatry.

When Tyre was befieged by Alexander, the Citizens bound the Statue of Apollo with Chains of Gold:

[d] From Leto, or Letoah, a Lizard.
[e] From Hores, the Deftroyer or Wafter.
[f] Apollo fignifies thefame.
[g] From Dei, fufficiency, comes Deione, Abundance,
[h] Selave in the Phænician fignifies Security, as alfo a Quail; hence they ufed the Quail to fignify the Thing. The Latin words Salus and Salvo are derive from hence,

but

but when that Conqueror took the place, he releafed the Deity, who thence obtained the Name of Philax-andrus, or the Friend of Alexander. At Rhodes, where he was worfhipped in a peculiar Manner, there was a Coloffal Image of him at the Mouth of the Harbour feventy Cubits high [i].

Phœbus [k] was very differently reprefented in different Countries and Times, according to the Character he affumed. To depict the Solar Light, the Perfians ufed a Figure with the Head of a Lion, covered with a Tiara, in the Perfian Garb, and holding a mad Bull by the Horns, a Symbol plainly of Egyptian Original. The latter People expreffed him fometimes by a Circle with Rays; at other Times by a Scepter with an Eye over it; But their great Emblem of the Solar Light, as diftinguifhed from the Orb itfelf, was the golden Seraph, or fiery flying Serpent [a]. The Hycropolitans fhewed him with a pointed Beard, thereby expreffing the ftrong Emiffion of his Rays downward; over his Head was a bafket of Gold, reprefenting the æthereal Height: He had a Breaft-Plate on, and in his Right Hand held a Spear, on the fummit of which ftood the Image of Victory (fo that Mars is but one of his Attributes): this befpoke him irrefiftible and ruling all Things: In his Left-hand was a Flower, intimating the vegetable Creation nourifhed, matured, and continued by his Beams: Around his Shoulders he wore a Veft depicted with Gorgons and Snakes; this takes in Minerva, and by it is expreffed the Virtue and Vigour of the Solar Warmth, enlivening the Apprehenfion and promoting Wifdom; whence alfo he is with great Propriety the Prefident of the Mufes: Clofe by were the expanded Wings of the Eagle, reprefenting the Æther, ftretched out from him, as from its proper

[i] We fhall fpeak of this hereafter.

[k] From Pheob, the Source, and ..ob, the overflowing, or the Source of the Inundation, the Egyptians expreffing the annual Excefs of the Nile by a Sun, with a River proceeding from its Mouth.

[a] Vide Macrob. Saturn. l. 1, c. 17.

Center

Center: At his Feet were three female Figures encircled by a Seraph, that in the midſt being the Emblem
of the Earth riſing in Beauty from the Midſt of Nature
and Confuſion (the other two) by the Emanation of
his Light, ſignified by the Seraph or Dragon.

Under the Character of the Sun, Apollo was depicted in a Chariot drawn by four Horſes, whoſe Names
the Poets have taken care to give us as well as thoſe of
Pluto. The Poets feigned each Night that he went to
reſt with Thetis in the Ocean, and that the next morning the Hours got ready his Horſes for him to renew
his Courſe (ſee Cramby's Telemaque for a Picture),
and unbarred the Gates of Day. It is no Wonder they
have been laviſh on a Subject, which affords ſuch ex-
tenſive Room for the Imagination to diſplay itſelf, as
the Beauties of the Sun riſing. When repreſented as
Liber Pater [b] he bore a Shield to ſhew his Protection of Mankind. At other times he was drawn as a
beardleſs Youth, his Locks diſhevelled, and crowned
with Laurel, holding a Bow in his Right-hand with his
Arrows, and the Lyre in his Left. The Palace of the
Sun has been admirably deſcribed by Ovid, as well as
his Car, in the ſecond Book of his Metamorphoſis.

CHAP. XXX. Of the Sons or Offspring of APOL-
LO, ÆSCULAPIUS, PHAETON, ORPHEUS, ID-
MON, ARISTÆUS, &c.

AS Apollo was a very gallant Deity, ſo he had a
very numerous Iſſue of which it is neceſſary to
give ſome Account, as they make a conſiderable Figure in poetical Hiſtory. The firſt and moſt noted of
his Sons was Æſculapius, whom he had by the Nymph
Coronis. Some ſay that Apollo ſhot his Mother, when

[b] Virgil gives him this Name in his firſt Georgic.
———Vos, O clariſſima Mundi
Lumina, labentem cœlo qui ducitis annum,
Liber & alma Ceres.

big with Child of him, on Account of her Infidelity; but repenting the fact faved the Infant, and gave him to Chiron to be inftructed [c] in Phyfick. Others report, that as King Phlegyas her Father was carrying her with him into Peloponnefus, her pains furprized her on the Confines of Epidauria, where to conceal her Shame fhe expofed the infant on a Mountain. However this be, under the Care of this new Mafter, he made fuch a Progrefs in the Medical Art, as gained him a high Reputation; fo that he was even reported to Raife the Dead. His firft Cures were wrought upon Afcles King of Epidaurus, and Aunes King of Daunia, which laft was troubled with fore Eyes. In fhort, his fuccefs was fo great, that Pluto, who faw the number of his Ghofts daily increafe, complained to Jupiter, who killed him with his Thunderbolts.

Cicero reckons up three of his Name. The firft the Son of Apollo worfhipped in Arcadia, who invented the Probe and Bandages for Wounds; the fecond the Brother of Mercury, killed by Lightning: and the third the Son of Arfippus and Arfinoe, who firft taught the Art of Tooth-drawing and Purging. Others make Æfculapius, an Egyptian King of Memphis, antecedent by a thoufand Years to the Æfculapius of the Greeks: The Romans numbered him amongft the Dii Adfcititii, or fuch as were raifed to Heaven by their Merit, as Hercules, Caftor, and Pollux, &c.

The Greeks received their knowledge of Æfculapius from the Phænicians and Egyptians. His Chief Temples were at Pergamus, Smyrna, at Trica, a City of Ionia, and the Ifle of Coos; in all which, votive Tablets were hung up [d], fhewing the Difeafes cured by his Affiftance; but his moft famous Shrine was at Epidaurus, where every five Years in the Spring, folemn Games were inftituted to him nine Days after the Ifthmian Games at Corinth.

[c] Ovid, who relates the Story of Coronis, in his fanciful Way tells us that Corvus, or the Raven, who difcovered her Amour, had, by Apollo, his Feathers changed from black to white.

[d] From thefe Tablets or votive Infcriptions, Hippocrates is faid to have collected his Aphorifms.   The

The Romans grew acquainted with him by an Accident; a Plague happening in Italy, the Oracle was consulted, and the Reply was, that they should bring the God Æsculapius from Epidaurus. An Embaſſy was appointed of ten Senators at the Head of whom was Q Ogulnius. Theſe Deputies on their Arrival, viſiting the Temple of the God, a huge Serpent came from under the Altar, and croſſing the City, went directly to their Ship and lay down in the Cabbin of Ogulnius, upon which they ſet ſail immediately; and arriving in the Tiber, the Serpent quitted the Ship, and retired to a little Iſland oppoſite the City, where a temple was erected to the God, and the peſtilence ceaſed

The Animals ſacrificed to Æsculapius were the Goats, ſome ſay on account of her nurſing him; others, becauſe this creature is unhealthy, as labouring under a perpetual Fever. The Dog and the Cock were ſacred to him on account of their Fidelity and Vigilance. The Raven was alſo devoted to him for its Forecaſt, and being ſkilled in Divination. Authors are not agreed as to his being the inventor of Phyſick, ſome affirming he only perfected that Part which relates to the Regimen of the Sick.

Let us now ſeek for the Origin of this Fable. The public Sign or Symbol expoſed by the Egyptians in their Aſſemblies, to warn the People to mark the Depth of the Inundation, in order to regulate the Ploughing accordingly, was the Figure of a Man with a Dog's Head carrying a Pole with Serpents twiſted round it, to which they gave the Names of Anubis [a] Thaaut [b], and Æsculapius [c]. In proceſs of time they made Uſe of this Repreſentation for a real King, who by the Study of Phyſick ſought the Preſervation of his Subjects. Thus the Dog and the Serpent became the Characteriſticks of Æsculapius amongſt the Romans and Greeks, who were entirely Strangers to the original meaning of theſe Hieroglyphicks.

[a] From Hannobeach, which in Phœnician ſignifies the Barker or Warner. Anubis.

[b] The Word Tayant, ſignifies the Dog.

[c] From Aiſh Man, and Caleph, Dog comes, Æſcaleph the Man-Dog, or AEſculapius.

G 3

Æsculapius

Æfculapius had, by his Wife Epione, two Sons, Machaon and Podalirius, both fkilled in Surgery, and who are mentioned by Homer at the Siege of Troy, and were very ferviceable to the Greeks. He had alfo two daughters, called Hygiœa and Jafo.

This Deity is reprefented in different Attitudes. At Epidaurus his Statue was of Gold and Ivory [a], feated on a Throne of the fame Materials, his Head crowned with Rays and a long Beard, having a knotty Stick in one Hand, the other entwined with a Serpent, and a Dog lying at his Feet. The Phliafians depicted him as beardlefs; and the Romans crowned him with Laurel, to denote his defcent from Apollo. The Knots in his Staff fignify the difficulties that occur in the Study of Medicine.

Phaeton was the Son of Apollo, and the Nymph Clymene. Having a difpute with Epaphus, the Son of Jupiter and Io, the latter upbraided him, that he was not really the fon of his Father, and that his Mother only made ufe of that Pretence to cover her Infamy. The Youth fired at this Reproach, by his Mother's Advice carried his complaint to his Father Phœbus, who received him with great Tendernefs and to allay his difquietude, fwore by Styx to grant him whatever he requefted, as a mark of his acknowledging him for his Son. Phaeton boldly afked the direction of the Solar Chariot for one Day. The Father at once grieved and furprized at the Demand, ufed all Arguments in vain to diffuade him from the Attempt; but being by his Oath reduced to fubmit to his obftinacy, he gave him the Reins, with the beft Directions he could how to ufe them. The Ambition of our young Adventurer was too fatal to himfelf. He loft his Judgment and way together; and Jupiter, to prevent the World being fet on Fire was obliged with his Thunderbolts to hurl him from his feat into the River Eridanus or Po. His fifters Phaethufa, Lampetia and Phæbe lamented his Lofs fo inceffantly up-

[a] This Image was the Work of Thrafymedes the Son of Ariftopius, a Native of Paris.

on the Banks that the Gods changed them into Black Poplar Trees whose juice produces the Electrum, or amber. Cygnus King of Liguria, no less grieved for his loss, was changed into a Swan, a Bird which became after sacred to Apollo. This Story makes a very considerable Figure in Ovid [a] who has out-done himself on this Subject.

A late Author offers an ingenious conjecture, with regard to this Fable [b]. Linen-Cloth was the great Manufacture of Egypt, and the bleaching of it consequently of great Importance. The Image exposed for directing this, was a Youth with Rays round his Head, and a Whip in his Hand, seated on an Orb, to which they gave the Name of Phaeton, [c], and Ben-Climmah, (d). Probably the months of May, June, and July, were the three sisters of Phaeton, because during these months they washed their linen white, of which Cygnus, or the Swan, the friend of Phaeton, is a further symbol. Now as the word Albanoth applied to these Months [e], signifies also Poplar Trees, it gave rise to this Metamorphosis.

Orpheus was the Son of Phœbus, by the Muse Calliope [g]. He was born in Thrace, and resided near Mount Rhodope, where he married Eurydice a Princess of that Country. Aristeus a neighbouring Prince, who fell in Love with her, attempted to surprize her and in her Flight, to escape his Violence, she was killed by the Bite of a Serpent. Her disconsolate Husband was so affected at his Loss, that he descended by the Way of Tœnarus to Hell, in order to recover her. As Music and Poetry were to him hereditary Talents he exerted them in so powerful a manner that

[a] Ovid Metamorph. Lib. II, in Principio.
[b] La Pluche Hist de Cieux.
[c] From Pha the Month, and Eton Linen, is made Phaeton; that is, the Inliction of the Linen Works.
[d] Ben-Climmah, the son of hot Weather. Hence the Story of Phaeton's burning the World.
[e] Albanoth, or Lebanoth, signifies the whitening Fields or Yards for Bleaching.
[g] Some make him the Son of Oeagrus and Calliope.

Pluto

Pluto and Proferpine were fo far touched, as to ref-
tore him his beloved Confort on one Condition that
he fhould not look back on her, till they came to the
Light of the World. His impatient Fondnefs made
him break this Article, and he loft her for ever.
Grieved at her Lofs he retired to the Woods and
Forefts, which it is faid were fenfible of his Harmony
[a]. But the Mœnades or Baccha, either incenfed
at his vowing a widowed Life, or as others-fay, infti-
gated by Bacchus, whofe Worfhip he neglected [b],
tore him in Pieces, and fcattered his Limbs about the
Fields, which were collected and buried by the Mufes
His Head and Harp, which were caft into the Hebrus,
were carried to Lefbos, and the former interred there.
His Harp was tranfported to the Skies, where it
forms one of the Conftellations. He himfelf was
changed into a Swan, and left a Son called Methon,
who founded in Thrace a City of His own Name. O-
vid has given this whole Story [c], but contrary to his
ufual Method, has broke the Thread of it, by interf-
perfing it in different parts of his Work.

It is certain that Orpheus may be placed as the earlieft Poet of Greece; where he firft introduced Aftronomy, Divinity, Mufick, and Poetry, all which he
had learned in Egypt. He wrote many Volumes in
natural Philofophy and Antiquities [d]. of which only a few imperfect Fragments have efcaped the Rage
of Time. In his Book of Stones he fays of himfelf,
' He could underftand the Flight and Language of
' Birds, ftop the Courfe of Rivers, overcome the poi-

____

[a] Ovid Metam. Lib. XI. in Principio.
[b] Others fay by Venus, on account of his defpifing her Rites
and that the Nymphs excited by her, tore him in Pieces in ftrug-
ling who fhould have him.
[c] In his Xth and XIth Books.
[d] He wrote a Book of Hymns and Treatifes on the Generation of the Elements; on the Giants War; on the Rape of Proferpine; on the Labours of Hercules; of Stones; on the Rites
and Myfteries of the Egyptians.

son of Serpents, and even penetrate the Thoughts
of the Heart [i].'

Let us seek the Origin of this Fable once more in E-
gypt, the Mother Country of Fiction. In July when
the Sun entered Leo, the Nile overflowed all the Plains.
To denote the publick Joy at seeing the Inundation
rise to its due height, they exhibited a Youth playing
on the Lyre or Sistrum, and sitting by a tame Lion.
When the Waters did not increase as they should, this
Horus was represented stretched on the back of a Lion
as dead. This Symbol they called Oreph or Orpheus
(k), to signify that Agriculture was then quite unsea-
sonable and dormant. The Songs they amused themselves with at this dull Season, were called the Hymns
of Orpheus; and as Husbandry revived immediately
after, it gave Rise to the Fable of Orpheus returning
from Hell. The Isis placed near this Horus they called
Eurydice (a), and as the Greeks took all these figures
in the literal and not the Emblematical Sense, they
made Eurydice the Wife of O pheus.

Idmon was the son of Apollo by Asteria, and attended the Argenauts in their Expedition to Colchis, being
famed for his Skill in Augury; but wandering from
his Companions, as they occasionolly landed, he was
killed by a wild Boar.

Another of the Children of Apollo was Linus, whom
he had by the Nymph Terpsichore. He was born at
Thebes, and eminent for Learning, if it be true that
Thamyris, Orpheus, and Hercules were all his Scho-
lars. Some say he was slain by the latter for ridiculing
him; but if Orpheus (as others affirm) lived a hundred Years before Hercules, it is rather probable that
Linus was the Disciple of Orpheus. However this be,

[i] This probably gave Rise to the Fable of his making Rocks
and Forests move to his Lyre.

[k] From Oreph, Occiput, or back part of the Head.

[a] From Eri, a Lion; and Dica, tamed, is formed Eridica,
Eurydice, or the Lion tamhd, i. e. the Violence or Rage of the Inundation overcome.

Linus

Linus wrote on the Origin of the World, the courses of the Sun and Moon, and the production of Animals

After all, Linus was only a Symbol of the Egyptians, which the Greeks according to Custom, personated. At the end of Autumn or Harvest, the Egyptians fell to their night work of making Linen Cloth [a], and the figure then exposed was called Linus [b] and denoted the sitting up or watching, during the Night.

Aristœus was the Son of Apollo, by Cyrene a virgin Nymph, who used to accompany him in Hunting, and whom he first fell in Love with on seeing her encounter a Lion. He was born in Lybia. He received his Education from the Nymphs, who taught him to extract Oil from Olives, and to make Honey, Cheese, and Butter; all which arts he communicated to Mankind. On this account he was regarded as a rural Deity. From Africa he passed into Sardinia and Sicily, from whence he travelled into Thrace, where Bacchus initiated him in his Mysteries. We have already mentioned how his Passion occasioned the Death of Eurydice, to revenge which the Wood-Nymphs destroyed his Bee-hives. Concerned at this Loss he advised with his Father, and was told by the Oracle, to sacrifice Bulls to appease her shade; and having followed this Advice, the Bees which issued from their Carcasses fully supplied the Damages he had sustained [c]. He died near mount Hœmus, and was deified on account of the Services he had done Mankind by his useful Inventions. He was also honoured in the Isle of Coos, for his calling the Etesian winds to relieve them at a time of excessive heat. Herodotus says that he appeared at Cyzicum after his death, and three hundred and forty years after, was seen in Italy at Metapontum, where he injoined the

[a] This was their chief Manufacture.

[b] Linus, from Lyn, to watch, whence our Word Linen, that is, the work, for the time of doing it.

[c] Virgil hath introduced this Story with great Elegance and Propriety, in his IVth Georgick, I. 314.

Inhabitants

Inhabitants to erect a Statue to him in a that of A-
pollo; which on consulting the oracle, they performed.

Circe was the Daughter of Phœbus, by Perfis the
Child of Oceanus, and a celebrated Sorceress. Her
first Husband was a King of the Sarmatæ, whom she
poisoned, for which she was expelled the Kingdom,
and fled to a Promontory on the Coast of Tuscany,
which afterwards took her Name. Here she fell in
love with Glaucus one of the Sea Deities, who pre-
ferring Scylla to her she changed her into a Sea Monster. Picus, King of the Latins, her next Favourite,
for rejecting her Addresses was metamorphosed into
a Woodpecker.

The most remarkable of Circe's Adventures, was
with Ulysses. This Prince returning from Troy, was
cast away on her coast, and his Men by a drink she
gave them, were transformed to Swine, and other
Beasts. Ulysses was preserved by Mercury, who gave
him the Herb Moly, to secure him from her inchant-
ments, and instructed him, when she attempted to
touch him with her wand, to draw his Sword, and
make her swear by Styx, she would use him as a
Friend, otherwise he would kill her. By this means,
he procured the Liberty of his Companions, and continued a Year with Circe, who bore him two Children
viz. Agrius and Latinus. Circe had a Sepulchre
in one of the Isles, called Pharmacusæ, near Sala-
mis.

Circe was no other than the Egyptian Isis whose
Horus, or attending Image, every Month assuming
some different Form, as a human Body, with the
Heads of a Lion, Dog, Serpent, or Tortoise, gave
Rise to the Fable of her changing Men by her In-
chantments into these Animals. Hence the Egyp-
tians gave her the Name of Circe, which signifies the
Ænigma.

Apollo had many other Children. Æthusa the
daughter of Neptune bore him Eluthcrus. By Evadne
he had Janus; by Atria, Miletus, Oaxes and Arabus,
who gave his Name to Arabia; by Melia he had
Isinenius

Ifmenius and Tanarus; by Aglaia, Theftor; by Manto, Mopfus; by Anathrippe, Chius; by Achalide, he had Delphus, and many others too tedious to enumerate.

CHAP. XXXI. Of the MUSES, and PEGASUS, the GRACES, and the SYRENS.

THESE celebrated Goddeffes, the Mufes, were the Daughters of Jupiter and Mnemofyne, though fome think them born of Cœlus. Their Number at firft was only three or four [e], but Homer and Hefiod have fixed it at Nine [f], which it has never fince exceeded. They were born on Mount Pierus, and educated by the Nymph Eupheme.

They had many Appellations common to them all, as Pierides from the place of their Birth ; Heliconides, from Mount Helicon in Bæotia ; Parnaffides, from the Hill of Parnaffus in Phocis ; Citherides from Mount Citheron, a place they much frequented ; Aonides, from Aonia ; Hippocranides, Agannipides, and Caftalides, from different Fountains confecrated to them, or to which they were fuppofed to refort.

In general they were the tutelar Goddeffes of al facred Feftivals and Banquets, and the Patroneffes of all polite and ufeful Arts. They fupported Virtue in Diftrefs, and preferved worthy Actions from Oblivion Homer calls them the Miftreffes and Correctreffes of Manners [g]: With regard to the Sciences, thefe

[e] Mneme, Aede, Melete, that is, Memory, Singing, and Meditation, to which fome add Thelxiope.

[f] Some affign as a Reafon for this, that when the Citizens of Sicyon directed three fkilful Statuaries, to make each three Statues of the three Mufes, they were all fo well executed, that they did not know which to chufe, but erected all the Nine, and that Hefiod only gave them Names.

[g] Hence old Bards and Poets were in fuch High Efteem, that when Agamemnon went to the Siege of Troy, he left one with Clytemneftra, to keep her Faithful, and Egifthus could not corrupt her, till he had deftroyed this Counfellor,

Sifters

Sisters had each a particular Province or department, though Poetry seemed more immediately under their united Protection.

Calliope (so called from the Sweetness of her Voice) presided over Rhetorick, and was reckoned the first of the Nine Sisters.

Clio, the Second (a), was the Muse of History, and takes her Name from her immortalizing the Actions she records.

Erato (b), was the Patroness of elegiac, or amorous Poetry, and the Inventress of Dancing. To Thalia (c), belonged Comedy, and whatever was gay, amiable, and pleasant. Euterpe, (named from her Love of Harmony) had the care of Tragedy.

Melpomene, (so styled from the Dignity and Excellency of her song) was the Guardian Muse of Lyric and Epic Poetry (d).

Terpsichore was the Protrectress of Musick, particularly the flute (e). The Chorus of the ancient Drama was her Province, to which some add Logick.

To Polyhymnia (g) belonged that Harmony of Voice and Gesture, which gives a Perfection to Oratory and Poetry, and which flows from just sentiments and a good memory.

Urania was the Muse whose Care extended to all divine or celestial Subjects such as the Hymns in Praise of the Gods, the Motions of the heavenly Bodies, and whatever regarded Philosophy or Astronomy (g).

The Muses, tho' said to be Virgins, were no Enemies to Love (h). We have already taken Notice of Calliope and Terpsichore yielding to the Addresses of

(a) From Kleos Glory (b), from Heros, Love (c), from Thalleie, to flourish or revive (d), from Melos poiein, to make a Concert or Symphony.

(e) Terpein tois chorois, to delight in Choruses.

(g) From Polus and Mneia, a great Memory.

(h) From Ouranos, Heaven.

(i) The Virginity or Chastity of the Muses, is a Point disputed by the Ancient Writers, though the Majority inclines in their Favour.

H

Apollo

Apollo. If their complaisance was solely owing to the Resentment of Venus, who inspired the Flames of Love, to revenge the Death of her favourite Adonis; it must be owned that the Muses have since been sufficiently devoted to her Service.

The Muses were themselves not wholly free from Revenge, as appears in the story of Thamyris. This Person was the Son of Philammon, and the Nymph Agriopa, and born at Odersæ, once a famous City of Thrace. He became so excellent a proficient in Musick that he had the Courage, or Vanity to contend (a) with the Muses; but being overcome, they not only punished him with the Loss of sight and Memory but caused Jupiter to cast him into Hell to expiate his Impiety.

The Muses were represented crowned with Flowers or Wreaths of Palm, each holding some Instrument or token of the Science or Art over which she presided. They were depicted as young, and the Bird sacred to them was the Swan [b].

To trace the Origin of these fabulous Deities, it is necessary to observe, that the nine emblematical Figures, which were exhibited among the Egyptians, to denote the nine Months, during which that Country was freed from the inundation, had each some instrument, or Symbol, peculiar to the Business of the Months, as a Pair of Compasses, a Flute, a Mask, a Trumpet, &c. All these Images were purely hieroglyphical, to point out to the People what they were to do, and to ascertain their Use; they were called the nine Muses [c]. The Greeks who adopted this Groupe of Emblems as so many real Divinities, took

[a] Thamyris wrote a Poem on the Wars of the Gods with the Titans, which exceeded every Thing that had appeared of the Kind before.

[b] Perhaps because it was consecrated to their master Apollo.

[c] From the Word Mose, that is, saved or disengaged from the Waters; whence the Name of Moses given to the Hebrew Lawgiver, so near did the Phænician and Egyptian Languages agree, with some small Difference of Pronunciation only, made two distinct Tongues.

Care to give each a particular Name, suited to the Instruments they bore, and which threw a new Disguise
over the Truth.

The Graces are also Attendants of the Muses, tho
placed in the Train of Venus [a]: Some make them
the Daughters of Jupiter and Eurynome, others of
Bacchus and Venus. They were three, Aglaia, Thalia and Euphrosyne, Names relative to their Nature
[b]. The Lacedemonians and Athenians knew but
two, to whom they gave different Appellations [c].
Eteocles, King of the Orchomenians, was the first who
erected a Temple to them.

Pegasus was a winged Horse produced by the
Blood which fell from Medusa's Head, when she was
killed by Perseus. He flew to Mount Helicon, the
Seat of the Muses, where, with a stroke of his Hoof,
he opened a fountain called Hippocrene, or the Horses Spring [d].

The unravelling these Figures, will convince us
how justly they belong to this Article, as they complete its Illustration. Near the nine female Figures,
which betokened the dry Season, were placed three
others representing the three Months of Inundation,
and were drawn sometimes swathed, as incapable of
using their Hands and Feet. These were called Charitout (e), or the Divorce. The Resemblance of this
word to the Greek Charites, which signifies Thanks-
givings or Favours, gave Rise to the Fable of the
Graces, or three Goddesses presiding over Benefits and
outward Charms.

[a] I chuse to place them here on account of the Explanation
of the Fable under one View.

[b] Aglaia, or Honesty, to shew that Benefits shou'd be bestowed freely : Thalia, or flourishing, to denote that the Sense of
Kindness ought never to de ; and Euphrosyne, or Chearfulness,
to signify that Favours should be conferred and received with mutual Pleasure.

[c] The Spartan Graces were Clito and Phaena; those of A-
thens, Auro and Hegemo.

[d] Fons Caballinus. See Persius, Satyr I.

[e] From Charat, to divide, comes Charitout the Separation
of Commerce.

 Yet

Yet, as during the Inundation, all Parts could not be so fully supplied, but that some commerce was necessary, they had recourse to small Barks, to sail from one City to the other. Now the emblematical Figure of a Ship or Vessel, in Egypt and Phœnicia, was a winged Horse (a) by which Name the Inhabitants of Cadiz, a Phœnician Colony, called their Vessels. Now if the Muses and Graces are the Goddesses which preside over Arts and Gratitude, this Emblem becomes unintelligible. But if we take the nine Muses for the three Months of Action and Industry, and the three Graces for the three months of inundation and rest, the winged horse, or Boat with sails, is a true picture of the End of Navigation, and the return of Rural Toils. To this Figure the Egyptians gave the name of Pegasus [b], expressive of its true meaning. All these images transplanted to Greece, became the Source of endless Confusion and Fable.

By the Latin and Greek Poets, the Graces are represented as beautiful young Virgins, naked, or but very slightly cloathed (c), and having Wings on their Feet. They are also joined Hand in Hand, to denote their Unity.

The Syrens were the Daughters of Achelous. Their lower Parts were like Fishes, and their upper like Women; but they were so skilled in Musick, that they insnared all who heard them to Destruction. Presuming to contend with the Muses, they were vanquished and stripped at once of their Feathers and Voices, as a punishment for their Folly.

The Egyptians sometimes represented the three Months of Inundation by Figures half Female and half Fish, to denote to the Inhabitants their living in the midst of the Waters. One of these Images bore

[a] Strabo Geograph. Lib. II. p. 99. Edit. Reg. Paris.
[b] From Pag to ccase, and Sus a Ship, Pegasus, or the Cessation of Navigation.
[c] Solutis Gratiæ Zonis.   Ode xxx. 5.
Junctæque Nymphis Gratiæ decentes.
Alterno terram quatiunt Pede. Horace, Lib. I. Ode iv. 5.

in

in her hand the Siftrum, or Egyptian Lyre, to fhew
the general Joy at the Floods arriving to its due
Height, which was the Affurance of a fucceeding
Year of Plenty. To thefe Symbols they gave the
Name of Syrens (a), expreffive of their real Meaning.
The Phœnicians, who carried them into Greece, re-
prefented them as real Perfons, and the Greeks and
Romans had too ftrong a tafte for the Fabulous, not
to embellifh the ftory (b).

CHAP. XXXII. Of DIANA, LUNA, or HECATE.

HAVING treated of the God of Wit and Harmony, with his Offspring and Train, let us now
come to his Twin Sifter Diana, the Goddefs of Chaftity, and the Daughter of Jupiter and Latona. Her
Father, at her Requeft, granted her perpetual Virginity, beftowed on her a bow and Arrows, appointed
her Queen of the Woods and Forefts (c), and affigned her a Guard of Nymphs to attend her (d). She
became the Patronefs of Hunting thus; Britomartis
a Huntrefs Nymph, being one Day entangled in her
own Nets, while the wild Boar was approaching her,
vowed a Temple to Dianna, and fo was preferved.
Hence Diana had the name of Dictynna. Others relate the ftory differently, and fay that Britomartis,
whom Diana favoured on account of her paffion for
the chafe, flying from Minus her Lover, fell into the
Sea, and was by her made a Goddefs.

The adventures of Diana make a pretty confiderable figure in poetical Hiftory, and ferve to fhew that
the Virtue of this Goddefs, if inviolable, was alfo
very fevere. Acteon experienced this Truth to his

[a] From Shur, a Hymn, and ranan to fing.
[b] Hence our imaginary Form of the Mermaid.
[c] Montium Cuftos nemorumque Virgo. Horat Lib. III.
[d] Sixty Nymphs, called Oceaninæ, and twenty of the Afiæ,

   Coft.

Coft. He was a young Prince, the Son of Ariftæus and Autonoe, the daughter of Cadmus, King of Thebes. As he was paffionately fond of that fport, he had the Misfortune one Day to difcover Diana bathing with her Nymphs. The Goddefs incenfed at the intrufion, changed him into a Stag; fo that his own Dogs miftaking him for their Game, purfued and tore him to pieces. Ovid has wrought up this fcene with great Art and Imagination (a).

The Truth of this fable is faid to be as follows: Actæon was a Man of Arcadia, a great lover of Dogs and Hunting, and by keeping many Dogs, and fpending his time in hunting on the mountains, he entirely neglected his domeftic Affairs, and being brought to Ruin was generally called the wretched Actæon, who was devoured by his own Dogs.

Meleager was another unhappy Victim of her Refentment, and the more fo as his punifhment was owing to no crime of his own. Oeneus his father, King of Ætolia, in offering facrifices to the Rural Deities, had forgot Diana. The Goddefs was not of a character to put up with fuch a Neglect. She fent a huge wild Boar into the fields of Caledon, who laid every thing wafte before him. Meleager, with Thefeus and the virgin Atalanta, undertook to encounter it. The Virgin gave the monfter the firft wound, and Meleager who killed it, prefented her the fkin, which his Uncles took from her, for which he flew them. Althæa his mother, hearing her two brothers had perifhed in this quarrel, took an uncommon Revenge. She remembered at the Birth of her fon, the fates had thrown a Billet into the Chamber, with an Affurance the boy would live as long as that remained unconfumed. The Mother had till now carefully faved a Pledge on which fo much depended; but infpired by her prefent fury fhe threw it in the flames, and Meleager inftantly feized with a confuming Difeafe expired as foon as it was burnt. His Sifters,

____
[a] Ovid Lib. iii. 131.

who

who exceffively mourned his Death, were turned into
Hen Turkies.   Ovid has not forgot to embellifh his
Collection with this ftory (a).

Others relate the ftory of Meleager thus: Diana
had, to avenge herfelf of Oeneus, raifed a War between the Curetes and Ætolians.   Meleager, who
fought at the Head of his Father's Troops, had always the Advantage, till killing two of his Mother's
Brothers, his Mother Althæa loaded him with fuch
Imprecations, that he retired from the field. The Curetes upon this advanced, and attacked the Capital
of Ætolia. In vain Oeneus preffes his fon to arm and
repel the Foe ; in vain his mother forgives and intreats
him.   He is inflexible till Cleopatra his wife falls at
his feet, and Reprefents their mutual danger. Touched at this, he calls for his Armour, iffues to the fight,
and repels the Enemy.

Nor was Diana lefs rigorous to her own fex.   Chione the daughter of Dædalion, being careffed both
by Apollo and Mercury, bore Twins, Philamon the
fon of Apollo, a famous Mufician, and Autolicus the
fon of Mercury, a fkilful Juggler or Cheat. The mother was fo imprudent to boaft of her fhame, and
prefer the Honour of being Miftrefs to two Deities, to
the modefty of Diana, which fhe afcribed to her
want of Beauty. For this the Goddefs pierced her
Tongue with an Arrow, and deprived her of the
Power of future boafting or calumny.

The River Alpheus fell violently enamoured of Diana, and having no hopes of fuccefs, had Recourfe to
Force. The Goddefs fled to the Letrini, where fhe
amufed herfelf with Dancing, and with fome Art fo
difguifed herfelf and her Nymphs, that Alpheus no
longer knew them. For this thefe people erected a
Temple to her.

During the Chafe one Day, Diana accidentally
fhot Chenchrius, Son of the Nymph Pryene, who be-

[a] Ovid Lib. viii. 26r.

wailed

walled him fo much that fhe was turned into a Fountain.

Diana had a great Variety of Names ; fhe was cal-
led Cynthia and Delia, from the place of her Birth ;
Artemis, on account of her Honour and modefty By
the Arcadians, fhe was named Orrhofia , and by the
Spartans, Orthia.   Her Temples were many, both in
Greece and Italy ; but the moft confiderable was at
Ephefus, where fhe was held in the higheft Venerati-
on.   The plan of this magnificent Edifice was laid by
Ctefiphon, and the ftructure of it employed for 220
Years, the ablett Architects and Statuaries in the
World. It was fet on Fire by Eroftratus, on the
day that Alexander the Great came into the World ;
but was foon rebuilt with equal Splendor under Dimo-
crates, who alfo built the City of Alexandria.

The Sacrifices offered to Diana, were the firft fruits
of the Earth, Oxen, Rams and white Hinds ; human
Victims were fometimes devoted to her in Greece, as
we find in the cafe of Iphigenia.   Her feftival was on
the Ides of Auguft, after which time all hunting was
prohibited.

Diana was reprefented of an uncommon high Stature, her hair difhevelled, a Bow in her hand, and a
quiver at her back, a Deer fkin faftened to her breaft,
and her purple Robe tucked up at the knees with
Gold buckles or clafps, and attended by Nymphs in a
Hunting-Drefs with nets and hounds.

Diana was alfo called Dea Triformis, or Tergemina,
on account of her triple character of Luna in Heaven,
Diana on Earth, and Hecate in the infernal Regions,
tho' the actions of the firft and laft are afcribed to her
under the fecond Name (a).

Luna was thought to be the daughter of Hyperion
and Theia The Egyptians worfhipped this Deity
both as Male and Female, the men facrificing to it
as Luna, the Women as Lunus, and each Sex on thefe

---

[a] Hefiod makes Luna, Diana and Heccate, three diftinct
Goddeffes.

occafions

Occasions, assuming the Dress of the other. Indeed this Goddess was no other than the Venus Urania, or Cœlestis of the Assyrians, whose Worship and Rites the Phænicians introduced into Greece. Under this Character Diana was also called Lucina, (a Name she held in common with Juno) and had the protection of Women in Labour [d], though some make Lucina a distinct Goddess from either [e]. By this Name she was adored by the Ægenenses and Eleans.

If Diana was so rigid in point of Chastity on Earth, her Virtue grew a little more relaxed when she got to the Skies. She bore Jupiter a Daughter there, called Ersa, or the Dew, and Pan, who was not the most pleasing of the Gods, deceived her in the shape of a white Ram. But her most celebrated Amour was with Endymion [f] the Son of Æthlius, and Grandson of Jupiter who took him up into Heaven; where he had the insolence to solicit Juno, for which he was cast into a profound sleep. Luna had the Kindness to conceal him in a Cave of Mount Latmos in Caria, where she had fifty Daughters by him, and a Son called Ætolus, after which he was again exalted to the Skies.

The Fable of Endymion had its Origin in Egypt. These people in the Neomenia, or Feast, in which they celebrated the ancient state of Mankind, chose a Grove or some retired shady Grotto, where they placed an Isis, with her Crescent or Moon, and by her side an Horus asleep, to denote the security and repose which Mankind then enjoyed. This Figure they called Endymion [g], and these Symbolical Fi-

[d] It is said she assisted Latona her Mother at the Birth of Apollo; but was so terrified at the Pains that she vowed perpetual Virginity.

[e] Some make Lucina the Daughter of Jupiter and Juno, and born in Crete.

[f] Others affirm, that Endymion was a King of Elis, much given to Astronomy and Lunar Observations, for which he was said to be in Love with the Moon, and caressed by her.

[g] From En, a Grotto or Fountain; and Dimion, Resemblance, is made Endimion, or the Grotto of the Representation.

gures,

gures, like the reft, degenerated into Idolatry, and became the Materials for fabulous Hiftory.

As the Moon, Diana was reprefented with a Crefcent on her head, in a filver Chariot drawn by white Hinds, with Gold Harnefs, which fome change to Mules, becaufe that Animal is barren [h]. Some make her Conductors a white and black Horfe [i]; others Oxen on account of the lunar Horns.

Hecate was the Daughter of Jupiter and Ceres.—— As to the Origin of the Name there is fome Variation [k]. She was the Goddefs of the infernal Regions, and on that account is often confounded with Proferpine. She prefided over Streets and Highways; for which caufe fhe was called Trivia; as alfo Propylæa, becaufe the Doors of Houfes were under her protection (a). The Appellation of Brimo was given her on account of her dreadful fhrieks, when Mars, Apollo, and Mercury, meeting her in the Woods attempted to ravifh her. She was alfo famous for Botany, efpecially in difcovering baneful and poifonous Herbs and Roots; as alfo for her fkill in Enchantments and magical Arts, in the practice of which her Name was conftantly invoked (b). Hefiod has given a very pompous Defcription of the Extent of her Power (c). She was ftyled in Egypt, Buhaftis.

As Hecate, Diana was reprefented of an exceffive Height, her Head covered with frightful fnakes, and her Feet of a ferpentine Form, and furrounded with Dogs, an Animal facred to her, and under whofe

---

[h] To exprefs that the Moon had no Light of her own, but what fhe borrowed from the Sun.

[i] To Exprefs the Wane and Full of the Moon.

[k] Either from ekathen at a diftance, becaufe the Moon darts her Rays afar off; or from Hekaton a Hundred, becaufe a Hecatomb was the ufual Victim.

(a) At every New Moon the Athenians made a Supper for her in the open Street, which in the Night was eaten by the poor People.

(b) So Dido in Virgil, calls on
Tergeminam Hecaten, tria Virginis ora Dianæ.   Æn. IV.

(c) Theogony, l. 411.

Form

Form she was sometimes Represented. She was also esteemed the Goddess of inevitable Fate.

If we have Recourse to the Egyptian Key, we shall find this threefold Goddess the same symbol with the Juno and Cybele we have already treated of. The Greek Sculptors had too good a Taste to endure the Head of the Bull or Goat on their Deities, which they borrowed from that Country. They therefore altered these hieroglyphical Figures to their own mode; but took care to preserve the Attributes by disposing them in a more elegant manner. The Lunar symbol amongst the Egyptians was called Hecate, or [a] Achete, and by the Syrians, Achot. The latter also styled her Deio, or Deione [b], and Demeter. The Crescent and Full Moon over her Head at the Neomeniæ, made her mistaken for that Planet, and the time of the Interlunia, during which she remained invisible, she was supposed to take a Turn to the invisible World, and so got the Name of Hecate. Thus the tripartite Goddess arose. The Meaning of the antient symbols was confounded and forgot, and a senseless Jargon of Fable and superstition introduced in its place, a point which can never be too exactly attended to on this occasion.

CHAP. XXXIII. Of MERCURY.

WE shall now give the History of a Deity neither famous for his Truth and Honesty, tho' he makes no inconsiderable Figure in the celestial catalogue. Mecury was the son of Jupiter and Maia, daughter of Atlas, and born on Mount Cyllene, in Arcadia. He was suckled by Juno, some of whose milk falling from his mouth on the Heavens, produced the Galaxy. He began to display early his Talent for

[a] Achate, the only or excellent or achet in [the Syriac] the Sister.

[b] Deio, or Deione, from Dei, sufficiency; or Demeter from Dei and Matar, Rain i. e. Plenty of Rain.

Theft,

Theft, as we have obferved under the article of Apollo. Being careffed, when an Infant in Vulcan's arms,
he ftole away his Tools.   The fame Day he defeated
Cupid at wreftling, and while Venus praifed him after
his Victory, he found Means to convey away her Ceftus.   He pilfered Jupiter's Sceptre, and had done the
fame thing by his Thunderbolts, but they were too
hot for his Fingers.   His manner of treating Battus
is worth relating.   This man faw him ftealing King
Admetus's cows from Apollo his herdfman.   To bribe
him to filence_be gave him a fine Cow, and the Clown
promifed to keep it fecret.   Mercury to try him, affumed another fhape, and offering a higher Reward,
the Fellow told all he knew, on which [a] the God
turned him into a touch-ftone.

Mercury had feveral appellations. He was called
Hermes [b] and Cyllenius, from his Temple upon
Mount Cyllene.   Nor were his Employments lefs various.   He was the Cupbearer to Jupiter till Ganymede took his place.   He was the meffenger of the
Gods, and the tutelar God of Roads and Crofs ways
[c], the inventor of Weights and Meafures, and the
Guardian of all merchandize and commerce, tho' this
office, feems but ill to agree with the actions afcribed to
him. He was in a peculiar manner the Protector of
learning, being the firft Difcoverer of Letters, and the
God of Rhetorick and Oratory   He was alfo famous
for his fkill in Mufick, and fo eloquent, that he was
not only the Arbitrator of all Quarrels amongft the
Gods, but in all leagues and Negociations particular
Regard was paid [d] to him.

[a] Ovid has given a fine Defcription of this Incident. Metam. Lib. 11. 680.

[b] Hermes, the interpreter, becaufe he imparted the minds f
the Gods to men.

[c] Where the Greeks and Romans placed certain Figures called Hermæ, from him, being of Marble or Brafs, with the Head
of a Mercury, but downwards of a fquare Figure.

[d] As the Feciales, or Priefts of Mars, proclaimed War; fo
the Caduceatores, or Priefts of Mercury, were employed in all
Embaffies and Treaties of Peace.

Together

Together with Tellus and Pluto, Mercury was invoked amongst the terrestrial Gods. In Conjunction with Hercules he presided over wrestling and the Gymnastick Exercises, to shew that Address on these Occasions should always be joined to force. He was also believed to preside over dreams, tho' Morpheus claims a share with him in this Department.

Annually in the middle of May a Festival was celebrated to his Honour at Rome, by the Merchants and Traders who sacrificed a Sow to him, intreating he would prosper their business, and forgive their Frauds. In all sacrifices offered to him, the tongues of the Victims were burnt which custom was borrowed from the Megarenses. Persons who escaped imminent Danger sacrificed to him a Calf with Milk and Honey. The Animals sacred to him were the Dog, the Goat and the Cock.

By his sister Venus he had a son called Hermophroditus, a great Hunter; a Wood Nymph, called Salmacis, fell in love with him, but had the mortification to be repulsed. Upon this, inflamed by her passion, she watched near a Fountain where he used to bathe, and when she saw him naked in the Water, rushed to embrace him: but the Youth still avoiding her, she prayed the Gods their bodies might become one, which was immediately granted: and what was yet more wonderful, the Fountain retained the Virtue of making all those Hermophrodites who used its Waters [a]

A late Author gives this story another Turn. He says, the Fountain Salmacis [b] being inclosed with high Walls, very indecent scenes passed there; but that a certain Greek of that Colony building an Inn there for the entertainment of strangers, the Barbarians, who Resorted to it, by their intercourse with the Greeks, became softened and civilized; which gave Rise to the fable of their changing their sex.

[a] See Ovid's Description of this Adventure. Metam. Book IV.

[b] In Caria, near the City of Halicarnassus.

Mercury

Mercury had other Children, particularly Pan, Dolops, Echion, Caicus, Erix, Bunus, Phares, and the Lares, with feveral others. Such was the Mercury of the Greeks and Romans.

But the Origin of this Deity muft be looked for amongft the Phænicians; whofe Image is the fymbolical Figure of their great Anceftor and Founder, and the proper Arms of that People. By the Bag of Money which he held, was intimated, the Gains of Merchandize. By the wings with which his Head and Feet were furnifhed, was fhadowed the fhipping of that people, their extenfive Commerce and Navigation. The Caduceus, with which [a] he was faid to conduct the fpirits of the Deceafed to Hades, pointed out the great Principles of the Soul's Immortality, a ftate of [b] rewards and Punifhments [c] after death, and a [d] Refufcitation of the Body. It is defcribed as producing three leaves together; hence called by Homer the golden three-leaved wand. The doctrine alluded to by this, was more diftinctly taught by the Emblems adorning the Hermetic Wand : For to the Extremity of it was annexed the Ball or CIRCLE. Two SERAPHS entwined the Rod; over which were EXPANDED WINGS, forming the compleat Hieroglyphic of THE MIGHTY ONES. The name of Mercury is a compound of the Celtic Merc, Merchandize [e]; and Ur, a man; and correfponds very exactly with the Hebrew Etymology, rendering the meaning of the Word Cnaan or Canaan, a Merchant or Trader.

This fymbolical figure (like many others, which at firft were very innnocent) became in time the Object of idolatrous worfhip to moft Nations. We are not to

[a] Virgaque levem coerces
——Aurea turbam.
[b] Tu pias lætis animas reponis
—— Sedibus.   HORACE.
[c] Hac alias fub trifta Tartara mittit.
[d] Dat fomnos adimitque.   VIRGIL.
[e] From Raçal, to trade, comes Marcolet, Merchandize.

Wonder that the Egyptians particularly, whofe Country was the Land of Ham, the Father of Canaan,
fhould do honour to this Figure, and apply it to their
Purpofes: For it is more than probable that, being fo
near at hand, he might be greatly affifting to his Brother Mizraim in the Settlement of that Country; befides the Confideration of their After-Obligations to
his Defcendant the Phænician, who is alfo called the
Ægyptian, Hercules.

CHAP. XXXIV Of VENUS.

THE next Deity that offers, is that powerful
Goddefs whofe influence is acknowledged by
Gods and Men. Cicero mentions four of this Name
[f]; but the Venus generally known is fhe who is fabled to have fprung from the Froth or Fermentation
raifed by the Genitals of Saturn, when cut off by his
Son Jupiter, and thrown into the Sea. Hence fhe
gained the Name of Aphrodite [g]. As foon as born
fhe was laid in a beautiful Couch or Shell, embellifhed
with Pearl, and by gentle Zephyrs wafted to the Ifle of
Cythera in the Ægean fea, from whence fhe failed to Cyprus which fhe reached in April. Here as foon as fhe landed, Flowers rofe beneath her Feet, the Hours received her, and braided her hair with golden Fillets, after which fhe was by them wafted to Heaven. Her
Charms appeared fo attractive in the Affembly of the
Gods, that fcarce one of them but what defired her in
Marriage. Vulcan, by the Advice of Jupiter, put Poppy in her Nectar, and, by intoxicating her gained
Poffeffion.

Few of the Deities have been fo extenfively worfhipped, or under a greater variety of Names. She

[f] The 1ft the Daughter of Cœlum; the 2d the Venus Aphro-
dita; the 3d born of Jupiter and Dione, and the Wife of Vulcan,
and the 4th Aftarte, or the Syrian Venus, the Miftrefs of Adonis;

[g] From Aphris, Froth, tho' fome derive it from aphranein to
run mad, becaufe all Love is Infatuation or Frenzy.

was

was called Cytherea, Paphia, Cypria, Erycina, Idalia, Acidalia, from the places where she was in a particular manner adored. Other Appellations were given her from her principal Attributes. She was styled Victrix [h], to denote her resistless sway over the Mind; Amica, from her being propitious to Lovers; Apaturia, from the Deceit and Inconstancy of her Votaries; Ridens, from her Love of Mirth and Laughter [i]: Hortensis, from her influencing the Vegetation of Plants and Flowers; Marina, from her being born of the Sea; Melanis, from her delighting in nocturnal [k] Amours; Meretrix, from the Prostitution of her Votaries; and Genetrix, from her presiding over the Propagation of Mankind. The Epithet of Migonitis, was given her from her power in the Management of Love (a), and that of Murcia and Myrtœa, on account of the Myrtle consecrated to her. She was named Verticordia, from her power of changing the Heart; for which Reason the Greeks styled her Epistrophia. The Spartans called her Venus Armata, because when besieged by the Messenians, their Wives unknown to their Husbands, raised the Siege. The Romans also termed her Barbata, because when a disease had seized the Women, in which they lost all their Hair, on their Prayers to Venus it grew again. A Temple was dedicated to her by the Appellation of Calva; because when the Gauls invested the Capitol the Women offered their Hair to make Ropes for the Engines. She had also the Epithet of Cluacida (b), from her Image being erected in the place where the Peace was concluded between the Romans and Sabines.

[h] Under this Character she is represented leaning on a Shield, and carrying Victory in her Right Hand, and a Scepter in her Left. At other Times with a Helmet, and the Apple of Paris in her Hand.

[i] Horace, Lib. I. Ode 2, Sive tu mavis Erycina ridens, Homer calls her Philomeides, or the Laughter-loving Queen.

[k] From melas, black, because Lovers chuse the Night.

(a) From mignumi, to mix or mingle; so Virgil,
——Mixta Deo Mulier.

(b) From Cluo to fight.

Let

Let us now enquire a little into the Actions ascribed
to this Goddess.   Her conjugal Behaviour we shall see
under the Article Vulcan, and find it was none of the
most edifying.   Her Amours were numerous.   Not to
mention Apollo, Neptune, Mars and Mercury, who all
boasted of her Favours [c].   She had Æneas [d] by
Anchises, but her principal Favourite was Adonis, the
Son of Cynaras, King of Cyprus and Myrrha, and a
youth of incomparable beauty, unfortunately in Hunting, killed by a wild Boar.   Venus who flew to his
assistance, received a prick in her Foot with a Thorn,
and the Blood which dropped from it produced the
Damask Rose [e]; but coming too late to save him,
she changed him into the Flower Anemone, which still
retains a Crimson Colour [f].   After this she obtained
of Proserpine, that Adonis should continue six Months
with her on Earth, and six Months remain in the lower Regions.

The most remarkable Adventure of Venus, was
her famous contest with Juno and Minerva for Beauty.   At the Marriage of Peleus and Thetis, the Goddess Discord resenting her not being invited, threw a
golden Apple amongst the company with this Inscrip-
tion, Let it be given to the fairest [g].   The Compe-
titors for this prize, were the three Deities above-
mentioned.   Jupiter referred them to Paris, youngest
Son to Priamus, King of Troy, who then kept his
Father's Flocks on Mount Ida.   Before him the
Goddesses appeared, as most say, naked, Juno of-

[c] By Apollo she had Electryon and five Sons; by Neptune,
Eryx, and Meligunis a Daughter; by Mars, Timor, and Pallor;
and by Mercury, Hermaphroditus.

[d] She immortalized AEneas, by purifying and anointing his
Body with ambrosial Essence, and the Romans deifiedhim by the
Nameof Indiges.   We have several ancient Inscriptions, Deo
Indigeti.

[e] Ovid, Lib X. 505.

[f] Some mythologized this Story, to signify by Adonis the Sun,
who during the Summer Signs, resides with Venus on the Earth,
and during the Winter with Proserpine.   The Wild Boar which
killed him is the Cold.

[g] Detur Pulchriori.

fered him Empire or Power; Minerva Wifdom; and Venus endeavoured to bribe him with the Promife of the Faireft Woman in the World. Fatally for himfelf and Family, the Shepherd was more fufceptible of Love, than of Ambition or Virtue, and decided the Point in favour of Venus. The Goddefs Rewarded him with Helen [a], whom he carried off from her Hufband Menelaus, King of Sparta, and the Rape gave Rife to that formidable Affociation of the Greek Princes, which ended in the Deftruction of his Family and the Ruin of Troy.

Venus, however propitious fhe was to Lovers, was very fevere to fuch as offended her. She changed the Women of Amathus in Cyprus, into Oxen for their Cruelty. The Propætides, who denied her Divinity, grew fo fhamelefsly impudent, that they were faid to be hardened into ftones [b]. Hippomenes and Atalanta, were another Inftance of her Refentment; for after fhe had affifted him to gain the Virgin, on their neglect to pay her the due Offerings, fhe infatuated them fo, that they lay together in the Temple of Cybele, who, for that Profanation, turned them into Lions [c].

Nor was fhe lefs favourable to her Votaries. Pygmalion a famous Statuary, from a Notion of the Inconveniencies of Marriage, Refolved to live fingle. He had, However, formed a beautiful Image of a Virgin, in Ivory, with which he fell fo deeply enamoured, that he treated it as a real Miftrefs, and continually folicited Venus, by Prayers and Sacrifices, to animate his beloved ftatue. His wifhes were granted, and by this enlivened Beauty he had a Son called Paphos, who gave his Name to the City of Paphos, in Cyprus [d].

[a] Such Helen was, and who can blame the Boy,
  Who in fo bright a Flame confumed his Troy?
                                    WALLER.

[b] See Ovid, Lib. X. I. 238.
[c] See the Article of Cybele, and Ovid, Lib. X. 560.
[d] Ovid, Lib. X. 245.

A God-

A Goddess so universally owned and adored could not fail of Temples. That of Paphos in Cyprus, was the principal. In that of Rome, dedicated to her by the Title of Venus Libitina, were sold all Things necessary for Funerals. She had also a magnificent shrine built for her by her son Æneas, on Mount Eryx in Sicily. The sacrifices usually offered to her were white Goats and Swine, with Libations of Wine, Milk, and Honey. The Victims were crowned with flowers or Wreaths of Myrtle. The Birds sacred to her were the Swan, the Dove, and the Sparrow.

So far for the Venus Pandemos, or Popularis, the Goddess of wanton and effeminate Love; but the Antients had another Venus whom they stiled Urania and Celistis, (who was indeed no other than the Syrian Astarte) and to whom they ascribed no Attributes but such as were strictly chaste and virtuous. Of this Deity they admitted no corporeal Resemblance, but she was Represented by the Form of a Globe ending conically [a], and only pure Fire was burnt on her Altars. Her sacrifices were called Nephalia, on account of their sobriety, only honey and wine being offered; but no Animal Victims except the Heifer, nor was the Wood of Figs, Vines or Mulberries suffered to be used in them.

This Distinction of two Venuses, the chaste and the Impure one, leads us to the true Explication of the Fable. In the different Attributes of the Egyptian Isis, we see those contradictory Characters explained. The Isis crowned with the Crescent Star or some of the Zodiacal Signs, is the celestial Venus. The Isis with the terrestial Symbols, such as the Heads of Animals, a Multitude of Breasts, or a Child in her Lap, became the Goddess of Fruitfulness and Generation, and consequently the Venus Pandemos. As the latter was regarded as a Divinity propitious to

[a] This Manner of Representation was borrowed from the Arabians and Syrians, who thought the Deity was not to be expressed by any corporeal Form.

Luxury

Luxury and Pleasure, it is no Wonder if she soon gained the Ascendant over her Rival. In Phænicia and Egypt, the young Girls [a] consecrated to the service of the terrestrial Isis, usually resided in a tent or Grove near the Temple, and were common prostitutes; whereas those devoted to the celestial Isis or Venus Urania, were strictly chaste. These Tabernacles were called the Pavillion of the Girls [b] and gave Rise to the Name of Venus, ascribed to the Goddess of Love. The Syrians also called the terrestrial Isis, Mylitta, or Illithye [c], and the Greeks and Romans adopted the same Name. Thus the symbolical Isis of Egypt, after producing the different Deities of Cybele, Rhea, Vesta, Juno, Diana, Luna, Hecate, and Proserpine, formed also the different Charactters of the common and celestial Venus; so easily do Superstition and Invention multiply the Objects of Idolatry.

As Venus was the Goddess of Love and Pleasure, it is no Wonder if the Poets have been lavish in the Description of her Beauties. Homer and Virgil have [d] given us fine Pictures of this Kind. Nor were the antient Sculptors and Painters negligent on so interesting a Subject. Phidias formed her statue of Ivory and Gold, with one Foot on a Tortoise [e]. Scopas

[a] They were called Kistophoroi, or Basket-Bearers, because they carried the Offerings.

[b] Succoth Venoth, the tabernacle of the Girls. The Greeks and Romans, who could not pronounce the word Venoth, called it Venos or Venus, and hearing the Tents of Venus so often mentioned, took it for the Name of the Goddess herself.

[c] From jeled, to beget comes Ilitta, Generation; which the Latins well expressed by Diva Genitrix, or Genitalis. See Horace, Carmen Seculare, l. 14.

[d] She said and turning round, her Neck she shew'd,
    That with celestial Charms divinely glow'd;
    Her waving Locks immortal Fragrants shed,
    And breath'd ambrosial Sweets around her Head:
    ' In flowing Pomp her radiant Robe was seen,
    ' And all the Goddess sparkled in her Mien.'
                PITT's Virgil Æneid I. 402.

[e] This Statue was at Elis, and the Tortoise was designed to shew that Women should not go much abroad, but attend their domestic affairs.   represented

Reprefented her Riding on a He-Goat, and Praxiteles
wrought her ftatue at Cnidos, of white Marble, half
opening her lips and fmiling.   Apelles drew her as
juft emerged from the fea, and prefling the water out
of her Hair, a piece that was reckoned ineftimable.
It were endlefs to mention the Variety of Attitudes
in which fhe is reprefented in Antique Gems and Medals [a] ; fometimes fhe is cloathed in Purple glittering with Gems, her Head crowned with Rofes, and
drawn in her Ivory Car, by Swans, Doves, or Spar-
rows.   At others fhe is reprefented ftanding with the
Graces attending her ; but in all pofitions Cupid her
fon is her infeparable Companion.   I fhall only add
that the ftatue called the Medicean Venus ; is the beft
figure of her which time has preferved.

CHAP. XXXV. Of the Attendants of VENUS,
viz. CUPID, HYMEN, and the HORÆ, or Hours.

BEFORE we clofe the Article of Venus, it is
neceffary to give fome Account of the Deities
who were ufually reprefented in her Train, and formed a Part of that State in which fhe ufually appeared.
The firft of thefe is Cupid.   Some make him one
of the moft ancient of the Deities, and fay he had no
Parents; but fncceeded immediately after Chaos. O-
thers Report, that Nox, or Night, produced an Egg,
which having hatched under her fable wings, brought
forth Cupid, or Love, who with golden Pinions immediately flew through the whole World [b]. But
the common Opinion is, that Cupid was the Son of

[a] See a great number of thefe in Mr. Ogle's Antiquities, il-
luftrated by ancient Gems, a Work, which it is a great Lofs to
the Publick, that ingenious and worthy Gentleman did not live
to finifh.

[b] Others make him the Son of Porus the God of Counfel,
who being drunk, begot him on Penia the Goddefs of Poverty.
Others the Son of Coelus and Terra, and fome of Zephyrus and
Flora.

Mars

Mars and Venus, and the Favourite Child of his
Mother who without his Aid, as she confesses in
Virgil, could do little execution. Indeed the Poets,
when they invoke the Mother, seldom fail to make
their joint Addresses to the Son (a). Perhaps this
Consciousness of his own Importance, rendered this
little Divinity so arrogant, that on many Occasions
he forgets his filial Duty. This Cupid belonged to
the Venus Paademos, or Popularis, and was called Anteros, or Lust.

But the Antients mention another Cupid, son of
Jupiter and Venus, of a nobler Character, whose delight it was to raise refined Sentiments of Love and
Virtue, whereas the other inspired base and Impure
Desires. His Name was Eros, or true Love. Eros
bore a golden Dart, which caused real Joy and Affection; Anteros a leaden Arrow, which raised a fleeting passion, ending in Satiety and disgust.

Cupid was Represented usually naked, to show that
Love has nothing of its own. He is armed with a
Bow and Quiver full of Darts, to shew his Power of
the mind; and crowned with Roses, to shew the delightful but transitory Pleasures he bestows. Sometimes he is depicted blind, to denote that Love sees no
[illegible]
faults in the object beloved; at others he appears with
a Rose in one hand and a Dolphin in the other; sometimes he is seen standing between Hercules and Mercury, to signify the Prevalence of Eloquence and Valour in Love; at others he is placed near Fortune, to
express how much the Success of Lovers depends on
that inconstant Goddess. He is always drawn with
Wings, to typify, that nothing is more fleeting than
the passion he excites.

The Egyptian Horus, which attended the terrestrial Isis, or the Venus Populatis, or Pandemos, was, according to the custom of the Neomeniæ, Represented with different attributes, sometimes with the wings
of the Etesian wind, at others, with the club of Hercules [b], the Arrows of Apollo, sitting on a Lion,

[a] See Horace, Lib. I. Ode xxx. & Passim.
[b] There is a Gem in Mr. Ogle answering this Description.

driving

driving a Bull, tying a Ram, or having a large Fish in his Nets. These signs of the different seasons of the year gave Rise to as many fables. The empire of Eros or love, was made to extend to Heaven and Earth, and even to the depths of the Ocean; and this little, but powerful child, disarmed Gods and Men.

Hymen the second attendant of Venus, was the God of marriage, and the Son of Bacchus and that Goddess [a]. He is said to be born in Attica, where he made it his business to rescue Virgins carried off by robbers, and to restore them to their Parents. On this account all Maids newly married offered Sacrifices to him; as also to the Goddess of Concord. He was invoked in the nuptial ceremony [b] in a particular Manner.

This God was Represented of a fair Complexion, crowned with Amaracus, or the Herb Sweet Marjoram, and robed in a Veil of Saffron Colour (representative of the Bridal Blushes) with a Torch lighted in his hand, because the Bride was carried always home by a Torch Light.

Every one knows it was a constant Custom of the oriental Nations, on the Wedding-day, to attend the Bridegroom and Bride with Torches and Lamps. The Chorus on these Occasions was Hu! Humeneh! Here he comes! This is the Festival (c)! The Figure exhibeted on this Occasion in Egypt, was a young Man bearing a Lamp or Torch, placed near the female Figure, which denoted the day of the Month fixed for the Ceremony.

The Graces, who always attended Venus, have been already described with the Muses under the article of Apollo.

The Horæ, or Hours, were the Daughters of Jupiter and Themis, and the Harbingers of Apollo. They were also the Nurses of Venus, as well as her Dressers, and made a necessary part of her Train.

[a] Hymen is thought to be the Son of the Goddess Venus Urania or the Celestial Venus.

[b] They repeated often the words, O Hymen! O Hymenæ.

[c] From Hu, lo! or here he is, and Meneh the Feast or Sacrifice, comes Hymenæus

CHAP.

CHAP XXXVI. Of Vulcan.

THOUGH the Husband should usually precede the Wife, yet Vulcan was too unhappy in Wedlock to obtain this Distinction. There were several of the Name [a], but the principal who arrived at the Honour of being deified, was the son of Jupiter and Juno, or as others say, of Juno alone: However this be, he was so remarkably deformed, that his Father threw him down from Heaven to the Isle of Lemnos, and in the Fall he broke his Leg [b]. Others Report that Juno herself, disgusted at his sight hurled him into the sea, where he was nursed by Thetis [c].

The first Residence of Vulcan on earth, was the Isle of Lemnos [d], where he set up his Forge, and taught men how to soften and polish Brass and Iron. From thence he removed to the Liparean Isles near Sicily, where, with the Assistance of the Cyclops, he made Jupiter fresh Thunderbolts, as the old grew decayed. He also wrought an Helmet for Pluto, which Rendered him invisible, a Trident for Neptune that shakes both Land and Sea, and a Dog of Brass for Jupiter, which he animated so, as to perform [e] all the natural Functions of the Animal. Nor is this a wonder; when we consider that at the Desire of the same God, he formed Pandora, who was sent with the fatal Box to Prometheus, as has been related in its

{a] The 1st, said to be the Son of Coelus; the 2d, the son of Nilus, called Opas; the 3d, the Vulcan, son of Jupiter and Juno, mentioned above; and the 4th, the son of Mænalius, who resided in the Vulcanean or Liparean Isles.

[b] He was caught by the Lemnians, or he had broke his Neck. It was added, he was a whole Day in falling.

[c] Others report he fell on the Land, and was nurse by Apes; and that Jupiter expelled him the Skies for attempting to rescue Juno, when she conspired against him.

[d] Because Lemnos abounds in Minerals and hot Springs.

[e] Jupiter gave this Dog to Europa, she to Procris, and by her it was given to Cephalus her Husband, and by Jupiter after turned to a Stone.

place

In short, Vulcan was the general Armourer of the Gods. He made Bacchus a golden Crown to prefent Ariadne, a chariot for the Sun, and another for Mars. At the Requeft of Thetis, he fabricated the divine Armour of Achilles, whofe fhield is fo beautifully de fcribed by Homer [a] ; as alfo the invincible Armour of Æneas, at the Intreaty of Venus. To conclude with an Inftance of his Skill this way, in Revenge for his Mother Juno's Unkindnefs, he prefented her a golden Chair managed by fuch unfeen Springs, that when fhe fat down in it fhe was not able to move till fhe was forced to beg her Deliverance from him.

Vulcan like the reft of the Gods had feveral names or appellations: He was called Lemnius, from the ifle of Lemnos, confecrated to him; Mulciber, or Mul·cifer, from his art of foftening Steel and Iron. By the Greeks, Hephaiftos, from his delighting in Flames or Fire; and Ætneus and Lipareus, from the Places fuppofed to be his Forges [b]. As to his Worfhip, he had an Altar in common with Prometheu· [c], and was one of the Gods who prefided over Marriage, becaufe he firft introduced the Ufe of Torches at the Nuptial Rites. It was cuftomary with many Nations, after Victory, to gather the Enemy's Arms in a heap, and offer them to Vulcan, His principal Temple was in a confecrated Grove at rhe foot of Mount Ætna, guarded by Dogs, who had the Difcernment to diftin-guifh his Votaries, to tear the Vicious and fawn upon the Virtuous.

The proper Sacrifice to this Deity was a Lion, to denote the refiftlefs Fury of Fire. His Feftivals were different: At thofe called Protervia (amongft the Romans) they ran about with lighted Torches The Vul-cania were celebrated by throwing living Animals in-to the Fire. The Lampadophoria were Races perfor-med to his Honour, where the contention was to car-

[a] See Iliad, Lib. 18
[b] On Account of the Volcanoes and fiery Eruptions there.
[c] Prometheus firft invented Fire, Vulcan the Ufe of it, in making Arms and Utenfils.

* I

ry lighted torches to the goal ; but whoever overtook
the person before him, had the privilege of delivering
him his torch to carry, and to retire with Honour.

Vulcan, however disagreeable his person was, was
ensible of Love : His first Passion was for Minerva,
and he had Jupiter's Consent to make his Addresses to
her, but his courtship was too ill-placed to be successful.   He was more fortunate in his Suit to Venus, tho'
he had no great Reason to boast his Lot.   The Goddess was too great a beauty to be constant, and Vul
can too disagreeable to be happy.   She chose Mars
for her Gallant, and the Intrigue for some time went
on swimmingly.   As Apollo or the Sun, had a friendship for the Husband, Mars was particularly fearful
of his discovering the Affair, and therefore set a Boy
called Alectryon, or Gallus, to warn him and his fair
Mistress of the Sun's Approach.   The Centinel unluckily fell asleep and the Sun saw them together, and
let Vulcan presently into the secret. The Black smith
God to revenge the Injury, against their next meeting, contrived so fine and imperceptible a Net Work,
that they were taken in their Guilt, and exposed to
the Ridicule of the Gods, till released at the intercession of Neptune.   Mars, to punish Alectryon for his neglect, changed him into a Cock, who to atone for his
Fault, by his crowing, gives constant notice of the
Sun rise [a].

This Deity, as the God of Fire, was represented
variously in different Nations.   The Egyptians depicted him proceeding out of an Egg placed in the
Mouth of Jupiter, to denote the radical or natural
heat diffused through all created Beings.   Some Historians make him one of the first Egyptian Kings, who
for his goodness was deified ; and, add, that King Menes erected a noble Temple to him at Thebes, with a
Colossal Statue seventy-five Feet high.   The Phani-
cians adored him by the name of Crysor, and
thought him the Author and Cause of Lightning, and
all fiery Exhalations.   Some Writers confound him

a] See Ovid, Lib. IV. 167.

with

with the Tubal Cain of Scripture.   In ancient Gems
and Medals of the Greeks and Romans, he is figured
as a lame, deformed, and squalid Man, Working at
the Anvil, and usually attended by his men, the Cyclops, or by some God or Goddess who comes to ask
his Assistance.

To examine into the Ground of this Fable, we must
have once more Recourse to the Egyptian Antiquities.
The Horus of the Egyptians was the most mutable figure on Earth ; for he assumed shapes suitable to all
Seasons of Time, and Ranks of People : To direct
the Husbandmen, he wore a rural Dress.   By a change
of Attributes, he became the Instructor of the Smiths
and other Artificers; whose Instruments he appeared adorned with.   This Horus of the Smiths
had a short or lame Leg, to signify, that Agriculture
or Husbandry halts without the Assistants of the Han-
dicraft or mechanic Arts.   In this Apparatus he was
called Mulciber [a], Hephaistos [b], and Vulcan [c],
all which Names the Greeks and Romans adopted
with the Figure, which as usual they converted from
a Symbol to a God.   Now as this Horus was removed from the side of the beautiful Isis (or the Venus
Pandemos) to make Room for the martial Horus, exposed in time of War, it occasioned the Jest of the assistants, and gave Rise to the Fable of Vulcan's being
supplanted in his Wife's Affections by the God of
War.

[a] From Malac, to direct and manage ; and Ber or Beer, a
Cave, or Mine, comes Mulciber, the King of the Mines or Forges.

[b] From Aph, Father, and Esto Fire, is form'd Ephaisto, or
Hepheftion the Father of Fire.

[c] From Woll, to work, and Canan, to hasten, comes Wol-
can, or Work finished.

CHAP. XXXVI.   Of the Offspring of Vulcan.

THOUGH Vulcan had no Iſſue by Venus, yet he had a pretty numerous Offspring We have already mentioned his paſſion for Minerva; This Goddeſs coming one Day to beſpeak ſome Armour of him, he attempted to raviſh her, and in the ſtruggle his ſeed fell on the Ground, and produced the Monſter Erichthonius [a].   Minerva nouriſhed him in her Thigh, and afterwards gave him to be nurſed by Aglauros, Pandroſus and Herſe, but with a ſtrict caution not to look in the Cradle or Coffer which held him. The firſt and laſt neglecting this Advice ran mad. Erichthonius being born with deformed, or as ſome ſay Serpentine Legs, was the firſt inventor of Chariots to ride in.   He was the 4th King of Athens, and a Prince of great Juſtice and Equity.

Cacus another ſon of Vulcan, was of a different Character.   He was a notorious Robber, and received his Name from his conſummate Villany [b]. He fixed himſelf on Mount Aventine, and from thence infeſted all Italy with his depredations; but having ſtolen ſome Oxen from Hercules, he dragged them backwards to his Cave [c], that the Robbery might not be diſcovered by the Track. Hercules, however paſſing that way, heard the lowing of his cattle, broke open the Doors, and ſeizing the Wretch put him to death.

A third ſon of Vulcan, Cæculus [d], ſo called from his little Eyes, reſembled his Brother Cacus, and lived by Prey. It is ſaid his Mother ſitting by the fire, a ſpark flew into her Lap, upon which ſhe conceived. Others ſay ſome Shepherds found him in the fire as ſoon as born.   He founded the City Præneſte.

[a] Derived from Eridos and Cthonos, or Earth and contention.
[b] From Kakos, bad or wicked.
[c] Virgil has given a fine Deſcription of this Cave, but he makes him but half a Man. See AEneid VIII. 194.
[d] It is thought the noble Roman Family of Cæcilii derive their Name from him. See Virgil, AEneid X. 544, and AEneid VII. 680.

By his wife Aglaia, one of the Graces, Vulcan had several sons, as Ardalus, the Inventor of the Pipe called Tibia. Brotheus, who being deformed like his Father, deftroyed himself in the Fire, to avoid the Reproaches he met with. Æthiops, who gave his Name to the Æthiopians, before called Æthereans, Olenus the Founder of a City of his own Name in Bœotia, Ægyptus from whom Egypt was called, Albion, Periphenus, Morgion, Acus and several others.

CHAP. XXXVIII. Of the CYCLOPS and POLYPHEMUS.

THE Cyclops were the Sons of Neptune and Amphitrite. The principal were Brontes, Steropes, and Pyracmon, though their whole Number was above a hundred. They were the journeymen of Vulcan. It is faid, as foon as they were born Jupiter threw them into Tartarus, but that they were delivered at the Interceffion of Tellus, and fo became the Affiftants of our God. They had each but one Eye [a] placed in the middle of their Foreheads, and lived on fuch Fruits and Herbs as the Earth brought forth without Cultivation. They are Reported to have built the Walls of Mycenæ and Tyrinthe with fuch maffy ftones, that the fmalleft required two Yoke of Oxen to draw it. The Dealers in Mythology fay, that the Cyclops fignify the vapours raifed in the air which occafion Thunder and Lightning.

With thefe we may clafs Polyphemus, though he was the fon of Neptune, having like the Cyclops but one eye; but of fo gigantick a Stature, that his very Afpect was terrible. His abode was in Sicily, where he furprized Ulyffes and his Companions, of whom he devoured three; but Ulyffes making him drunk, blinded him with a firebrand, and fo efcaped with the

[a] From Kuklos Circulus, and Ops Oculus, that is the one-ey'd Man.

reft.   Virgil hath given us a fine Defcription of this Scene [a].

CHAP. XXXIX Of MINERVA or PALLAS.

WE come next to Minerva or Pallas, one of the moft diftinguifhed of the Dii Majores, as being the Goddefs of Sciences and Wifdom. Cicero mentions five [b] of this Name; but the moft confiderable was the Daughter of Jupiter, not by any infamous Amour, nor even by the conjugal Bed, but the Child of his Brain. It is faid her Father feeing Juno barren through Grief, ftruck his Forehead, and three Months after came forth Minerva [c]. On tne Day of her Nativity it rained Gold at Rhodes [d]. Her firft Appearance on Earth was in Libya, where beholding her own Beauty in the Lake Triton, fhe from thence gained the Name of Tritonis [e].

[a] See Virgil AEneid, Lib. III. 620, but the whole Defcription, tho' admirable, is too long to be copied here.

[b] The 1ft the Mother of Apollo, or Latona; the 2d produced from the Nile, and worfhipped at Sais in Egypt; the 3d the Child of Jupiter's Brain; the 4th the Daughter of Jupiter and Corypha, who invented Chariots with Four Wheels; and the 5th the Child of Pallas whom fhe killed, becaufe he attempted her Chaftity.

[c] It is faid Vulcan was the Midwife, by cleaving his Skull with a Hatchet; but that feeing an armed Virago come out inftead of a Child he ran away. Others report, that when Jupiter fwallowed Metis, one of his Wives, he was with Child of Pallas

[d] Hence the Rhodians were the firft who worfhipped her, as Claudian remarks.

> Auratas Rhodiis imbres, nafcente Minerva
> Induxiffe Jovem ferunt.

Some fay it was becaufe fhe taught them the Art of making Coloffal Statues.

[e] An annual Ceremony was performed at this Lake by the Virgins, who in diftinct Bodies attacked each other with various Weapons. The firft that fell was efteemed not a Maid, and thrown into the Lake; but fhe who received moft Wounds was carried off in Triumph.

She

She had besides several other appellations amongst the Greeks and Romans. She was called Pallas from the brandishing her Spear in War. Athena, because she was born full grown, and never suckled; whence also she obtained the name of Ametrois, or Mother-less. The Epithet of Parthenis, or the Virgin, was given her on account of her perpetual Chastity; that of Ergatis, or the Workwoman, for her Excellency in Spinning and Weaving; Musica, from her inventing the Pipe; Pylotis, because her Image was set up in the Gates; and Glaucopis, or green-ey'd, because her eyes were of that cast [a], like those of the Owl.

Minerva was the Goddess of War, Wisdom and Arts, such as Weaving, the making Oil, Musick, especially the Pipe (b); of building Castles, over which she presided; and, in short, was the Patonness of all those Sciences, which render Men useful to Society and themselves, and intitle them to the Esteem of Posterity.

We have already had occasion to observe how this Goddess vowed a perpetual Virginity, and in what manner she rejected the addresses of Vulcan. She was indeed very delicate on this point, for she deprived Tiresias of his sight, because he accidentally saw her bathing in the fountain of Helicon; but at the intercession of his mother Chariclo, she relented so far, that to compensate his loss, she endued him with the Gift of Prophecy (c). Nor was she less severe to Medusa, who being ravished by Neptune in her temple, she revenged the Sacrilege, by turning her Locks into Snakes, and causing all who beheld her after to be changed into stones.

She was equally jealous of her Superiority in the Arts she invented. Arachne, a Lybian Princess, the

[a] Yet Homer and all the Poets call her the blue-ey'd Maid. See Pope.

[b] It is said, seeing her Cheeks reflected in the Water as she played, she threw away the Pipe with this Expression; That Musick was too dear if purchased at the Expence of Beauty.

(c) Ovid relates the Story of Tiresias very differently; for which see Metamorp. Lib. III. 316.

Daughter

Daughter of Idmon, had the presumption to challenge her at Spinning. The Folly cost her dear; for Minerva struck her with the Spindle on the Forehead, for which attempting to hang herself through Despair, the Goddess turned her into a Spider, in which shape she still exercises the Profession she so much boasted [a]. The Reader may consult Ovid, if he would see this Story set in a beautiful Light.

As Conduct is opposite in military Affairs, to brutal Valour, so Minerva is always by the Poets placed in Contrast to Mars. Thus we see Homer makes her side with the Greeks in the Trojan War, while the other Deity takes the part of the Enemy. The Success is answerable to this Disposition [b], and we see Prudence and Discipline victorious over Valour without Counsel, and Force under no direction.

One of the most remarkable of Minerva's Adventures, was her Contest with Neptune, of which Notice has been taken under the Article of that Deity. When Cecrops founded Athens, it was agreed, that whoever of these two Deities should produce the most beneficial Gift to Mankind, should give Name to the new City. Neptune with a stroke of his Trident formed a Horse; Pallas caused an Olive to spring from the Ground, and carried the Prize. The meaning of this Fable was to point out, that Agriculture was to a rising Colony of more importance than Navigation.

Minerva was highly honoured, and had several Temples both in Greece and Italy. The Athenians, who always had a particular Devotion to her, as the Patroness of their City, in the flourishing State of their Republick erected a magnificent Temple to her by the Name of Parthenis, or the Virgin Goddess, in whih they placed her Statue of Gold and Ivory thirty-nine Feet high, wrought by the Hands of Phidias. She had a stately Temple at Rome on Mount Aventine, where her Festival called Minervalia or Quinquatria, was celebrated for five Days successively

[a] See Ovid, Lib. VI. 1.
[b] See the Preface to Mr. Pope's Homer.

in

in the month of March. She had sometimes her Altars in common with Vulcan, sometimes with Mercury. The usual victim offered her was a white Heifer never yoked. The Animals sacred to her were the Cock, the Owl, and the Basilisk.

We must not here omit the Palladium (a), or that sacred statue which fell down from Heaven, and was preserved in Troy, as a treasure on whose safety that of the City depended. Diomedes and Ulysses found means to steal it, and the City was soon after taken and destroyed [b]. However, it is certain that Æneas brought either this or another of the same Kind with him into Italy, and deposited it at Lavinum, from whence it was removed to Rome, and placed in the Temple of Vesta. When this Edifice was consumed by fire Metellus a noble Roman, rushed in and brought it off, though with the loss of his Eyes, in Recompence for which heroic Action, he had the Privilege of coming to the Senate in a Chariot, that the Honour might in some degree allay the sense of his misfortune. The Romans indeed, vain of their Trojan descent, regarded the Palladium in the same Light with their Ancestors, and thought, the Security and Duration of their Empire were annexed to the possession of this Guardian Image.

Come we next to enquire into the mythological Birth and Origin of this fabled Goddess, who is no other than the Egyptian Isis under a new Dress or Form, and the same with the Pales or Rural Goddess of the Sabines [d]. The Athenians, who were an Egpptian Colony from Sais, followed the Customs of

[a] Authors differ as to this Palladium, some making it of Wood, and adding, it could move its Eyes and shake its Spear. Others say it was composed of the Bones of Pelops, and sold by the Scythians to the Trojans.

[b] Some assert it was a Counterfeit Palladium the Greek Generals stole away, and that AEneas saved the true One. Others make two Palldaiums.

[c] To whose Honour th Feasts called Palilia were celebrated Now this Word is manifestly of Egyptian Derivation, being taken from Pillel to govern the City ; whence comes Pelilah, the public Order

their

their anceſtors, by particularly applying themſelves to raiſing Flax for Linen Cloth, and the cultivation of the Olive (a).   Now the figure worſhipped at Sais, as preſiding over theſe Arts, was a Female in compleat Armour.   This as Diodorus tells us, was becauſe the Inhabitants of this Dynaſty, were both the beſt Huſbandmen and Soldiers in Egypt.   In the Hand of this Image they placed a ſhield with a full Moon depicted on it ſurrounded by ſerpents, the Emblems of Life and Happineſs.   And at the Feet of this ſymbol they placed an Owl, to ſhew it was a nocturnal Sacrifice.   To this they gave the Name of Meduſa, (b) expreſſive of what ſhe was deſigned to repreſent.   The Greeks who were ignorant of the true Meaning of all this, did not think fit to put ſuch a favourable ſenſe on the Head of Meduſa, which ſeemed to them an Object of Horror, and opened a fine Field for poetical Imagination.   The preſſing of the Olives did indeed turn Fruit into ſtones, in a literal ſenſe; hence they made the Ægis or ſhield of Minerva petrify all who beheld it.

To remind the People of the Importance of their Linen manufactory, the Egyptians expoſed in their Feſtivals another Image, bearing in her Right Hand the Beam or Inſtrument round which the Weavers Rolled the Warp of their Cloth.   This Image they called Minerva (c).   Now there are antient Figures of Pallas extant which correſpond with this Idea (d).   What ſtill heightens the Probability of this is, that the Name of Athene given to this Goddeſs, is the very Word in Egypt for the flaxen thread (e) uſed in their Looms.   Near this Figure, which was to Warn the Inhabitants of the Approach of the Weaving or Winter-ſeaſon, they placed another of an Inſect, whoſe

[a] The City of Sais derived its Name from this Tree, Zaith or Sais ſignifying the Olive.

[b] From Duſh, to preſs comes Meduſha or Meduſa the Preſſing. See Iſai. xxv. 10.

[c] From Minevra, a Weaver's Loom.

[d] In the Collection of Prints made by M. De Crozat.

[e] Atona, Linen Thread. See Prov. vii. 16.

Induſtry

Induftry feems to have given rife to this Art, and to
which they gave the Name of Arachne [a], to denote
its Application.   All thefe emblems tranfplanted to
Greece, by the Genius of that People, fond of the
marvellous were converted into real Objects, and indeed afforded Room enough for the Imagination of
their Poets to invent the Fable of the Transformation of Arachne into a Spider.

Minerva, by the Poets and Sculptors, is ufually Reprefented in a ftanding Attitude completely armed,
with a compofed but fmiling countenance, bearing a
golden Breaft plate, a Spear, in her Right Hand, and
her terrible Ægis in her Left, having on it the Head
of Medufa entwined with fnakes.   Her Helmet was
ufually entwined with Olives, to denote Peace is the
end of War, or rather becaufe that Tree was facred
to her.   See her Picture in Cambray's Telemaque.
At her Feet is generally the Owl, or the Cock; the
former being the Emblem of Wifdom, the latter of
War.

CHAP. XXXIX.   Of MARS and BELLONA.

MARS was the fon of Juno alone, who being
chagrined that Jupiter fhould bear Minerva
without her help, to be even with him confulted
Flora, who fhewed her a flower in the Olenian fields,
on touching of which fhe conceived, and became the
Mother of this dreadful Deity (b).   Thero, or Fiercenefs, was his Nurfe, and he received his Education
amongft the Scythians, the moft barbarous nation in
the World, amongft whom he was adored in a particular manner, though they acknowledged no other
God.

This Deity had different appellations.   The Greeks
called him Ares (c), either from the Deftruction he

(a) From Arach, to make Linen Cloth.
(b) Others make him the Son of Jupiter and Juno, or of Jupiter and Erys.
(c) Either from arein, to kill, or from areo to keep filence.

caufes,

caufes, or the filence and vigilance obferved in War. He had the Name of Gradivus from his Majeftick Port; of Quirinus, when on the defenfive, or at reft. By the ancient Latins he was ftiled Salifubfulus, or the Dancer, from the Uncertainty that attends all martial enterprizes.

Mars was the God of War, and in high Veneration with the Romans, both on account of his being the Father of Romulus their Founder, and becaufe their own Genius always inclined to conqueft. Numa though otherwife a pacific Prince, having implored the Gods, during a great Peftilence, received a fmall Brafs Buckler, called Ancile, from Heaven, which the nymph Egeria advifed him to keep with the utmoft care, the Fate of the Roman People and Empire depending on its Confervation. To fecure fo valuable a Pledge, Numa caufed eleven more fhields of the fame Form to be made, and intrufted to the Care of thefe to an Order of Priefts he inftituted, called Salii, or the Priefts of Mars, in whofe Temple the twelve Ancilia were depofited. The Number of thefe Priefts was alfo twelve, chofen out of the nobleft Familes, who on the 1ft of March annually, the Feftival of Mars, carried the Ancilia with great ceremony round the City, clafhing their Bucklers, and finging hymns to the Gods, in which they were joined by a chorus of Virgins chofen to affift on this occafion, and dreffed like themfelves. This Feftival was concluded with a grand Supper [b]

Auguftus erected a magnificent Temple to Mars at Rome, by the title of Ultor, which he vowed to him, when he implored his Affiftance againft the Murderers of Julius Cæfar. The Victims facrificed to him were the Wolf for its Fiercenefs, the horfe on ac count of its ufefulnefs in war, the Woodpecker and Vulture for their ravenoufnefs; the Cock for his Vigila ce. He was crowned with Grafs, becaufe it grows in Cities depopulated by war, and thickeft in Places moiftened with human Blood.

[b] Called Cœna Saliaris.

The History of Mars furnishes new Adventures. We have already related his Amour with Venus, by whom he had Hermione, contracted to Orestes, and afterwards married to Pyrrhus King of Epirus.

By the Nymph Bistonis, Mars had Tereus, who reigned in Thrace, and married Progne the Daughter of Pandion, King of Athens. This Princess had a Sister called Philomela, a great Beauty; and being desirous to see her, she requested her Husband to go to Athens and bring her Sister, with her Father's Permission, to her. Tereus, by the Way, fell in Love with his Charge, and on her rejecting his Solicitations, ravished her, cut out her Tongue, and enclosed her in a strong Tower, pretending to his Wife she died in the Journey. In this condition the unhappy Princess found means to embroider her Story, and send it to her Sister, who transported with Rage, contrived how to revenge the injury. First she brought her Sister home privately; next she killed her Son Itys, and served up his Flesh to his Father for Supper: After he had eat it, she exposed the head and told him what she had done; Tereus, mad with Fury, pursued the Sisters, who in their Flight became transformed, Progne to a Swallow, and Philomela to a Nightingale. Itys was by the Gods changed to a Pheasant, and Tereus himself into a Lapwing. Ovid has [d] given us this Story with his usual embellishments.

Mars married a Wife called Nerio, or Nerione [e], which in the Sabine tongue signifies valour or strength. He had several Children the principal of whom were Bythis, who gave his Name to Bythinia; Thrax, from whom Thrace was so called; Ænomaus, Ascalaphus, Biston, Chalybs, Strymon, Parthenopæus, Tmolus, Pylus, Euenus, Calydon, &c.

This Deity having killed Halirothus the Son of Neptune, was indicted before the Assembly of the Gods for the Murder as well as for the Crime of de-

___

[d] See Ovid. Lib VI. 413.

[e] Hence the Claudian Family at Rome are said to derive the Sirname of Nero.

K   bauching

bauching Alcippe, fifter to the deceafed. Twelve Gods were prefent, of whom fix were for acquitting him, fo that by the Cuftom of the Court, when the Voices were equal, the favourable fide carrying it, he came off. Some fay this Trial was in the famous Areopagus, or Hill of Mars, at Athens, a Court, which in fucceeding Time gained the higheft Reputation, for the Juftice and Impartiality of its proceedings [a].

Mars was neither invulnerable nor invincible; for we find him in Homer both wounded and purfued by Diomedes, but then it muft be confidered that Homer was fo good a Patriot, that he always affects to difgrace the Gods, who took the Trojan's Part.

Mars, whatever his appearance be, was of Egyptian Original. This Nation was divided into three claffes, the Priefts, the Hufbandmen, and the Artificers; of thefe the firft were by their Profeffion exempt from War, and the laft reckoned too mean to be employed in Defence of the State; fo that their Militia was wholly taken from the fecond Body. We have already obferved, that in the Sacrifices which preceded their military Expeditions, their His appeared in a warlike Drefs, and gave Rife to the Greek Pallas or Minerva. The Horus which accompanied this Figure, was alfo equipped with this Helmet and Buckler, and called by the Name of Harits [b], or the formidable. The Syrians foftened this word to Hazis (c); the Greeks changed it to Ares; the Gauls pronounced it Hefus; and the Romans, and Sabines, Warets or Mars. Thus the military Horus of the Egyptians became perfonified and made the God of Combats or War.

[a] Thefe Judges were chofen out of Perfons of the moft blamelefs Characters. They fuffered no verbal Pleadings before them, left a falfe Eloquence might varnifh a bad Caufe; and all their Sentences were given in writing and delivered in the Dark.

[b] From Harits violent or enraged. See Job xv. 20.

[c] Hazis (Syr) the terrible in War. Pfalm xxiv. 8. The Syrians alfo called him Ab Guereth, or the Father of Combats; whence the Romans borrowed their Gradivus Pater.

Mars is ufually defcribed in a Chariot drawn by fu-rious Horfes, compleatly armed, and extending his Spear with the one hand, while with the other Hand he grafps a fword embrued in blood. His Afpect is fierce and favage. Sometimes Difcord is reprefented as preceding his Car, while Clamour, Fear, and Ter-ror appear in his Train. Virgil has given a Defcripti-on of this God pretty much agreeable to this Idea [a].

Bellona is ufually reckoned the fifter of Mars, tho' fome call her both his fifter and wife. As her Incli-nations were equally cruel and favage, fhe took a plea-fure in fharing his dangers, and is commonly depicted as driving his chariot with a bloody whip in her hand. Appius Claudius built her a Temple at Rome where in her Sacrifices called Bellonaria, her Priefts u-fed to flafh themfelves with Knives. Juft oppofite ftood the Columna Bellica, a Pillar from whence the Herald threw a Spear, when War was proclaimed a-gainft any nation. She is faid to be the Inventrefs of the needle [b], from whence fhe took her name.

This Goddefs is reprefented fometimes holding a lighted Torch or Brands, at others with a trumpet, her Hair compofed of Snakes clotted with Gore, and her Garments ftained with Blood, in a furious and diftracted Attitude.

CHAP. XL. Of Ceres.

IT may not be improper now to pafs to fofter Pic-tures, whofe agreeablenefs may ferve as a contraft to the ftronger Images juft difplayed. As plenty and abundance Repair the Wafte and Havock of War, we fhall next to Mars introduce Ceres, a Divinity friendly and beneficent to Mankind.

This Goddefs was the daughter of Saturn and Rhea. Sicily, Attica, Crete, and Egypt, claim the Honour of her Birth, each Country producing its

[a] Virgil Æneid \ III. 700.
[b] From Belone, a Needle.

 Reafons

Reafons, though the firft has the general fuffrage. In her Youth fhe was fo beautiful, that her Brother Jupiter fell in Love with her, by whom fhe had Proferpine. Neptune next enjoyed her, but the Fruit of this amour is controverted, fome making it a daughter, called Hira, others a horfe, called Arion. Indeed as this laft Deity careffed her in that Form, the latter Opinion feems beft founded. However this be, fhe was fo afhamed of this laft Affair, that fhe put on mourning garments, and retired to a Cave, where fhe continued fo long, that the World was in danger of perifhing for want [a]. At laft Pan difcovered her Retreat, and informed Jupiter, who by the interceffion of the Parcæ, or Fates, appeafed her, and prevailed on her to Return to the World.

For fome time fhe took up her Abode in Corcyra, from whence fhe removed to Sicily, where the Misfortune befel her of the Rape of Proferpine her daughter, by Pluto. The difconfolate Mother immediately carried her complaints to Jupiter, upbraiding him with his permitting fuch an injuftice to be committed efpecially on the Perfon of his own Daughter. But obtaining little fatisfaction, fhe lighted her Torches at Mount Ætna, and mounting her Car drawn by winged Dragons, fet out in fearch of her beloved Daughter. As her Adventures in this Journey were pretty Remarkable, we fhall mention them in their Order.

Her firft ftop was at Athens, where being hofpitably received by Celeus, fhe in Return taught him to fow Corn, and nourifhed his Son Triptolemus with celeftial Milk by day, at night covering him with fire, to Render him immortal. Celeus out of Curiofity difcovering this laft particular, was fo affrighted, that he cried out and Revealed it himfelf, on which the Goddefs killed him. As to his fon, Ceres lent him her Chariot, and fent him thro' the World to inftruct Mankind in the Art of Agriculture.

[a] Becaufe during her Abfence the Earth produced no Corn or Fruits.

She

She was next entertained by Hypothoon and Meganira [a] his Wife, who set Wine before her, which
she refused, as unsuitable to her mournful Condition;
but she prepared herself a Drink from an Infusion of
Meal or Corn, which she afterwards used. Iambe [a]
an attendant of Meganira, used to divert the Goddess
with stories and jests, which she repeated in a certain
kind of Verse. It happened, during a sacrifice made
her here, that Abas, son to Meganira, derided the ceremony, and used the Goddess with opprobrious
Language, whereupon sprinkling him with a certain
mixture she held in her Cup, he became a Newt or
Water Lizard. Erisichton also for cutting down a
Grove consecrated to her, was punished with such an
insatiable hunger that nothing could satisfy him, but
he was forced to gnaw his own flesh.

From thence Ceres passed into Lycia, where being
thirsty and desiring to drink at a Spring, the Clowns
not only hindered her, but sullied and disturbed the
Water, reviling her for her Misfortunes, upon which
she turned them into Frogs. These Frogs tho' alrea;
dy punished for affronting his sister, had the Folly to
ask Jupiter to grant them a King. He sent them a
Frog whom they rejected, and desired another, upon
which the God sent them a Water Serpent, who devoured them, and effectually convinced them of their
Weakness.

It is disputed, who first informed Ceres where her
Daughter was; some ascribe the Intelligence to Triptolemus, and his Brother Eubuleus; but the most part
agree in giving the Honour of it to the Nymph Are-
thusa (a Fountain in Sicily) [c], who flying in the
pursuit of the River Alpheus, saw this Goddess in the
Infernal Regions.

We have but one Amour of Ceres recorded. Finding Jasion the son of Jupiter and Electra asleep in a

[a] Hypothoon was the son of Neptune and Asope.

[b] The Daughter of Pan and Echo, and the inventress of I-
ambic Verse.

[c] The Daughter of Norcus and Doris, and a Companion o f
Diana.

K 3

Fickl

Field newly ploughed up, fhe acquainted him with her paffion, and bore him Plutus the God of Riches ; but Jove incenfed to fee his fon become hir Rival, killed him with a Thunderbolt.

Ceres had feveral Names; fhe was called Magna Dea, or the Great Goddefs, from her Bounty in fupporting Mankind ; Melaina, from her black Cloathing; Euchlæa, from her Verdure ; Alma, Altrix, and Mammofa, from her nourifhing and impregnating all Seeds and Vegetables, and being as it were the common Mother of the World. The Arcadians, by way of Excellence, ftyled her Defpoina, or the Lady. She was alfo honoured with the peculiar Epithet of Thefmophoris, or the Legiflatrefs, becaufe Hufbandry firft taught the ufe of Land-marks, and the Value of Ground, the Source of all Property and Law.

It muft be owned this Goddefs was not undeferving the higheft Titles given her, confidered as the Deity who firft taught Men to plow and fow, to reap and houfe their Corn, to yoke Oxen, to make Bread, to cultivate all forts of Pulfe and Garden ftuff (except Beans) tho' fome make Bacchus the firft Inventor of Agriculture. She alfo inftructed mankind to fix Limits or Boundaries, to afcertain their Poffeffion.

There was none of the celeftial Affembly, to whom more folemn Sacrifices were inftituted than to Ceres. The place where fhe was principally worfhipped, was at Eleufis, where her Rites were performed in the moft folemn and myfterious Manner. They were celebrated only once in five Years ; all the matrons initiated, were to vow a perpetual Chaftity. At the Commencement of the Feftival, a Feaft was kept for feveral Days, during which, Wine was banifhed the Altars. After this the Proceffion began, which confifted in the Carriage of the facred Bafkets or Cannifters, in one of which was inclofed a Child with a golden Seraph, a Van, Grains, Cakes, &c. The Reprefentation of the Myfteries, during which a profound Silence [a] was to be obferved, concluded thus : Af-

---

[a] It was Death to fpeak, or to reveal what paffed in thefe religious Rites.

ter a horrid Darkness; Thunder, Lightning, and whatever is moft awful in Nature, fucceeded a calm and bright Illumination, which difcovered four perfons fplendidly habited. The firft was called the Hierophant, or the Expounder of facred Things, and reprefented the Demiurgus; or Supreme Being: The fecond bore a Torch, and fignified Ofiris; the Third ftood near the Altar, and fignified Ifis; the Fourth, whom they called the Holy Meffenger, perfonated Mercury [a]. To thefe Rites none were admitted but perfons of the firft Character; for Probity or Eminence. Only the Priefts were fuffered to fee the Statue of the Goddefs. All the Affembly ufed lighted Torches; and the folemnity concluded with Games, in which the Victors were crowned with Ears of Barley.

According to Herodotus, thefe Rites were brought from Egypt to Greece, by the daughters of Danaus. Others fay that Eumolpus the fon of Triptolemus and Driope, transferred them from Eleufis to Athens.

The Thefmophoria; or leffer Feftivals of Ceres, were celebrated annually at Argos, and in many points refembled the Eleufinian myfteries, tho' they fell fhort of them very much in the Dignity and Grandeur of the Celebration.

Q: Memmius the Ædile firft introduced thefe Rites into Rome by the Title of Cerealia [b]. None were admitted to the Sacrifices guilty of any Crime; fo that when Nero attempted it, the Roman Matrons expreffed their Refentment, by going into Mourning. This Feftival was clofed by a Banquet and publick Horfe Races.

The Ambarvalia were Feafts celebrated by the Roman Hufbandmen in Spring to render Ceres propiti-

[a] The whole Purport of this Reprefentation, was defigned to allegorize the defolate State of Mankind after the Flood, and fhew the Benefits of Agriculture and Induftry.

[b] This appears from a Medal of this Magiftrate, on which is the Effigies of Ceres holding in one Hand three Ears of Corn; in the other a Torch, and with her left Foot treading on a Serpent.

ous,

ous, by luſtrating their Fields. Each Maſter of a family furniſhed a Victim with an Oaken Wreath round its Neck, which he led thrice round his Ground followed by his Family ſinging Hymns, and dancing in Honour of the Goddeſs. The Offerings uſed in the Luſtration were Milk and new Wine. At the cloſe of the Harveſt there was a ſecond Feſtival in which the Goddeſs was preſented with the firſt Fruits of the Seaſon, and an Entertainment provided for the Relations and Neighbours.

The beginning of April the Gardeners ſacrificed to Ceres, to obtain a plentiful produce of their Grounds which were under her Protection. Cicero mentions an antient Temple of hers at Catanea in Sicily, in which the Offices were performed by Matrons and Virgins only, no man being admitted. The uſual ſacrifices to this Goddeſs were a Sow with Pig, or a Ram. The Garlands uſed by her in her Sacrifices were of Myrtle or Rapeweed : But Flowers were prohibited, becauſe Proſerpine was loſt as ſhe gathered them The Poppy alone was ſacred to her, not only becauſe it grows amongſt Corn, but becauſe in her Diſtreſs Jupiter gave it her to eat, that ſhe might ſleep and forget her troubles.

Let us now endeavour to find ſome Explanation of this Hiſtory of Ceres. If we have Recourſe to our former Key, we ſhall find the Ceres of Sicily and Eleuſis, or of Rome and Greece, is no other than the Egyptin Iſis, brought by the Phœnicians into thoſe Countries. The very Name of Myſtery [a] given to the Eleuſinian Rites, ſhews they are of Egyptian Origin. The Iſis which appeared at the Feaſt appointed for the Commemoration of the State of Mankind after the Flood, bore the Name of Ceres [b], ſuitable to her Intention. She was figured in Mourning, and with a Torch, to denote the Grief ſhe felt for the Loſs of Perſephone [c] her favourite Daughter, and

[a] From Miſtor, a Veil or Covering.
[b] From Cerets. Diſſolution or Overthrow, Jer. xlvi. 20.
[c] From Peri, Fruit or Corn, and Saphan loſt, comes Perſephoneh, or the Corn loſt.

the Pains she was at to recover her. The Poppies
with which this Isis was crowned, signified the joy
Men received at the first abundant crop [a]. Triptolemus was only the Attendant Horus [b], bearing in
his hand the Handle of a Plough, and Celeus his father was no more than [c] the Name of the Tools u-
sed in forming this useful Instrument of Agriculture.
Eumolpus expressed [d] the Regulation or Formation of the People to industry and tillage ; and Proser-
pina or Persephoneh being found again, was a lively
Symbol of the Recovery of Corn almost lost in the
deluge, and its Cultivation with Success. Thus the
Emblems, almost quite simple of the most important
Event which ever happened in the World, became,
when transplanted to Greece and Rome, the sources of
the most ridiculous Fable and grossest Idolatry.

Ceres was usually represented of a tall Majestick
Stature, fair Complexion, languishing Eyes, and yel-
low or flaxen Hair ; her Head crowned with Poppies
or Ears of Corn, her breasts full and swelling, holding
in her Right Hand a bunch of the same Materials with
her Garland, and in her Left a lighted Torch. When
in a Car or Chariot, she is drawn by winged Dragons,
or Lions.

CHAP. XLI. Of BACCHUS.

AS corn and wine are the noblest gifts of Nature;
so it is no wonder, in the Progress of idolatry
if they became deified, and had their Altars. It is
therefore no unnatural Transition, if from Ceres we
pass to Bacchus.

[a] Boho signified a double Crop, and is also the Name for the
Poppy.
[b] From Tarap, to break, and Telem a Furrow, comes Trip-
tolem, or the act of Ploughing.
[c] Celeus. from Celi, a Tool or vessel.
     Virgea præterea Celei vilisque supellex. Virg. Geo.
[d] From Wam, People, and Alap, to learn, is derived Eu-
molep or Eumolpus, i. e. the People regulated or instructed.

This

This Deity was the Son of Jupiter and Semele (as has been observed in the article of Jupiter) and was born at Thebes. Cicero mentions five [a] of the Name. It is said the Nymhps took care of his Education, tho' some ascribe this Office to the Horæ or Hours: others to the Naiades. Mercury after this carried him into Eubæa, to Macris, the Daughter of Aristeus (b), who anointed his lips with Honey; but Juno incensed at his finding Protection in a place sacred to her, banished him thence; so that Macris fled with him into the country of the Phænicians, and nourished him in a Cave. Others say, that Cadmus, Father to Semele, discovering her crime, put her and the child into a wooden ark, which by the tides was carried to Oreatæ a town of Laconia, where Semele being found dead, was buried with great Pomp, and the Infant nursed by Ino in a cave. During this Persecution, being tired in his flight, he fell asleep, and an Amphisbena or two-headed Serpent, of the most poisonous Kind, bit his Leg; but awaking he struck it with a Vine Twig, and that killed it.

In his infancy some Tyrrhenian Merchants found him asleep on the shore, and attempted to carry him away; but suddenly he transformed himself into monstrous shapes; at the same time their masts were encompassed with Vines, and their Oars with Ivy, and struck with Madness, they jumped into the Sea, where the God changed them into Dolphins. Homer has made this the subject of one of his Hymns.

Bacchus, during the Giants War, distinguished himself greatly by his Valour in the form of a Lion, while Jupiter, to encourage his son used the Word Euhoe, which became afterwards frequently used in his Sacrifices. Others say, that in this Rebellion the Titans cut our Deity to pieces; but that Pallas took his

[a] The first son of Jupiter and Proserpine; the 2d the Egyptian Bacchus the Son of Nile, who killed Nysa; the 3d the son of Caprius, who reigned in Asia; the 4th the Son of Jupiter and Luna; the 5th born of Nisus and Thione.

[b] Others say Mercury carried him to Nysa, a City of Arabia near Egypt.

Heart

Heart while yet panting, and carried it to her father, who collected the Limbs and re-animated the
Body, after it had slept three Nights with Proserpine (a).

The moſt memorable Exploit of Bacchus was his
Expedition to India, which employ'd him three years.
He ſet out from Egypt, where he left Mercurius Trif-
megiſtus to aſſiſt his Wife in quality of Co-Regent
and appointed Hercules his Viceroy. Buſiris he conſtituted Preſident of Phœnicia, and Antæus of Lybia,
after which he marched with a prodigious Army, carrying with him Triptolemus and Maro, to teach mankind the arts of Tillage and planting the Vine.   His
firſt Progreſs was Weſtward (b), and during his courſe
he was joined by Pan and Luſus, who gave their
Names to different Parts of Iberia. Altering his views
he returned thro' Ethiopia, where the Satyrs and
Muſes increaſed his Army, and from thence croſſing
the Red Sea, he penetrated through Aſia to the re-
moteſt parts of India, in the Mountains of which
Country, near the Source of the Ganges, he erected
two Pillars, to ſhew that he had viſited the utmoſt
Limits of the habitable World [c]. After this, returning Home with Glory, he made a triumphant
entry into Thebes, offered part of his ſpoils to Jupiter, and ſacrificed to him the richeſt ſpices of the
Eaſt.   He then applied himſelf ſolely to Affairs of
Government, to reform Abuſes, enact good Laws,
and conſult the happineſs of his people, for which he
not only obtained the Title of the Law-giver by way
of excellence, but was deified after Death.

[a] The Mythologiſts ſay, that this is to denote the cuttings of
Vines will grow, but that they will be three Years before they
come to bear.

[b] Pan gave his Name to Spain, or Hiſpaniola, Luſus to Luſi-
tania, or Portugal.

[c] In his Return he built Nyſa, and other Cities, and paſſing
the Helleſpont he came into Thrace, where he left Mars, who
founded the City Maronœa. To Macedo he gave the Country
from him called Macedonia, and left Triptolemus in Attica to
inſtruct the People.

JUNO

Juno having ſtruck him with Madneſs, he had be-fore this wandered through part of the World. Proteus, King of Egypt, was the firſt who received him kindly. He next went to Cybella in Phrygia, where being expiated by Rhea, he was initiated in the Myſteries of Cybele. Lycurgus, King of the Edoni, near the River Strymon, affronted him in this Journey, for which Bacchus deprived him of his Reaſon; ſo that when he thought to Prune his Vines, he cut off the Legs of his Son Dryas and his own. By Command of the Oracle, his Subjects impriſoned him, and he was torn in pieces by wild Horſes. It is eaſy to ſee how inconſiſtent theſe Accounts of the ſame perſon are, and that the Actions of different Bacchuſes are aſcribed to one

We have two other Inſtances recorded of the Reſentment of this Deity. Alcithoe a Theban Lady derided his Prieſteſſes, and was transformed into a Bat; Pentheus the Son of Echion and Agave, for ridiculing his Solemnities (called Orgia), was torn in pieces by his own Mother and Siſters [a], who in their madneſs took him for a wild Boar.

The favourite Wife of Bacchus was Ariadne, whom he found in the iſle of Naxos, abandoned by Theſeus, he loved her ſo paſſionately, that he placed the Crown ſhe wore as a Conſtellation in the Skies. By her he had Staphilus, Thyonæus, Hymenæus, &c.

Ciſſus, a Youth whom he greatly eſteemed, ſporting with the Satyrs was accidentally killed. Bacchus changed him into the Plant Ivy, which became in a peculiar manner conſecrated to his Worſhip. Silenus another of his Favourites, wandering from his Maſter, came to Midas King of Phrygia, at whoſe Court he was well received. To requite this Favour, Bacchus promiſed to grant whatever he Requeſted. The Monarch, whoſe ruling paſſion was Avarice, deſired all he touched might be turned to Gold; but he ſoon felt the Inconveniency of having his wiſh granted, when he found his Meat and Drink converted into

[a] Ovid Lib. II. 630.

Metal

Metal. He therefore prayed the God to recall his Bounty and releate him from his Misery. He was commanded to wash in the River Pactolus, which from that time had Golden Sands [a].

[b] Bacchus had a great variety of Names; he was called Dionysius [c], from his Father's Lameness, while he carry'd him in his Thigh: The Appellation of Biformis was given him, because he sometimes was represented as old, sometimes as young; that of Brisæus, from his inventing the Wine press [d]; that of Bromius, from the crackling of fire heard when Semele perished by the Lightning of Jupiter; that of Bimater, from his having two Mother's or being twice born. The Greeks styled him Bugenes, or born of an Ox, because he was drawn with Horns: and for the same Reason the Latins called him Tauriformis. He was named Dæmon bonus, because in all Feasts the last glass was drank to his Honour. Evius, Evous, and Evan, were Names used by the Bacchanals in their wild Processions, as were those of Eleus, and Eleleus. He was styled Iacchus, from the Noise made [e] by his Votaries in their drunken Frolicks; Lenæus, because Wine assuages the Sorrows and Troubles of Life (f); Liber, and Liber Pater, because he sets Men free from Constraint, and puts them on an Equality; and on the same Account he was sirnamed Lyæus, and Lycœus (g); Nyctilius was an Appellation given him, because his Sacrifices were often celebrated in the Night: from his Education on

[a] Ovid. Lib. xi. 86.

[b] From Bachein, to run mad, because Wine inflames, and deprives Men of their Reason.

[c] From Dios, God, and nusos, lame or crippled.

[d] Some derive it from Brisa, his Nurse; others from the Promontory, Brisa in the Isle of Lesbos, where he was chiefly worshipped.

[e] From iachno, to exclaim or roar. See Claudian's Rape of Proserpine.

[f] From Lenio, to soften; but Servius gives the Epithet a Greek Etymology, from lenos, a Wine-Press. The first Conjecture is best supported by the Poets.

   Cura fugit multo diluiturque mero.   OVID.

[g] From luo, to unloose or set free.

     L   Mount

Mount Nyfa, he gained the Epithet of Nifæus, as alfo that of Thyoneus, from Thyo, his Nurfe; and that
of Triumphus, from his being the firft who inftituted
Triumphs.

The principal Feftivals of Bacchus were the Ofco-
phoria, inftituted by the Phænicians. The Treiteri-
ca [h] celebrated in Remembrance of his three Years
Expedition to India. The Epilænea were Games appointed at the Time of Vintage, in which they contended who fhould tread out moft Muft or Wine, and
fung Hymns to the Deity. The Athenians obferved
a certain Feaft called Apaturia; as alfo others called
Afcolia and Ambrofia. Thefe latter were celebrated
in January, the Month facred to Bacchus; the Romans called them Brumalia, and kept them in February and Auguft [i]; but the moft confiderable of the
Romans, with regard to this God were the Baccha-
nalia, Dionyfia or Orgia, folemnized at Mid-day in
February, by Women only at firft; but afterwards by
both Sexes. Thefe Rites were attended with fuch a-
bominable Exceffes and Wickednefs, t' it the Senate
abolifhed them by a public Decree [k].

The Victims, agreeable to Bacchus, were the Goat
and the Swine, becaufe thefe Animals are deftructive
to the Vines; the Dragon and the Pye on Account
of its chattering. The Trees and Plants ufed in his
Garlands were the Ivy, the Fir, the Oak, and the
Herb Rapeweed; as alfo the Flower Daffodil or Narciffus.

Bacchus was the God of Mirth, Wine, and good
Cheer, and of fuch the Poets have not been fparing
in his praifes. On all Occafions of Pleafure and focial Joy they never failed to invoke his prefence, and
to thank him for the Bleffings he beftowed. To him
they afcribed the forgetfulnefs of their Cares, and the
foft Tranfports of mutual Friendfhip and chearful

[h] Virgil, Æneid IV. 303.
[i] See Cœl. Rhodeg. Lib. XVII. cap. 5.
[k] See Horace, Book II. Ode XIX. wholy confecrated to his
Praife.

Con-

Converſation. It would be endleſs to repeat the Compliments paid him by the Greek and Latin Poets who, for the moſt part, were hearty Devotees to his Worſhip.

Bacchus, by the Poets and Painters, is repreſented as a corpulent Youth (a) naked, with a ruddy Face, wanton Look, and effeminate Air. He is crowned with Ivy and Vine Leaves, and bears in his Hand a Thyrſus (b) encircled with the ſame. His Car is drawn ſometimes by Lions, at others, by Tygers, Leopards, or Panthers, and ſurrounded by a Band of Satyrs and Mænades, or Wood-Nymphs, in frantick Poſtures; and, to cloſe the mad Proceſſion, appears, old Silenus riding on an Aſs, which was ſcarcely able to carry ſo fat and jovial a Companion.

But on the great Sarcophagus of his Grace the Duke of Beaufort, at Badminton, he is expreſſed as a young Man mounted on a Tyger, and habited in a long Robe. He holds a Thyrſus in one Hand, and with the other pours wine into a Horn. His Foot reſts upon a Baſket. His Attendants are the ſeaſons, properly repreſented and intermingled with Fauns, Genies, &c.

To arrive at the true Original of this fabled Deity, we muſt once more reviſit Egypt, the Mother Country of the Gods, where he was indeed no other than the Oſiris of that People. Whence ſprung another Bacchus, diſtinguiſhed from him, as will preſently appear. We have already had ſufficient Occaſion to Remark how their Horus changed his Name and Attributes according to the Seaſons, and the circumſtances or Operations he was intended to direct. To commemorate the antient State of Mankind, he appeared under the Symbol of a Child, with a Seraph by his ſide, and aſſumed the Name of Ben Semele (c). This was

(a) Bacchus was ſometimes depicted as an old Man with a Beard, as at Elis in Greece, and it was only then he had horus given him ſometimes he was cloath'd with a Tyger's Skin.
(b) The Thyrſus was a wooden Javelin with an iron Head.
(c) Ben-Semele, or the Child of the Repreſentation.

L 2

an Image of the Weakness and Imperfection of Husbandry after the Deluge. The Greeks, who knew nothing of the true Meaning of the Figure, called it the fon of Semele, and to heighten its Honour, made Jupiter his Father, or according to the Eaftern Style (a), produced him out of his Thigh. They even embellifhed the Story with all the marvellous circumftances of his Mother's death, and fo effectually compleated the Fable.

Let us add to this, that in all the antient Forms of Invocation to the Supreme Being, they ufed the Expreffions afterwards appropriated to Bacchus, fuch as io Terombe (a)! io Bacche (b)! or io Baccoth! Jehova! Hevan, Hevoe, and Eloah (c)! and Hu Efh! Atta Efh (d). Thefe exclamations were repeated in after-ages by the People, who had no longer any fenfe of their true fignification, but applied them to the objects of their Idolatry. In their Huntings they ufed the Outcries of io Saboi (g), io Niffi, which with a little Alteration became the Titles of the Deity we are fpeaking of. The Romans or Latins, of all thefe, preferred the name of Baccoth, out of which they compofed Bacchus. The more delicate Ear of the Greeks, chofe the Word io Niffi, out of which they formed Dionyfius. Hence it is plain that no real Bacchus ever exifted, but that he was only a Mafque or Figure of fome concealed Truth. In fhort, whoever attentively reads Horace's inimitable Ode to Bacchus (h), will fee that Bacchus meant no more than the improvement of the World, by the Cultivation of Agriculture, and the planting of the Vine.

[a] See Genefis xlvi. 26, fpeaking of Jacob's Children, or who came out of bis Thigh.

(b) Io Terombe I Let us cry to the Lord! Hence Dithyrambus

[c] Io Baccoth! God fee our Tears! whence Bacchus.

[d] Jehovah! Hevan or Hevoe, the Author of Exiftence; Eloch the mighty God! Hence Evoe, Evous, &c.

(e) Hu Efh! Thou art the Fire! Atta Efh! Thou art the Life! Hence Attes and Ves.

[g] Io Saboi! Lord thou art an Holt to me! Io Niffi! Lord be my guide! Hence Sabafius and Dionyfius, the Names of Bacchus.

[h] Horace, Lib. II. Ode xix.

CHAP.

CHAP. XLII. *Of the* Attendants *of* BACCHUS;
SILENUS, SYLVANUS, and the MÆNADES, or
BACCHÆ, the SATYRS, FAUNI and SILENI.

AS Bacchus was the God of Good-Humour and
convivial Mirth, so none of the Deities appear
with a more numerous or splendid Retinue.

Silenus, the principal person in his Train, had been
his Preceptor, and a very suitable one for such a Deity; for the old Man had a very hearty Affection for
his bottle; yet Silenus distinguished himself in the
Giants War, by appearing on his Ass, whose braying
put those daring Rebels into Confusion (a). Some
say he was born at Malea a City of Sparta; others,
at Nysa in Arabia; but the most probable Conjecture
is, that he was a Prince of Caria, noted for his Equity
and Wisdom [b]. However this be, he was a constant Attendant and Companion of his Pupil in all
his Expeditions. Silenus was a notable good Moralist
in his cups, as we find in Virgil, who has given us a
beautiful Oration of his on the noblest subjects [c],
in the fine Eclogue which bears his Name.

Silenus is depicted as a short corpulent old Man,
bald headed, with a flat Nose, prominent Forehead,
and big Ears. He is usually described as over-loaden
with Wine, and seated on a saddle-back'd Ass, upon
which he supports himself with a long staff; and in
the other Hand carries a Cantharus or Jug, with the
Handle worn out almost, by frequent use.

Sylvanus was a rural Deity, who often appears in
the Train of Bacchus; some suppose him the son of
Saturn; others, of Faunus. He was unknown to
the Greeks, but the Latins received the Worship of

[a] For which it was raised to the Skies, and made a Constellation.

[b] On this Account arose the Fable of Midas lending him his
Ears. It is said, that being once taken Prisoner, he purchased his
Liberty with this remarkable Sentence, ' That it was best not to
be Born; and next to that most eligible to die quickly.'

[c] Virgil, Eclouge VI. 14.

L 3

him

him from the Pelasgi, who upon their Migration into Italy, confecrated Groves to his Honour, and appointed folemn Feftivals, in which Milk was offered to him. Indeed the Worfhip of this imaginary Deity feems wholly to have rifen out of the ancient facred Ufe of Woods and Groves.

The Mænades were the Prieftefles and Nymphs who attended Bacchus, and were alfo called Thyades, from their Fury; Bacchæ, from their Intemperance; and Mimallones, from their Difpofition to ape and mimic others, which is one of the Qualities of drunken People. Thefe bore Thyrfufes bound with Ivy, and in their Proceffions fhocked the ear and eye with their extravagant Cries and ridiculous and indecent contortions.

The Life Guards or Trained-Bands of Bacchus, were the Satyrs. It is uncertain whence thefe half Creatures fprung; but their ufual Refidence was in the Woods and Forefts, and they were of a very wanton and luftful difpofition; fo that it was very dangerous for a ftray Nymph to fall into their hands. Indeed it was natural for them to ufe compulfion, for their Form was none of the moft inviting, having deformed Heads, armed with fhort Horns, crooked Hands, rough and hairy Bodies, Goats Feet and Legs and Tails as long as Horfes.

We are now to feek fome explanation of this Groupe of Figures, and to do this we muft have Recourfe to the Egyptian Key. As Idolatry improved, the Feafts or Reprefentations of thofe People grew more pompous and folemn, fhow degenerated into Mafquerade, and Religion into Farce or Frenzy. The Een femele, or Child of Reprefentation, mentioned in the Explanation of Bacchus, became a jolly Rofy Youth, who, to adorn the Pomp, was placed in a Chariot, drawn by Actors in Tigers or Leopards fkins, while others dreffed in thofe of Bucks, or Goats, furrounded him; and to fhew the Dangers they had gone through in Hunting, they fmeared their Faces with Dregs of Wine, or Juice of Mulberries, to imitate the blood of the beafts they killed. Thefe Af-

fiftants

fiftants were called Satyrs (a), Fawns (b), and Thyades [c], and Mænades (d), and Baffarides (e). To clofe the Proceffion, appeared an old Man on an Afs, offering Wine to the tired Youth, who had returned from a profperous Chafe, and inviting them to take fome Reft. This Perfon they called Silen (g), or Sylvan, and his Drefs was defigned to fhew that old men were exempt from thofe Toils of Youth, which by extirpating Beafts of Prey, fecured the approaching harveft.

All thefe Symbols were by the Greeks and Romans adopted in their Way, and the Actors or Mafks of Egypt, became the real Divinities of Nations, whofe inclination to the marvellous made them greedily embrace whatever flattered that Prepoffeffion.

CHAP. XLIII. Of HERCULES, and his Labours.

HAVING gone through the Dii Majores, or celeftial Deities of the firft Rank; we fhall proceed to the Demi-Gods, who were either thofe Heroes whofe eminent Actions and fuperior Virtues raifed them to the Skies, or thofe terreftrial Divinities, who for their Bounty and Goodnefs to Mankind, were claffed with the Gods.

To begin with the former, Hercules undoubtedly claims the foremoft Place. There were feveral of this Name (h); but he to whom, amongft the Greeks, the greateft Glory is attributed, was the Son of Jupiter and Alcmena, Wife of Amphitryon, King of Thebes. This Monarch being gone on an Expedition

[a] From Satur, hidden or difguifed.
[b] From Phanim, a Mafque or falfe Face.
[c] From Thouah, to wander, or run about wildly.
[d] From Mainoma, to intoxicate or drive mad.
[e] From Batfar to gather the Grapes.
[g] From Selav, Safety or Repofe.
[h] The Egyptian Hercules is reckoned the eldeft of thefe; who fignalized himfelf in the Giants War, and was one of the principal Divinities of that Country.

againft

gainft the Ætolians, Jove affumed his Form, and under that fafe Difguife eafily enjoyed his defires. It is faid he was fo enamoured, that he prolonged the Darknefs for three Days and three Nights fucceffively. Hercules was the Fruit of this extraordinary Amour, and at the fame time Alcmena bore twins to her Hufband, Laodamia, and Iphiclus, who was remarkable for his extraordinary Swiftnefs.

This Intrigue of Jupiter, as ufual, foon came to the Ears of his jealous wife, who from that Moment meditated the Deftruction of Hercules. A favourable Occafion offered to her Refentment. Archippe, the Wife of Sthenelus, King of Mycene, being pregnant at the fame time with Alcmena; Jupiter had ordained, that the Child firft born fhould have the fuperiority, or Command over the other. Juno caufed Archippe to be delivered, at the end of feven months of a fon, called Euryftheus; and to retard the Labour of Alcmena in the Form of an old Woman fhe fat at the Gate of Amphitrion's Palace, with her Legs acrofs and her Fingers interwoven. By this fecret Inchantment, that Princefs was feven Days and Nights in extreme Pains, till Galanthis one of her Attendants feeing Juno in this fufpicious Pofture, and conjecturing the caufe ran haftily out with the news that her Miftrefs was delivered. The Goddefs ftarting up at the News, Alcmena was that moment freed of her burthen; but Juno was fo incenfed at Galanthis, that fhe changed her into a Weefel.

During his Infancy Juno fent two Serpents to deftroy him in his Cradle, but the undaunted Child ftrangled them both with his Hands. After this, as he grew up he difcovered an uncommon Stature and Strength of Body [a], as well as heroic Ardour of Mind. Thefe great Qualities of Nature were improved by fuitable Care, his education being intrufted

____

[a] Some fay when he arrived at Manhood he was four Cubits high and had three Rows of Teeth.

to the greatest Masters (a) ; so that it is no Wonder if, with such considerable advantantages, he made such a shining Figure in the World.

His extraordinary Virtues were early put to the Trial, and the Tasks imposed on him by Eurystheus, on account of the Danger and Difficulty which attended their Execution, received the Name of the Labours of Hercules, and are commonly reckoned to be twelve in Number.

1. The first Labour or Triumph of Hercules, was the death of the Nemæan Lion. It is said that this furious Animal, by Juno's Direction, fell from the Orb of the Moon, and was invulnerable. It infested the Nemæan Woods, between Philus and Cleone, and did infinite Mischief. The Hero attacked it both with his Arrows and Club, but in vain, till perceiving his Error, he first strangled and then tore it in pieces with his Hands. The Skin he preserved, and constantly wore as a token of his Victory.

2. His next enterprise was against a formidable Serpent, or Monster, which harboured in the Fens of Lerna, and infected the Region of Argos with his poisonous Exhalations. The Number of Heads assigned this Creature is various (b); but all Authors agree, that when one was cut off another succeeded in its place, unless the Wound was immediately cauterised. Hercules not discouraged, attacked this Dragon, and having caused Iolaus to cut down Wood sufficient for flaming Brands, as he cut off the Heads, applied them to the Wounds, and by that Means obtained the conquest, and destroyed the Hydra. Some explain this fable, by supposing Lerna a Marsh, much

(a) Linus the Son of Appollo instructed him in Philosophy; Eurytus taught him Archery; Eumolpus, Musick, particularly the Art of touching the Lyre; from Harpalycius the Son of Mercury, he learned Wrestling and the Gymnastick Exercises; Castor shewed him the Art of managing his Weapons; and to compleat all, Chiron, initiated him in the Principals of Astronomy and Medicine.

(b) Some make the Heads of the Lernæan Hydra to be Seven, others nine; others fifty.

infested.

infested with Snakes and other poisonous Animals, which Hercules and his companions deftroyed, by fetting Fire to the Reeds. Others imagine he only drained this Fen, which was before unpaffable. O-thers make Lerna a Fort or Caftle of Robbers, under a Leader called Hydra, whom Hercules extirpated. However this be, in Confideration of the Service of Iolaus on this Occafion, when he grew decripid with old Age, his Mafter, by his Prayers, obtained him a Renewal of his Youth.

3. The next Tafk impofed on him by Euryftheus, was to bring him alive a huge wild Boar, which rava-ged the Foreft of Erymanthus, and had been fent to Phocis by Diana, to punifh Oeneus for neglecting her Sacrifice [a]. In his way he defeated the Centaurs who had provoked him, by infulting Pholus, his hoft. After this he feized the fierce Animal in a Thicket, furrounded with Snow, and, purfuant to his injuncti-on, carried him bound to Euryftheus, who had like to have fainted at the Sight.

4. This Monarch after fuch Experience of the Force and Valour of Hercules, was refolved to try his Agility : For this end he was commanded to take a Hind which frequented Mount Mænalus, and had brazen Feet and golden Horns. As fhe was facred to Diana, Hercules durft not wound her, and it was not very eafy to run her down : This Chafe coft him a whole Year's Foot-Speed. At laft, being tired out, the Hind took to the Receffes of Mount Artemefius, but was in her way overtaken, as fhe croffed the Ri-ver Ladon, and brought to Mycene.

5. Near the Lake Stymphalus in Arcadia, harbour-ed certain Birds of Prey, with Wings, Beaks, and Talons of Iron, who preyed on human Flefh, and de-voured all who paffed that way. Thefe Euryftheus fent Hercules to deftroy. Some fay he killed them with his Arrows (b); others, that Pallas lent him

(a) This Story has a near Refemblance with the Boar of Ca-lydon, mentioned in the Article of Diana.

(b) There is an antient Gem expreffive of this. See Ogle's Antiquities.

some brazen Rattles made by Vulcan, the sound of which frightened them to the Island of Aretia. Some suppose the birds called Stymphalides, a Gang of desperate Banditti, whose Haunts were near that Lake.

6. His next expedition was against the Cretan bull. Minos, King of that Island, being formidable at Sea, had forgot to pay Neptune, the worship due to him, and the Deity to punish his Neglect, sent a furious Bull, whose Nostrils breathed Fire, to destroy the Country Hercules brought this terrible Animal, bound to Eurystheus, who, on account of his being sacred let him loose in the Territory of Marathon, where he was afterwards slain by Theseus. Some reduce the Story to this, that Hercules only was sent to Crete, to procure Eurystheus a Bull for breeding out of.

7. Diomede, King of Thrace the son of Mars and Cyrene, was a Tyrant possessed of a Stud of Horses, so wild and fierce, that they breathed Fire, and were constantly fed with human Flesh, their Master killing all Strangers he could meet with for Provender for his cattle. Hercules having vanquished him, gave him as a prey to them, and killing some, brought the rest to Eurystheus.

8. The next employment of Hercules, seems a little too mean for a Hero, but he was obliged to obey a severe Task-master, who was so sensible of his own Injustice in these injunctions, that he did not care to trust himself in the Power of the person who commanded [a]. Augeus, King of Elis, had a stable intolerable from the stench arising from the Dung and Filth it contained, which is not very surprising if it be true, that it sheltered three thousand Oxen, and had not been cleaned for thirty Years. This Place Eurystheus ordered Hercules to clear in one Day; and Augeas promised him, if he performed it, to give

[a] It is said Eurystheus never would suffer Hercules to enter Mycene, but notified his Commands to him over the Walls, by Capreas an Herald.

him

him a Tenth Part of the Cattle. Hercules, by turning the Course of the River Alpheus through it executed his defign; which Augeas feeing, refufed to
ftand by his Engagements. The Hero, to Reward
his Perfidy, flew him with his Arrows, and gave his
Kingdom to Phyleus his Son, who had fhewed his
Abhorrence of his Father's Treachery. Some add
that, from the Spoils taken at Elis, Hercules inftituted the Olympic Games to Jupiter, celebrated every
fifth year, and which afterwards gave rife to the Grecian Æra.

9. Euryftheus defirous to prefent his Daughter Ad-
meta with the Belt or Girdle worn by Hippolyte,
Queen of the Amazons, Hercules was fent on this expedition; he was but flenderly provided, having but
one fhip; but Valour like his was never deftitute
of Refources in Diftrefs. In his way he defeated and
killed Mygdon and Amicus, two Brothers who oppo-
fed his paffage, and fubduing Bebrycia, gave it to Ly-
cas, one of his Companions, who changed its Name
to Heraclea, in Memory of his Benefactor. On his
Approach to Themifcyra, he learnt that the Amazons
had collected all their forces to meet him. The firft
Engagement was warm on both Sides, feveral of the
braveft of thefe Viragoes were killed, and others made
Prifoners. The Victory was followed by the total
extermination of that female Nation, and Hippolyte,
their Queen, was by the Conqueror given to Thefeus
as a Reward for his Valour. Her belt he brought to
Euryftheus.

10. His fucceeding exploit was againft Geryon,
King of Spain, who had three bodies, and was the fon
of Chryfaoris and Calirrhoe. This Monarch had a
Breed of Oxen, of a purple Colour, who devoured
all Strangers caft to them, and were guarded by a
Dog with two heads, a Dragon with feven befi es a
very watchful and fevere Keeper. Hercules killed
both the Monarch and his Guards, and carried the
Oxen to Gadira, or Cadiz, from whence he brought
them to Euryftheus. It was during this expedition
that, among the eternal Monuments of his Glory,
erected

erected two Pillars at Calpe and Abyle, upon the utmoft Limits of Africa and Europe. Some give a more fimple Turn to the whole, by faying Geryon was a King of Spain, who governed by Means of three Sons famous for Valour and Prudence, and that Hercules having raifed an Army of mercenary Troops in Crete, firft overcame them, and fubdued that Country.

11. The next tafk enjoined him by Euryftheus, was to fetch him the golden Apgles of the Hefperides (a) which were guarded by a Dragon with an hundred Heads. The injunction was not eafy, fince Hercules was even ignorant of the place where they grew. The Nymphs of Eridanus, whom he confulted, advifed him to go to Prometheus [b], who gave him the Information and Direction he wanted, after which he vanquifhed the Dragon, and brought the precious Fruit to his Mafter.

12. The laft command of Euryftheus was for him to go down to Hell, and bring away Cerberus, Pluto's Maftiff. Hercules having facrificed to the Gods, entered the infernal Regions, by a Cavity of mount Tænarus, and on the Banks of Acheron found a white Poplar-Tree, of which he made him a Wreath, and the Tree was ever after confecrated to him; paffing that River he difcovered Thefeus and Pirithous chained to a Stone. The former he releafed, but left the latter confined. Mænetius, Pluto's Cow-herd, endeavouring to fave his Mafter's Dog, was crufhed to Death. Cerberus, for Refuge, fled beneath Pluto's Throne, from whence the Hero dragged him out, and brought him upon Earth by way of Træzene. At fight of the Day, the monfter vomited a poifonous matter, from whence fprung the Herb Aconite, or Wolf's Bane; but being prefented to Euryftheus,

(a) Juno, on her Marriage with Jupiter, gave him thefe trees, which bore golden Fruit, and were kept by the Nymphs AEgie, Arethufa, and Hefperethufa, Daughters of Hefperus, who were called the Hefperides.

[b] Or as others fay, to Nereus, who eluded his Enquiry, by affuming various Shapes.

M

he

he ordered him to be dimiffed, and fuffered to Return to Hell.

It would be almoft endlefs to ennmerate all the Ac-tions of this celebrated Hero of Antiquity, and there-fore we fhall only touch on the principal He deli-vered Creon, Kieg of Thebes, from an unjuft Tribute impofed on him by Erginus and the Myniæ, for which Service that Prince gave him his Daughter Megara, by whom he had feveral fons; but Juno ftriking him with Frenzy, he flew thefe Childien, and on reco-vering his fenfes, became fo fhocked at his Cruelty, that he abftained from all human fociety for fome Time. In his Return from the expedition againft the Amazons, Laomedon, King of Troy, by the promife of fome fine Horfes, engaged him to deliver his daughter Hefione, expofed to a vaft Sea-monfter fent by Nep-tune; but when he had freed the Princefs, the deceit-ful monarch retracted his word. Upon this, Hercu-les took the City, killed Laomedon, and gave Hefione to Telamon, who firft fcaled the walls [a]. After this he flew Tmolus and Telegonos, the fons of Proceus, two celebrated wreftlers, who put to Death all whom they overcame. He alfo killed Sarpedon, Son of Neptune, a notorious Pirate.

During his African expedition, he vanquifhed Cye-nus, King of Theffaly, the Son of Mars and Cleobuli-na, a favage Prince, who had vowed to erect his Fa-ther a Temple with the Heads or Sculls of the Stran-gers he deftroyed. In Lybia, he encountered the fa-mous Antæus, the fon of Earth, a Giant of immenfe ftature, who forced all whom he met to wreftle with him, and fo ftrangled them. He challenged Hercules, who flung him thrice, and thought each Time he had killed him; but on his touching the Ground he renewed his Strength. Hercules being apprized of this, held him up in the Air, and fquee-zed him in fuch a manner, that he foon expired (b). In his Progrefs from Lybia to Egypt, Bufiris, a cru-

[a] This Princefs redeemed her Brother Priamus, who was afterwards King of Troy.

[b] This is finely expreffed in a double Atique Statue belong-ing to the Earl of Portfmouth, at Hifbourne in Hampfhire.

c.!

of Prince, laid an Ambuscade to surprize him but was himself, and his son Amphiadamus, sacrificed by the Victor on the Altars he had profaned. In Arabia, he beheaded Emathion, the son of Tithonus, for his want of hospitality; after which, crossing Mount Caucasus, he delivered Prometheus. In Calydon, he wrestled with Achelous, for no less a prize than Deianira, daughter to King Oeneus. The contest was long dubious, for his Antagonist had the Faculty of assuming all shapes; but as he took that of a Bull, Hercules tore off one of his horns, so that he was forced to submit, and to redeem it by giving the Conqueror the Horn of Amalthœa, the Daughter of Harmodius; which Hercules filled with a variety of Fruits, and consecrated to Jupiter. Some explain the Fable thus: Achelous is a winding River of Greece, whose stream was so rapid, that it overflowed the Banks, Roaring like a Bull. Hercules forced it into two Channels; that is, he broke off one of the Horns, and so Restored Plenty to the Country.

This Hero reduced the Isle of Coos, and put to Death Eurylus, King of it, with his sons, on account of their injustice and cruelty; but the Princess Chalchiope, his Daughter, he married, by whom he had a son named Thessalus, who gave his Name to Thessaly. He subdued Pyracemos, King of Eubœa, who, had, without a Cause, made War on the Bœotians —— In his way to the Hesperides, he was opposed by Albion and Borgia, two Giants, who put him in great Hazard, his Arrows being spent. Jupiter, on his Prayer, overwhelmed them with a shower of Stones, whence the Place was called the stoney field. It lies in the Gallia Narbonensis. Hercules did great service in Gaul, by destroying Robbers, suppressing Tyrants and Oppressors, and other Actions truly worthy the Character of a Hero, after which, it is said, he built the City Alesia, and made it the capital of the Celtæ, or Gauls. He also opened his way through the Alps into Italy, and by the Coasts of Liguria and Tuscany, arrived on the Banks of the Tyber, and slew the furious Robber Cacus, who from his Den on Mount A-

 ventine

ventine, infested that Country. Being denied the Rites of Hospitality, he killed Theodamas the Father of Hylas, but took the latter with him, and treated him kindly.

Hercules, however intent on Fame or Glory, was like other Heroes, but too susceptible of Love. We find an instance of this in Omphale, Queen of Lydia, who gained such an Ascendant over him, that he was not ashamed to assume a Female Dress, to spin a-mongst her Women, and submit to be corrected by her according to her caprice.

His favourite wife was Deianira, before mentioned, and whose Jealousy was the fatal Occasion of his Death. Travelling with this Princess through Æto-lia, they had Occasion to pass a River swelled by the sudden Rains. Nessus, the Centaur, offered Hercules his service to carry over his Consort, who accepting it, crossed over before them. The Monster, seeing the Opportunity favourable, offered violence to Deianira, upon which her Husband, from the opposite Bank, pierced him with one of those dreadful Arrows, which being dipped in the Blood of the Lernæan Hydra, gave a Wound incurable by Art. Nessus expiring, gave the Princess his Garment, all bloody, as a sure Remedy to Recover her Husband, if ever he should prove unfaithful. Some Years after Hercules having subdued Oechalia, fell in Love with Iole, a fair Captive, whom he brought to Eubœa, where having erected an Altar to sacrifice to Jove for his victory, he dispatched Lycus to Deianira, to carry her the News, and inform her of his approach. This Princess, from the Report of the messenger, suspecting her Husband's Fidelity, sent him as a present the coat of Nessus, which he no sooner put on, but he fell into a delirious Fever, attended with the most excru-ciating Torments. Unable to support his Pains he retired to Mount Oeta, and erecting a Pile of Wood, to which he set Fire, threw himself into the Flames, and was consumed (a). Lycus, his unhappy
Friend

[a] There is at Wilton, the Seat of the Earl of Pembroke, amidst a Multitude of other valuable Curiosities, a small Marble

Friend and Companion, in his Agony, [he first hurled into the River Thermopolis, where he became a rock. his Arrows he bequeathed to Philoctetes, who buried his Remains in the River Dyra.

So perished this great Hero of Antiquity, the Terror of oppressors, the Friend of Liberty and Mankind, for whose Happiness (as Tully observes) he braved the greatest Dangers, and surmounted the most arduous toils, going through the whole earth with no other view than the establishing Peace, Justice, Concord and Freedom. Nothing can be added to heighten a Character so glorious as this.

Hercules left several Children: by Deianira he had an only Daughter, called Macaria; by Melita, who gave her Name to the Isle of Malia, he had Hylus, Afer, Lydus, and Scythes, his sons, who are said to have left their Appellation to Africa, Lydia, and Scythia. Besides which, he is said to have had fifty sons by the fifty Daughters of Thestius. However, his Offspring were so numerous, that above thirty of his Descendants bore his Name, whose Actions being all attributed to him, produce the Confusion we find in his History.

Eurystheus, after his Death, was so afraid of these Heraclidæ, that by his ill Usage he forced them to fly to Athens, and then sent an Embassy to that City to deliver them up, with menaces of a war in case of Refusal. Iolaus, the Friend of Hercules, who was then in the shades, was so concerned for his master's posterity, that he got Leave from Pluto to return to Earth, and kill the Tyrant, after which he willingly returned to Hell.

Hercules, who was also called Alcides, was, after his death, by his Father Jupiter, deified, and with great Solemnity married to Hebe, his half sister, the Goddess of Youth. At first sacrifices were only offered to him as a Hero; but Phœstius coming into

---

ble Statue of Lycus, supporting the dying Hercules, of inimitable workmanship, in which the Chissel appears to be infinitely superior to the Pencil.

 Sycionia

Syconia altered that Method. Both the Greeks and Romans honour'd him as a God, and erected Temples to him in that Quality. His Victims were Bulls or Lambs, on account of his preseving the Flocks from Wolves, i. e. delivering Men from Tyrants and Robbers. He was called also Melius, from his taking the Hesperian Fruit, for which Reason Apples were used [a] in his Sacrifices. Mehercule, or by Hercules, was, amongst the Romans, an Oath only used by the Men.

Many Persons were fond of assuming this celebrated name. Hence Diodorus reckons up three; Cicero six; others to the Number of forty-three. But the Greeks ascribed to the Theban Hercules the Acts of all the rest. But the Foundation of all was laid in the Phænician or Egyptian Hercules. For the Egyptians did not borrow the Name from the Grecians; but rather the Grecians, especially those who gave it to the Son of Amphitryon, from the Egyptians: principally because Amphitrion and Alcmena, the Parents of the Grecian Hercules, were both of Egyptian descent (b). The Name too is of Phœnician Extraction (c), a name given to the discoveries of new Countries, and the Planters of Colonies there; who frequently signalized themselves no less by civilizing the inhabitants, and freeing them from the wild Beasts that infested them than by the Commerce which they established; which (no doubt was the source of ancient Heroism and war d). And however the Phœnician and Egyptian Hero of this name may have been distinguished by a multitude of Authors; I am fully persuaded, after the most diligent enquiry, that they were indeed one and the same person: Of whose history let us take a short Review.

About the year of the World 2131, the Person distinguished by the Name of Hercules Assis (e), suc-

[a] From melos, an Apple.
[b] Herodotus in Euterpe.
[c] Harokel, a Merchant.
[d] Banier's Mythology, Vol. 4. p. 72.
[e] Assis the valiant: So that Hercules Assis is the heroic
rchant.

ceeded Janias, as King of Lower Egypt, being the laſt
of the Hycſos, or Shepherd Kings from Canaan;
who had held the Country 259 Years. He continued
the War with the Kings of Upper Egypt 49 Years,
and then by Agreement withdrew, with his Subjects,
to the Number of 240,000. In his Retreat he is ſaid
to have founded firſt the City of Jeruſalem [a]; and
afterwards that of Tyre, where he was called Melcarthus [b]. From Egypt he brought the Computation
of 365 Days to the Year, and ſettled it in his own
Kingdom, where it continued many Ages. In his
Voyages he viſited Africa, where he conquered An-
tœus, Italy, France, Spain, as far as Cadiz, where
he ſlew Geryon; and proceeded thence even to the
Britiſh Iſlands, ſettling Colonies and raiſing Pillars,
wherever he came, as the ſtanding Monuments of
himſelf and of the Patriarchal Religion which he
planted: For Pillars placed on Eminences in circular
Order, were the Temples of thoſe early Times, and
as yet we find no Footſteps of Idolatry, either in E-
gypt or Phænicia. To his Arrival in theſe Iſlands
(and not in Liguria) muſt be applied whatever is related of his Encounter with Albion and Bergion, and
of his being aſſiſted, when his Weapons were ſpent,
by a Shower of Stones from Heaven. Albion is the
Name given afterwards to this Country; and by the
miraculous Shower of Stones no more is intended,
than that the Inhabitants were at leaſt reconciled to
him on account of the divine Religion which he
taught, and the great Number of theſe open Temples
of Stones erected by him. He is ſaid to have been attended by Apher, the Grandſon of Abraham, whoſe
Daughter he married, and by whom he had a Son
named Dodorus [c]. To him the Phænicians were indebted for the gainful Trade of Tin, which gave

---

[a] Manetho apud Joſepdum, l. 1. contra Apion.

[b] Or King of the City, from Melek, King, and Cartha,
City.

[c] Joſephus, from Polyhiſter and Cleodemus. Idem in Antiq. l.
Shindler's Lexicon. See Stukely's Account of Abury and Stonehenge; and Cooke's Enquiry into the Patriarchal Religion.

Name

Name to thefe Iflands [a]. He found out alfo the Purple Dye, and feems to have been the firft who applied the Loadftone to the Purpofes of Navigation, thence called Lapis Heraclius. He is fuppofed to have been drowned at laft, and became afterwards one of the firft Objects of Idolatry amongft his Countrymen. The Solemnities were performed to him in the Night, as to one who after all his great Fatigues and Labours, had at length gained a Time and Place of Reft. Manetho calls him Arcles.

Hercules is ufually depicted in a ftanding Attitude, having the fkin of the Nemæan Lion thrown over his Shoulders, and leaning on his Club, which is his infeparable Attribute. The Judgment of this Hero, or his preference of Virtue to Vice, who both follicit him to embrace their Party, makes one of the fineft Pictures of Antiquity. The Choice he made does no Difhonour to his Memory.

It may not be amifs to add the Explanation of the Fable of the Hefperides, as given by a late ingenious Author [b], and which fufficiently fhews how the moft important and ufeful Truths, reprefented under the plaineft Symbols, became difguifed or disfigured by Error and Fiction. The Phænicians were the firft Navigators in the World, and their Trade to Hefperia and Spain, was one of the nobleft Branches of their Commerce. From hence they brought back exquifite Wines, rich Ore of Gold and Silver, and that fine Wool to which they gvae fo precious a Purple Dye. From the Coaft of Mauritania they drew the beft Corn, and by the way of the Red Sea, they exchanged Iron Ware and Tools of fmall Value for Ivory, Ebony, and Gold Duft. But as the Voyage was long, the Adventurers were obliged to affociate and get their Cargoes ready in Winter, fo as to fet out early in Spring. The publick Sign, expofed on thefe Occafions, was a Tree with golden Fruit to denote the Riches arifing from this Commerce. The Dragon

<hr>

[a] Britannia is from Barat-anoc, the Land of Tin.
[b] Le Pluche's Hiftory of the Heavens, Vol. II. 150.

which

which guarded the Tree, fignified the Danger and Difficulty of the voyage. The Capricorn, or fometimes one Horn placed at the Root expreffed the Month or Seafon ; and the three Months of Winter, during which they prepared for the expedition, were Reprefented by three Nymphs, who were fuppofed to be be Proprietors of the tree, and had the Name of Hefperides (a) ; which fully fhewed the meaning of this emblematical Groupe, from whence the Greeks miftaking its defign and ufe, compofed the Romance of the Hefperian Gardens.

CHAP. XLIV. Of HEBE and GANYMEDE.

HEBE, the Goddefs of Youth, was, according to Homer, the Daughter of Jupiter and Juno.— But the Generality of Writers relate her Birth thus : Juno being invited to an entertainment by Apollo, eat very eagerly fome wild Lettuces, upon which fhe conceived, and inftantly brought forth this Goddefs.—— Jove was fo pleafed with her beuaty, that he made her his Cup bearer, in the difcharge of which Office, fhe always appeared crowned with Flowers. Unluckily, at a Feftival of the Gods in Ethiopia, Hebe being in waiting, flipped her Foot, and got fo indecent a fall, that Jupiter was obliged to Remove her from her ufual Attendance. To repair this Difgrace, as well as the Lofs of her poft, Jupiter, upon Hercules being advanced to the Skies, married him to Hebe, and their nuptials were celebrated with all the Pomp becoming a celeftial Wedding. By this Union fhe had a Son named Anicetus, and a Daughter called Alexiare.

Hebe was held in high veneration amongft the Sicyonians, who erected a Temple to her by the Name of Dia. She had another at Corinth, which was a

[a] From Efper, the good Share or beft Lot. See 2 Samuel, vi. 19

Sanctuary

Sanctuary for Fugitives; and the Athenians confecrated an Altar in common to her and Hercules.

Ganymede, who fucceded to her Office, was the
Son of Tros, King of Phrygia or Troy, and a Prince
of fuch Wifdom and perfonal Beauty, that Jupiter,
by the Advice of the Gods, refolved to Remove him
from earth to the Skies. The Eagle difpatched on
this Commiffion, found him juft leaving his Flock of
Sheep, to hunt on Mount Ida, and feizing him in his
Talons, brought him unhurt to the Heavens, where
he entered on his new office of filling Nectar to Jupiter
tho' others fay he was turned into that Conftellation,
or fign of the Zodiac, which goes by the name of A-
quarius (a).

The Mythologifts make Hebe fignify that mild tem-
perature of the Air, which awakens to Life the Trees,
Plants and Flowers, and cloaths the earth in vegetable
beauty; for which caufe fhe is called the Goddefs of
perpetual Youth. But when fhe flips or falls, that is,
when the flowers fade. and the autumnal leaves drop,
Ganymede, or the Winter, takes her place.

CHAP. LXV.   Of CASTOR and POLLUX.

WE have already, under the Article of Jupiter,
mentioned his Amours with Leda the Wife of
Tyndarus, King of Sparta, in the Form of a Swan, on
which Account he placed that Figure amongft the
Conftellations. Leda brought forth two Eggs, each
containing Twins, from that impregnated by Jupiter,
proceeded Pollux and Helena, both immortal; from
the other Caftor and Clytemneftra, who being begot
by Tyndarus, were both mortal. They went, however, all by the common name of Tyndaridœ, and
were born and educated in Paphnus, an Ifland belong-
ing to Lacædemon, tho' the Meffinians difputed this
Honour with the Spartans. The two Brothers, how-

[a] The Winter being attended with frequent Rains, it is not
improbable that Ganymede fhould be the Sign Aquarius.

ever.

ever differing in their nature and temper (a), had entered into an inviolable Friendship, which lasted for Life. Jove soon after sent Mercury to remove them to Pellene, for their further Improvement. As Jason was then preparing for his Expedition to Colchis in search of the Golden Fleece, and the nobleft Youth of Greece crowded to become Adventurers with him, our two Brothers offered their fervices and behaved during the Voyage, with a Courage worthy of their Birth. Being obliged to water on the coaft of Babrycia, Amycus, fon to Neptune, King of that Country, challenged all the Argonauts to box with him; Pollux accepted the bravado, and killed him. After their Return from Colchis, the two brothers were very active in clearing the feas of Greece from Pirates. Thefeus in the mean time had ftolen their fifter Helena, to Recover whom, they took Athens by Storm, but fpared all the inhabitants, except Æthra, Mother to Thefeus, whom they carried away Captive. For this Clemency they obtained the Title of Diofcuri (b); yet Love foon plunged them in the fame Error they had fought to punifh in the perfon of Thefeus, Leucippus and Arfinoe had two beautiful Daughters called Phœbe and Talayra. Thefe Virgins were contracted to Lynceus and Ida, the Sons of Aphareus. The two brothers without Regard to thefe Engagements, carried them off by force. Their Lovers flew to their Relief, and met their Ravifhers with their Prize near mount Taygetus. A fmart conflict enfued, in which Caftor was killed by Lynceus, who in Return fell by the Hands of Pollux. This immortal brother had been wounded by Ida, if Jupiter had not ftruck him with his Thunder. Pollux, however, was fo touched with his lofs, that he earneftly begged of this Deity to make Caftor immortal; but that Requeft being impoffible to grant, he obtained Leave to fhare his own Im-

---

[a] This Particular we learn from Horace;
    Caftor gaudet Equis: Ovo prognatus eodem
    Pugnis Quot capitum vivunt totidem Studiorum
    ———— millia.   HORAT.
[b] The Sons of Jupiter.

mortality with his Brother; so that they are said to live and die alternately every day [a]. They were buried in the Country of Lacedemon, and forty years after their decease translated to the skies, where they form a Constellation called Gemini (one of the signs of the Zodiac) one of which Stars rises as the other sets. A Dance of the martial kind was invented to their Honour, called the Pyrhic or Castorean dance.

Castor and Pollux were esteemed as Deities propitious to Navigation; the Reason was this: When the Argonauts weighed from Sigæum (b), they were overtaken with a Tempest, during which, Orpheus offered Vows for the safety of the ship; immediately two lambent Flames were discovered over the Heads of Castor and Pollux, which Appearance was succeeded with so great a calm, as gave the Crew a Notion of their divinity. In succeeding Times these Fires often seen by the Mariners were always taken as a good or favourable Omen. When one was seen alone it was reckoned to forbode some Evil, and was called Helena (c).

The Cephalenses (or the Inhabitants of Cephalonia) placed these two Deities amongst the Dii Magni. The Victims offered them were white Lambs. The Romans paid them particular Honours for their Assistance in an engagement with the Latins, in which they appeared on their side, mounted on white Horses, and turned the scale of victory in their Favour. For this a Temple was erected to them in the Forum. Amongst the Romans, Æcastor was an oath peculiar to the Women, but Ædepol was used indiscriminately by both Sexes.

Castor and Pollux were represented as two beautiful Youths, completely armed, and riding on white horses with Stars over their Helmets. These Deities were unknown to the Egyptians or Phœnicians.

[a] Virgil alludes to this;
Si Fratrem Pollux alterna Morte redemit.
————— Itque reditque viam.   Virg. Æneid VI.
[b] This Cape lies near Troy.
[c] The first Helena carried off by Theseus.

C H A P.

CHAP. XLVI. Of Perseus, and Bellerophon.

PERSEUS was the Son of Jupiter and Danae, whose Amour has been already mentioned, and is inimitably described by Horace (a). Acrisius her Father, on hearing of his Daughter's disgrace, caused her and the Infant to be shut up in a Chest and cast into the Sea, which threw them on the isle of Seriphus, governed by King Polydectes, whose Brother Dictys being a fishing took them up, and used them kindly. When Perseus, for so he was called, was grown up, Polydectes, who was enamoured of his Mother, finding he would be an obstacle to their courtship, contrived to send him on an exploit, he judged would be fatal to him, this was to bring him the head of Medusa, one of the Gorgons. This inchantress lived near the Tritonian Lake, and turned all who beheld her into stone. Perseus in this Expedition was favoured by the Gods; Mercury equipped him with a Scimeter and the wings from his heels; Pallas lent him a shield, which reflected Objects like a Mirror; and Pluto granted him his Helmet, which gave him the Privilege of being invisible. In this manner he flew to Tartessus in Spain, where directed by his mirror, he cut off Medusa's head, and putting it in a Bag lent him by the Nymphs, brought it to Pallas. From the Blood arose the winged Horse Pegasus, and all Sorts of serpents. After this the Hero passed into Mauritania, where his interview with Atlas has been already spoken of under its proper article (b).

In his Return to Greece (others say, at his first setting out) he visited Ethiopia, and mounted on Pegasus, delivered Andromeda daughter of Cepheus, King of that Country, who was exposed to a sea Monster. After his death, this Princess and her Mother Cassiope, or Cassiopeia, were placed amongst the Celestial Constellations.

(a) Horat. Lib. III. Ode XVI.
(b) See the Article of Atlas.

Perseus was not only famous for Arms, but Literature, if it be true that he founded an Academy on Mount Helicon. Yet he had the misfortune inadvertently to commit the Crime of Paricide, for being reconciled to his Grandfather Acrisius, and playing with him at the Discus or Quoits, a game he had invented, his Quoit bruised the old King in the Foot, which turned to a mortification, and carried him off. Perseus interred him with great solemnity at the gates of Argos. Perseus himself was buried in the way between Argos and Mycenæ, had divine Honours decreed him, and was placed amongst the Stars.

Bellerophon the son Glaucus, King of Ephyra, and Grandson of Sisiphus, was born at Corinth. Happening accidentally to kill his Brother, he fled to Prætus, King of Argos, who gave him a hospitable Reception; but Sthenobæa his Queen, falling enamoured with the beautiful Stranger, whom no Intreaties could prevail on to injure his Benefactor, accused him to her husband, who unwilling to take violent [measures, sent him into Lycia, with Letters to Jobates, his Father-in-Law (a), desiring him to punish the Crime, This Prince, at the Receipt of the Order, was celebrating a Festival of nine Days, which prevented Bellerophon's Fate. In the mean time he sent him to subdue the Solymi and Amazons, which he performed with success, Jobates next employed him to destroy the Chimæra (b), a very uncommon Monster. Minerva or as others say Neptune, compassionating his Innocence exposed to such repeated dangers, furnished him with the Horse Pegasus by whose Help he came off victorious. Jobates, on his Return, convinced of his Truth and Integrity, and charmed with his virtues gave him his daughter Philonoe, and associated him in his throne Sthenobæa hearing how her malice was disappointed, put an end to her Life. But like other Princes, Bellerophon grew foolish with too

[a] King in his History makes Jobates his Son in-Law.
[b] The Chimæra was a Monster with the Fore-part like a Lion, the middle like a Goat, and the Tail like a Serpent.

much Profperity, and by the Affiftance of Pegafus,
refolved to afcend the fkies; Jupiter, to check his
Prefumption, ftruck him blind in the flight, and he
fell back to the Earth, where he wandered till his
death in Mifery and Contempt. Pegafus, however,
made a fhift to get into Heaven, where Jupiter placed him amongft the conftellations.

Let us once more try to give fome Explanation of
thefe two Fables. The fubjects of Cyrus, who before
this time had been known by the name of Cuthœans
and Elamites, thenceforward began to be diftinguifhed
by that of the Perfians (a) or Horfemen. For it was
he who firft inured them to Equeftrian Exercifes; and
even made it fcandalous for one of them to be feen
on foot. Perfes, or Perfeus, then is a Horfeman, one
who had learned the Art of Horfemanfhip from the
Phœnicians, who attended Cadmus into Greece. The
wings at his Heels, with which he is faid to have
been fupplied by Mercury, were the fpurs he wore;
by the affiftance of which he made fuch fpeed. The
Pegafus was no more than a Reined Steed (b). His
Rider, Bellerophon, is the Captain of the Archers or
Lancemen (c). The Chimæra, having the Form of
a Lion before, or of a Dragon behind, and a Goat between, is but the innocent Reprefentative of three
Captains of the Solymi (a Colony of the Phænicians in
Pifidia), whofe names in the Language of that Peo-
ple, happened to fignify thefe three Creatures (d).
And the very place in the Country of the Argives,
where Bellerophon mounted his Horfe and fet forward
the Greeks called Kenthippe (e). From fuch trifling
Grounds the induftrious Greeks, according to their
Cuftom, wove this wondrous Tale!

[a] Perfim, Horfemen.
[b] From Pega, a Bridle, and Sus, a Horfe.
[c] From Bsal, a Lord or Captain, and Harovin, Archer or
Lancemen.
[d] Ary, a Lion; Tfoban, a Dragon; and Azal or Uzil, a
Kid.
[e] From kenteo to ftimulate or fpur, and hippos an Horfe. See
Bochart's Hierozoicon, l. 2. c. 6. p. 99.

N 2

CHAP.

CHAP. XLVII. Of JASON and the GOLDEN FLEECE.

THIS ancient Greek Hero was the Son of Æson, King of Thessaly and Alcimede; and by the Father's Side allied to Æolus. Pelias his Uncle, who was left his Guardian, sought to destroy him; but he was conveyed by his Father's Friends to a cave, where Chiron instructed him in physic; whence he took the name of Jason [a]. Arriving at Years of maturity, he returned to his Uncle, who, probably with no favourable intention to him, first inspired him with the notion of the Colchian expedition, and agreeably flattered his Ambition with the view of so tempting a prize as the Golden Fleece.

Athamas, King of Thebes, by his first wife had Helle and Phrixus. Ino his second, fell in Love with Phrixus her Son in Law, but being rejected in her advances, she took the opportunity of a great famine to indulge her Revenge, by persuading her Husband, that the Gods could not be appeased till he sacrificed his Son and Daughter. But as they stood at the Altar, Nephale their Mother [b], invisibly carried them off, giving them a Golden Ram she had got from Mercury to bear them through the Air. However, in passing the Streights, between Asia and Europe, Helle fell into the Sea, which from thence was called the Hellespont. Phryxus continued his course to Colchis, where Æta, King of that Country, entertained him hospitably; after which he offered up his Ram to Jupiter, [c], and consecrated the skin or hide in the Grove of Mars. It was called the Golden fleece from its colour [d], and guarded by bulls breathing Fire, and a watchful Dragon that never slept, as a pledge of the utmost importance.

[a] Or Healer, his former Name being Diomede.
[b] Nephele, in Greek signifies a Cloud.
[c] Who placed it it amongst the Constellations.
[d] Some make the Fleece of a purple colour, others white.

Jason,

Jason being determined on the Voyage, built a Veffel at Colchos in Theffaly, for the expedition [a]. The Fame of his defign foon drew the braveft and moft diftinguifhed Youths of Greece, to become Adventurers with him, though Authors are not agreed as to the names or number of the Argonauts, for fo they were called [b]. The firft place which Jafon touched at was the Ifle of Lemnos, where he continued fome time with Hipfipile the Queen, who bore him Twins. He next vifited Phineus King of Paphlagonia, from whom, as he he had the gift of Prophecy, he received fome informations of fervice to him in his Enterprize. After this, fafely paffing the Cyanean rocks [c], he entered the Euxine, and landing on the banks of the Phafis, repared to the Court of King Æta, and demanded the Golden Fleece. The Monarch granted his Requeft provided he could overcome the difficulties, which lay in his way [d], and which appeared not eafily furmountable. Jafon was more obliged to Love than Valour for his conqueft. Medea daughter to Æta, by her enchantments laid the Dragon afleep, taught him to fubdue the Bulls, and fo by night he carried off the Prize, taking with him the Princefs, to whofe Aid he was chiefly indebted for his Succefs (e).

Æta enraged at the trick put upon him, purfued the Fugitives; and it is faid, that to elude his Fury, Medea tore in pieces her young brother Abfyrtes, and fcattered the Limbs in his way, to ftop his Pro-

[a] Argos a famous Shipwright was the Builder, whence fhe was called Argo.

[b] Some make the number Forty nine, others more. The principal were Ancæus, Idmon, Orpheus, Augias, Calais, Zethus, Caftor, Pollux; Tiphys was their Pilot, and Lynceus remarkable for his quick fight, their look-out in cafe of danger. It is faid Hercules was with them.

[c] Cyanean Rocks, called the Symplegades, were fo called becaufe they floated and often crufhed fhips together. The Argonauts efcaped this Danger by fending out a Pidgeon, and lying by till they faw her fly through.

[d] Such as killing the brazen-footed Bulls and the Dragon.

[e] Ovid, Lib. VII. 159

                          grefs

grefs (a). After this, Jafon returned fafely to Greece, and foon heard that Pelias had deftroyed all his friends and made himfelf mafter of the kingdom. To revenge this Action, Medea failed home before him, and introducing herfelf to the Daughters of Pelias, under the character of a Prieftefs of Diana, fhewed them feveral furprizing inftances of her magical Power. She propofed making their Father young again, and to convince them of the poffibility of it fhe cut an old Ram in pieces, and feething it in a Cauldron, produced a young Lamb. The daughters ferving Pelias in the fame manner killed him (b), and fled the Country. Jafon-having notice of this, arrived in Theffaly, and took poffeffion of the Kingdom; but afterwards, he gene roufly reftored it to Acaftus fon of Pelias, who had accompanied him in the Colchian expedition, and with Medea went and fettled at Corinth.

Here Jafon finding himfelf cenfured for cohabiting with a Sorcerefs, and a Stranger, quitted her and married Creufa, daughter to Creon, King of theCountry. Medea feemingly approved the match, but meditated a fevere Revenge. She firft privately killed the 2 Children fhe had by him and then fent theBride a prefent of a Robe and gold Crown tinged in Naptha, which fet fire to her and the whole Palace. The Enchantrefs then afcending her Car (c) drawn by Dragons, efcaped through the Air to Athens, where fhe married King Ægeus, by whom fhe had a Son named Medus. But attempting to poifon Thefeus his eldeft Son, and the defign being revealed, fhe with her fon Medus fled to Afia, where he left his Name to Media (d).

[a] Others fay that AEte, to obftruct their Return, ftationed a Fleet at the Mouth of the Euxine Seas, and fo obliged Jafon to come Home by the Weft of Europe.

[b] Some Authors relate the Story differently, and fay that this Experiment was tried by Medea on AEfon, Jafon's Father. See Ovid in the place cited.

[c] Given her by Phœbus, or the Sun.

[d] A Region of Perfia.

Jafon

Jafon had feveral Temples erected to him, particularly one at Athens, by Parmenio, of polifhed Marble. The place where he was chiefly worfhiped was at Abdera in Thrace.

If we feek for the real Truth of the Argonautic Expedition, we fhall find it to be this: The Value of the Royal Treafury at Colchis had been greatly extolled; and the Pillage of it was the Thing aimed at by the Argonautic Expedition. The Word Gaza, in the Colchian Language (the fame, according to Herodotus with the Egyptian), fignifies a Fleece as well as a Trea. fure. This gave Occafion of the Circumftance of the Golden Fleece. The Word Sor is alfo a Wall and a Bull; Nacafh, Brafs and a Serpent. So this Treafure being fecured by a double Wall and Brazen Doors, they formed hence the Romantic Story of its being a Golden Fleece guarded by two Bulls and a Dragon [a]. The Mariner's Compafs is fuppofed [b] to have made Part of this Treafure (and if fo, this was of itfelf a Curiofity of infinite Value); whence the Ships of Phrixus and Jafon, which carried it, are faid to have been oracular and to have given Refponfes.

CHAP. XLVIII. Of THESEUS and ACHILLES.

WITH thefe two great Men we fhall clofe the Lifts of the Demi-Gods or Heroes.

Thefeus was Son to Ægeus, King of Athens and Æthra. In his Youth he had an early Paffion for Glory; and propofed Hercules for his Model. Sciron, a notorious Robber, who infefted the Roads between Megara and Corinth, was by him thrown down a Precipice, as he was accuftomed to treat fuch as fell into his Hands. Procruftes, a famous Tyrant of Attica, he faftened to a bended Pine, which being loofed tore him afunder [c].

[a] Bochart in Phaleg. l. 4. c. 31. p. 289.
[b] Stukeley's Stonehenge.
[c] He was a Tyrant of Attica, who feized all Strangers, and meafured them by his Bed; if they were too Long for it, he cut them fhorter; if too Short, he ftretched them till they died.

His

His first distinguishing Adventure, was the Destruction of the Cretan Minotaur. Minos King of that Island, had made War on Ægeus, because the Athenians had basely killed his Son, for carrying away the Prize from them. Being victorious, he imposed this severe Condition on the vanquished, that they should annually send seven of the noblest Youths, chosen by Lot, into Crete; to be devoured by the Minotaur [a]. The fourth Year of this Tribute, the choice fell on Theseus, Son to Ægeus, or as others say, he intreated to be sent himself. However this be, on the Arrival of Theseus at the Court of Minos, Ariadne his Daughter fell deeply in Love with him; and gave him a Clue, by which he got out of the Labyrinth. This done he sailed with his fair Deliverer for the Isle of Naxos, where he ungratefully left her [b], and where Bacchus found her and took her for his Mistress.

The Return of Theseus, through his own Neglect, became fatal to his Father. The good King at his Departure had charged him, as he sailed out with black Sails, to return with the same in case he miscarried, otherwise to change them to White. Impatiently he every Day went to the Top of a Rock that overlooked the Ocean, to see what ships appeared in View. At last his Son's Vessel is discovered, but with the sable Omens he dreaded; so that through Despair he threw himself into the Sea, which still retains his Name [c]. The Athenians decreed Ægeus divine Honours, and sacrificed to him as a Marine Deity, the adopted Son of Neptune.

Theseus performed after this several considerab'e Actions; he killed the Minotaur; he overcame the Centaurs; he subdued the Thebans, and defeated the

[a] Pasiphae, Wife to Minos King of Crete, and Daughter of the Sun, instigated by Venus, conceived a brutal Passion for a Bull. To gratify her, Dœdalus contrived an artificial Cow, in which placing her, she had her desire. The Fruit of this Bestial Amour was the Minotaur, who was kept in a Labyrinth made by the same Dœdalus, and fed with human Flesh.

[b] For this Story See the Article of Bacchus.

[c] The AEgean Sea.

Amazons

Amazons. He affisted his friend Pirithous, in his enterprize to the infernal world, to carry off Proserpine; but in this Expedition he failed, being imprisoned and fettered by Pluto, till released by Hercules. No doubt was the Story of Theseus divested of the marvellous, it would make a very considerable figure (a).

Theseus had several Wives; his first was Helena Daughter of Tyndarus, whom he carried off; the second Hippolita, Queen of the Amazons, given him by Hercules; the last was Phædra, Sister to Ariadne, whose Lewdness sufficiently punished him for his infidelity to her sister. This Princess felt an incestuous flame for her son in law Hippolitus (b), a Youth of uncommon Virtue and Chastity. On his repulsing her Solicitations, her Love turned to Hatred, and she accused him to his Father for an attempt to ravish her. Theseus now grown old and uxorious, too easily gave ear to the Accusation. The Prince informed of his danger fled in his Chariot; but his Horses being frighted by the Phocæ, or Sea-Calves, threw him out of his feat, and his Feet being entangled, he was dragged thro' the Woods and torn in pieces (c). Phædra, tormented with Remorse, laid violent hands on herself; and soon after, Theseus being exiled from Athens, ended an illustrious Life in Obscurity.

To explain the Story of the Minotaur: It is said that Pasiphae fell in love with a young Nobleman of the Court, named Taurus: That Dædalus lent his House for the better carrying on of their Intrigue, during a long Illness of Minos; and that the Queen in due time was delivered of two children, one of which resembled Minos the other Taurus; whence the Minotaur: And the Athenians have aggravated the story, from their extreme Prejudice to Minos.

[a] He first walled Athens, and instituted Laws; together with that democratic Form of Government which lasted till the Time of Pisistratus.

[b] Son of Hippolita, Queen of the Amazons.

[c] Some say Æsculapius restored him to Life, and that he came into Italy, where he changed his Name to Virbius, i. e. twice a man.

But

But what became of the Athenian Youth, the tax of whom was three times paid ? The Cretan King had instituted Funeral Games in Honour of Androgeos, wherein those unhappy Slaves were assigned as the Prize of the Conqueror. The first who bore away all the Prizes was Taurus, of an insolent and tyrannical disposition, and particularly severe to the Athenians delivered up to him; which contributed not a little to the Fable. These Wretches grew old in Servitude, and were obliged to earn their living in the most painful drudgery under Taurus, the subject of Minos; and may therefore with some propriety be said to be devoured by him. But it is certain they neither fought at those Games, nor were destroyed by the cruelty of a monster which never existed (a).

Of the same stamp is the tale of the Centaurs. The Thessalians pretty early distinguished themselves from the rest of Greece, who fought only on Foot or in Chariots, by their Application to Horsemanship To acquire the more agility in this exercise, they were wont to fight with Bulls, which they pierced with Darts or Javelins; whence they obtained the Name of Centaurs (b) and Hippocentaurs (c). As these Horsemen became formidable by their Depredations, the Equivocation, which appeared in the Name made them to be accounted Monsters, compounded of two Natures. The Poets catched at this Idea, which gave the story the Air of the Marvellous: And they who made Oranges to pass for Golden Apples, Shepherdesses for Nymphs, Shepherds in disguise for Satyrs, and ships with sails for winged Dragons, would make no difficulty in calling Horsemen Centaurs (d).

Achilles was the offspring of a Goddess. Thetis bore him to Peleus (e), and was so fond of him, that she took herself the charge of his Education. By day

<hr>

[a] Abbe Banier's Mythology, Vol. 3. p. 500.
[b] From Kenteo to prick or lance, and Tauros, a Bull.
[c] From Hippos, a Horse.
[d] See the Abbe Banier's Mythology, Vol. 3. p. 536.
[e] King of Thessaly.

she

she fed him with Ambrosia, and by Night she covered him with celestial Fire to render him immortal (a). She also dipped him in the Waters of Styx, by which his whole Body became invulnerable, except that part of his heel by which she held him. She afterwards intrusted him to the care of the Centaur Chiron (the Master of so many Heroes) who fed him with Honey and the marrow of Lions and wild Boars, to give him that Strength and Force necessary for martial toil.

When the Greeks undertook the siege of Troy, Chalcas the Priest of Apollo, foretold the City could never be taken, unless Achilles was present. Thetis his Mother, who knew what would be his Fate if he went there, had concealed him in a Female disguise in the Palace of Lycomedes, King of the Isle of Scyros. Ulysses, who had engaged to bring him to the Greek Camp having discovered the place of his Retreat, used the following Artifice. Under the Appearance of a Merchant, he is introduced to the daughters of Lycomedes, and while they were studiously intent on viewing his Toys, Achilles employed himself in examining an Helmet and some other Armour, which the cunning Politician had purposely thrown in his way. Thus was Achilles prevailed on to go to Troy, after Thetis had furnished him with a suit of impenetrable armour made by Vulcan (b). His actions before Troy, as well as his Character, are so finely described by Homer, that it would be doing them injustice to repeat them here. It is sufficient to say he could not escape his fate, being treacherously killed by Paris (c), who with an Arrow wounded him in the only part that was vulnerable. The Greeks after the cap-

[a] See the Story of Triptolemus, under the Article of Ceres Upon Peleus discovering this, Thetis parted from him.

(b) The description of his shield in Homer is one of that Poets Master pieces.

[c] The Case was thus; Achilles enamoured with Polyxena, desired her of Priam, who consented to the Match. The Nuptials were to be solemnized in the Temple of Apollo, where Paris had privately concealed himself, and took the Opportunity to kill Achilles.

ture of Troy, endeavoured to appeafe his Manes, by facrificing Polyxena. The oracle at Dodona decreed him divine Honours, and ordered annual Victims to be offered at his Tomb. In purfuance of this the Theffalians brought thither yearly two Bulls, one Black, the other White, crowned with Wreaths of flowers, and water from the Rvier Specchius.

CHAP. XLIX. Of Cadmus, Europa, Amphion, and Arion.

AGENOR, King of Phœnicia, by the Nymph Melia, had a Daughter called Europa, one of the moft beautiful Princeffes of her age. She could hardly then be fuppofed to efcape the Notice of Jupiter, whofe Gallantries extended to all Parts of the World. To feduce her, he affumed the Form of a white Bull, and appeared in the Meadows where fhe was walking with her Attendants. Pleafed with the Beauty and Gentlenefs of the Animal, fhe ventured on his Back, and immediately the God triumphant, bore her off to Crete (a), where laying afide his Difguife, he made the Bull a Conftellation in the Zodiac, and to honour his new miftrefs gave her name to the fourth part of the World.

In the mean Time, Agenor, difconfolate for his daughter's lofs, fent his fons Cadmus and Thafus with different Fleets in Search of her (b). Thafus fettled in an Ifland of the Ægean Sea, to which he gave his Name (c). Cadmus enquiring of the Delphic Oracle for a fettlement, was anfwered, That he fhould follow the direction of a Cow, and build a City where fhe laid down. Arriving amongft the Phocenfes, here one of Pelagon's Cows met him, and conducted him through Bœotia, to the Place where

[a] Ovid, Lib. II. P 35.
[b] With an Injunction not to return without her under Pain of Banifhment.
[c] It was before called Plate.

Thebes

Thebes was afterwards built. As he was about to
facrifice his guide to Pallas, he fent two of his Company to the Fountain Dirce for Water, who were
killed by a Dragon. Cadmus foon revenged their
Death by flaying the Monfter; but fowing his teeth,
according to Pallas's advice, there fprung up a number of men armed, who affaulted him to Revenge
their Father's Death. It feems the Goddefs of Wifdom had only a Mind to frighten him; for on his
cafting a ftone amongft them, thefe upftart Warriors
turned their weapons on each other with fuch Ani-
mofity that only five furvived the combat, who proved very ufeful to Cadmus in founding his new City.
After this, to recompenfe his toils, the Gods gave
Cadmus, Harmonia, or Hermione, the Daughter of
Mars and Venus, and honoured his nuptials with peculiar Prefents and marks of favour. But their pofterity proving unfortunate, they quitted Thebes to Pentheus, and went to govern the Eclellenfes, where in
an advanced age, they were turned to Serpents (a),
or as others fay, fent to the Elyfian fields in a Chariot
drawn by ferpents. The Sidonians decreed divine
Honours to Europa, and coined Money in Memory
of her, with the figure of a woman crofling the fea on
a Bull.

The Greeks were indebted to Cadmus for the Invention of Brafs, and the firft ufe of Arms. In the
Phœnician Tongue, the two words, which the Greeks
tranflated Serpent's teeth, fignified as well Spears of
Brafs (b). The Ambiguity of another Word helped
on the fable (c), which from the difference of pronunciation fignified either the number five, or one
ready for Action: And fo the fame fentence which,
with the Phœnicians, intended only that he commanded a difciplined Body of men armed with Spears of
Brafs, was rendered by thefe miracle-mongers, he
made an army of five men out of the teeth of a Ser-

[a] Ovid, Lib. IV. 562.
[b] Sheni Nacafh.
[c] Chemifh.

pent

pent [a]. Cadmus being an Hivite, a name of near affinity with that of a Serpent, gave further occasion to that part of it, which says that his Men sprung from a Serpent, and that himself and his wife were changed into this Animal. Thus industrious were the Greeks to involve the most simple facts in the most mysterious confusion.

The Phœnicians with Cadmus, expelled their country by Joshua, first introduced amongst the Greeks the practice of consecrating statues to the Gods; and the use of letters; thence called Phœnician or Cadmœan letters. For the Greek characters are manifestly taken from the Samaritan or Phœnician Alphabet. Cadmus and Og, or Ogyges, are the same: Whence any thing very ancient was termed Ogygnian by the Thebans. The Gophyrœi, settled at Athens, were Phœnicians that came with him, and preserved the memory of him by the Name of Ogyges; as from his name Cadmus or Cadem [b], was their famous place of learning, and thence every other, named Academia [c].

Amphion, the Son of Jupiter and Antiope, was instructed in the Lyre by Mercury, and became so great a proficient, that he is reported to have raised the walls of Thebes by the Power of his Harmony. He married Niobe, whose insult to Diana occasioned the loss of their Children. The unhappy Father, in despair, attempted to destroy the Temple of Apollo, but was punished with the loss of sight and skill, and thrown into the infernal Regions.

Arion was a Native of Methymna, and both a skilful Musician and a good Dithyrambic Poet. He lived in the time of Periander, King of Corinth. After passing some time in Italy and Sicily, and acquiring an easy fortune by his profession, he sailed from Tarentum in a Corinthian vessel homeward-bound. When they were got to sea, the avaricious Crew agreed to

[a] Bochart de Coloniis Phœnicum, cap. 19.
[b] Signifying the East. He was so called because he came hence.
[c] Stillingfleet's Origines sacræ.

throw

throw Arion over-board, in order to share his money. Having in vain used all his eloquence to soften them, he played a farewell Air (called Lex Orthia) and crowned with a Garland, with his Harp in his hand, plunged into the Sea, where a Dolphin, charmed with his melody, received him and bore him safe to Tœnarus near Corinth. Having informed Periander of his story, the King was incredulous, till the ship arrived, when the Mariners being seized and confronted with Arion, owned the Fact, and suffered the punishment due to their Perfidy. For this Action the Dolphin was made a Constellation.

CHAP. L. Of ÆOLUS and BOREAS.

IN the Multiplication of Fabulous Deities, the ancients not only assigned each Element, and part of Nature its tutelar God, but even idolized the passions. No wonder then if we see a God or chief of the Winds too, controuling all the rest. This Province was naturally assigned to that which was the most violent and uncontroulable itself. For this Imaginary Deity they borrowed a name from the Phœnicians, and called him Æolus [a] the son of Jupiter, by Acasta or Sigesia the daughter of Hippotus. He reigned in the Liparœan isles near Sicily, from whence perhaps the fable took its original (b); but his Residence was at Strongyle, now called Strombolo [c]. Here he held these unruly Powers enchained in a vast Cave, to prevent their committing the like Devastation they had been guilty of before they were put under his direction [d].

[a] From Aol for Alol a storm, whirlwind or tempest.
[b] These Islands being greatly subject to winds and storms.
[c] Famous for its Vulcano, tho' some place his Residence at Reggio in Calabria.
[d] They had disjoined Italy from Sicily, and by disuniting Europe from Africa, opened a passage for the Ocean to form the Mediteranean Sea.

According to some Authors, the Æolian or Liparæan isles were uninhabited, till Liparus the son of Ausonis settled a Colony here, and gave one of them his name. Æolus the son of Hippotus, who married his daughter, peopled the rest, and succeeded him in the Throne. He ruled his subjects with equity and mildness, was an hospitable good Prince, and being skilled in Astronomy, by means of the Reflux of the Tides, which is remarkable near those Islands, as well as by observing the nature of the Volcanos with which they abound, he was able to foretell the Winds that should blow from such a quarter [a].

We are indebted to Virgil for a fine poetical Description of this God, when Juno visits his cave to desire his assistance to destroy Æneas in his voyage to Italy.

Boreas was of uncertain Parentage; but his usual Residence was in Thrace (b). When Xerxes, King of Persia, crossed the Hellespont with his numerous Armada, to invade Greece, the Athenians invoked his assistance, and he scattered and destroyed the greatest part of their fleet. This Deity, notwithstanding his Rage, was not inflexible to love. He debauched Chloris the daughter of Arcturus, by whom he had Hyrpace, and carried her to Mount Niphates, (called the bed of Boreas) but since known by the Name of Caucasus: But his favourite mistress was Orithya the daughter of Erictheus, King of Athens. By this Princess he had two sons, Zetes and Calais, who attended Jason in the Colchic expedition, delivered Phineus from the Harpies [c]; and were afterwards killed by Hercules: as also four daughters, Upis, Laxo, Hecaerge, and Cleopatra. Perhaps the North wind, or Boreas alone, was deified, because of the regular winds it is the most tempestuous and raging that blows.

[a] It is said that before a southerly wind blows, Lipara is covered with a thick Cloud, but when it changes to the North the Volcano emits clear Flames with a remarkable noise.

[b] Probably because this Country is much subject to cold Northerly winds.

[c] Some say out of Envy for their Swiftness; others, because their Father had by a Tempest destroyed the Isle of Cos.

CHAP.

CHAP. LI. Of MOMUS and MORPHEUS.

MOMUS was the God of Pleasantry and Wit; or Rather the Jester of the celestial Assembly, for like other great Monarchs, it was but reasonable that Jupiter should have his fool. We have an instance of his sarcastic Humour in the contest between Neptune, Minerva, and Vulcan, for skill. The First had made a Bull; the Second a House; and the third a Man; Momus found Fault with them all; He disliked the Bull, because his Horns were not placed before his eyes, that he might give a surer blow; he condemned Minerva's House, because it was immoveable, and so could not be taken away if placed in a bad Neighbourhood. With Regard to Vulcan's man he said he ought to have a window in his breast. Hesiod makes Momus (a) the son of Somnus and Nox.

Morpheus (b) was the God of Dreams, and the Son of Somnus, whom Ovid calls the most placid of all the Deities. Mr. Addison observes that he is still represented by the antient Statuaries under the figure of a Boy asleep, with a bundle of Poppy in his hand : And black Marble, from the Relation which it bears to night, has with great propriety been made use of.

CHAP. LII. Of ORION.

THE Original, or Birth of Orion, borders a little on the Marvellous. Hyricus, a Citizen of Tanagra, in Bœotia, was so hospitable to Strangers, that Jupiter, Neptune, and Mercury were resolved, under the character of benighted Travellers, to know the Truth. Their Entertainment was so agreeable, that discovering their Quality, they offered the old

[a] From Momos, cavilling or finding Fault
[b] From Morphe, a Form or vision.

Man whatever he should ask; his Request was a son [a]. The Gods to gratify his wish called for an Ox Hide, in which having deposited their Urine, they bid him keep it under ground for ten months, at the Expiration of which time, he found it produced a Boy, who was at first called Urion, to express his Origin; but after, for Decency's Sake, his name was changed to Orion.

He was a remarkable Hunter, and kept a fleet pack of Hounds. Neptune gave him the Power of walking on the surface of the Waters, with the same Speed that Iphiclus did (b) over the Ears of Corn.— This Faculty seemed needless, if it be true that Orion was so tall, that the deepest Seas could not cover his shoulders. As a proof of this, he crossed from the Continent of Greece to the Isle of Chios, where, attempting to vitiate Ærope, the Wife of King Oenopion, that Monarch deprived him of his Sight (c). From Chios he proceeded and found his way to Lesbos, where Vulcan received him kindly, and gave him a guide to the palace of the Sun, who restored him to sight. He then made war on Oenopion, who concealed himself under ground to escape his vengeance; so that frustrated of his design he went to Crete where he pursued his favourite exercise of Hunting. But having by some means offended Diana [d], that Goddess put him to death (e); but afterwards relenting, prevailed on Jupiter to raise him to the skies, where he forms a constellation (g) remarkable for predicting Rain and tempestuous Weather.

[a] His wife having left him childless, whom on her Death Bed, he promised never to marry again.

[b] Brother to Hercules   See the Article of that God.

[c] His Pursuit of the Pleiades has been mentioned under the Article of Atlas.

[d] Either for attempting her Chastity, or for boasting his superior Skill in the Chace; others say for endeavouring to debauch Opis one of her Nymphs.

[e] Either by her Arrows, or as others say, raising a Scorpion, which gave him a mortal wound.

[g] Virgil calls it Nimbosus Orion, on account of the showers which attend his Rising.   Æneid l. 535 Lib. IV. 52.

CHAP.

CHAP. LIII.   Of the Marine Deities, OCEANUS,
NEREUS, TRITON, INO, PALEMON, and GLAU-
CUS.

AS the antient Theogony took Care to people the
Heavens and Air with Deities, fo the Sea naturally came in for its Share, nor was it juft to leave
the extended Realms of water without Protection and
Guardianſhip. Neptune, though Monarch of the
deeps, could not be prefent every where, and it was
proper to affign him Deputies, who might relieve him
of ſome part of the weight of Government.

Nereus, ſon to Oceanus, fettled himſelf in the Æ-
gean Sea, and was regarded as a Prophet. He had
the faculty of affuming what Form he pleafed. By
his wife Doris he had fifty Nymphs, called Nereids
[a], who conftantly attended on Neptune, and when
he went abroad ſurrounded his Chariot.

Triton was the fon of Neptune and Amphitrite (b),
and was his Father's Herald. He fometimes delighted
in mifchief, for he carried off the Cattle from the
Tanagrian Fields, and deftroyed the fmall coafting
Veffels; fo that to appeafe his Refentment, thofe
People offered him Libations of new wine. Of this
he drank fo freely that he fell afleep, and tumbling
from an eminence, one of the natives cut off his head.
He left a daughter called Triftia, by whom Mars had
a fon named Menalippus.

This God is reprefented of a human Form, from
the waift upwards, with blue eyes, a large mouth and
Hair matted like wild Parfley. His ſhoulders were
covered with a Purple Skin, variegated with fmall
Scales, his Feet refembling the fore Feet of a
Horfe, and his lower parts turned like a Dolphin with
a forked tail. Sometimes he is drawn in a Car with

[a] By which are meant the Rivers which empty themſelves
in the Ocean.

[b] Some fay of Neptune and Cœleno, others of Nereus or O-
ceanus.

Horſes

Horses of a Sky Colour. His Trumpet is a large Couch, or Sea Shell. Ovid [a] has given two very beautiful Descriptions of him. There were indeed many Tritons, who composed the numerous Equipage of Neptune, and were reckoned as Deities propitious to Navigation.

Ino was the daughter of Cadmus and Harmonia, and married to Athamas King of Thebes. This Prince having the misfortune to lose his Senses killed his son Learchus in one of his mad Fits, upon which his Queen to save Melicertes, her remaining Boy, leaped with him from the Rock Molyris into the Sea. Neptune received them with open Arms, and gave them a Place amongst the marine Gods, only changing their Names, Ino being called Leucothea, and Melicertes Palæmon (b); for this we are indebted to the fertile invention of the Greeks, Melicertes being no other than the Melcarthus or Hercules of Tyre, who, from having been drowned in it, was called a God of the Sea, and from his many Voyages, the Guardian of Harbours.

Glaucus was a Fisherman, whose Deification happened in an odd Manner. His Parentage and Country [c] are variously reported; but he was an excellent Swimmer, and a skilful Fisherman. Having one Day taken a large Draught in his Nets, he observed with surprize, that the Fishes on tasting a certain Herb jumped into the sea again. Upon trying the experiment himself, he followed them, and became a Sea God. Some ascribe to Glaucus, the Gift of Prophecy. Ovid has not forgot his Transformation amongst his Metamorphoses (d). Virgil has given an elegant list of these Deities in his fifth Æneid (e)

[a] Ovid Metamorp Lib. I.

[b] The Romans called him Portunus; and painted him with a Key in his hand, to denote him the Guardian of Harbours. To Ino they gave the Name of Matuta, being reputed the Goddess that ushers in the morning.

(c) Some make him the Son of Mercury, others of Neptune others of Anthadon; on account of his skill in Swimming he was called Pontius.

[d] Ovid, Lib. XIII. 899.

[e] Æneid, Lib. V. 822.

C H A P.

CHAP LIV. Of PROTEUS and PHORCYS, with the GRÆÆ and GORGONS, SCYLLA and CHARYBDIS.

PROTEUS, the fon of Neptune, by the Nymph Phænice, was by his Father appointed Keeper of the Phocæ, or Sea Calves. His Refidence was at Alexandria, in Egypt, from whence in a Journey he made to Phlegra, [a], he married the Nymph Torone, who bore him Tmolus and Telegonus, both killed by Hercules for their cruelty to Strangers. Their Father Proteus, who left them on account of their in-hofpitable Temper, it is faid, was not much concerned at their death. By Torone he had alfo three daughters, Cabera, Retia, and Idothea. Proteus had the art of affuming all Forms [b]; as alfo the gift of prophecy or divination; Orpheus calls him the univerfal Principle of Nature.

Hiftorians make Proteus King of Carpathus [c]; who, on account of his great Charafter for Wifdom, and Equity, was chofen King of Egypt, and deified after his death. According to Herodotus, Paris and Helena in their flight from Sparta, were received at his Court, where Helen continued all the time of the Trojan Siege, after which he Reftored her honourably to Menelaus.

Proteus is ufually Reprefented in a chariot drawn by Horfes, in the Form of Tritons.

His half Brother Phorcys or Phorcus, was the fon of Neptune, by the Nymph Thefea [d]. He married his fifter Ceto, by whom he had the Phorcydes and Goigons, Thoofa [e] and Scylla. He was vanquifhed by Atlas, who threw him into the fea, where his Father raifed him to the Rank of a Sea God.

[a] A Town in Campania.
[b] See Ovid Lib. VIII. 730.
[c] An Ifland in the AEgean Sea, between Rhodes and Crete now called Scarpanto.
[d] Others call him the fon of Pontus and Terra.
[e] By whom Neptune had the Cyclops Polyphemus.

The

The Gorgons were in all four fifters, of whom Medufa was the Chief. They had hair like Snakes, Tufks like wild Boars, brazen hands, and golden wings. On the death of their fifter, they purfued Perfeus, who faved himfelf by putting on the Helmet lent him by Pluto, and which rendered him invifible.

The Graæ were their fifters, and are reprefented as three old Women, who lived in Scythia, and had but one Eye and Tooth in common amongft them, which they ufed as they had occafion, and afterwards laid it up in a coffer. For the Prefervation of this valuable Legend we are indebted to Palæphatus.

Scylla (a), another daughter of Phorcys by her familiarity with Glaucus, excited the jealoufy of Circe, daughter of the Sun, who by magick Spells, or Poifon, fo infected the Fountain in which fhe bathed, that fhe became a Monfter (b), upon which thro' defpair at the lofs of her beauty, fhe threw herfelf into the fea, and was changed into a Rock [c], which became infamous for the multitude of Ship-wrecks it occafioned. Thofe who would fee a beautiful defcription of Scylla will find it in Virgil [d].

Care muft be taken not to confound this Scylla with another of the fame name, and daughter of Nifus King of Megara. Minos had befieged this Monarch in his Capital, but the Oracle had pronounced Nyfus invincible, while he preferved a Purple Lock of Hair which grew on his Head. Scylla, who was fecretly in Love with Minos, betrayed both her Father and

[a] Some make her the daughter of Phoronis and Hecate, and fay that her misfortune was owing to the jealoufy of Amphitrite for her cohabiting with Neptune.

[b] Authors difagree as to her Form ; fome fay fhe retained her beauty from the Neck downwards, but had fix Dogs Heads ; others maintain, that her upper parts continued entire, but that fhe had below the body of a Wolf, and the Tail of a Serpent.

[c] It lies between Sicily and Italy, and the noife of the waves beating on it, gave Rife to the Fable of the Barking of Dogs and Howling of Wolves, afcribed to the Monfter.

[d] Virgil makes her changed to a Rock, which confounds her with the other Scylla. AEneid, Lib. III. 424.

Country

Country into his Hands, by cutting off the Lock; but the Conqueror detecting her Treachery, banished her his sight. Unable to bear the Treatment she so justly merited, she cast herself into the Sea, and was changed into a Lark [a]. Her Father, transformed into an Hawk still pursues her for her ingratitude and Perfidy.

Charybdis was a female Robber, who it is said stole Hercules's Oxen, and was by Jupiter, on that account changed into a whirlpool [b], which is very dangerous, to Sailors, and lying opposite to the Rock Scylla, occasioned the Proverb, of running out of one danger to avoid another [c].

CHAP. LV. Of Pan and Faunus. Of the Nymphs and the Goddesses, Feronia and Pales.

IT is now time to revisit the Earth again, and see the numerous train of the inferior Deities, appropriated to the Forests, Woods, and those Recesses of Nature whose prospect fills the imagination with a kind of religious Awe or Dread.

Pan the principal of these, is said to be the son of Mercury and Penelope (d) the wife of Ulysses, whom while she kept her Father's flocks on mount Taygetus he deflowered in the Form of a white Goat. As soon as born, his Father carried him in a Goat Skin to Heaven, where he charmed all the Gods with his Pipe; so that they associated him with Mercury in the post of their messenger. After this he was educated on Mount Mænalus, in Arcadia, by Sinoe and the other Nymphs, who, attracted by his Music, followed him as their Conductor.

Pan, though devoted to the Pleasures of a Rural

[a] Ovid, Lib. VIII. 142.
[b] An Eddy, or Whirlpool, on the Coast of Sicily, as you enter the Fare of Messina. . See Virgil, AEneid III. 420.
[c] Incidit in Scyllam qui vult vitare Charybdim.
[d] Some say of Penelope and all her Lovers, whence he was called Pan.

Life

Life, diftinguifhed himfelf by his Valour.   In the
Giants War he entangled Typhon in his Nets, as we
have already obferved ; he attended Bacchus in his
Indian expedition with a body of Satyrs, who did
good fervice.   When the Gauls invaded Greece, and
were about to pillage the Temple of Delphos, he
ftruck them with fuch a fudden confternation by night,
that they fled without any body to purfue them [c].
He alfo aided the Athenians in a fea fight gained by
Miltiades over the Perfian fleet, for which they dedicated a Grotto to his Honour under the Citadel.

This Deity was of a very amorous Conftitution. In
a conteft with Cupid, being overcome, that little God
punifhed him with a paffion for the Nymph Syrinx,
who treated him with difdain.   But being clofely
purfued by him, and ftopped in her flight by the River Ladon, fhe invoked the Naiades, who changed
her into a tuft of Reeds, which the difappointed Lover
grafped in his arms.   Contemplating a transformation fo unfavourable to his defires, he obferved the
Reeds tremble with the wind, and emit a murmuring
found.   Improving this hint, he cut fome of them,
and formed the Pipe for which he became fo famous.
His other Amours were more fuccefsful.   He charmed Luna, or the Moon, in the fhape of a beautiful
Ram. In the difguife of a Shepherd, he became a fer-
vant to the Father of Dryope [b] in order to gain accefs to his miftrefs. By the Nymph Echo [c] he had a
daughter called Irynge, a famous Sorcerefs, who fupplied Medea with her Philtrum ; but Pan afterwards
flighting her, fhe retired to the Recefles of the Hills,
where fhe pined with grief till fhe dwindled to a fha-
dow, and had nothing left but a voice [d] , others afcribe the change of Echo to another caufe.

Pan,

[a] Hence the expreffion of a Pannick, for a fudden Fear and
Terror.

[b] Dryope rejected his Suit ; but was afterwards changed into the Lotus Tree.   See Ovid Met. Lib. IX. 325.

[c] Some fay that Echo fell in Love with Narciffus, and was
flighted by him.

[d] It is reported, that Juno punifhed Echo in this manner for
her Loquacity, becaufe when Jupiter was engaged in any new
Amour

Pan was properly the God of Shepherds and Hunters, and as he was a Mountain Deity the Flocks and Herds were under his immediate Protection and Care. He was likewise honoured by the fishermen, especially those who inhabited the Promontories washed by the Sea.

He was chiefly esteemed in Arcadia, his Native Country, where the Shepherds offered him milk and honey in wooden Bowls. If successful in Hunting, they allotted him part of the Spoil; but if otherwise they whipped his Image heartily. At Molpeus, a town near the City Lycosura, he had a Temple by the title of Nomius, because he perfected the Harmony of his Pipe on the Nomian Mountains.

The Romans adopted him amongst their Deities by the Names of Lupercus and Lycæus. His Festivals called Lupercalia, and celebrated in February, were instituted by Evander, who being exiled Arcadia, fled for Refuge to Faunus King of the Latins, and was by him allowed to settle near Mount Palatine (a). Romulus made some Addition to these Ceremonies, in which the Luperci, or Priests of Pan, ran naked thro' the City, striking those they met with Things made of Goat Skins, particularly the Women, who fancied that it helped their easy conception, or speedy Delivery.

Pan is represented with a smiling ruddy Face, and thick Beard covering his Breasts, two Horns on his Head, a Star on his Breast, with the Nose, Feet, and Tail of a Goat. He is cloathed in a spotted Skin, having a Shepherd's crook in one Hand, and his pipe of unequal Reeds in the other, and is crowned with Pine, that Tree being consecrated to his service.

Pan, however, said to be the Offspring of Penelope, was indeed one of the most ancient, being of the first eight of the Egyptian Gods; and was looked upon as the symbol of Nature. His Horns, say the My-

Amour, he sent this Nymph to amuse his jealous Spouse with her Chat.

(a) Where he had a Temple built afterwards.

P   thologists,

thologifts, reprefent the Rays of the Sun, and the Vivacity and Ruddinefs of his Complexion, the brightnefs of the Heavens; the Star on his Breaft, the Firmament; and his Feet and Legs overgrown with hair, denote the inferior part of the World, the Earth, the Trees and Plants (a).

Faunus was the fon of Picus, King of the Latins, who was cotemporary with Orpheus. He reigned in Italy at the time that Pandion ruled Athens, and introduced both Religion and Hufbandry into Latium. He deified his Father, and his Wife Fauna or Fatua (b). He had the Gift of Prophecy. His Son Stercutius was alfo honoured on account of his fhewing how to improve Land by dunging or manuring it. The Faunalia were kept in December, with Feafting and much mirth, and the Victims offered were Goats.

The Fauni, or Children of Faunus, were vifionary Beings much like the Satyrs, and were ufualy crowned with Pine. Both Faunus and they were the only Deities regarded in Italy, and wholly unknown to the Greeks.

The Fauni were the Hufbandmen, the Satyrs the Vine dreffers, and the Sylvani thofe who cut Wood in the Forefts, who as was ufual in thofe early times, being drefied in the fkins of beafts, gave rife to thofe fabulous Deities.

The Terreftrial Nymphs were divided into feveral Claffes. The Heathen Theology took care that no part of Nature fhould remain uninformed or unprotected. The Oreades, or Orefteades, prefided over the Mountains (c). Of thefe Diana had a Thoufand ready to attend her at her pleafure. It is faid they firft reclaimed Men from eating or devouring each other, and taught the Ufe of vegetable Food

[a] Abbe Banier's Mythology, Vol. I. p. 540.
[b] Some add fhe was his Sifter, and a Prieftefs. He whipped her to Death with Myrtle Rods for being d.unk, and then made her a Goddefs: for which Reafon no Myrtle was ufed in her Temples; the Veffels were covered, and the Wine offered was called Milk.
[c] Some make them five only, and call them the Daughters of Hecatæus; but Homer ftiles them the offspring of Jupiter.

Meliffa,

Melissa, one of these, was the Inventress of Honey [a].
The Napeæ were the tutelar Guardians of Vallies and
Flowry Meads.   The Dryades inhabited the Forests
and Woods, residing in their particular Trees, with
which they were thought to be coeval, as several Instances prove [b]. The Oak was generally their choice
either from its Strength or Duration.   Some were
called Hamadryades, whose Existence was insepara-
bly united to that of the Tree they animated.   The
Naiades were the Nymphs of the Brooks and Rivers:
the Limniades frequented the Lakes; and the Ephy-
driades delighted in Springs and Fountains.   Thus all
the Face of Nature became enlivened by the Force of
Imagination, and the Poets did not fail to improve so
ample a field for description.   The Mythologists destroy all this fine Landscape, by making the Nymphs
only signify the universal Moisture which is diffused
through all Nature.

There were also celestial Nymphs of a higher Rank,
who attended the Dii Majores.   Jupiter boasts of his
in Ovid [c].   The Muses were the Nymphs or Attendants of Apollo, as the Bassarides, or Mænades, belonged to Bacchus. Juno had fourteen who waited on her
[d] person ; and Neptune had no less than fifty Nere-
ides at his beck, on which account he was called Nym-
phagater, or the Captain of the Nymphs [e].

The usual Sacrifices to these Deities were Goats ;
but more commonly Milk, Oil, Honey, and Wine.
The Nymphs were always represented as young and
beautiful Virgins, and dressed in such a manner as was
most suitable to the character ascribed to them.

To the Train of Pan we may join two rural Goddesses, of whom the first is Feronia, or the Goddess of
Woods and Orchards [f].   The Lacedemonians first

[a] Whence the Bees are called Melissæ.
[b] Arcas preserving a decayed Oak, by watering the Roots,
was rewarded by marrying the Nymph who resided in it.
[c] Ovid Metam. Lib. I.
[d] Virgil, Æneid l 75.
[e] See Hesiod and Pindor.
[f] From Fero, to bear or produce.

P 2

introduced

introduced her Worſhip into Italy under Evander, and built her a Temple in a Grove near Mount Soracte. This Edifice being ſet on Fire, and extinguiſhed, the Neighbours reſolved to remove her Statue, when the Grove became green of a ſudden [a]. Strabo tells us, that her Prieſts or Votaries could walk barefoot over burning coals unhurt. Slaves received the Cap of Liberty in her Temple, on which Account they regarded her as their Patroneſs.

Pales was the protecting Deity of Shepherds and Paſturage. Her Feſtival was obſerved by the Country people in May, in the open fields, and the Offerings were Milk, and Cakes of Millet, in order to engage her to defend their Flocks from wild Beaſts, and infectious Diſeaſes. Theſe Feaſts were called Palilia, Some make Pales the ſame with Veſta or Cybele. This Goddeſs is repreſented as an Old Woman.

Both theſe Deities were peculiar to the Romans, and wholly unknown in Greece.

CHAP. LVI. Of Priapus and Terminus.

PRIAPUS was, as the Generality of Authors agree, the Son of Bacchus and Venus [b]. This Goddeſs meeting him in his Return from his India expedition, their amorous Congreſs produced this Child, who was born at Lampſacus (c), but ſo deformed, that his Mother, aſhamed of him, abandoned him (d). Being grown up, the inhabitants of that place baniſhed him their Territory, on account of his Vices; but being viſited with an epidemical Diſeaſe, upon conſulting the Oracle of Dodona, he was recalled (e).

[a] This Miracle is aſcribed to other Deities.
[b] Some make him the Son of Bacchus and Nais ; others ſay Chione was his Mother.
[c] A City of Myſia at the Mouth of the Helleſpont.
(d) Some ſay that Juno being called to aſſiſt at the Labour, out of Hatred to Bacchus the Son of her Rival Semele, ſpoil the Infant in the Birth.
(e) Others ſay, that the Women of Lampſacus prevailed on their Huſbands to recall him.

And

And Temples were erected to him as the tutelar Deity of Vineyards and Gardens, to defend them from Thieves and Birds destructive to the fruit.

Priapus had several Names. He was called Avistupor for the Reason just mentioned. The Title of Hellespontiacus was given him, because Lampsacus was seated on that Streight or Arm of the Sea. It is uncertain how he came by the Epithet of Bonus Deus ascribed to him by Phurnitius. Those of Phallus and Fascinum were assigned him on a very obscene account, and indeed his whole Figure conveyed such an idea of ugliness and lewdness, that the Poets generally treat him with great contempt (a). The Sacrifice offered him was the Ass, either because of the natural Uncomeliness of that Animal, and its strong propensity to venery, or because as some say, Priapus attempting the Chastity of Vesta when asleep, she was awakened by the braying of old Silenus his Ass, and so escaped the injury designed her.

This Deity is usually represented naked and obscene with a stern countenance, matted hair, and carrying a wooden sword (b), or sickle in his hand. His Body ended in a shapeless Trunk or Block of Timber.

Some of the Mythologists make his Birth allude to that radical Moisture, which supports all vegetable productions, and which is produced by Bacchus and Venus, that is the Solar Heat, and the water or liquid Matter, whence Venus is said to spring. The Worship of this infamous Deity was taken from the Syrians of Lampsacus.

With Priapus we may associate Terminus, a very antient Deity amongst the Romans, whose Worship was first instituted by Numa Pompilius, who erected him a Temple on the Tarpeian Hill (c). This Deity was thought to preside over the stones or landmarks, called Termini, which were held so sacred, that it was Sacrilege to move them, and the Criminal becoming

(a) Horat, Satyr VIII.
[b] Virgil, Georg. IV.
[c] Which was open at Top.

P 3   devoted

devoted to the Gods, it was lawful for any Man to kill him.

The Feasts called Terminalia, were celebrated annually about the end of February, when the antient Termini, or Landmarks, were carefully visited and crowned with Garlands. At first the Sacrifices to these rural Deities were very simple, such as Wheat Cakes and the first fruits of the Field, with Milk (a); but in later times the Victims were Lambs, and Sows that gave suck, whose blood was sprinkled upon the stones.

The Roman Termini were square stones, or Posts, much resembling our Mile Stones [b].

CHAP. LVII. Of FLORA.

THE Poets make this Goddess the same with Chloris the Wife of Zephyrus (c), mentioned by Ovid; but the Historians agree that she was a celebrated Roman Courtezan, who having amassed a considerable Fortune by her profession, made the Roman People her Heirs, on Condition that certain Games, called Floralia, might be annually celebrated on her Birth Day. The Senate, to give a Gloss to so infamous a Prostitution of Religion, pretended this Festival was designed in honour of Flora, a certain Sabine Goddess, who presided over Flowers. These Sports were held in the Campus Martius, and proclaimed by Sound of Trumpet. No Women appeared at them, but the most immodest of the Sex [d]. Yet when Cato, during his Censorship, came to behold them, they suspended the ceremonies through shame, till he thought fit to withdarw; such an influence had the Virtue of one Man over a corrupt and dissolute Multitude.

[a] To shew that no force or violence should be used in settling mutual Boundaries.
[b] Ovid Fasti Lib II.
[c] Ovid Fasti.
[d] Juvenal, Sat. VI.

Flora's Image, in the Temple of Caſtor and Pollux was dreſſed in a cloſe Habit, holding in her Hands the Flowers of Peas and Beans; for at the Celebration of her Rites the Ædiles ſcattered theſe and other Pulſe amongſt the People [a]. The modern Poets and Painters have ſet off her charms in a more laviſh, Manner, and not without Reaſon, ſince no part of Nature affords ſuch innocent and exquiſite entertainment to the Sight and Smell, as the variety which adorns, and the Odours which embalm the floral World.

CHAP. LVIII. Of POMONA and VERTUMNUS]

THE Goddeſs Pomona was a Latian Nymph, whom that Nation honoured as a tutelar Deity of Orchards and Fruit Trees. Vertumnus (the Proteus of the Roman Ritual) [b] was the God of Tradeſmen, and from the Power he had of aſſuming any ſhape, was believed to preſide over the Thoughts of Mankind. His Feſtivals called Vertumnalia, were celebrated in October.

Vertumnus his courtſhip makes one of the moſt elegant and entertaining ſtories in Ovid [c]. Under the diſguiſe of an old Woman he viſited the Gardens of Pomona, whom he found employed in looking after her Plantations. He artfully praiſes the beauty of her Fruit, and commends the care which produced it. Thence from the view of the Vine, ſupported by the Elm, he inſinuates to her the neceſſity and pleaſure of a married Life. The Goddeſs heard all his eloquence with an indifferent Ear. Her Heart remained untouched till throwing off his diſguiſe, the God aſſumed his youthful beauty, and by his Form ſoon gained the Goddeſs's conſent.

[a] See Valerius Maximus, Lib. II.
[b] Becauſe of the Turns or Fluctuations to which Trade is ſubject.
[c] Ovid, Lib. XIV. 622.

Some imagine Vertumnus an Emblem of the Year; which though it assumes different Dresses, according to the different Seasons, is at no time so agreeable as in Autumn, when the Harvest is crowned, and the richest Fruits appear in their full perfection and lustre. The Historians say, that this God was an antient Tuscan Prince, who first taught his subjects to plant Orchards, and to graft and prune fruit trees; whence he is said to have married Pomona.

Both these Deities are unknown to the Greeks, and are honoured only by the Romans.

CHAP. LIX.   Of the Lares and Penates, and Genii.

THE Lares were the Offspring of Mercury. The Nymph Lara having offended Jupiter, by disclosing some of his intrigues to Juno, that Deity ordered her tongue to be cut out, and banished her to the infernal mansions. Mercury, who was appointed to conduct her into exile, ravished her by the way, and she brought forth the Lares (a).

These Deities not only presided over the Highways and the Conservation of the publick safety, but also over private Houses, in most of which the Romans had a particular place called Lararium, where were deposited the Images of their domestic Gods, the statues of their Ancestors, and the Lares.

Their Festival, called Compitalia, was celebrated in January, in the open Streets and Roads. At first Boys were sacrificed to them, but that savage custom was soon disused, and Images of Wool and Straw (b), with the first Fruits of the Earth, Wine, Incense, and Garlands of Flowers were the Offerings. When the Roman Youth laid aside the Bulla, (an Ornament

---

[a] Ovid Fast. Lib. ii.
(b) They hung up as many Images as there were Persons of all Sexes and Ages in the Family, and a woollen Ball for every Servant.

they

they conftantly wore (a) till fourteen Years of Age]
they confecrated or hung it up to the Lares, who were
regarded as infernal as well as domeftic Deities.

The Antients fuppofed, (according to fome Authors) that the Souls of Men after Death became a
kind of Demons, called Lemures [b]. Thefe they
fubdivided into claffes, the one benevolent and friendly to Mankind, which they termed Lares; the other,
who being wicked during Life, retained a malicious
Difpofition in their difembodied State, they ftyled
Larvæ.

The Lares were reprefented as young Boys with
Dogs Skins about their Bodies (c), and with their
Heads covered, which was a fign of that Freedom and
Liberty which men ought to enjoy in their own Houfes. They had always the Image of a Dog near them,
to denote their Fidelity in preferving the Places allotted to their charge, on which account this Animal
was peculiarly confecrated to them. Some confound
thefe with the Penates and Genii.

CHAP. LX. Of the PENATES.

THE Penates (d) were the Deities who prefided
over new born Infants. The antient Hetrufci
called them Confentes, or Complices, though otheis
make of them four of the Dii Majores (e). But there
were three Claffes or Ranks of them: Thofe who
prefided over Empires and States (g); who had the

(a) The Bulla was a golden Ornament fhaped like a Heart, but
Hollow.

(b) So called from Romus, Brother of Romulus, whofe Ghoft
haunted his Brother. The Lemuralia were celebrated in the middle of May, during which it was unlawful to Marry.

[c] Some fay the Imiges were like Dogs.

[c] So called, from Penus, within, either becaufe they prefide over our Lives, or were placed in the innermoft Parts of the
Houfe.

[e] Viz. Jupiter, Juno, Minerva and Vefta. Some drop
Vefta: Others make them only Two, Neptune and Apollo: O-
thers, Cœlum and Terra

[g] Virgil, AEneid III. 148.

Protection

Protection of Cities; who took the Care or Guardi-
anship of private Families, and were called the leſſer
Penates [a].

These Domeſtic Gods were placed in the utmoſt
Receſs of the Houſe, thence called Penetrale [b].—
Dardanus brought them from Samothracia to Troy,
whence, on the Deſtruction of that City, Æneas tranſ-
ported them to Italy.   They were reckoned ſo ſacred
that the expreſſion of driving a Man from his Penates
[c] was uſed to ſignify his being proſcribed or expelled his Country.

Dionyſius of Halicarnaſſus, Lib. 1. ſays, that he had
ſeen them at Rome under the Figure of two young
men ſitting, with Spears in their Hands.

CHAP. LXI.   Of the Genii.

SOME do not diſtinguiſh between theſe and the
Penates, or Lares; but they were very different.
The Antients aſſigned to every Thing its Guardian or
peculiar Genius; Cities, Groves, Fountains, Hills,
were all provided with Keepers of this Kind, and to
each Man they allotted no leſs than two, one Good,
the other Bad (d), who attended him from the Cradle
to the Grave.   The Greeks called them Dæmons.—
They were named Præſtites, from their ſuperinten-
ding human Affairs

The Sacrifices offered theſe Divinities were Wine
(e) and Flowers, to which they joined incenſe, parched Wheat, and Salt.   Sometimes the Victim was a
Swine [g], though Animal offerings were not uſual to
them.   The Genii were repreſented under various
Figures, ſuch as thoſe of Boys, Girls, old Men, and

[a] AEneid VIII. 543.
[b] See Horace, Lib. IV. Ode 4. 26.
[c] Virgil; AEneid iv. 21.
[d] Horace, Lib. ii. Epiſt. 2.
[e] Perſius, Sat. vi.
(g) Some aſſert no Blood was ſuffered to be ſpilt in their Sacrifices.

even

even Serpents. Thefe Images were crowned with Plane Tree Leaves, a Tree confecrated to the Genii.

By Genius is meant the active Power or Force of Nature, from whence the Nuptial Bed is ftiled Genial, and the fame Epithet given to all occafions wherein focial Joys and Pleafures are felt. Hence alfo the Expreffions of indulging our Genius, that is, living happily, or according to our inclinations, confulting our Genius, for examining how far our Capacity extends, and the Term of a great Genius for an exalted or comprehenfive Mind. The later Romans in the degenerate Days of the State, introduced the fervile Flattery of fwearing by the Genii of their Emperors, and the Tyrant Caligula put feveral to death for refufing to take the Oath.

CHAP. LXII. Of Isis, Osiris, and Orus.

THESE Three have been much fpoken of already, as having given Rife to almoft all the different Divinities of Greece and Rome. Ifis is faid to have been the fifter of Ofiris [a], the Daughter of Saturn, and a Native of Egypt. She married her Brother, and fhared his Throne. They governed with great Equity and Wifdom, civilizing their fubjects, and inftructing them in Hufbandry and other ufeful Arts. Thefe inftructions were delivered in Verfe, and were called the Poems of Ifis [b].

Ofiris, having conferred the greateft benefits on his own Subjects, made the neceffary difpofition of his Affairs, committing the Regency to Ifis, and fet out with a Body of Forces in order to civilize the reft of Mankind. This he performed more by the Power of Perfuafion, and the foothing Arts of Mufick and Poetry, than by the terror of his Arms. He marched firft into Ethiopia; thence to Arabia and India. Having traverfed Afia, he croffed the Hellefpont, and fpent

[a] Diodor. Sic. l. 1.
[b] Plato, de leg. Dialog. 2.

fome

some time in Europe. Returning to Egypt, he was
slain by his Brother Typhon; of whom we have spoken sufficiently in the Chapter of the Giants.

When the news of this reached Coptus, where Isis
then was, she cut her Hair, and in deep Mourning
went every where in search of the dead Body; which
she found at length, and concealed it at Butus. But
Typhon hunting by Moonlight found it there and
tore it into many pieces, which he scattered abroad.
Isis then traversed the Lakes and watery places, in a
boat made of the Papyrus, seeking the mangled limbs
of Osiris: Where she found one, there she buried it.
Hence the many Tombs ascribed to Osiris. Thus Plutarch. But Diodorus Siculus says that she joined the
Fragments, embalmed and buried them at Memphis;
prevailing on the Egyptian Priests to promote his Deification, in consideration of a third part of the Kingdom given to them.

Isis afterwards, with the assistance of her Son Orus,
vanquished Typhon; reigned happily over Egypt to
her death, and was also buried at Memphis. At Bu-
siris a most superb Temple was raised to her. She was
succeeded by her son Orus, who completed the Reign
of the Gods and Demigods in Egypt.

To do the greater Honour to these their Favourites,
the Egyptians made them to represent the objects of
their idolatrous Worship. The Attributes of Isis indeed, when exposed as the public sign of their Feasts,
differed according to the different Purposes to which
they applied the Figure. But at other times this Goddess was represented with a flowing Veil, having the
Earth under her Feet, her Head crowned with Towers (like the Phrygian Mother) the Emblem of Height
and Stability; and sometimes with upright Horns,
equally expressive of Dominion and Power; next
to these the Crescent; then the Sun; and above all,
expanded Wings. She has also Wings, and a Quiver on her shoulders. Her left Hand holds a Cornucopia, her right a throne charged with the cap and
sceptre of Osiris, and sometimes a flaming Torch;
and her Right Arm is entwined by a Serpent. The

Imagi

Imagination of the Reader will prefently conceive this
to be the Symbol of the Æther, the natural Parent
and Spirit of the Univerfe, comprehending and pervading the whole Creation. As fuch fhe is eafily confounded with Nature, which is defined by Balbus in
Cicero [a] to be " That which contains and fuftain
" the whole World." In Herodotus, fhe is the fame
with Ceres; in Diodorus, with Luna, and Ceres and
Juno; in Plutarch, with Minerva, Proferpine, Luna,
Thetys. By Apuleius, fhe is called the Mother of the
Gods, and is the fame with Minerva, Venus, Diana,
Proferpine, Ceres, Juno, Bellona, Hecate, Rhamnufia;
hence termed fometimes murionumos, or " The Goddefs "of a thoufand Names." Being a female Figure,
and thus principally honoured, fhe was denominated
Ifis [b].

So likewife in Herodotus, Ofiris and Bacchus are the
fame; in Diodorus, Sol, Ofiris, Serapis, Dionyfius,
Pluto, Ammon, Jupiter, Pan; in Plutarch, Sol, Ofiris, Pluto, Bacchus, Serapis, Apis, Oceanus, Sirius.
Hence we fee him in Gems with a radiated Crown and
a Bafket on his Head, having the Horns of Ammon;
and in his Hand a Trident entwined by a Serpent. He
is the great Emblem of the Solar Body.

Orus is the Symbol of Light, as the Name im-
ports [c]; and is generally figured as a winged Boy,
ftanding between Ofiris and Ifis. He is the Herws of
the Greeks, and the Cupid of the Romans: The Son
of Ofiris and Ifis, whofe paffion for each other is faid
to have commenced in the Womb, where they embraced; and Orus was the Fruit of this early Conjunction. The whole containing this fimple Truth,
that Light, " has began to flow from the Body of the
" Sun, from its firft Exiftence, thro' the Midft of
" Æther." But thefe themfelves were but natural Emblems. Plutarch therefore refers us higher: affirming, that Ofiris fignifies the active Principle, or the

[a] Natura eft quæ contineat mundum omnem eumque tuea-
tur. De Nat Deor. l. 2.
[b] Or Ifha the Woman, Kat' exochen.
[c] From Aor, Light.

Qmoft

moſt Holy being; Iſis the Wiſdom or Rule of his Operation; Orus the firſt Production of his Power [a], the Model or Plan by which he produced every Thing, or the Archetype of the World [b].

EXPLANATION

Of the three folloinw g Plates of Isis, Osiris, and Orus.

THESE three following Plates, viz. of Iſis, Oſiris, and Orus, were taken originally from the Bembine or Iſiac Table in the Bodleian Library. This Table or Altar Plate is of Braſs, full of Hieroglyphics inlaid in Silver and Enamel, which conſtitute an Epitome of the Egyptian Theology. It has been deſcribed, copied and elaborately explained by the learned Jeſuit, Athanaſius Kircher, in his OEdipus Ægyptiacus, vol. 3. p. 80, & ſeq Romæ 1654. 7 Hor. Apoll.

In this of Iſis, the Top Cornice over her abounds with Flames, diffuſed like riſing Serpents, indicating Light and Life ſupernal and diſtant from the Contagion of groſs Matter. In thoſe underneath, is the Circle with expanded Wings, the emblem of Æther. The Architraves are ſupported by two Columns, with alternate ſquare Diviſions of black and white, crowned with the Head of Iſis. At ſome diſtance on the Outſides are two Pilaſters, decorated with Flowers, from which riſe two Aſpics, Symbols of Warmth and Moiſture conjoin'd, the ſecondary Cauſe of Life. In the Midſt of this magnificent Throne is the Goddeſs ſeat-

[a] De Iſid. and Oſirid. p. 354. See Ramſay's Theology of the Pagans.

[b] The Bull Apis was the Subſtitute of Oſiris; the Name of the latter Sor, or Sur, ſignifying a Bull, and Apis, the moſt Mighty. But the Bull Apis had particular Marks; and they added, that the Apis was animated by the Soul of Oſiris. The Greeks gave the Article and the Termination to the Word Oſiris, ö disguiſing it, that the Egyptians knew it not again.

ed

ed, to denote ftability and power. From the Navel
to the Foot her Habit is compofed of Wings, reprefenting the Velocity and Sublimity of the Æther, dif-
fufing itfelf univerfally. Thence upwards to the
Breaft, fhe is full of Paps, fhewing the body of the
World, or the univerfal Machine to be thence nourifhed and fupported. The Collars round her Neck
are the celeftial Orbs. The great variety of created
Beings, is aptly fignified by the party coloured Feathers of the African Hen, which covers her Head, in
a flying Attitude. The Bafket on the Back of this
Bird is the Emblem of Plenty, from which, on each
fide, fprings a leaf of the Egyptian Peach; and two
Horns, which point out the Crefcent Moon, inclofing a Circle marked with the Figure of the Scarabæ-
us, or Beetle, reprefenting the Sun.

The Gefture of her Left-Hand is commanding and
monitory; Her Right holds a fceptré of the flowering
Lotus. Her feat is adorned with the Figure of a Dog
fitting; to intimate her Dominion, according to Diodorus, refulgent in the Dog-Star. Within the Table
beneath the Throne, is the body of a Lion with the
Head of an Hawk, at his Forefeet a Canopus, fupporting upright wings; emblems of earth, fire, water,
and air. Over the Back of the Lion Hawk is the
Serpent, tranfmitted through a Circle, with expanded
wings, explained in the Chapter of Mercury, page 98
of whofe Caduceus thefe are the Attributes; and on
his Head a Crefcent, with the Sun over that. By the
fmall hieroglyphic Characters near the Ifis, fhe is faid
to be the fpirit of the World, penetrating all things
with the Eye of Divine Providence; and the Bond of
the fuperior and inferior worlds.

Explanation of the Plate of Ofiris.

Ofiris is reprefented here feated on a teffellated
Throne, to exprefs Dominion and the Viciffitudes of
Day and Night, which depend upon him. He has the
Head of an Hawk, a Bird from his ftrength of Vifion
by which he is faid to look fteady on the Meridian

Sun,

Sun, frequently depicted for the Symbol of the Solar Orb.
He is crowned with a Mitre, full of small Ores, to
intimate his Superiority over all the Globes. The
Gourd upon the mitre implies his Action and Influence
upon moisture, which, and the Nile particularly, was
termed by the Egyptians the Efflux of Osiris. The
lower part of his Habit is made of descending Rays,
and his Body is surrounded with Orbs. His Right
Hand is extended in a commanding Attitude, and his
Left holds a Thyrsus or Staff of the Papyrus, pointing out the principle of Humidity, and the Fertility
thence flowing under his Direction.

Explanation of the Figure of Orus.

The Figure of Orus, which is the Emblem of the
Solar Efflux, is Juvenile, as perpetually renewed and
renewing Youth and Vigour. He stands to denote
the unabated Activity of Light: And is habited in a
sort of network, composed of Globules of Light push-
ing and intersecting each other every way. He holds
a Staff crossed, expressing his Power in the four Elements; and on it the Head of the Houp, a transient
Bird, to represent the continual Change of Things
which he produces by those Elements. This Staff,
the Symbol of his Rule, is further adorned with a
Gnomon and a Trumpet, indicating Season and Sym-
metry, Harmony and Order. At his Back is a Trian-
gle, with a Globe fixed to it; shewing the regular Being of the world to depend upon him. The sides of
the Portal, which he stands in are decorated with the
celestial Bodies, and on the Top of it is the circle with
expanded Wings. The Hieroglyphics engraven on
the Base, call him, The Parent of vegetable Nature;
the Guardian of Moisture; Protector of the Nile; A-
verter of Evils: Governor of the Worlds; the many-
figured God; the Author of Plenty.

CHAP.

CHAP. LXIII.   Of the CABIRI.

BOCHART says, that the Cabiri were the Gods of the Phænicians, and observes justly, that Cabir signifies, both in the Hebrew and Arabic tongues, Great or Mighty; So that Cabiri, in the Plural, are THE GREAT or MIGHTY ONES He that ministred in holy Things went by the Appellation of Cohes, a manifest Corruption of the Hebrew, Cohen, a Priest, or Intercessor.

They are spoken of by the Names of Axieros, Axiocherfos and Axiocherfa; as three distinct persons: And in them our Author thinks that he has found Ceres, Proserpine and Pluto; the Abbe Pluche, Osiris, Orus, and Isis; others, Jupiter, Ceres, and Bacchus. To these, the Scholiast upon Apollonius has added a Fourth Casmilus or Cadmilus; the same, says he, is Hermes or Mercury, whom Varro declares to be only a Minister Attendant on the Cabiri.

Several Authors have confined the Appellation of Cabiri to Jupiter, Minerva and Juno. Nor is it at all improbable that these should have been so called in After-Ages, when the World in general had forsaken the worship of the Creator for that of the creature, and understood by these Terms those Things which must indeed be allowed the most proper and significant emblems of the Divine Personalities [a]: The Solar Fire being meant by Jupiter [b]; by Minerva, darting from the head of him, the Light thence springing; and by Juno, the Æther, (including the Air) the natural Representative of the SACRED SPIRIT.—— These are indeed the same with the Egyptian Osiris, Orus and Isis.

But in the earlier Times it was judged an act of irreverence to pronounce their Names; which was the Case of the Tetragrammaton with the Jews. They

[a] Sic Homines novere Deos, quos arduus Æther.
Occulit, & colitur pro Jove formi Jovis.   OVID.
[b] Macrob. l. 1. c. 23. Plato in Phæd. Orpheus, &c.

W. C

were therefore only ſpoken of by the general Denomination of Dioſcouroi, or ſprung from Jove; a title afterwards conferred upon Caſtor and Pollux.

Even Children were initiated into theſe myſteries, and thought by their Parents to be afterwards ſecure from Dangers of any Kind. Such as were permitted to partake of the Ceremonies, were wont to aſſemble in a Wood or Grove, which was held ſacred and became a ſanctuary. By the Initiation men were believed to become more holy, juſt and pure: and it is ſaid that none ever duly performed the ceremonies, without being amply rewarded for his Piety.

As to what is ſaid of a Man's being ſacrificed in theſe Myſteries upon ſome extraordinary occaſion; I cannot find the Aſſertion to be well-grounded. Julius Firmicus intimates, that the Cabiri were three Brothers, one of whom was ſlain by the other Two, and then deified; and ſpeaks of his Worſhippers, as holding up their bloody Hands to the once bleeding; which may refer either to their Hands being embrued in the blood of the ordinary Victims, or to the Warlike Diſpoſition of that conquering People (Macedonians). But, if the Thing be Fact, it muſt have proceeded from an aſſurance, that ſuch a Sacrifice was one Day or other to promote the Happineſs of Mankind (c).

CHAP. LXIV. Of the inferior DEITIES attending Mankind from their Birth to their Death.

IT would be a Taſk almoſt endleſs to enter into a minute Detail of the inferior Deities acknowledged by the Greeks and Romans. The Names of theſe viſionary Beings occur ſo ſeldom in the Claſſic Authors, that it is ſufficient barely to mark their Denominations.

[c] This was alſo the leading Opinion of the Britiſh Druids; Pro Vita Hominis niſi Vita Hominis reddatur, non poſſe aliter Deorum immortalium numen placari arbitrantur. Cæſ Comm. l. 6. c. 15.

During

During Pregnancy, the tutelar Powers were the God Pilumnus (a), and the Goddesses Intercidona (b), and Deverra (c). The signification of these names seems to point out the Necessity of Warmth and Cleanliness to Persons in this condition.

Besides the superior Goddesses Juno Lucina, Diana, Ilythia and Latona, who all presided at the Birth, there were the Goddesses Egeria (d), Prosa (e), and Manageneta (g), who with the Dii Nixii (h), had all the care of Women in Labour.

To Children, Janus performed the Office of Door-keeper or Midwife, and in this quality was assisted by the Goddess Opis, or Ops (i); Cunia rocked the cradle, while Carmenta sung their Destiny; Levana lifted them from the Ground (k); and Vegitanus took care of them when they cried; Rumina [l] watched them while they suckled; Potina furnished them with Drink; and Educa with Food or Nourishment; Ossilago knit their Bones; and Carna (m) strengthened their Constitution; Nundina (n) was the Goddess of Children's Purification; Statilinus or Statanus, instructed them to walk, and kept them from falling Fabulinus learnt them to prattle; the Goddess Paven-

---

[a] Either from Pilum, a Pestle; or from Pello, to drive away, because he procured a safe Delivery.

[b] She taught the Art of cutting Wood with a Hatchet to makes Fires.

[c] The Inventress of Brooms.

[d] From casting out the Birth.

[e] Aulus Gellius, cap. xix.   [g] AElian.

[h] From Enitor, to struggle. See Ausonius, Idyll. 12.

[i] Some make her the same with Rhea or Vesta.

[k] Amongst the Romans the Midwife always laid the Child on the Ground, and the Father, or Somebody he appointed, lifted it up; hence the Expression of tollere Liberos, to educate Children

[l] This Goddess had a Temple at Rome, and her offerings were Milk.

[m] On the Kalends of June Sacrifices were offered to Carna, of Bacon and Bean-Flower Cakes; whence they were called Fabariæ.

[n] Boys were named always on the 9th Day after their birth Girls on the 8th.

tia preserved them from Frights (a); and Camœna learnt them to sing.

Nor was the Infant, when grown to riper Years, left without his protectors; Juventus was the God of Youth; Agenoria excited men to action, and the Goddesses Stimula and Strenua inspired courage and Vivacity; Horta (b) inspired the Love of Fame or Glory; and Sentia gave them sentiments of Probity and Justice; Quies was the Goddess of Repose or Ease [b]; and Indolena, or Laziness, was deify'd by the name of Murcia [d]; Vacuna protected the Idle; Adeona and Abeona secured People in going abroad and returning [e], and Vibilia, if they wandered, was so kind to put them in the right Way again; Fessonia refreshed the Weary and Fatigued; and Meditrina healed the sickly [g]; Vitula was the Patroness of mirth and frolick [h]; Volupia the Goddess who bestowed Pleasure [i]; Orbona was addressed, that Parents might not lose their Offspring; Pellonia averted Mischiefs and Dangers: and Numeria taught People to cast and keep Accounts; Angerona [k] cured the Anguish or Sorrows of the Mind; Hæres-Martia secured Heirs the Estates they expected; and Stata, or Statua Mater secured the Forum, or Market Place, from Fire; even the Thieves had a Protectress in Laverna (l), Averruncus prevented sudden Misfortunes; and Consus was always disposed to give good advice to such as wanted it, Volumnus in-

[a] From Paverem avertendo.
[b] She had a Temple at Rome, which always stood open.
[c] She had a Temple without the Walls.
[d] Murcia had her Temple on Mount Aventine.
[e] From Abeo to go away, and Adeo to come.
[g] The Festival of this Goddess was in September, when the Romans drank new Wine mixed with old by way of Physick.
[h] From Vitulo, to leap or dance.
[i] From Voluptas.
[k] In a great Murrain which destroyed their Cattle, the Romans invoked this Goddess, and she removed the Plague.
[l] The Image was a Head without a Body, Horace mentions her, Lib. I. Epist XVI. 60. she had a Temple without the Walls, which gave name to the Porta Lavernalis.

spired

spired Men with a Disposition to do well ; and Honorius raised them to Preferment and Honours.

Nor was the Marriage State without its peculiar
Defenders. Five Deities were esteemed so necessary,
that no Marriages were solemnized without asking their
Favours : these were Jupiter-perfectus, or the Adult,
Juno, Venus, Suadela (a), and Diana

Jugatinus ty'd the Nuptial Knot, Domiducus usher-
ed the Bride home; Domitius took Care to keep her
there, and prevent her gadding abroad ; Manturna
preserved the conjugal Union entire; Virginensis (b)
loosed the Bridal Zone or Girdle; Viriplaca was a
propitious Goddess ready to reconcile the married
Couple in Case of any accidental Differences; Matuta was the Patroness of Matrons, no Maid Servant being suffered to enter her Temple ; Mena and Februa
(c) were the Goddesses who regulated the Female
Katamenia; the Goddess Vacuna (d) is mentioned by
Horace (e) as having her Temple at Rome ; the Rus-
ticks celebrated her Festival in December, after the
Harvest was got in (f);

The Antients assigned the particular Parts of the
Body to peculiar Deities ; the Head was sacred to Jupiter, the Breast to Neptune, the Waist to Mars, the
Forehead to Genius, the Eyebrows to Juno, the Eyes
to Cupid, the Ears to Memory, the Right Hand to Fides
or Veritas, the Back to Pluto, the Reins to Venus,
the Knees to Misericordia, or Mercy, the Legs to
Mercury, the Feet to Thetis, and the Fingers to Minerva (g).

The

____

(a) The Goddess of Eloquence, or Persuasion, who had always
a great Hand in the Success of Courtship.

(b) She was also called Cinxia Juno.

(c) From Februo, to purge.

(d) She was an old Sabine Deity. Some make her the same
with Ceres ; but Varro imagines her to be the Goddess of Victory, the Fruits of which are Ease and Repose.

(e) Horace, Lib. I. Epist. X. 49.

(f) Ovid Fast. Lib VI.

(g) From this Distribution arose, perhaps, the Scheme of our
modern Astrologers, who assign the different Parts of the Body

to

The Goddess who presided over Funerals was Libitina (a) in whose Temple at Rome, the Undertakers furnished all the Neceffaries for the Interment of the Poor or Rich; all dead bodies were carried through the Porta Libitina, and the Rationes Libitinæ, mentioned by Suetonius, very nearly anfwer our Bills of Mortality.

C H A P. LXV.   Of the inferior Rural DEITIES.

THE Romans were not content with the great Variety of Gods, which filled their Ritual. They were daily inventing new Deities of an inferior Order, to anfwer the demands of Superftition and increafe the Kalender. Rufina thus became the Name for a Goddefs, who prefided over the Country in general. Collina had the Charge of the Hills, and Vallona the Infpection of the Vallies; Hippona was the Guardian of Stables and Horfes; and Bubona took Care of the Oxen; Seia, or Sogetia watched the Seed till it fprouted; and Runcina weeded the young Corn; Sarritor was the God of Sowing, and Occator of Harrowing; Robigus kept the Blights or Mildew away (b); Stercutius manured or dunged the Ground; Nodotus, or Nodofus took Care to ftrengthen and knit the ftalks of the Corn; Volufia watched the Blade; Patelina unfolded the Ear; Lactucina filled it; and Matura brought it to due Ripenefs; Hoftilina produced a plentiful Crop; and Tutelina took Care to reap and get it fafe in; Pilumnus kneaded the Bread;

to the celeftial Conftellations, or Signs of the Zodiac; as the Head to Aries, the Neck to Taurus, the Shoulders to Gemini, the Heart to Cancer, the Breft to Leo. the Belly to Virgo, the Reins to Libra, the Secets to Scorpio, the Thighs to Sagotarius the Knees to Capricorn, the Legs to Aquarius, and the Feet to Pifces.

(a) Some confound this Goddefs with Proferpine, others with Venus.

(b) His Feftival called Robigalia, was celebrated in the begining of May.

and Fornax [a] baked it: Mellona was the Goddess
of Honey; but the Truth is, these fanciful Deities
are so little mentioned in Authors, that we may call
them the Refuse or Scum of the Gods.

CHAP. LXVI.   Of THEMIS, ASTREA, and NE-
MESIS.

THEMIS was the Daughter of Cœlum and Terra, and the Goddess of Laws, Ceremonies
and Oracles. Jupiter consulted her in the Giant's
War, and afterwards espoused her; she instructed
Deucalion how to re-people the World after the Deluge, and was rather indeed a moral than an historical
Deity, as she signifies that Power which rewards Virtue and punishes Vice.

To Jupiter, Themis, besides a numerous Offspring
already spoken of, bore the Goddess Astræa, who resided on Earth during the Golden Age, and inspired
Mankind with the Principles of Justice and Equity;
but as the World grew corrupted, she returned to
Heaven [c] and become that Constellation in the Zodiac, which is called Virgo. This Goddess is represented with her eyes bound or blinded, having a
Sword in one Hand, and in the other a pair of ballan-
ces equally poised.

Nemesis was the daughter of Jupiter and Necessity
[c]. She had the Title of Adrastea, beeause A-
drastus, King of Argos, first raised an Altar to her.
She had a magnificent Temple at Rhamnus in Attica,
with a Statue. She is represented with a stern Aspect,
having in one Hand a Whip, in the other a Pair of
Scales.

[a] Ovid Fasti, Lib. VI.
[b] Terras Astræa reliquit.
[c] Others say of Oceanus and Nox.

CHAP.

CHAP. XII. Of the Goddefs FORTUNA, or FORTUNE, and the other VIRTUES and VICES deified by the Antients.

FORTUNE was thought to have fo great a fhare in human Affairs, that it is no Wonder the Romans made her a Goddefs. Juvenal, however, is not a little fevere upon his countrymen (a) for this choice; and Horace exprefles, if not an abfolute Contempt for (b), yet at beft a very mean Opinion of this Deity. But whatever Sentiments the Philofophers or Poets might entertain of her, they did not leffen her in the Sight of the Vulgar, who paid her much Veneration.

This Goddefs had a variety of Epithets; fhe was termed Regia, and Aurea, from an Image of her ufually kept in the Apartment of the Cæfars. In the Capital fhe was worfhipped by the Title of Bona, but her Temple at the Efquilia was confecrated by the Name of Mala. She was called Confervatrix, Manens, and Felix, in antient Infcriptions, to denote the Happinefs fhe beftows. Domitian confecrated her a Chapel by the Style of Redux, and in fome antient monuments fhe is called Stata. The Names of Barbata and Pan were given her by Survius Tullius, who dedicated a fhrine to her [c]: fhe was alfo termed Cæca, not unjuftly, on Account of the injudicious diftribution of her Favours. She was honoured at Rome by the Title of Fortuna Equeftris (d). In a Temple fhe had near that of Venus, fhe bore the Appellations of Mafcula and Virilis. At other Times fhe was named Mammofa (e), Primogenia (g), and

[a] Satyr X.
[b] Lib. I. Ode XXXIV. 14
[b] He alfo called her Obfequens, from her favouring his wifhes Horace calls her Sæva on a quite contrary account.
[d] This Temple was erected in purfuance of a Vow of the Prætor Q. Fulvius Flaacus, for a Victory he obtained in Spain, by means of his Cavalry.
[e] Either from her having large Breafts, or the Plenty fhe fupplies.
[g] From her giving Birth to the City and Empire.

Privata,

Privata, or Propria (a). In the quality of Fortuna-Virgo, Coats of young Children were offered to her before they put them on ; and she was stiled Viscata, or Viscosa (b), on account of her alluring or attracting people by her deceitful kindness.

The principal Temple of this Goddess was at Præ-neste, whence she was called Præneftina. She is usually represented blind, standing on a wheel in a moving Attitude, and holding a Cornucopia, from whence she pours Wealth and all the Emblems of Prosperity. Horace has given a very masterly Picture of her in an Ode to Mæcenas (c).

She is sometimes figured in a flying Attitude, with broad Wings, sounding a Trumpet, and her flying Robe wrought over with Eyes, Ears and Tongues, to denote the Surprize, Attention, and Discourse she excites. Virgil (d) has given an inimitable Description of her, nor does Ovid fall much short of him [e].

Peace is a blessing so universally esteemed, that it is no wonder if she was deified. The Athenians (according to Plutarch) erected her an Altar with her Statue, attended by that of Pluto the God of Riches, to shew that she was the source of Plenty. At Rome she had a magnificent temple in the Forum (g), which was consumed by fire in the Reign of Commodus.

On Medals, this Goddess is represented before an Altar, setting Fire with a Torch in her left Hand to a Pile of Arms, and with the other holding an Olive branch. Behind her, on a Column, appears the Image of a naked Boy or Man extending his Arms in a rejoicing Posture (h). The Poets generally introduce her

[a] From her favouring particular Persons. These two last Appellations were given her by Servius Tullius, a very great Admirer of her Divinity.

[b] From Viscus, Birdlime. Hence Seneca says, Beneficia sunt viscosa, Obligations are catching.

[c] Horace, Lib. III. Ode XXIX 49.

[d] Virgil Æneid I.

[e] Ovid Met. XII. 42. 63.

[g] Begun by Claudius, and finished by Vespasian.

[h] The Legend of this Medal, which was struck by Vespa-

sian

her in company with the moſt ſhining Virtues [a].—
And Virgil repreſents her as the common Wiſh of
Mankind [b]. Claudian has compoſed her Panegyrick
in a very diſtinguiſhed manner. Sometimes ſhe appears like a Matron holding a bunch or ears of corn,
and crowned with Olive, or Roſes.

The Goddeſs Concordia or Concord, was another
Divinity of the Romans. At the Requeſt of his Mother Livia, Widow of Auguſtus, a Temple was dedicated to her by Tiberius at Rome. She had ſeveral o-
ther magnificent Temples ; in one of theſe were de-
poſited the rich ſpoils of the Temple of Jeruſalem.

Virtue and Honour had their Temples at Rome.
That to Virtue was erected by M. Marcellus (c), and
was the only paſſage to the Temple of Honour, to
ſhew that worthy actions were the true foundation
of laſting fame. The ſacrifices to Honour were performed by the Prieſts bare headed.

Virtue was repreſented like an elderly Matron ſitting on a ſquare ſtone ; in antient Medals they appear
jointly: However, upon ſome of Gordian and Nu-
menian, ſhe is found in the figure of an old Man with
a Beard.

Fides, or Faith, had a Temple near the Capitol,
founded by Numa Pompilius. No Animals were offered, or Blood ſpilt in her ſacrifices ; during the performance of her Rites, her Prieſts were cloathed in
white Veſtments, and their Heads and Hands covered with Linen Cloth ; to ſhew that Fidelity ought to
be ſecret. Her Symbol was a white Dog, and a figure where two women are joining Hands, repreſents
the Goddeſs.

Hope is another of the Paſſions deify'd by the Romans. She had a Temple in the Herb-Market, which
was conſumed by Lightening. On Medals ſhe appears

ſion on the Conqueſt of Judæa, is Paci Orbis Terrarum   On a
Medal of his Son Titus, ſhe is ſeen with a Palm in one Hand and
a Sceptre in the other, the Inſcription Pax AEterna.
[a] Horace, Carmen See 57.
[b] AEneid XI. 362.
[c] Son to Auguſtus

in a standing attitude, with her Left-Hand holding up
lightly her loose Robes, and leaning on her Elbow;
in her Right she has a Plate, on which is placed a Ci-
borium, or Cup, fashion'd like a Flower, with this in-
scription, Spes, P R. the Hope of the Roman People
[a] In the modern Statues and Paintings, her Cha-
racteristick is a Golden Anchor.

Piety, or filial affection, had a Chapel at Rome, consecrated by the Duumvir Attilius, Glabrio, on a remarkable Occasion: " A man being sentenced to
" hard imprisonment, his Daughter, who was then a
" Nurse, daily visited him, and was strictly search'd
" by the Gaoler, to see she brought no Food to the
" Prisoner. At last a discovery was made, that she
" supported him with her Milk. This instance of
" Piety gained her Father's freedom. They were both
" afterwards supported at the publick expence, and
" the place was consecrated to this Goddess [b]."

Pudicitia, or Chastity, was honoured at Rome under two names. Into the Temple of Pudicitia Patricia
none were admitted but Ladies of noble Birth. Virginia the Daughter of Aulus having married a Plebi-
an, so offended these, that they excluded her their af-
semblies: Upon which Virginia calling a meeting of
the Plebeian Matrons dedicated a Chapel to this Goddess by the name of Pudicitia Plebeia (c). Her speech
on this occasion was truly great. " I dedicate, says she,
" this Altar to Pudicitia Plebeia, and desire you will
" adore Chastity as much as the Men do Honour;
" and I wish that this Temple may be frequented by
" purer Votaries (if possible) than that of Pudicitia
" Patricia." In both these Temples no Matron was
permittted to sacrifice unless she had an unblemish'd
Character, and was but once married. In Medals this
Deity is represented under the Figure of a Woman
veiled, pointing with the Fore Finger of her Right-

[a] The Reverse is a Head of Adrion.
[b] Pliny's Nat. Hist. Lib. VII cap. 36.
[c] All Matrons who married but once, were honoured with
the Corona Pudicitiæ, or Crown of Chastity.

R 2

Hand

Hand to her Face, to fignify that fhe had no Reafon to blufh.

Mercy, or Clemency had an Altar at Athens, erected by the Kindred of Hercules. At Rome was a Temple dedicated to the clemency of Cæfar (a). Both the Romans and Greeks gave the name of Afylum to the Temples each had erected to this Goddefs.

Truth, according to Plutarch, was the Daughter of Saturn and Time, and the Mother of Virtue, and was reprefented as a beautiful young Virgin of a proper Stature, modeftly clad in a Robe, whofe Whitenefs refembled that of Snow. Democritus, to give an idea of the difficulty of her being found, fays that fhe is concealed in the bottom of a well.

Liberty was fo much the delight of the Romans, that it was but natural for them to imagine her a Goddefs, and to confecrate to her Temples and Altars.— She was reprefented in the Form of a Virgin cloathed in White, holding a Sceptre in her Right-Hand, and a Cap in her Left.

Good Senfe or Underftanding, [Men] was honoured with an Altar in the Capitol, by M. Æmilius, and Atilius the Prætor erected her a Chapel.

Fauftitas, or the publick Felicity and Welfare, had many Altars, and was adored both by the Greeks and Romans; the former honour'd this Goddefs under the names of Endaimonia and Macaria. The Athenians confulting an Oracle on the fuccefs of a battle, were informed, that they fhould win the victory, if one of the Children of Hercules would fubmit to a voluntary death; on this Macaria, one of his daughters, kill'd herfelf, and the Athenians becoming victorious, paid her Adoration under the name of Felicity. She was reprefented in painting, as a Lady cloathed in a purple Veftment trimmed with filver, fitting on an Imperial Throne, and holding in one hand a Caduceus, and in the other a Cornucopia.

Victory was honoured by feveral Nations as a Goddefs. According to Hefiod, fhe was the daughter of

[a] This Temple was built by a Decree of the Senate, after the Death of Julius Cæfar.

Styx

Styx and Pallas ; she was painted by the Ancients in the Form of a Woman clad in Cloth of Gold, and is represented on some Medals with Wings, flying thro' the Air holding a Palm in one hand, and a Lawrel Crown in the other ; in others she is to be seen standing upon a Globe, with the same Crown and Branch of Palm.

The Goddess Salus, or Health, had a Temple at Rome near the Gate, from thence called Porta Salutaris, and as the Blessings she bestows are known to all, so no doubt but she had a great number of Votaries. She was represented by a woman sitting on a Throne, and holding a Globe in her Hand. Near her stood an Altar, with a Snake entwined round it. In this Temple was performed the Augurium Salutis, a Ceremony which Augustus revived from Desuetude: It was a day set apart annually, for enquiring of the Gods by Divination, whether they would allow the People to pray for Peace ? On this day, the Roman Armies were forbid to march or engage. It is worthy of Remark, that the Priests of this Temple had arrogated to themselves the sole Privilege of offering supplications for the Health of every Individual, as well as for the State.

The Good Genius was ador'd by the Greeks, and, according to Pausanias, had a Temple in the Road leading to Mount Mænalus. At the close of Supper a Cup was always offered him of Wine and Water, and call'd the Grace-Cup.

Wealth has such an Influence on the affairs of Life, that it has in all Ages been the Object of publick Worship, or of secret Idolatry. Thus the Romans deified both Plutus and Pecunia, or Money. Menander wittily observes on this subject ; " That if you " can possess this Deity, you may ask and have what " you please : Even the Gods themselves shall be at " your devotion.

Silence was, amongst the Romans, both a Male and Female Deity, by the names of Harpocrates and Angerona ; but the latter seems only to have been a Female Imitation of the former, whom they borrowed from the Egyptians. He was the Son of Isis, begotten by Osiris after his Death, and on that Account said to have been a weakly Child. His Statue was placed at some small distance from those of Osiris, Orus and Isis, with his finger on his Mouth; intimating to the Worshippers, that not a Word was to be said that those Deities had once been mortal. The Greeks and Romans appropriated to themselves this Symbol of Silence, but in general were ignorant of its original Intention.

Nor were these the only visionary Deities erected by the Heathens. Fear, Hope, Diseases, Calamities and even Vices, were honoured with a view of averting their Visitation, or allaying their noxious influences. Thus Febris, or the Fever, had her Altars at Rome. Hostilius Tullus vowed a Temple to the Goddesses Terror and Paleness. M. Marcellinus, after escaping a storm near Sicily, built a Chapel to the God Tempestas, without the gate of Capena. And Poverty and Art were both deified by the people of Godora because necessity is the Mother of Invention. Envy was a Goddess whose person and abode are inimitably described by Ovid (a).

Calumny had an Altar erected to her by the Athenians. We have a very remarkable Picture of this mischievous Goddess, as drawn by the hand of the great Apelles. Credulity, represented by a man with large open ears, invites this Deity to him, extending his Hand to receive her. Ignorance and Suspicion stand just behind him. Calumny (the principal Figure of the Piece) appears advancing, her Countenance ruffled with passion, holding in her left-hand a lighted torch, and with her right dragging along a Youth, who lifts up his hands supplicating the Gods. Just before her goes Envy pale and squinting. On her Right-Side are Fraud and Conspiracy. Behind her follows Repentance with her cloaths torn, and looking backwards on Truth, who slowly closes up the Rear [b]. Contumely and Impudence, were also

____
(a) Metam. Lib. II. 762.   [b] Lucian.

honoured

honoured by the Athenians under the figure of Partridges, esteemed a very bold Bird. Discord is reprefented as a Goddess by Petronius Arbiter, whose Defcription of her is worthy so masterly a Pencil: And Virgil has given us a Picture of Fury, a Deity much of the same ftamp. It is now time to clofe the particular account, and to proceed to a Confideration at large of the Heathen Theology.

A DIS-

A DISSERTATION

ON THE

THEOLOGY OF THE HEATHENS.

THE Religion of Mankind was at firſt One like the Object of it. But when the latter was changed, the Mode and Ceremonial of Worſhip continued ſtill the ſame: For Idolatry, that WORST of things, was but in its Origin, the corruption of true Religion which is the BEST? We are not therefore to wonder if we ſee the ſame uſage of Temples, Altars, Prieſts, Sacrifices, Firſt-fruits &c. common to the Patriarchs and Unbelievers. We even behold, in theſe and many other inſtances, the ſame religious cuſtoms amongſt the Heathens, which it pleaſed the divine Being to enforce the continuance of by the Moſaic Diſpenſation; a convincing argument that they muſt have been uncorrupt and innocent in their original.

Nor did Mankind in general loſe ſight of the original Object ſo ſoon, or ſo totally, as is commonly apprehended. Since we find amongſt the Eaſtern Nations, and indeed amongſt ſeveral of the Greeks and Romans, the moſt exalted notions of the Supreme Being, the Creator of Heaven and Earth.

According to the Egyptians (a), Eicton, or the firſt God, exiſted in his ſolitary Unity before all Beings. He is the fountain and original of every thing that either has Underſtanding, or is to be underſtood. He

[a] Jamblicus de Myſt. Egypt, Ed. Lugd. 1552. p. 153. 4.

is the firſt Principle of all Things, ſelf ſufficient, incomprehenſible, and the Father of all Eſſences. Hermes ſay likewiſe, that this ſupreme God has conſtituted another God, called Emeph. to be Head over all Spirits, whether ethereal, empyrean, or celeſtial; and that this ſecond God, whom he ſtyles the Guide, is a Wiſdom that transforms and converts into itſelf all ſpiritual Beings. He makes nothing Superior to this God Guide, except the firſt intelligent, and firſt Intelligible, who ought to be adored in Silence. He adds, that the Spirit which produceth all Things, has different Names, according to his different Properties and Operations; that he is called in the Egyptian Language Amoun, as he is wiſe; Ptha, as he is the Life of all Things, and Oſiris, as he is the Author of all Good [a].

Let us proceed to the Greeks, amongſt whom Orpheus claims the firſt place in Right of his Antiquity, and to whoſe theological Sentiments the Preference is always given by the early Writers in Favour of Chriſtiany.

" There is one unknown being, exalted above, and
" prior to, all Beings [b], the Author of all Things,
" even of the Æther, and of every Thing that is be
" low the Æther; this exalted being is LIFE, LIGHT
" and WISDOM: which three Names expreſs only
" One and the ſame Power, which drew all Beings,
" viſible and inviſible, out of nothing."

Thus alſo the divine Plato; " That which [c]
" gives Truth and Reality to Things known, and
" endues the Knower with the power of Underſtand
" ing: This call thou the Idea of the GOOD ONE,
" the Source of Wiſdom and Truth." But GOD is every where diſtinguiſhed throughout the Works of this illuſtrious Philoſopher as the BEAUTIFUL, the GOOD, the JUST ONE.

[a] See Ramſay's Theology, annex'd to Cyrus, 4to Ed. p. 14 and 17.

[b] Suid do Orph. p 352. & Cedrenus, p. 47.

[c] De Repub. lib. 6.

Would

Would you fee the Being and the Providence of God demonſtrated from the Order and Adminiſtration of the World? You will no where find it more convincingly than the Reaſoning of Balbus in Cicero; and from which Obſervations you muſt of Neceſſity draw the ſame Concluſion which he does, that [a] "All "Things in the World are wonderfully directed by a "divine Mind and Counſel, to the Safety and Con- "ſervation of the Whole."

Theſe Sentiments are alſo the Reſult of Seneca's Enquiries. "By Jove, ſays he [b], the wiſe Men amongſt the Ancients did not mean ſuch a One as we ſee in the Capitol and other Temples, but the Guardian and Ruler of the Univerſe, a MIND and SPIRIT, the Maſter and Artificer of this Mundane Fabric, whom every Title ſuits. Would you call him Fate? you would not err: For he it is on whom all things depend the CAUSE of CAUSES. Would you call him Providence? You are in the Right: For by his Wiſdom is the World directed; hence it moves unſhaken, and performs its every Office. Wou'd you call him Nature? 'Tis not amiſs; Since from him all Things proceed, and by his Spirit we live: Or the World? 'Tis well: For he is All in All, and exiſting by his own Power."

Innumerable are the Inſtances which might be brought from the Ancients to this purpoſe. But theſe may ſuffice. And from an attentive conſideration of theſe it will appear, that the Philoſophers endeavoured to eſtabliſh a particular Syſtem with Relation to the Origin of Idolatry, which tends very much to leſſen the ſuppoſed Abſurdity of it. They maintained [c] that the Idea which the wiſe Men of Antiquity had formed to themſelves of GOD, was that of a being ſuperior to whatever exiſts; of a SPIRIT preſent in all the Bounds of the Univerſe, who animates all, who is the Principle of Generation and communicates Fer-

[a] Sic undique omni Ratione concluditur, Mente Conſilioque Divino omnia in hoc Mundo ad ſalutem omnium conſervationemque admirabiliter adminiſtrari.   De Nat. Deor. l. 2. c. 53.
[b] Natural. Quæſt. l. 2. c. 45.
[c] See Banier's Mythology, Vol. I. p. 171.

tility to every Being, Of a FLAME, lively, pure, and always active: Of an INTELLIGENCE, infinitely wife; whole providen e continually watches and extends over all: In a Word, an Idea of a Being to whom they had given different Names anfwering to his fuperior Excellence; yet fuch as always bore the Stamp of that fupreme Right of Poffeflion, which is only inherent in the abfolute Lord, and in him from whom all Things flow.

It is, however, too fatally true to be denied that, as the corruption of the Heart of Man dilated and enlarged itfelf, a Difrelifh of Spiritual Things gradually came on, and the Mind grew more devoted to fenfible Objects. Of all created Things within his Profpect, the Sun was the moft glorious and the moft likely to engage his Attention firft, and next his Wonder and his Worfhip. Accordingly it had been confidered from the Beginning as the great or primary Emblem of the Divinity, being not only the moft beautiful of all Bodies in its appearance, but the moft beneficent in its Effects; the Regulator of the Seafons, and the natural Parent of Light and Fertility. Hence Plato [a] calls it the " The Offspring of the GOOD ONE, which " the GOOD ONE produced analogous to Himfelt " it is termed by others [b] " the Eye of Jove," and " The Mind of Jove, of Heaven, of the World " In fine, whoever will be at the Pains to confult Macrobius, may fee that the Figures of all the Heathen Deities were but fo many different Expreflions of the Qualities and Attributes of the Sun, or of the Seafons which depended on and were governed by him: to whom his Votaries afcribed Omnipotence, and whom in their Invocations they faluted as " The Power, " the Light, and the Spirit of the World [c]."

[a] De Repub. l. 6.
[b] Apuleius de Mundo, Macrobius Saturnal l. 1. cap. 17. ufque ad finem cap 23.
[c] Potentiam folis ad omnium poteftatum fummitatem referri indicant theologi; qui in facris hoc breviffima precatione demonftrant dicentes. Helie pantokrator kofmon præuma, kofmon dunamen, fofmonphos. Ibid. c. 23.

The

The Solar Body, before Writing, could not more properly be reprefented than by the Figure of a Circle; a fymbol fo plain and inoffenfive, that, one would think, it fhould not eafily be perverted to the ufes of Idolatry. It was accordingly fubftituted in Hieroglyphicks as the Artificial (its Principal the Sun being the great Natural) Emblem of the Divinity, and became the Figure of all the open Temples; the earlieft Places of Religious Worfhip. Thefe Circles or Difcs are the Sun-Images mentioned in Scripture (a), and are at this Day the Symbols of Royalty, Glory and Divinity: And it may be worth while perhaps to remark that the word from which this is fupplied (b), is ufed to fignify Idolatry in general, from the near Relation which it bears to the original object of it (c), whofe Derivative it is.

When religious Worfhip began to be transferr'd from the Divinity to his Emblem, from the Creator to the Creature; then that particular day of the Week which had ever been kept fecret to the Creator of all Things, began likewife to be fet apart and dedicated to the Honour of this Luminary, was thence termed Sunday, and continu'd to be had in efpecial Reverence above the reft. Hence celebrated by one of the moft ancient Writers, as " An holy Day, becaufe it was " the Birth-Day of Apollo, or the Sun (d)" Which indeed was fo far true, that it was the Commemoration of that day, on which the human Eye was firft bleffed with the profpect of that glorious Object. For it requires no extraordinary Sagacity, but only a little attention, however generally and unaccountably this point has been overlooked, to fee and be convinced that the firft Holy Seventh Day was the particular ftated day of the Chriftian Sabbath. It appears from the original Account of it, that the work of the Creation took up Six Days, and that the laft created Being was

[a] Hamminchem, Sun-Images.
(b) Hamen, Idolatry.   [c] Hamah the Sun.
[d] Hefiod.

Man

man; who was therefore in all probability formed on the evening of the Sixth Day. That which immediately succeeded was the First of Adam's Life, as well as the first Sabbath. It was the first day of his first Week, and Month and Year, i. e. the First in Man's Accompt of Time. On the Expiration of this first Sabbath, he began to Number his secular Days, as they advanced in Order, till he had told six. The next was again his Holy Seventh; yet the first Day of his second week, for his weeks were ascertained by the Return of the Sabbaths. Thus it obtained duly in all ordinary and civil Computations to be the First Day of the Week, at the same Time that it was distinguished with a Retrospect to the Work of the Creation, as an Holy Seventh Day. And it is remarkable that the most ancient of the Heathen Writers, while they speak of it as such, have rendered the very same Reason for it [a], which the Jewish Legislator had before given; namely, that "On it all things were "ended or completed." This then being of ancient and Patriarchal Usage, was not confined to any particular nation or Set of Men, like the Jewish Sabbath, but extended to all mankind, and was universally observed as the Birth-Day of the World: But being at length abused and desecrated to the Purposes of Idolatry, it pleased the divine Being, when he delivered his People from the Bondage of the Egyptians, to consecrate another Day to his peculiar Worship. This was the self same Day in which he brought them forth with their Armies from the Land of Egypt. Which was therefore to be a Memorial of their Deliverance [b], as long as their State and Polity should

[a] Vide Clement. Alev. Strom. l. 5. p. 560. & Polii. Synops ad Genes. xi. 2.

[b] Deuteronom, c. v. 15.

S

last

laft, and a Sign (a) and Covenant that the moft high GOD was their GOD.

But to refume our Subject, from which, we hope, the Reader will excufe this litte Digreffion, if fuch it be. Another Emblem of the Divinity, in a manner univerfally received, was the Seraph or fiery-flying Serpent, the *Salutis Draco* (b), the great Symbol of Light and Wifdom, of Life and Health. Why the Figure of this Animal was thus honoured, feveral Reafons may be affigned; as, the annual Renovation of its youth and beauty; its Sinuofity, which enabled it to put on various forms; the acutenefs of vifion, and extraordinary fagacity afcribed to it; and its colour, which is that of vivid Flame, or burnifhed Brafs. Its name of Seraph particularly is fo expreffive (c) of that Blaze of Brightnefs which it feemed to furnifh when reflecting the fplendor of the Sun-Beams; that it has been transferred to a fuperior Order of Angels; and is once made ufe of to denote even the glorious appearance of the Cherubim (d). This is the fame fymbol which was erected by Mofes in the Wildernefs. But this alfo was at length proftituted to abominable purpofes, and made the attribute of all the Egyptian Deities (e).

Expanded Wings made a third emblem of the Divinity. This was the Hieroglyphic fubftituted for the Æther, which was confidered as the natural fymbol of the divine fpirit, and, as fuch, fucceeded to a fhare of idolatrous worfhip (g). In fome of the original open Temples, particularly in that wonderful

One

[a] Ezekiel, c. xx. 10, 11, 12, 13.
[b] Macrobius.   [c] Seraph a Flame or Burning.
[d] Ifaiah vi.   [e] Orus Apollo; ad initium.
(g) Platon. Epinomis.
Zenoni & reliquis fere Stoicis AEther videtur fummus Deus, mente præditus, qua omnia regantur. *Ciceron Academ.* Quæft. l. 4. c. 41.

One of Abury in Wiltshire, the complex Figure of the Circle, and Seraph with expanded Wings, was represented entire.

Such were the natural Emblems of the Divine Being; and so plain and simple their hieroglyphical Represen tations; the original intent of which is explained to us by Kircher [g] from a piece of Antiquity in the Phœ nician Language; " Jove, says this Fragment, is a " figured Circle; from it is produced a Serpent: The " Circle shews the Divine Nature to be without be " ginning or end; the Serpent his Word, which ani- " mates the World and makes it prolific: his Wings " the Spirit of God, which gives Motion to the whole System."

The Commencement of Idolatry, avowed and aiming at some Establishment, must bear date from the extraordinary Project set on foot at Babel.. The design as appears from the original Account of it [h] was to build a City and a Tower, the Citadel or commanding part of which was to be erected to these Powers, which are there distinguished as the Shemin, or Heavens. The Supposition of its being to reach unto the Heavens is an Addition of the Translators. The confusion there spoken of, was the Confusion of the Lip, or religious Confession. The true Believers on this Occasion separated from the Idolaters, whom they left behind in Assyria to proceed in their mad enterprize, and dispersed themselves in the adjoining Countries, carrying with them the same Language and the same Patriarchal Religion, where we find both for a considerable Time after. The Confusion of Tongues, as it is called, was but the natural, and by no Means the immediate consequence of this Dispersion.

Cleanthes autem, qui Zenonem audivit, tum ultimum & altissimum atque undique circumfusum, & extremum omnia longentem atque complexum ardorem, qui Aether nominatur; certissinum Deum judicat. Id. de Nat. Deor. l 1. c. 14. See Chap. 62. of Isis, Osiris and Orus.

[g] Obel. Pamph p. 403.

[h] Gen. xi. 4. The Original runs strictly thus; " Let us " erect to us a City and a Tower, and the chief Place of it to the Heavens."

Next we find the Solar Body and its natural Symbol, the Fire worshipped at Ur of the Chaldees, thence denominated. The same Symbol was held in especial Reverence afterwards by the Persians, but never worshipped, in the proper sense of the Expression. The Species of Idolatry relating to the Worship of the human Figure was not introduced till long after: Nor was the Temple, which Ninus is said to have built, erected to his Father Belus, as many have asserted, but to Bel or Baal Shemim, the Lord of the Heavens, meaning the Sun.

Thus Idolatry in Assyria was prior to the Time of Abraham [a]; but it was confined to that Country: For neither in his Time, nor for some Time after, do we find any Traces of it in Arabia, Phœnicia, or Egypt. We may rest assured that Ishmael, the Father of the Arabians, and his Brethern by Keturah, adored the God of their Father, and established his Worship in the East Country, whither they were sent (Gen. xviii. 19). In Phœnicia we find Abimelech, the King of the Philistines, believing in God, favoured with a divine Intercourse, and pleading to the heavenly Vision the Righteousness of his Nation. Their Behaviour with Isaac afterwards leaves no Room to doubt that they continued then in the same Faith [b]. God himself declares to Abraham, that his Children shall not possess that Land till the fourth Generation after him, because the Iniquity of its inhabitants was not yet full. Whence it is but rational to conclude, that till the fourth Generation after, or till about the Time of the Exodus, they had not, at least generally, swerved into Idolatry. Sir Isaac Newton [c] imagines that they continued in the true Religion till the Death of Melchizedeck; but that afterwards they began to embrace Idolatry spreading thitherward from Chaldæa. They could not, however, in any short Time after, have amongst them more than the Beginnings of Idolatry though I presume, they sunk into it apace after

[a] Joshua xxiv. 2.　　[b] Gen. xxvi. 28, 29. & seq.
[c] Chronology of ancient Kingdoms amended, p. 188.

the

the Departure of Joseph's Brethern with their Families into Egypt.   When the Patriarch came into this last-mentioned Country also, GOD is said to have sent Judgments upon Pharaoh's Family, because of Abraham's Wife; and the King of Egypt seems to have been no Stranger to the true God, but to have had the Fear of him before his Eyes, and to have been influenced by it in all his actions [a].   Abraham was entertained by him without the Appearance of any indisposition towards him, or any the least sign of their having a different Religion.   Even the Heathen writers give Hints, that the Egyptians were at first Worshippers of the true GOD.   Plutarch testifies, that in upper Egypt, the Inhabitants paid no part of the Taxes raised for the idolatrous Worship; asserting themselves to own no mortal Being for GOD (b), but professing to worship their GOD CNEPH only.——— Porphyry calls this Egyptian CNEPH ton Demi on, the Creator of the Universe.

I cannot persuade myself that Joseph, when long after this he flourished at the head of the Egyptian Ministry, had that People deserted the Worship of the true God, would have married into the family he did, or that the zealous Patriarch would have held so sacred and inviolable the Lands and Endowments of an idolatrous Priesthood.   With Justice therefore has the great Grotius remarked [c] that in the age of Joseph no certain Footsteps of Idolatry are to be discerned in Egypt. I would give it to the Reader as a conjecture highly probable, that Idolatry was not established by Law in any part of that country till the disgrace of Moses at the court of Egypt, when he first retired to his Brethern in Goshen; about forty years before the Exodus. This is countenanced by a passage of scripture, where it is said of the children of Israel, that they sacrificed unto Devils, not to GOD;

[a] See Shuckford's Connection, Vol. l. p. 281, and 312.
[b] De Iside & Osiride.
[c] Vide Poli Synopsin in Gen. 46. verf. ultim.

they

to Gods whom they knew not, to new Gods that came newly up whom their Fathers feared not [a].

So that Eusebius, Lactantius, Cassian, Lucian, with many of the Jewish Rabbies, as well as Vassius; the Abbe Banier, and the Moderns in general, appear to have been grosly mistaken, in making either Phœnicia or Egypt the Birth-place of Idolatry. But this symbolical and hieroglyphical Divinity, proceeded from Assyria thro' Phœnicia to Egypt. But it was the Phœnician commerce which spread it in the remotest Quarters of the World: And it is observed, that in all the Religions we know, even in the East and West Indies, there is not one of them, whose Theology is not full of the like Emblems.

It must be confess'd that the multiplication of symbols became at length an inexhaustible Fund of Idolatry. Those Characters which, before the knowledge of Letters were innocent and even necessary, being by that rendered in short time useless, generally neglected understood by few, and at last grievously perverted, were the occasion of infinite errors. This may be well exemplified by a short account of the Zodiac [b].

The Crab, an Animal walking backwards or obliquely, seemed a proper emblem of the Sun, who arriving at this sign begins his Retrogradation (c). The wild Goat on the contrary, whose Custom is to feed as he climbs, was chosen to denote the Sun, who on coming to this point of the Heavens, quits the lowest part of his Course to regain the highest. The Ram, the Bull and the two Kids gave name to the three celestial Houses, thro' which the Sun passes in Spring. This distinguish'd the different Kinds of young Cattle, produced in this season, as they naturally succeeded each other : The Lambs appearing first, the Calves next, and the Kids last. Two of these latter were chosen, on account of the peculiar Fruitfulness of the Goat which generally bears 'Twins. But these the Greeks

[a] Deuter. 32. 17.
(b) See Abbe Pluche's History of the Heavens, Vol. 1. p. 10. & eq.   [c] Macrob. Saturn. l. 1. c. 17.

difplaced, fubftituting the Twin Brothers, Caftor and Pollux. The Fury of the Lion juftly expreffed the Heat of the Sun, on his leaving Cancer. The Virgin crown'd with Ears of Corn, was an emblem of the Harveft, ufually ending about that time. Nothing could better denote the equality of days and nights under the Autumnal Equinox, than the ballance Libra. The difeafes, confequent upon the fall of the Leaf, were characterifed by the Scorpion. The chafe of wild Beafts, annually obferved at that time, was not improperly diftinguifhed by Sagittarius, a man on horfeback, armed with a Bow and Arrow. Aquarius reprefented the Rains of Winter: And the two Fifhes bound together or inclofed in a Net, indicated the feafon for fifhing, ever beft at the approach of Spring. What could be more fimple and ufeful than this Divifion of the Sun's annual courfe into twelve equal portions, expreffed by fo many vifible figns, which ferved to regulate and defcribe the feafons and the bufinefs proper to each. Thefe rude Delineations of the celeftial Houfes probably gave birth to painting. But then thefe Images prefented to the mind a meaning very different from the Idea conveyed to the Eye. And when this meaning was loft, the Imagination was quickly at work to fupply another more agreeable to its own Corruption.

The Kingdom of Egypt, on account of its peculiar fituation, became the great fchool of this fymbolical Learning; and thence, in procefs of time, the grand Mart of Idolatry. It is not improbable, that the Priefts might endeavour to ftem the torrent of fuperftition that enfued from it, till finding all their ftrength ineffectual, they fubmitted to the times, and from views of Avarice and Ambition became public Defenders of thofe errors, which fecretly they condemned. For, it is certain, that while they thus complied with the popular Languages, they yet ftudied all they could collect of the ancient and real fignification of the fymbolical Figures, taking care to require a profound fecrecy of all perfons whom they inftructed in this kind of knowledge. And for this reafon Sphin-

ge

ges were placed at the entrances of their Temples, in
timating to thofe who approached, that they were to
look for a further meaning in what they fhould fee;
for that all was myfterious there.

Such was the Origin of thofe Initiations fo much
fought after in Egypt, Afia, and afterwards in Greece.
Indeed thefe Myfteries themfelves were in the End
moft grofsly abufed; yet there is no queftion, but
that in their primary inftitution they were intended to
explain the natural and divine things conched under
thofe Reprefentations. For they did not only unfold
the nature of Things, tho' this feems to have had (a)
the greateft fhare in them; but inculcated alfo the
immortality of the foul, a future ftate of [b] Rewards
and Punifhments, the confequent Neceffity of Virtue,
and the other great truths of Religion which had been
handed down from the earlieft ages.

Thus the antient Eaftern Nations had a referved
Meaning in all their emblematical Figures; which it
is frequently in our Power, even at this diftance of
time, to make out. Much of the Language fpoken
by them is ftill exifting: By the means of which,
matters of fo remote antiquity may in a great meafure
be difengaged from the myfterious darknefs in which
the ignorance of fome Ages and the Folly of others

[a] Omitto Eleufinam fanctam illam & auguftam,
  Ubi initiantur gentes orarum ultimæ :
  Prætereo Samothraciam, eaque
                ——— Quæ Lemni
  Nocturno aditu occulta coluntur
  Sylveftribus fepibus denfa :
  Quibus explicatis, ad rationemque revocatis, rerum magis
Natura cognofcitur, quam Deorum. Cicero de Nat. Deor. l. I.
c. 42.
(b) Mihi cum multa eximia divinaque videntur Athenæ peperiffe
atque in vita hominum attuliffe, tum nihil melius illis myfteriis,
quibus ex agrefti immanique vita exculti ad humanitatem & mi-
tigati fumus: initiaque, ut appellantur, ita re vera principia vitæ
cognovimus; neque folum cum lætitia vivendi rationem accepi-
mus, fed etiam cum fpe meliore moriendi. Cicero de Legibus
l. 2. c. 14.

have

have involved them. I shall be easily understood to speak this of the Hebrew Tongue; so much of which I say, is yet remaining to us, as will easily by a comparison with other Languages, manifest it to be an Original: And all others, on examination, will discover how largely they have drank of this Fountain —— The names of Animals, so intimately expressive of their properties, bespeak it to have been given by the great Author of Nature; and those of the first Men (a), so nicely applied to their respective conditions and circumstances, leave no Room to doubt that they were coæval with the persons themselves. The Greeks borrowed their Idolatry from Phænicia and Egypt, which indeed the innovating spirit of that people improved in the most extravagant manner: And it is not possible to explain their religious Antiquities without having Recourse to the Language of those Countries from which they were transplanted. When therefore this is done without force or constraint, proposing an Interpretation natural and easy; not to receive it, were to reject the only means (in many cases) of information, which remain to us at this immense distance of time. The Reader, will consider this as an Apology for the free use which is made of this tongue in the preceding Sheets; where he will find a great number of strange and otherwise unaccountable stories, having their foundation solely in the different meanings of the same word. So that an account, in itself innocent and easy, by being perversely rendered, became frequently the source of idle wonder, and at length of idolatrous veneration. It is not from the fabulous Greeks themselves that we are to expect full Satisfaction in these matters. Very few of them gave themselves the trouble to enquire into the meaning of their own Ceremonies. Every thing that was but Egyptian was readily adopted: And the very names of the Gods they worshipped were originally taken upon Trust. For the Pelasgians, as Herodotus in-

[a] See Origin of Languages by Dr. Gregory Sharpe.

forms

forms us, [a], had formerly sacrificed and prayed to Gods in general, without attributing either name or sirname to any Deity, which in those times they had never heard of: But they called them Gods, because they disposed and governed all actions and countries. After a long time the names of the other Gods were brought among them from Egypt, and last of all that of Bacchus: Upon which they consulted the Oracle of Dodona, still accounted the most ancient, and then the only Oracle in Greece, and having enquired whether they should receive these names from the Barbarians, the Oracle answer'd, they should. So from that time they invoked the Gods in their sacrifices under distinct Names; and the same were afterwards received by the Greeks from these Pelasgians. This says my author, I had from the Priestesses of Dodona.

It is said to the Honour of Moses, that he was learned in all the wisdom of the Egyptians. Whence is it then that greater absurdities in Religion have been ascribed to this wise People; than have been met with amongst the most barbarous and unciviliz'd Nations? This could only proceed from the travelling Greeks who understood little of what they saw, and made the worst use of what they carried home; which by their Poets was afterwards enlarged and diversified with all the wantonness of a licentious imagination. Thus that Idolatry, which had its foundation in the vanity and corruption of the human heart, was chiefly indebted to its fabulous bulk amongst the Greeks to the warm and plastic imaginations of the Poets, and was still further improved by the boldness of the Pencil, the fine expression of the Chissel, and the Licence of the Stage.

When the human Figure was first made the object of idolatrous Veneration, may perhaps be difficult to determine. We read of Graven Images in the Land of Canaan in the time of Moses and Joshua. But these in all Probability were extremely rough and inartificial, and perhaps nothing more than upright

Stones or standing Pillars. Such as they were, how-ever, Cadmus is said to have carried the Use of them into Greece. I should imagine that they were not worshipped in Egypt till long after; especially if that be true, which Clemens of Alexandria quotes Leo as affirming [b], in his Treatise of the Egyptian Gods, that their celebrated Isis lived not till the Time of Lynceus, in the eleventh Generation after Moses.

It has been generally allowed that the Persons, whose Memory was thus religiously preserved, were such as had been greatly distinguished for the Invention of useful Arts, and their Beneficence to Mankind [c]. But to make this Species of Idolatry go down with the People, something more than a pretended Deification seems to have been necessary; because in order to secure this extravagant Honour to their Favourites, we find the Egyptians arraying their Images with various Ensigns and Attributes; thus making them the Representatives of such natural Things as were adored already by the superstitious Herd. Thus we find Osiris adorned with the emblems of the Sun, Isis decked with those of the Æther, and the golden Seraph inseparable from Orus [d]. Granting therefore that there were such Persons in the World, as Jupiter, Apollo, Bacchus, Isis, &c. yet we must allow the Attributes given, and the Ceremonies paid to them, to be solely applicable to the Luminaries, or to the natural Causes and Effects, which, it is manifest, were represented by them.

Or it may be that Mankind were not altogether so eager and so hasty in their Corruptions: that the Consecration of eminent and virtuous Men was no more in the first place than a Sort of Canonization; and that the Worship paid to them was only considered as a public Testimony of their Belief, that such Persons

---

[b] Stromat. l. 1. p. 322.

[c] Sofcepit autem vita hominum, confuetudoque communis, ut beneficiis excellentes viros in cœlum fama ac voluntate tollerent. Cicero de Nat Deor. l. 2. c. 24.

[d] Infantemque vident, exporrectumque Draconem. OVID. See Chap. 61. of Isis, Osiris, and Orus.

were

were received into the Abodes of the Blessed, and numbered among the Sons of God. This at least was the Opinion of Cicero (a). For that the Law commands those who were consecrated from amongst Men, to be worshipped; it shews indeed, says he, that the Souls of all Men are immortal; but that those of the Brave and the Good are divine.

May we not therefore conclude, with Regard to the ancient Egyptians particularly, that they were not ignorant of the ONE SUPREME BEING, who by his Knowledge conceived the World, before he formed it by his Will: But to comply with the growing Corruptions of Mankind, in which compliance they were extremely guilty, allow'd them to adore (and in this no Doubt they found their Account) the different Attributes of his Essence, and the different Effects of his Goodness under the Symbols of the heavenly Powers, of renowned Personages, and at last even of the terrestrial Bodies, as Plants and Animals; thus wilfully laying the Foundation of the grossest Superstition and Idolatry.

How little the besotted Greeks had to say for themselves on this Head, and how ignorant indeed they were of their own religious Rites, has been remarked already. As these took their Gods so fondly from the Egyptians, so did the Romans theirs chiefly from them. This appears at large in the preceding Sheets. It must be confess'd at the same Time, that as some of these last refer the whole Multitude of their Divinities to the Sun, the original Object of Idolatry, thence called the Universal One (b), so did others of them to the GREAT AUTHOR OF NATURE, affirming "Jupiter " to be the Soul of the World (c), who formed the

---

[a] Quod autem ex hominum genere confecratos, ficut Herculem & ceteros, coli lex jubet, indicat omnium quidem animos immortales effe, fed fortium bonorumque divinos. De Legibus l. 2. c xi.

[b] Diverfæ virtutes folis nomina Diis dederunt: unde eu to pan fapinetum principes prodiderunt. Macrob. Saturn. l. 1. c. 17.

[c] St. Auguftin de Civitate Dei, c 11. Tome 5. p 42, 43

" Univerfe

" Universe of the four Elements, and fills and moves
" it thus compacted." In the Æther he is Jupiter;
in the air Juno; in the Sea Neptune; in the lower
parts of the Sea, Salacia; in the Earth, Pluto; in
Hell, Proserpine; in domestic Fires, Vesta; in the
Working-Furnace, Vulcan; in the Heavenly Bodies,
the Sun, Moon and Stars; amongst Diviners, Apollo
in trade, Mercury; in Janus, the Beginner; in boundaries, the Terminator; in time, Saturn; in War,
Mars and Bellona; Bacchus in the Vintage; Ceres
in the Harvest; in the Woods, Diana; in the Sciences, Minerva; and is himself, in fine, the whole multitude of vulgar Gods and Goddesses. These are all
the one Jupiter, whether they be considered, according to some, as Parts of Himself, or according to o-
thers as his Virtues and Attributes. This is exactly
of a Piece with the Reasoning of Seneca; who af-
serts that GOD may have names in number equal to
his Gifts (a).

Notwithstanding this, we find on some occasions,
even among these, the monstrous absurdity of making
new Gods arrived to such a Pitch, that Temples have
been every now and then vowed and erected by Ma-
gistrates, and Commanders, even to Creatures of their
own sudden imagination; such as the chance of war,
or their own wishes or Fears had raised. So that
Pliny's Observation (b), with some allowance for the
Latitude of Expression, may seem to have been not
ill founded; that the Extravagance of human Passions and Affections had made more Gods than there
were men.

[a] Jovem illum optimum ac maximum rite dices & tonantem
& statorem quod stant beneficia ejus omnia, stator stabilitorque
est. Quæcunque voles illi nomina proprie aptabis, vim aliquam
effectumque cœlestium rerum continentia. Tot appellationes e-
jus possunt esse, quot munera. Hunc & Liberum Patrem & Herculem, ac Mercurium nostri putant. Quia omnium parens sit :
Quia vis ejus invicta sit. Quia ratio penes illum est numerusque,
& ordo, & Scientia, &c. De Benef. l. 4. c. 7. 8.
[b] Nat. Hist. Lib. ii. c. 7.

Yet upon the Whole, the Hiftory of Religion is not fo darkened with Error, but that, thro' all thefe fhades of Folly, an attentive Enquirer may ftill difcern the difpenfations of God, from the firft Offence of man to this Day, to have been regular and uniform, and directed to one great End, namely, his own fupreme Glory in the Happinefs of his Creatures.

Let us therefore adore this ever gracious Being with humble fincerity. Let us acknowledge his infinite mercies with a due fenfe of our own Demerits: And beware, above all Things, that we attempt not to fet up our own weak Reafon in oppofition to the declared Will and Commandments of God. This has been the great Stumbling Block in all Ages: And from fuch Demeanour, Confufion of every fort muft neceffarily enfue.

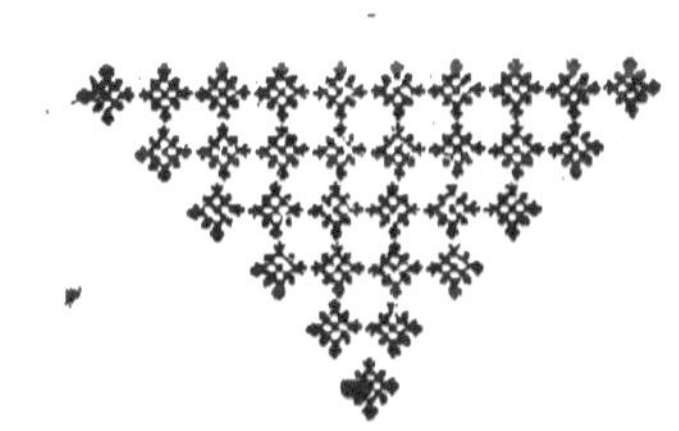

MYTHOLOGY *of the* HEATHENS.

HAVING confidered the Theology of the Heathens, we fhall next give fome Account of their Mythology; a fubject already touched upon in the Hiftory of the Deities themfelves. We fhall now enter into the Nature of the Pagan Fables, their religious fentiments, and the manner of their Worfhip. Here we fhall find Truth blended with error, and obfcured by fiction, which has wrapt in clouds the moft important Doctrines, fuch as the Creation of the World, the fall of Man, the deftruction of the human Race by an univerfal deluge, the change produced in nature by that great event, the Origin of natural and moral Evil, and the final Reftitation of all things to their primitive Glory and Splendor. This will lead us to a fhort view of their moral fentiments, as well as the nature of their Worfhip.

Notwithftanding the great Corruption which had crept into the Worfhip of all nations, we have feen that the men of Learning and Reflection generally maintained honourable Notions of the Deity, and the moft juft and rational Ideas of the Obligations of moral Virtue. Philofophers frequently arofe, and by their Inftructions difperfed the Clouds of Darknefs, if not from the minds of the Poor and Vulgar, at leaft from thofe who had Leifure and Oppertunity to attend their Lectures, or to read their Works. By thefe morality was made a Science, and Ethics became the moft valuable branch of Philofophy. As the Greeks and Romans had received their Divinities from

T 2

Eg)pt,

Egypt, and by miſtaking the Manners, the Cuſtoms and Language of that Nation, had made Gods of the common Symbols which they employed to teach the People to honour one God, the Author of all Good, to live in Peace, to expreſs the Times and Seaſons for the Performance of the common Occurrences of Life, and to expect a better State to come; ſo their Religion became obſcured by Fables, and a variety of fictions, which, while the Vulgar underſtood in a literal ſenſe, their ſages endeavoured to explain and reduce to ingenious Allegories, and thereby to render the Heathen Worſhip conſiſtent with all the natural notions of a ſupreme Deity, the wiſe Governor of the World, and by accounting for the introduction of moral Evil, to vindicate the Rules of his Providence, and to juſtify the ways of God to Man.

Fables are indeed a very ancient Method of conveying Truth, and are therefore to be conſidered as Veils of ſo fine a Texture, as not wholly to conceal the Beauties that lie beneath them.   Thus, ſays Origen; (a) " The Egyptian Philoſophers have ſublime Noti-
" ons with regard to the divine Nature, which they
" keep ſecret, and never diſcover to the People, but
" under the veil of Fables, and Allegories.   All the
" Eaſtern Nations, the Perſians, the Indians, the Sy-
" rians, conceal ſecret myſteries under their religious
" Fables.   The wiſe men of all Nations (b) ſee into
" the true ſenſe and meaning of them, whilſt the vul-
" gar go no further than the exterior ſymbol, and ſee
" only the bark that covers them."

This was frequently the caſe when foreign and diſtant Nations adopted what they but imperfectly underſtood.   Allegories became Objects of Faith.—Thus could any thing give a more lively Idea, of the

<hr>

(a) Origen contra Celſum, Lib. I. p. 11.
[b] " Thoſe who are acquainted with theſe Myſteries," ſays Iſocrates, inſure to themſelves very pleaſing Hopes againſt the " Hour of Death and which extend to a whole Eternity." Theſe " Myſteries," ſays Epictetus, " were eſtabliſhed by the Ancients " to regulate the Lives of Men, and to baniſh diſorders from the " World.

ftate of Retribution, and the Rewards or Punifhments which follow upon a Life of Virtue or Vice, than the Ceremonies with which the Egyptians buried their dead. The Greeks and Romans ftruck with the ideas that were io ftrongly conveyed, took the type for the Reality: The Boat which was to convey the Body to the place of Burial, which was with the Egyptians an Emblem of Death, and was called Tranquility, becaufe it carried over none but the juft, was reprefented by the Greeks and Romans as a boat to carry fouls. Cerberus, an Hieroglyphic, carved out of wood or Stone, to exprefs the Lamentations beftowed on the Virtuous, became an animated Monfter. The Lake of Acherufia became a vifionary River of Tartarus, and was called Acheron. The Judges that decided the merit of the Deceafed, were reprefented as configning the fpirit to final Happinefs or Mifery, and the flowery Field where the Righteous alone were buried, into that Place of Joy which the Elizout of the Egyptians was only defigned as a faint Reprefentation. Yet notwithftanding the fables into which thefe Myfteries were turned, this very important truth was ftill conveyed, that there would be a State of Judgment in which the Virtuous would be rewarded, and the Vicious punifhed, according to their Deferts. The very Prayer or form of Abfolution, which was given by the Egyptian Priefts to the Relations of the deceafed, contained a ufeful Leffon to the Living, as it exhibited a concife Syftem of thofe Morals which were to entitle them to the divine Favour, and to a decent Burial in the Plains, on the Confines of the Lake Acherufia. This Prayer was preferved by Porphyry, who copied it from Euphantes, whofe Works are now loft, and is as follows: "O Sun, thou firft Divi-
" nity! and ye celeftial Gods, who gave life to man!
" Vouchfafe to receive me this Day, into your holy
" Tabernacles. I have endeavoured, to the beft of
" my Power, to render my Life agreeable to you;
" I have behaved with the higheft veneration towards
" the Gods, with whom I was acquainted in my In-
" fancy; I have never failed in my Duty to thofe

T 3

" wha

" who brought me into Being, nor in natural Affec-
" tion to the Womb that bore me. My Hands are
" pure from my Neighbour's Blood ; I have main-
" tained an inviolable Regard to Truth and Fidelity
" and may I not appeal to the filence of Mankind,
" who have nothing to lay to my Charge, as a fure
" and certain Teftimony of my Integrity ? If, howe-
" ver, any perfonal and fecret Fault has efcaped me,
" and I have offended in eating or in drinking, let
" thefe Entrails bear all the blame." Here the Entrails of the deceafed were produced by the Relations
and immediately thrown into the Lake.

But however ufeful thefe Ceremonies might be, as
practifed among the Egyptians, yet being confidered
as Realities by the Greeks, and rendered more ridiculous by the Abfurdity of their Fables, it is no wonder that they loft their efficacy, and became, as Juvenal informs us, difbelieved even by their children.

But it is not at all ftrange, that this fhould be the
cafe with the Greeks, when the Egyptians themfelves
were fallen into Idolatry, and thofe fimple Emblems,
once fo well known to this People, were become the
Medium of their Prayers and Adorations. Every
Thing had an Air of Myftery, and thefe Myfteries
were underftood by none but the Priefts, or thofe to
whom they were pleafed to explain them, which was
always done under the Seal of Secrefy. The Vulgar
were fuffered to continue in their errors, fince it might
have been dangerous even for their Prieft to attempt
to open their eyes, and to reduce their worfhip to the
fimplicity of the ancient Practice.

But here I cannot help obferving, that notwithftanding all that has been faid to the contrary, there
is far from being fufficient Reafon for our believing,
that they were fo loft to Reafon and common Senfe,
as to pay adoration to the Ox, the Goat, the Crocodile, or the Produce of their Gardens ; the paffages
brought from Scripture to prove it, are far from being fatisfactory, fince they are capable of a very different interpretation. Would the Children of Ifrael
while in the Wildernefs, have hankered after the O-
nions

nions of Egypt, if they had been there an object of
Worſhip.   It is as abſurd to ſuppoſe it, as to imagine
that the Egyptians could be guilty of ſo ſenſeleſs a
kind of Adoration.   The Character that is given of
this people in Holy Writ, ſeems ſtrongly to contradict
it, when it is mentioned to the Praiſe of Moſes, that
he was learned in all the Wiſdom of the Egyptians.
They were indeed univerſally allowed to be the wiſeſt nation on Earth, which they could not have been
were they ſo ſtupid as to worſhip Beaſts, Birds, Fiſhes,
Reptiles, Inſects, and Plants.   However, their having
theſe on their ſymbols, added to their dreſſing up a
Ram with flowers, and having a Feſtival on the Sun's
Entrace into Aries, and the ſame ceremony of dreſſing up a Bull at his entering Taurus, and ſo of the o·
ther ſigns, might give Room to Strangers to entertain
this opinion ; eſpecially as theſe might be practiſed
after the original meaning was forgot : But who, that
has ever ſeen a Company of young Men and Women
in the Country of England, dancing round a Maypole,
adorned with green Bows and Garlands, could be ſo
abſurd as to imagine that this Diverſion was performed in Honour of the Goddeſs Flora. The Abſurdity of the ſuppoſition is not leſs in the former caſe
than in the latter, ſince the Beaſt dreſſed up in honour
of the ſign into which the Sun was ſuppoſed to enter
was not regarded as an object of Worſhip, though the
Sun or the Stars might be adored as the Emblems,
or the Reſidence of the Deity

   Nothing has ever contributed more to diſguiſe the
Truth, and to corrupt the worſhip of the Greeks and
Romans than the Multitude of Fictions introduced
by their Poets.   It is this that has principally occaſioned that jumble of Images, that indecorum in characters, and that Abſurdity in their Fictions, which
are ſo juſtly condemned by their wiſeſt Philoſophers.

   It is the Province of Poetry to change the Face of
Nature, to give Life and Activity to inanimate Beings
Subſtance and form to Thought ; to deify the Paſſions, and to create a World of its own. The Poet
is

is not bound by the same Laws as other Men; he has a Power that enables him to create and deftroy at Pleafure, and with the fame eafe he forms Gods [a], Heroes, Men and Monfters. He makes quick Tranfitions from Reality to Fiction; from Fiction to Reality, and from thofe which he believes to thofe of his own creating: and from hence arifes a principal fource of that confufion which has given fuch different interpretations to, and which renders it fo difficult to explain the ancient Mythology. The Greek and Roman Poets have almoft always preferred the marvellous and the fparkling, to the fimplicity of naked Truth. I a Princefs died of Grief for the lofs of her Hufband or her Child, fhe was changed into a Rock or Fountain; inftead of faying, that Cephalus rofe with the Sun, Aurora muft be in Love with the Youth, and force him abroad. To reprefent the long Life of Iolaus, the Goddefs of Health muft renew his Age. Inftead of faying that Endymion ftudied on the Mountains of Caria, the Courfe of the Moon, they tell us, that he had there an Interview with Diana; and that her ftaying with her Gallant was the caufe of Eclipfes. But as thefe Amours could not laft for ever, they were obliged to invent a new Fable, to account for them another way, and therefore they feigned that fome Sorcerefs of Theffaly, by her Enchantment, drew down the Moon to the Earth. To account for the perpetual Verdure of the Laurel, they talked of the Amours of Apollo and [b] Daphne. To exprefs the agility and fwiftnefs of Periclymenus, they affirmed that he was able to affume all fhapes, and at laft turned himfelf into an Eagle. Amphion, by his Oratory, prevailed on a barbarous people to build a City, and to dwell in Society; he is therefore faid to raife up the walls of Thebes by the found of his Lyre, and Orpheus to charm the Lions and Tyger, and to move the Rocks and Trees by his

[a] The ancient Heroes were fuppofed to be a middle kind of Beings, that partook both of the Nature of Gods and Men.
[b] The Laurel was called by the Greeks, Daphne.

Har-

Harmony; becaufe nothing could withftand his perfuafion, or refift the force of his eloquence.

Who would imagine that by the wings of Dædalus
and Icarus, were fignified a fhip under fail ? That all
the Changes of Ach elous were only frequent Inundations? That by the combat of Hercules with the God
of that River, was only meant a Bank that was raifed
to prevent its overflowing ? That Hercules encountering the Hydra of Lerna, fignified no more than a
man's draining a marfhy Country ; or that Hercules
feparating with his Hands the two Mountains Calpe
and Abyla, when the Ocean rufhed in with violence,
and found a paffage into the Mediterranean, meant
no more, perhaps, than that in the Time of one Hercules, the Ocean by the affiftance of an Earthquake
broke a Neck of Land, and form'd the Straits of Gi-
braltar ? Or that the Fable of Pafiphae contains nothing but an Intrigue of the Queen of Crete with a
Captain named Taurus ?

Who could believe that Scylla and Charybdis, thofe
dreadful monfters that devoured all paffengers, were
only two dangerous Rocks near the Ifland of Sicily,
rendered famous by their being frequently fatal to
Mariners ? That the frightful Monfter which ravaged
the plains of Troy, was the Inundations of the Sea ;
or that Hefione's being expofed to this Monfter,
meant no more than that fhe was to be given to him
who put a ftop to thefe inundations ?

Thus, fays the Abbe Banier, if we would diftinguifh
truth from fiction, whenever a Poet brings a God upon the Stage, he ought to be fet afide : What Homer
and Virgil afcribe to Minerva, is to be attributed to
prudence and good conduct. It is no longer the exhalations that produce Thunder, but Jupiter armed
to affright mortals. If a Mariner perceives a rifing
ftorm, it is angry Neptune fwelling the Waves. Echo
ceafes to be a mere found, and becomes a Nymph be-
wailing the lofs of her Narciffus.

Thus by the Cloud with which Minerva concealed
Ulyffes, is meant the darknefs of the Night, which
fuffered him to enter the Town of the Phænicians
without

without being difcovered : and when Priam is conducted by Mercury into the tent of Achilles, we are
only to underftand, that he fet out to obtain Hector's
Body in the Dark, with a Prefent to appeafe his Anger If the delights of the Country of the Lotophagi
detain the Companions of Ulyffes, we are told by Homer, that the Fruits of that Ifland made thofe who
tafted them lofe all Remembrance of their Families,
or their Native Country, This is an ingenious Fidion intended to convey this important truth, that the
Love of Pleafure debauches the mind, and banifhes
from the Heart every laudable Affection. If they
loiter at the Court of Circe, and abandon themfelves
to Riot and Debauchery, this pretended Sorcerefs,
with great elegance and ftrength of expreflion is faid
to turn them into Swine. Thus he elegantly conveys
this moral Sentiment, That as the principal Diftinction between a Brute and a reafonable Creature confift
in a power to exercife his Reafon, when this is loft he
is rather a Brute than a Man, and therefore inftead
of fimply faying, that the Defires and Affections are
become brutal, he mentions the Body as affuming
that Form which beft fuits with the difpofition of the
mind. The Narration would be thought too fimple
and unadorned was he to fay, that Ulyffes was expofed to feveral ftorms; he muft have Neptune's Refentment, who takes this method of reverging the
death of his fon Polyphemus. What an apparatus
of fiction is introduced before Achilles can kill Hector !
His Armour is made by Vulcan; his Mother, to render him invulnerable, had dipped him in the River
Styx. Minerva affumes the form of Deiphobus, that
Hector may be deceived by imagining that he had the
affiftance of his Brother ; Jupiter takes the fcales,
weighs the Deftinies of the two Heroes, and feeing
Hector's fink, abandons him to his Fate, and then Achilles takes away his life. Homer, inftead of informing
us, that after the bloody battle fought on the banks
of the Xanthus, that River being choaked up with
dead bodies, overflowed the plain, till taking them out
of the water, they kindled a funeral pile, and confumed
them

them to Afhes: Inftead of this, what a Variety of
Machinery is employed! The River feeling himfelf
oppreffed, utters his Complaints to Achilles, but receiving no Satisfaction, fwells againft him, and pur-
fues him with fuch Rapidity, that he would certainly
have been drowned, if Neptune and Minerva had
not been commiffioned by Jupiter to moderate his
Wrath, by promifing him a fpeedy Satisfaction. When
this great Poet would let us know, that after the Retreat of the Greeks an Inundation from the Sea deftroyed the famous Wall they had built during the Siege
of Troy, to protect them from the Enemy: He fays,
that Neptune enraged at the Greeks, begs of Jupiter
to fuffer him to beat it down with his Trident; and
having prevailed on Apollo to give him his Affiftance,
they labour in Concert to perform this arduous Tafk.
So when Turnus caufed the Fleet of Æneas to be fet
on Fire, Virgil introduces Cybele, who inftantly tranf-
forms the Veffels into Nymphs.

If the Poet, fays Lactantius, found it for his Inter-
eft to flatter or confole a Prince for the Lofs of his Son,
it was but giving him a place amongft the Stars. Shepherds were all Satyrs or Fauns, Shepherdeffes, Nymphs
or Naiads; Ships, flying Horfes; Men on Horfeback,
Centaurs; every lewd Woman was a Syren or a Har-
py; Oranges were Apples of Gold; and Arrows and
Darts, Lightning and Bolts of Thunder.

The Rivers and Fountains had their tutelary Deities, and fometimes were reprefented as being Deities
themfelves; the uniting their Streams was called Marriage, and Brooks and Canals were ftiled their Children. If they would fpeak of the Rainbow, that too
muft be a Goddefs dreffed in the richeft Colours; and
as they were at a Lofs how to account for the Production of this feeming Phænomenon, it was called the
Daughter of Thaumas, a poetical Perfonage, whofe
Name fignifies Wonderful.

Sometimes a Concern for the Honour of the Ladies became a Source of Fables. If a Princefs proved
too frail to withftand the Attempts of her Lover, her
Flatterer, to fkreen her Reputation, immediately cal-

led in the Affistance of some enamoured God; this was easily believed by the ignorant Vulgar; for they could suppose none but a divine Person could presume to attempt one of her Rank, or could be able to thaw the Coldnefs of the infensible Fair Thus her Reputation was unfullied, and instead of becoming infamous she was highly honoured, and the Hufband himself instead of being offended, partook of her Glory A great number of Fables were derived from this Source. Nor is the Story of Rhea Sylvia [a], the Mother of Rhemus and Romulus, and of Paulina [b], the only Inftances to be found in Hiftory of the Credulity of Hufbands and Parents From this Source, and the Lewdnefs or Corruption of the Priefts, were doubtlefs derived many of the Fables relating to the Amours of the Gods.

At other Times, the ftrangeft Transformations fprung only from a Similitude of Names, and confifted in a Play of Words; thus Cygnus was transformed into a Swan; Picus, into a Wood pecker; Hierafe, into a Spar Hawk; the Cercopes, into Monkies; and Alopis, into a Fox

Thus the ancient Poets gave Rife to innumerable Errors, and indeed the Painters and Statuaries have employed all their Skill to confirm and ftrengthen the Delufion. The Poets have fpread an Air of Fiction

[a] Her Uncle Amulius, having found means to get into her Apartment, Numitor, her Father, fpread a Report, that the Twins of which fhe was delivered, proceeded from the Embraces of the God of War. Dion. de Halic, Ant. Rom. Lib. I. Tit. Liv. Lib. I.

[b] A young Roman Knight, called Mundus, falling in Love with Paulina, and finding all his Eudeavours to conquer her Virtue prove fruitlefs, corrupted the Priefts of Anubis, who perfuaded her to believe that the God was ftruck with her Beauty, on which fhe was that very Night led by her Hufband to the Temple. A few days after, feeing Mundus, whom fhe happened accidentally to meet, he let her into the fecret; Paulina, enraged and filled with indignation, carried her complaint before Tiberius, who ordered the Statue of Anubis to be thrown into the Tiber, his Priefts to be burnt alive, and Mundus to be fent into Exile

over

over ferious Hiftories, difguifed and altered Facts [a]; and rendered the divineft Truths fabulous. This in nothing appears more evident, than in the Account they have left us of the Origin of the World, which feems partly compofed of Traditions handed down from the Sons of Noah, partly of the Fictions and Ornaments introduced by the Poets, and partly from their endeavouring to reconcile confufed and imperfect Traditions with popular Opinions, and the Corruptions introduced into religious Worfhip. This, it is proper for us particularly to examine, as it is an Enquiry abfolutely neceffary to explain many of the Pagan Fables, and to give us juft Ideas of their religious Sentiments, which will be found much plainer expreffed by their Philofophers than their Poets.

The ancient Opinion, that the World was formed from that Chaos, or a confufed Concourfe of Matter which Hefiod calls the Father of the Gods, probably had its Rife from a literal Interpretation of the Beginning of that fublime Defcription, which Mofes gives us of the Creation [b]; where, before the Formation of any part of the Univerfe, it is faid, The Earth was without Form, and void, and Darknefs was upon the Face of the Deep, as the latter Part of the Verfe, where the Spirit of God is reprefented as moving or hovering over the Waters, might give the

[a] The Abbe Banier, from whom we have borrowed many of thefe Remarks, fays, " That Homer of a faithlefs Proftitute, " has made his chafte Penelope, and Virgil, of a Traitor to his " Country, has given us the pious Hero, of a Renegado, who " loft his Life in a Battle againft Mezentius, he has made a Con " queror and a Demi-God. The fame Poet has not yet even " fcrupled to reflect Difhonour on Dido, a Princefs of ftrict Vir " tue and divefted her of the Reputation fhe had acquired for " Chaftity and Courage, has reprefented her as indulging an " infamous Paffion, and a Cowardice capable of Defpair. Almoft " all of them have confpired to make Tantalus pafs for a Mifer, " and have fet him in the Front of the Avaricious, in the Center " of Hell: where he is reprefented as fuffering a Punifhment " proportionable to his Guilt. Thus they have treated a Man, " who, acording to Pindar, was a religious and a generous " Prince." Banier Vol. I. Book I; c. 4.
[b] Gen. i. 2.

U

Egyptians

Egyptians, the Phænicians, the Chaldeans, the Perſians, and the Indians, the Idea which they mean to expreſs when they talk of the Egg of the World.

But it was not ſufficient for Heſiod to make a God of Chaos, to deſcribe the Order that ſprang from this Confuſion ; Chaos muſt have an Offspring, and therefore inſtead of ſaying like Moſes, that Darkneſs was upon the Face of the Deep ; he ſays, Chaos brought forth Gloomineſs and Night ; and to continue the Genealogy, inſtead of ſaying with the inſpired Writer, God divided the Light from the Darkneſs, he expreſſes ſomething like the ſame Idea, by adding, that from Night ſprang Air and Day. Moſes ſays that God ordered the dry Land to appear, and created the Firmament which he called Heaven ; Heſiod ſays, that the Earth begat Heaven, the high Mountains and the Caves He then informs us of the Ocean, who was the Father of Springs and Rivers, of the Birth of the Sun and Moon, and ſeveral other Gods of the like Kind.

It is very evident, that this whole account is nothing more than an allegorical Hiſtory of the Formation of all Things, in which the various parts of Nature are perſonated ; but the Hand of the great Architect is wanting Ovid treats this Subject in a more intelligible Manner, and with great Beauty introduces the Creator, whom he calls God, or Nature, forming the various Parts with the utmoſt Regularity and Order. But in nothing does he come ſo near to Moſes, as in the Account he gives of the Formation of Man, which as well as Moſes, he makes the laſt Work of the Creation, and introduces Prometheus, or Council, forming him of Clay, in the Image of the Gods.

A Creature of a more exalted Kind,
Was wanting yet. and then was Man deſign'd,
Conſcious of Thought, of more capacious Breaſt,
For Empire form'd, and fit to rule the reſt[a].

[a] Ovid, Lib. I.

From

From this introduction it will not admit of a doubt but that Ovid underſtood the ſtory of Prometheus in the literal Senſe. And as to the circumſtances which he omits, of his taking fire from Heaven to animate the lumpiſh Form; what is this, ſays a modern Author, but God's breathing into his Noſtrils the breath of Life.

Father Litſiteau (a) gives us an account of a very whimſical opinion maintained by the Iroquois, one of the moſt conſiderable of all the Savage nations. They believe that in the beginning there were ſix men [b]; but as yet there being no Earth, theſe men were carried about in the Air at the Mercy of the Winds. As they had no Women they foreſaw that their Race muſt ſoon come to an End; at laſt they learned that there was one in Heaven, on which it was agreed, that one whom they fixed upon ſhould go and fetch her from thence; the attempt was dangerous, but it was accompliſhed by the aſſiſtance of the Birds, who wafted him thither on their Wings. Upon his Arrival he waited for the Woman's coming out to draw Water, and as ſoon as ſhe appeared, he ſeduced her by offering her a preſent. The Lord of Heaven knowing what had paſſed, baniſhed this Woman, and a Tortoiſe received her on its Back; when the Otter and the Fiſhes drawing up mud from the Bottom of the Water, formed of the body of the Tortoiſe a ſmall Iſland, and this encreaſing by Degrees was the original of the Earth. The Woman had at firſt two Sons, one of whom arming himſelf with offenſive weapons, ſlew his Brother, and that after this ſhe had ſeveral Children, from whom ſprang the reſt of Mankind.

Wild and extravagant as this Tradition is, yet it ſeems at leaſt to be founded on a Remnant of the primitive Hiſtory of the World, the baniſhment of Eve from the terreſtrial Paradiſe, and the Murder of Abel

[a] Manners of the Savages, Vol. 1.
[b] The People of Peru and Brazil agree upon the ſame number.

by Cain his Brother. Thus they altered the Tradition 'tho' part of it was ftill retained.

And here it cannot be improper to mention a Fable, which Plato puts into the Mouth of Ariftophanes [a]; " The Gods, fays he, formed man at firft of a
" round figure, with two bodies, two faces, four legs
" four Feet, and both Sexes. Thefe men were of
" fuch extraordinary Strength, that they Refolved to
" make War upon the Gods; Jupiter, incenfed at
" this Enterprize, would have deftroyed them as he
" had done the Giants; but feeing that by this means
" he muft have deftroyed the whole human Race, he
" contented himfelf with dividing them afunder? and
" at the fame time ordered Apollo to ftretch over the
" Breaft, and other parts of the Body, the fkin, as
" it is at prefent. Thefe two parts of one body thus
" disjoined, want to be re-united; and this is the o-
" rigin of Love."

Ovid mentions only the Formation of Man, without taking the leaft notice of Eve, in which he evidently copies the account given us by Mofes, who omits mentioning this in his general Hiftory of the Creation. And the hint of this Fable was probably taken from this Circumftance, where the Scripture fays (b), God created Man, and then adds, Male and Female created he them; and the circumftance of their being cut afunder, the clofing up the Flefh, and the Reafon given for conjugal Love, from Eve's being made of a Rib taken out of Adam's fide, and his faying upon this, She is Bone of my Bone, and Flefh of my Flefh; therefore fhall a man leave his Father and Mother, and cleave unto his Wife (c).

From hence it feems at leaft probable, that the Writings of Mofes were not unknown to the Greeks, which makes it the more likely, that thefe Writings or a more antient Tradition, gave Rife to the different Reprefentations the Pagans have given us of an original State of Innocence, which was an Object of

---

[a] Plato in his Banquet.   [b] Gen. i. 27.
[c] Gen. ii. 21, 22, 23, 24.

Faith

Faith amongſt all civilized Nations: This has been
painted in the moſt beautiful Colours, by the Heathen
Poets, under the diſtinction of the golden Age, or
the Reign of Saturn. This was the pre-exiſtent ſtate
of Pythagoras, and of all the Eaſtern Nations ; from
whence it is eaſy to ſee that the Abbe Banier muſt be
greatly miſtaken, when he ſays (a), that the golden
Age had only a Relation to the antient Inhabitants of
Latium, after the arrival of Janus, who, according to
him, ſoftened the Ferocity of their Manners, gave
them Laws, and brought them to live together in Cities and Villages Plato, ſpeaking of the Creator of
the World, ſays (b), " This Architect had a Model,
" by which he produced every thing, and this Model
" is himſelf. The world was perfect in its conſtitution,
" perfect in the various parts that compoſe it ; and
" was ſubject neither to the Diſeaſes nor to the Decay
" of Age. God was then the Prince ; the common
" Parent of all ; he governed the World by himſelf,
" as he governs it now by inferior Deities : Rage and
" Cruelty did not then prevail upon Earth, War and
" Sedition were entirely unknown, God himſelf took
" care of the ſuſtenance of Mankind, and was their
" Guardian and Shepherd : There were no Magiſ-
" trates, no civil Polity as now. In thoſe happy
" Days Men ſprung from the boſom of the Earth,
" which produced them of itſelf, as it produces
" Flowers and Trees. The fertile Fields yielded
" Corn and Fruit, without the Labour of Tillage.—
" Mankind being troubled with no inclemency of the
" Seaſons, had no need of Raiment to cover their
" Bodies ; they took their Reſt on Beds of ever ver-
" dant Turf [c] ; every Thing was beautiful, harmo-
" nious and tranſparent ; Fruits of an exquiſite taſte
" grew ſpontaneouſly ; and it was watered with Ri-
" vers of Nectar ; they there breathed the Light as
" we breathe the Air, and drank Waters which were
" purer than Air itſelf."

[a] Banier, Vol. ii. p. 271.   [b] Plato in Timæus, p. 1047.
[c] Plato in Timæus, p. 537, 538.

Theſe

'Thefe were the Sentiments not only of the Greeks
and Romans, but of all the [a] Eaft.   The ancient
Chinefe Authors diftinguifh the two ftates of Man before and after the Fall, by the two Heavens, and defcribing the firft ; " All things fay they, were then in
" an happy ftate, every thing was beautiful, every
" thing was good, all Beings were perfeft in their
" Kind.   In this happy age, Heaven and Earth em-
" ployed all their virtues jointly to embellifh Nature.
" Tnere was no jarring in the Elements, no Inclemen-
" cy in the Air ; all things grew without Labour : an
" univerfal Fertility reigned.   The active and paffive
" Virtues confpired together to produce and perfect
" the Univerfe." And again, " Whilft the firft ftate
" of Heaven lafted, a pure pleafure and perfect tran-
" qullity reigned over all nature. There were neither
" labour nor pain, nor forrow nor crimes (b)."

But as the Heathens could not believe that it was
confiftent with the Goodnefs of a wife and infinitely
benevolent Being, to create a World in the diforder-
ed State in which this Earth is at prefent, fo nothing
perplexed them more than the difficulty of accounting
for the Introduction of natural and moral evil. The
Story of Pandora and her Box, though it feems to
have fome Relation to that of Eve, as fhe was created
by the fame Prometheus, was the firft Woman, and
the firft who introduced mifery and death into the
World, yet could not give Satisfaction to any reafonable Mind. Hefiod had given it too much the air of a
fiction, and indeed it feems only a fine Allegory, to
fhew the confequences of difobedience in things, to appearance, the moft indifferent ; that from hence fpring

[a] The Bramins of India teach, " That Souls were origin-
" ally created in a State of Purity ; but having finned, were
" thrown down into the Bodies of men or of beafts according to
" their refpective Demerits ; fo that the Body where the Soul
" refides is a fort of Dungeon or Prifon."   Vide A. Rogers on
the Religion of the Bramins.
    [b] Duhald's Hift. of China, in his Abftract of the Chinefe
Claffes.

innumerable

innumerable Evils; while Hope, which only can alleviate them, stays behind. It was doubtless in this light that this fable was considered by the men of sense and understanding. It could give no satisfaction to the penetrating genius of the Philosophers, and therefore Pythagoras adopted the notion of transmigration and of a pre-existent State which he learnt from the Egyptians, Opinions which Plato sometimes seems firmly to believe, and at others mentions only as an ingenious Allegory: However, with these sentiments each of these great men attacked the opinions of those, who on account of the introduction of Evil, denied a providence, by proving that the disorder of the World, and the Misery and Death to which man is subject, are only the consequences which Men have brought upon themselves by their crimes. " Our " Alienation from God, says Pythagoras, [a], and " the loss of the Wings which used to Raise us up " to heavenly Things, have thrown us down into " the Region of Death, which is over-run with all " Manner of Evils; so the stripping ourselves of " earthly affections, and the Revival of our Virtues, " make our Wings grow again, and raise us up to the " Mansions of Life, where true Good is to be " found without any Mixture of Evil." This is more fully explained by Plato, who says, " That the " etherial Earth, the ancient abode of Souls, is placed " amongst the Stars in the pure Regions of Heaven; " but that, as in the Sea, every thing is altered " and disfigured by the Salts that abound in it; so in " our present earth, every thing is deformed, cor- " rupted, and in a Ruinous Condition, if compared " with the primitive Earth." In other Places he endeavours to account for this imaginary Change in the Residence of Man; he represents the Universe, as filled with innumerable Worlds inhabited by free Spirits qualified to enjoy the double Felicity of contemplating the eivine Presence, and of admiring him in his works. But as the sight of the supreme

[a] Hierocl Comm. in aurea Carm. p. 187.

Good

Good muſt neceſſarily engage all the Love of his Creatures, the Will could never offend while the Soul had an immediate view of the divine eſſence ; he therefore ſuppoſes, that at ſome certain Intervals theſe ſouls quitted the divine Preſence, to ſurvey the beauties of Nature, and to feed on the more proper Food of infinite beings, and that then it became poſſible for them to adhere to theſe, and to ſuffer themſelves to be alienated from the Love of the Supreme, when they were thrown into ſome Planet fitted for their Reception, there to expiate their guilt in human bodies, till they are cured and recovered to Virtue by their ſufferings; that Souls leſs degraded than others dwell in the bodies of Philoſophers; and the moſt deſpicable of all animate the bodies of Tyrants; and that after Death they will be more or leſs happy, according as they have in this Life loved Virtue or Vice.

Though theſe Sentiments are not comformable to the Moſaic Account of the Fall, yet they are nevertheleſs very ſublime and have a natural Tendency to promote that Love of God, that Reſignation to the divine Will, and that Rectitude of Life, which was ſo ſtrongly inculcated in the Old and New Teſtament.— In ſeveral Things, however, both Moſes and Heathen Philoſophers agree ; they equally aſſert, that Man was created in a ſtate of Innocence, and conſequently in a ſtate of Happineſs, but that debaſing his Nature, and alienating himſelf from God, he became guilty, ſubject to pain, diſeaſes and death, and to all thoſe afflictions which are neceſſary to awaken his Mind, and to call him to his duty : That we are no Strangers here, that this is a State of Trial, and that it is as much our Intereſt as Duty, to fit ourſelves by a Courſe of Virtue and Piety, for a nobler and more exalted State of Exiſtence. The Egyptians [a] and Perſians [b] had other Schemes, wherein the ſame

important

---

[a] The Egyptians derive their Source of natural and moral Evil, from a wicked ſpirit whom they call Typhon.

[b] The Perſians deduce the Origin of all the Diſorder and

Wicked-

important Truths were conveyed, tho' according to
the genius of those Countries, they were wrapped up
in Allegories. Plutarch has given us his sentiments on
the same subject, and they are too just and rational
to be omitted. " The World, at its Birth, says he (a)
" received from its Creator all that is good : What-
" ever it has at present, that can be called wicked or
" unhappy, is an indisposition foreign to its nature.
" God cannot be the cause of evil, because he is so-
" vereignly good : Matter cannot be the Cause of E-
" vil, because it has no active Force ; but evil comes
" from a third principle, neither so perfect as God,
" nor so imperfect as matter."

The Indian and Chinese Authors are still more ex-
plicit in their account of the Fall of Man, than the
Philosophers we have mentioned, and speak of this
great Event in such Terms, as must raise the Admiration of every Reader. One of their Authors [b]
speaking of the latter Heaven, or the World after the
fall, says, " The Pillars of Heaven were broken, the
" Earth was shaken to its Foundation ; the Heavens
" sunk lower towards the North ; the Sun, the Moon
" and the Stars, changed their motions ; the Earth
" fell to pieces ; the waters enclosed within its bosom
" burst forth with violence, and overflowed it. Man
" rebelling against Heaven, the System of the Uni-

Wickedness in the World from evil Spirits, the chief of whom
they call Abrim or Arimanius. Light, say they can produce
nothing but Light, and can never be the Origin of Evil : It produced several Beings, all of them spiritual, luminous and powerful ; but Arimanius their Chief had an evil Thought contrary to the Light : He doubted, and by that doubting became
dark ; and from hence proceeded whatever is contrary to the light.
They also tell us that there will come a time when Arimanius
shall be compleatly destroyed, when the Earth shall change its
Form, and when all Mankind shall enjoy the same Life, Language
and Government. See Dr. Hyde's ancient Religion of the Per-
sans.

(a) Plutarch de Anim. form. p . 1015.

(b) The Philosopher Hoinantese. See an Account of his works
in Duhald's Hist. of China.

" verse

" verſe was quite diſordered." Other Authors (a) ſtill more ancient expreſs themſelves thus : " The u-
" niverſal Fertility of Nature degenerated into an
" ugly Barrenneſs, the Plants faded. the Trees with-
" ered away, diſconſolate Nature refuſed to diſtribute
" her uſual Bounty. All Creatures declared War a-
" gainſt one another ; Miſeries and Crimes overflow-
" ed the Face of the Earth. All theſe Evils aroſe
" from Man's deſpiſing the Supreme Monarch of the
" Univerſe : He would needs diſpute about Truth
" and Falſhood, and theſe diſputes baniſh'd the eter-
" nal Reaſon He then fixed his looks on terreſtrial
" Objects and loved them to exceſs ; hence aroſe the
" Paſſions ; he became gradually transform'd into the
" Objects he loved, and the celeſtial Reaſon entirely
" abandoned him."

It was the Opinion of Socrates and Pluto, that the Soul only was the Man, and the the body nothing more than a priſon, a dwelling-place, or a garment ; and conſequently, that they had no neceſſary connection with each other ſince the Soul being entirely diſ-tinct from matter, might live, and think, and act, with-out the aſſiſtance of ſuch groſs organs, and would only begin to exert itſelf with its native Freedom, when the Clog of the Body was ſhaken off and deſtroyed. The mind then, in his Eſteem, was the only part worthy of our care ; and that our principal ſtudy ſhould therefore be to raiſe and exalt its Faculties. to improve in Virtue and in Piety, and in all thoſe Diſpoſitions which will bring us to a nearer Reſemblance to the ſupreme and only perfect mind.

And here it cannot be amiſs to obſerve, that the Notion of good and bad Dæmons, which was almoſt univerſally believed, had a very near Relation to our Ideas of Angels and Devils, as they were a middle Claſs of Beings, ſuperior to Men and inferior to the Gods ; the one Species endeavoured to inſpire Motives to Virtue, and to ſhield from

---

[a] Wentſe and Licentſe. See Duhald.

Dæm-

Danger the other leading to Sin and Ruin. Plato and Jamblicus, who as well as Socrates, believed the Exiſtence of theſe tutelarly Deities, denied that wicked Spirits had any Influence on human Affairs. Theſe Philoſophers maintained the Liberty of the Will, and at the ſame Time endeavoured to prove the Neceſſity Man frequently ſtood in of being favoured with the divine Aſſiſtance, which they imagined they partook of by the intervention of theſe Beings. They believed that (a) " Every Man " had one of theſe Genii, or Dæmons for hisGuardian, " who was to be the Witneſs, not only of his Actions, " but of his very Thoughts ; that at Death the Genius " delivered up to Judgment the perſon who had been " committed to his Charge ; that he is to be a Witneſs for or againſt him, and according to his Deciſion his Doom is to be pronounced."

The Notion of Guardian Angels has been contended for by many Chriſtians, who alledge ſeveral Paſſages of Scripture, that ſeem to favour this Doctrine, while others have turn'd all that has been ſaid of theſe Genii into Allegory; and aſſert, that by the two Dæmons, the one good and the other bad, are meant the Influences of Conſcience, and the Strength of Appetite.

It is very evident, however, that the Greeks had an Idea of theſe Beings, and that their Exiſtence was generally believed. Hence according to Plutarch, came their Fables of the Titans and Giants, and the Engagements of Python againſt Apollo ; which have ſo near a Reſemblance to the Fictions of Oſiris and Typhon. Theſe were beings ſuperior to Men, and yet compoſed of a ſpiritual and corporeal Nature ; and conſequently capable of animal Pleaſures and Pains. The Fictions relating to the Giants, in Mr. Banier's Opinion [b], took their Riſe from a Paſſage in Geneſis ; where it is

[a] Apuleius on the Dæmon of Socrates.
[b] Banier, Vol. I. 121. 122.

faid, that the [a]Sons of God, whom the Ancients fuppofed to be the Guardian Angels, became enamoured
with the Daughters of Men, and that their Children
were mighty Men, or Giants, the Word in the Original fignifying either Giants, or Men become monftrous
by their Crimes; their Heads inftead of their Guilt,
were faid to reach to the Clouds, while the Wickednefs of their Lives might not improperly be termed
fighting againft God, and daring the Thunder of
Heaven. But however this be, it will hardly be
doubted, but that this Paffage might give Rife to the
Amours of the Gods and Goddeffes, and their various
Intrigues with Mortals. As the frequent appearance
of real Angels to the Patriarchs, and the hofpitable
Reception they met with under the difguife of Travellers, might give Room for the Poets to Form, upon
the fame Plan, the Tales of Baucis and Philemon, and
to contraft that beautiful Picture of humble Content,
and of the Peace that bleffed the homely Cottages of
the innocent and good, with the Story of Lycaon, who
wanting Humanity, and being of a favage inhofpitable
Temper, is, with great Propriety, faid to change his
Form into one more fuitable to the Difpofition of his
Mind. The Moral of this Fable is, that Humanity is
the Charaftciftick of Man; and that a Cruel Soul in
a human Body is only a Wolf in difguife.

It is certain that the Traditions relating to the univerfal Deluge, have been found in almoft all Nations;
and though the Deluge of Deucalion fhould not appear
to be the fame as that of Noah, it cannot be doubted
but that fome Circumftances have been borrowed from
Noah's Hiftory, and that thefe are the moft ftriking
Parts of the Defcription. Lucian, fpeaking of the ancient People of Syria, in the Country where the Deluge of Deucalion is fuppofed to have happened, fays
[b] that "The Greeks affert in their Fables, that the

---

[a] Gen. vi. 2. By the Sons of God, is here undoubtedly
meant the Defcendents of Seth, whofhad probably this Title given
them, to diftinguifh them from the Defcendents of Cain, who
were called the Sons of Men.
[b] De Dea Syria.

" firft

" firſt Men being of an inſolent and cruel diſpoſition,
" inhuman, inhoſpitable, and regardleſs of their Faith
" were all deſtroyed by a deluge; the Earth [a] pour-
" ing forth vaſt ſtreams of water, ſwelled the Rivers,
" which together with the Rains; made the Sea riſe
" above its banks and overflow the land, ſo that all
" was laid under Water, that Deucalion alone ſaved
" himſelf and Family in an Ark, and two of each
" kind of wild and tame Animals, who loſing their a-
" nimoſity, entered into it of their own accord. That
" thus Deucalion floated on the Waters till they be-
" came aſſuaged, and then repaired the human
" Race."

We are alſo informed, that this Veſſel reſted on a
high Mountain; and Plutarch even mentions the
Dove, and Abydinus ſpeaks of a certain Fowl being
let out of the Ark, which finding no place of Reſt returned twice into the veſſel. We are told too that
Deucalion, a perſon of ſtrict Piety and Virtue, offered Sacrifice to Jupiter the Saviour. Thus the ſacred
Writings inform us, that Noah offered Sacrifices of
clean beaſts in Token of gratitude to God, for having
graciouſly preſerved both him and his Family.

The Chaldean Authors have alſo related a Tradition, which undoubtedly can only refer to this celebrated Event; and which, for its ſingularity, deſerves
to be mentioned [b]. Chronus (or Saturn, ſay they)
appearing to Xiſuthrus in a dream, informed him, that
on the Fifteenth of the Month Dæſius, a deluge would
deſtroy Mankind, at the ſame time enjoining him to
write down the Origin of the Hiſtory, and end of all
Things, and then to conceal the Writing in the Earth
in the City of the Sun, called Sippara. He was next
enjoined to build a ſhip, to provide neceſſary Proviſi-
ons, and to enter into it himſelf with his Friends and
Relations, and to ſhut in with them the Birds and
four footed beaſts. Xiſuthrus obeyed the Orders that
had been given him, and made a ſhip two furlongs in

(a) The ſame though it is expreſſed by Moſes, who ſays, The
Fountains of the great Deep were broken up.
[b] See Syncell. Chronolog. p. 38.

X

Breadth;

breadth, and five in length; which he had no fooner entered than the Earth was overflowed.

Some time after, perceiving that the Waters were abated, he let out fome Fowls, but finding neither Food nor Refting Place, they returned into the Veffel. In a few days more he fent out others, who returned with mud in their claws; but the third time he let them go they returned no more: From whence he concluded, that the Earth began to appear; He then made a window in the veffel, and finding fthat it had refted on a mountain, came forth with his Wife, his Daughter and the Pilot, and having paid Adoration to the Earth, raifed an Altar and offered a Sacrifice to the Gods; when he and they who were with him inftantly difappeared. The Perfons in the fhip finding they did not return, came out and fought for them in vain: At laft they heard a Voice faying, " Xifu- " thrus, on account of his Piety is, with thofe who " accompanied him, tranflated into Heaven and num- " bered among the Gods." They were then, by the fame Voice, exhorted to be religious, to dig up the Writing that had been buried at Sippara, and then to repair to Babylon.

Thus it appears, that Idolatry and Fables being once fet on Foot, the People, who ftill retained confufed Ideas of fome anient Truths, or the moft remarkable Particulars of fome paft Tianfactions, adapted them to the prefent mode of Thinking, or applied them to fuch Fables as feemed to have any Relation thereto. By this means truth and falfhood were blended together; and thus it happens that we fiequently find fome Traces of Hiftory intermingled with the moft ridiculous Fictions, and remarkable Tranfactions fometimes pretty exactly related, though at the fame time confounded with the grofleft Abfurdities

It is very evident that the divifion of time into feven days could only be a Tradition conftantly preferved and handed down from the moft early Ages. This appears to be the moft antient method of reckoning time, fince it was very early obferved by the
Egyptians.

Egyptians. But of this we have said enough in the preceding Differtation, to which it properly belongs.

We might here add a number of other Circumftances in which there feems to be fome Refemblance between the facred Hiftory and the Fictions of the Pagans; this indeed has opened fo wide a field for the conjectures of men, that there is hardly a Perfon in the Old Teftament, but on account of fome Incident in his Life, has been thought to be the Model of a correfpondent Character in the Heathen Poets.

But notwithftanding the difficulty of difcovering the Origin of Fables, when fome are founded on Tradition, others on Hiftory, others on the Strength of a warm and lively Imagination; and others, perhaps, on a mixture of all thefe together: Yet it muft be confeffed, that they are generally filled with the nobleft Sentiments, and the Morals which the Poets intended to be conveyed, are frequently obvious to the meaneft Capacities. Virtue is painted in the moft beautiful Colours, and Vice in its native Deformity. All Methods are taken to render Villany hateful, and undiffembled Goodnefs amiable in the Eyes of Men. Who can read the picture Ovid gives of Envy (a), without detefting the hateful Perverfion of the Paffions? The very Defcription of the Field muft have a greater Force than all the Arguments of a long and laboured Difcourfe.

> Livid and meagre were her Looks, her eye
> In foul diftorted Glances turn'd awry;
> A hoard of Gall her inward Parts poffefs'd,
> And fpread a greennefs o'er her canker'd breaft:
> Her teeth were brown with Ruft, and from her Tongue,
> In dangling drops the ftringy poifon hung.
> She never fmiles, but when the wretched weep,
> Nor lulls her malice with a moment's fleep.
> Reftlefs in fpite, while watchful to deftroy,
> She pines and fickens at another's Joy,
> Foe to herfelf.——— ADDISON.

[a] Ovid Metam. l. 2.

 It

It is is eafy to fee the Advantage of fuch Portraits as thefe, where the Virtues and Vices are coloured with fuch Juftice and ftrength of Fancy.

The Story of Deucalion and Pyrrha teaches, that Piety and Innocence will always infure the divine Protection.

That of Phaeton, that a too exceffive Fondnefs in the Parent is Cruelty to the Child.

That of Narciffus, that an inordinate Self Love, which renders us cruel to others, is fure to be its own Tormentor.

That of Pentheus, that Enthufiafm is frequently more cruel than Atheifm, and that an inordinate zeal deftroys the effects it would produce.

That of Minos and Scylla, the Infamy of felling our Country; and that even they who reap Advantage from the Crime, deteft the Criminal.

The Story of Cippus, is adapted to infpire that noble Magnamity and true greatnefs of Soul, which made him prefer the Publick Welfare to his own private Grandeur, while with an exemplary generofity, he chofe rather to live a private Freeman than to command Numbers of Slaves.

From the ftory of Tereus we learn, that he who is guilty of one Crime lays the Foundation of another and that he who begins with Luft may poffibly end with Murder.

From the Avarice of Midas we learn that Covetoufnefs is its own Punifhment, and that nothing would prove more fatal to us than the Completion of our Wifhes, and the Gratification of our fondeft Defires.

As the Morals of the Greeks and Romans were generally founded on the Conftitution of the human Frame, and our various Relations as animal, as rational, and unaccountable Beings, they came very near to the Morals or Chriftianity. They fprang from the Seeds of eternal Truth originally fown in the Mind, by the great Creator himfelf. They were founded in Nature, and confequently muft fo far as they were uncorrupted, be agreeable to every Revelation that

could

could possibly proceed from the God of Nature : For
the Dictates of unbiassed and unprejudiced Reason
can never deviate far from the Truth. The Laws of
Justice and Humanity are so level to the Understanding
and so conformable to the Impulses of the moral Sense
that a serious Enquirer can never be much mistaken
unless his Heart be corrupt. " According to the O-
" pinions of the greatest and wisest Philosopher, says
" Cicero [b], the Law is not an an Invention of the
" human Mind, or the arbitrary Constitution of Men;
" but flows from the eternal Reason that governs the
" Universe, The Rape which Tarquin committed up-
" on Lucretia, was not less criminal from there being
" at that Time no written Law at Rome against such
" Acts of Violence ; the Tyrant was guilty of a breach
" of the eternal Law, whose Origin is as ancient as
" the divine Intellect ; for the true, the primitive, and
" the supreme Law, is nothing else but the soveeign
" Reason of the great Jove." Can any thing be more
just and more rational than this Sentiment !

The Philosophers, the Historians and the Poets,
some few instances excepted, were unanimous in the
Cause of Virtue. The Philosophers laid down the
nicest Rules for the Regulation of the moral Conduct;
for the exercise of Humanity, and the manner in
which benefits ought to be conferred ; they employed
themselves in making good Laws, they inculcated a
Love of the Gods, a Love of their Country, a Contempt for Luxury, and for the mean Gratifications of
Sense. And these were inforced by the brightest Conjectures relating to a happy immortality. The Historians generally wrote of Virtue as if they felt it, and
expressed a Love and Admiration of it by their Manner of describing great, generous, and good Actions ;
and those that were mean, selfish and cruel. The
Honours of the first, and the Infamy of the last, they
transmitted down to future Ages. The Poets have
dressed up Piety and Virtue, in all the Instances of
Life in the brightest and most lively Colours ; here

[b] Cicero de log. l. 2. p. 1194.

X 3

their

their Numbers flow with the foftest, mildest, and most melodious Harmony, while all the Thunder of Poetry was employed to blast the falfe Joy of the Wicked.

Pindar writes in a Strain of exalted Piety, and endeavours to wipe off the Afperfions which ancient Fables had thrown on their Deities. Virtue and Religion are the Subjects of his Praifes, and he fpeaks of the Rewards of the Juft with a warm and lively Affurance.

Juvenal eftablifhes the Diftinctions of Good and Evil, and builds his Doctrines on the unmoveable Foundations of a fupreme God, and an over ruling Providence: His Morals are fuited to the Nature and Dignity of an immortal Soul, and like it derive their Original from Heaven.

He afferts [c], that the indulgence of a fecret Inclination to Vice, though never ripened into Action, ftains the Mind with Guilt, and juftly expofes the Offender to the Punifhment of Heaven. What a Scene of Horror does he lay open [d], when he expofes to our View the Wounds and Anguifh of a guilty Confcience! With what Earneftnefs does he exhort his Reader [e] to prefer Confcience and Principle to Life itfelf, and not to be reftrained from the Exercife of his Duty by the Threats of a Tyrant, or the Profpect of Death, in all the Circumftances of Cruelty and Terror! How juftly does he expofe the fatal Paffion of Revenge [f], from the Ignorance and Littlenefs of the Mind that is carried away by it; from the Honour and Generofity of paffing by Affronts, and forgiving Injuries; and from the Example of thofe who had been remarkable for their Wifdom and their Meeknefs, and efpecially from that of Socrates, who was fo great a Proficient in the beft Philofophy, that being fenfible that his Perfecutors could do him no Hurt, had not the leaft Wifh to do them any: Who juft before he was going to die, talked with that eafy and chearful,

[c] Juv. Sar. 13. v. 208.
[d] Ib. v. 192, 210.
[e] Sat. 8. v. 79, 85.   [f] Sat. 13. v. 181.

Compofure

Compofure, as if he had been going to take poffeffion of a Crown [a], and drank of the poifonous bowl,
as a potion that was to help him forward to a happy
immortality.

Thus did the Teftimony of a good Confcience fupport the wife and virtuous of the Heathens in their
laft moments, while Guilt was fure to dwell upon the
mind, and deprive it of all confidence in God. What
Plato fays to this purpofe is admirably good (b).
" Know, Socrates, fays he, that when any one is at
" the point of Death, he is filled with anxious doubts
" and Fears, from a Reflection on the Errors of his
" paft Life; then it is that the Pains and Torments
" referved in the other World for the guilty, which
" he had before ridiculed as fo many idle Fables, be-
" gin to affect his foul, and to fill him with dreadful
" apprehenfions left they fhould prove real. Thus,
" whether it be that the mind is enfeebled with age,
" or that having death nearer at hand, he examines
" things with greater attention, his Soul is feized
" with Fear and Terror, and, if he has injured any
" one finks into defpair, while he, who has nothing
" to reproach himfelf with, feels the fweet Hope
" fpringing up in his Soul, which Pindar calls The
" Nurfe of old Age."

Socrates traces all the Principal Duties to God and
Man (a) in fuch a manner, as is moft likely to engage
and prevail upon the mind. He made as many Im-
provements in true Morality, as was poffible to be
made by the utmoft Strength of human Reafon, and
in fome places he feems as if enlightened by a Ray
from Heaven. In one of Plato's dialogues he prophe-
fies that a Divine Perfon, a true Friend and Lover of
mankind, would come into the World, to inftruct

[a] Socrates being afked by his Friends to give them the Reafon of this ferene Joy and noble intrepidity; ' I hope, he replied,
" to be re-united to the good and perfect Gods, and to be affocia-
" ted with better men than thofe I leave upon the Earth." Plato's Dialogues, p. 48. 51.

[b] De Rep. 1. 5.

[c] Zenophon's memorable Things of Socrates.

them

them in the moſt acceptable Way of addreſſing their Prayers to the Majeſty of Heaven, and deſcribes him by the Great and Providential title of One that taketh Care of us.

Theſe were the Sentiments of ſome of the moſt celebrated of the Pagan Philoſophers, whence Chriſtianity receives this Teſtimony of its Truth, that the Purity of its moral Precepts, is confirmed by the Dictates of the unprejudiced Reaſon, and unbiaſſed Judgments, of the wiſeſt and beſt Men in all Ages. Can any thing be a greater Confirmation of its Divinity, than its bearing thoſe Signatures of eternal Reaſon, which are ſtamped on all Hearts? And that while the Works of the Heathens, however excellent, are mingled with Uncertainty and Miſtake, this alone has the moſt remarkable Credentials of that eternal Truth which is always conſiſtent with itſelf, and at the greateſt Diſtance from Error.

But here it may be aſked, how are theſe ſublime Conceptions conſiſtent with Idolatry : with the Blindneſs of Men who paid Adoration to ſenſeleſs Statues, who were continually adding to the Number of their Gods, and who were ſo ſtupid, as not only to build a Temple to Public Faith, to Virtue, and other Deities of the like Kind; but even to worſhip the Fever, and to build an Altar to Fear?

To reconcile theſe ſeeming Contradictions, it is neceſſary, in a few words, to throw what has already been ſaid upon this Subject, in one point of View.

It appears from the Account we have given of the Theology of the Ancients, that the Egyptians, Greeks and Romans worſhipped only one Almighty, independent Being, the Father of Gods and Men, with a ſupreme Adoration; and that the ſeveral ſuperior Deities publickly worſhipped, were only different Names, or Attributes of the ſame God. This is aſſerted not only by ſeveral of the Pagans, but even by St. Auſtin. Whether this Diſtinction was maintained by the Bulk of the People amongſt the Greeks and Romans, is not ſo eaſy to determine ; it is probable, that they might imagine them diſtinct Beings ſubordinate to the Su-

preme

preme. However, there were others univerfally allowed to be of an inferior Clafs, and thefe were the
national aad tutelary Deities, among which laft number we may reckon the good Dæmons, or houfhold
Gods, which the Romans upon conquering any nation or City, invited to take up their Refidence a-
mongft them. Thefe were undoubtedly worfhipped
with an inferior Kind of Adoration. Since the Stoic
and Epicurean Philofophers, who allowed their Exiftence, believed them to be mortal, and that they
were to perifh in the general conflagration, in which
they imagined the world was to be confumed by fire.
To this Pliny alludes, when defcribing the darknefs
and horror that attended the Eruption of Vefuvius,
he fays, that fome were lifting up their hands to the
Gods; but that the greater part imagined, that the
laft and eternal night was come, which was to deftroy
both the Gods and the World together.

This Diftinction may be juftified by the united Teftimony of the ancients; and indeed it in a great meafure removes the abfurdity of their continually introducing what were called new Gods; that is, new
mediators, and new methods or Ceremonials to be
added, on particular occafions to the ancient Worfhip.

The Idolatry of the Pagans, did not confift in
paying a direct Adoration to the Statues, but in
making them the (n) Medium of Worfhip; and
there-

[n] The Folly of reprefenting the Infinite and Omniprefent
Spirit, by a fenfible Image, is obvious from a very fmall Degree
of Reflection; and from hence arifes the Crime of Idolatry, or
reprefenting him by the Works of Nature, or thofe of Mens
Hands, as it is a Degradation of the Deity and an affront to the
Being, whofe glorious Effence is unlimitted and unconfined; from
hence proceeds that Exclamation of the Prophet, Whereunto
fhall ye LIKEN me, faith the Lord, &c.

When the Ifraelites made the Golden Calf, and cried out,
This is the God that brought us out of the Land of Egypt, they
muft be fuppofed to mean, This reprefents the God that brought
us out of the land of Egypt. They bad lately left a Country fond
of Symbols, where they had been ufed to fee one Thing reprefented

therefore, whether the feveral Deities were reckoned
to be inferior beings, or only different Names or Attributes of one Supreme, yet their Symbols, the Sun,
Moon and Stars, or the Statues erected to the Honour
of their Gods, were never (except amongft the loweft
and moft ignorant of People) acknowledged as the ultimate Objects of Worfhip In thefe Statues, however, the Deity was fuppofed to refide in a peculiar
Manner.

But even this was not always the Cafe: it is very
evident, that the Statues erected to the Paffions, the
Virtues, and the Vices, were not of this Clafs. The
Romans had particular Places for offering up particular
Petitions; they offered up their prayers for Health.
in the 'Temple of Salus; they prayed for the Prefervation of their Liberties before the Statue of Liberty,
and offered their Sacrifices to the Supreme before a
Figure expreffive of their Wants. Fever, in the
Opinion of the moft ftupid of the Vulgar, could never
be confidered as a God, yet at the Altar of Fever they
befought the Supreme, to preferve them from being
infected with this Difoider, or to cure their Friends
who were already infected by it: And at the Altar of
Fear, they put up their Supplications, that they might
be preferved from the Influence of a fhameful Panic
in the day of Battle.

As this appears evidently to be the Cafe, it is no
Wonder, that the Number of thefe Kind of Gods became very great. Some of thefe, by the Parade of
Ceremonies that attended this Method of Devotion,
were found to have a mighty Effect on the Minds of
the Vulgar: So that when any Virtue began to lofe

fented by another; and the Sun, the moft glorious Image of the
Deity, when he enters into Taurus, reprefented by a Bull. Had
they been fo ftupid as to Imagine this Calf which they had juft
made to be the God of their Fathers, the God that had wrought
fo many Mirac'es for them even before they had given him Exiftence; their Folly would be entirely inconfiftent with the rational
Nature of Man, and they muft have been abfolutely incapable
both of Moral and Civil Government, and could only be accounted Idiots or Madmen.

Ground,

Ground, a Temple, or at leaft an Altar erected to its Honour, was fure to raife it from its declining ftate, and to re-inftate its influence on the Heart of Man.

This appears to be a true Reprefentation of the cafe, from the account which Dionyfius of Halicarnaffus gives (a) of the Reafons, which induced Numa Pompilius to introduce Faith into the number of the Roman Divinities, and which, doubtlefs, gave Rife to all the other Deities of the fame kind, that were afterwards introduced. " To engage his People to " mutual Faith and Fidelity, fays he, Numa had re " courfe to a method hitherto unknown to the moft " celebrated Legiflators ; publick contracts, he ob " ferved were feldom violated, from the regard paid " to thofe who were Witneffes to any engagement, " while thofe made in private though in their own " Nature no lefs indifpenfable than the other, were " not fo ftrictly obferved ; whence he concluded,that " by deifying faith, thefe contracts would be ftill " more binding : Befides, he thought it unreafonable, " that while divine Honours were paid to Juftice, " Nemefis and Themis; faith the moft facred and " venerable Thing in the World, fhould receive nei " ther publick nor private Honour; he therefore " built a Temple to publick faith, and inftituted Sa " crifices, the Charge of which was to be defrayed by " the Publick. This he did with the Hope, that a " Veneration for this Virtue being propagated thro' " the City, would infenfibly be communicated to " each Individual. His Conjectures proved true, " and faith became fo revered, that fhe had more " force than even Witneffes and Oaths; fo that it " was the common method, in cafes of intricacy, for " Magiftrates to refer the Decifion to the faith of the " contending Parties."

Thus it appears evident, that thefe kind of Gods, and the Temples erected to their Honour, were founded not only on political, but on virtuous Principles. This was undoubtedly the cafe, with refpect to the

(a) Dion. Halic. l, 2. c. 75.

Greeks

Greeks as well as the Romans : For a propofal being made at Athens, to introduce the Combats of the Gladiators; firft throw down, cried out an Athenian Philofopher from the midft of the Affembly, throw down the Altar, erected by our Anceftors above a thoufand years ago to Mercy   Was not this to fay that they had no need of an altar to infpire a Regard to mercy and compaffion, when they wanted publick Spectacles to teach a Savage cruelty and hardnefs of Heart.

APPENDIX.

CONTAINING

An account of the various Methods of Divination by Aftrology, Prodigies, Magic, Augury, the Arufpices and Oracles : with a fhort account of Altars, facred Groves and Sacrifices, Priefts and Temples.

I. Of ASTROLOGY.

WE fhall now unfold the methods, by which the Names of the Heathen Gods laid the foundation of feveral pretended Sciences : and this we think the more neceffary in this place, as it is a fubject which has a clofe connection with the Origin of Idolatry. And here we muft again turn our eyes to the Ancient Egyptians, who were not only the Inventors of Arts, but the Authors of the groffeft Superftitions. We have already accounted for the Names given to the figns of the Zodiac, which, in their firft Inftitution, had an expreffive meaning, and which one would hardly imagine capable of producing the multitude of fuperftitious ceremonies, and extravagant opinions which refulted from them ; ceremonies and opinions diffufed over the whole Earth, and propagated with fuccefs in almoft every Nation.

Aftrology was doubtlefs the firft method of Divination, and probably prepared the mind of Man for the other no lefs abfurd ways of fearching into Futurity : And therefore a fhort view of the Rife of this pretended Science cannot be improper in this Place, efpecially as the Hiftory of thefe Abfurdities is the beft method of confulting them. And indeed as this

Y

Trea-

Treatife is chiefly defigned for the Improvement of Youth, nothing can be of greater Service to them than to render them able to trace the Origin of thofe pretended fciences, fome of which have even ftill an Influence on many weak and ignorant minds. But to proceed.

The Egyptians becoming ignorant of the Aftronomical Hieroglyphics, by degrees looked upon the names the figns, as exprefling certain Powers with which they were invefted, and as Indications of their feveral offices. The Sun on account of its fplendor and enlivening influence, was imagined to be the great mover of nature; the moon had the fecond Rank of Powers, and each fign and conftellation a certain fhare in the government of the world; the Ram had a ftrong influence over the young of the flocks and herds; the Ballance could infpire nothing but inclinations to good order and juftice; and the Scorpion excite only evil difpofitions: And, in fhort, that each fign produced the good or evil intimated by its name. Thus, if the child happened to be born at the inftant when the firft Star of the Ram rofe above the Horizon, (when in order to give this nonfenfe the air of a fcience, the ftar was fuppofed to have its greateft influence) he would be rich in Cattle: and that he who fhould enter the World under the crab, fhould meet with nothing but difappointment; and all his affairs fhould go backwards and downwards. The people were to be happy whofe King entered the world under the fign Libra; but compleatly wretched if he fhould light under the horrid fign Scorpio: The Perfons born under Capricorn, efpecially if the Sun at the fame time afcended the Horizon, were fure to meet with fuccefs and to rife upwards like the wild Goat, and the Sun which then afcends for fix months together, the Lion was to produce Heroes; and the Virgin with her ear of corn, to infpire chaftity, and to unite virtue and abundance. Could any thing be more extravagant and ridiculous! " This way of arguing, fays an inge-
" nious modern Author, is nearly like that of a
" man, who fhould imagine, that in order to have
" good

" good Wine in his Cellar, he need do no more than
" hang a good Cork at the Door."

The Cafe was exactly the fame with refpect to the Planets, whofe Influence is only founded on the groundlefs fuppofition of their being the Habitation of the pretended Deities, whofe Names they bear, and the Fabulous Characters the Poets have given them.

Thus to Saturn they imputed languid and even deftructive influences; for no other Reafon, but becaufe they had been pleafed to make this Planet the Refidence of Saturn, who was painted with gray hairs and a Scythe.

To Jupiter they attributed the Power of beftowing Crowns, and diftributing long Life, Wealth and Grandeur, meerly becaufe it bears the Name of the Father of Life.

Mars was fuppofed to infpire a ftrong inclination for War; becaufe it was believed to be the Refidence of the God of War.

Venus had the power of rendering Men voluptuous, and fond of pleafure, becaufe they had been pleafed to give it the Name of one, who, by fome, was thought to be the Mother of Pleafure.

Mercury, though almoft always invifible, would never have been thought to fuperintend the Profperity of States, and the Affairs of Wit and Commerce, had not Men, without the leaft Reafon, given it the Name of one who was fuppofed to be the inventor of civil Polity.

According to the Aftrologers, the power of the afcending Planet is greatly increafed by that of an afcending Sign; then the benign influences are all united, and fall together on the Head of all the happy Infants which at that Moment enter the World [b]; yet can

Y 9   any

[b] " What compleats the Ridicule, fays 'he Abbe La Pluche,
" to whom we are obliged for thefe judicious Obfervations is,
" that what Aftronomers call the firft Degree of the Ram, the
" Ballance, or of Sagitarius, is no longer the firft Sign, which
" gives fruitfulnefs to the Flocks, infpires Men with a Love of
" Juftice or forms the Hero. It has been found that all the ce-
" leftial

any Thing be more contrary to Experience ; which
shews us that the Characters and Events produced
by Persons born under the same Aspect of the Stars,
are so far from being alike, that they are directly opposite.

Thus, it is evident, that Astrology is built upon no
Principles, that it is founded on Fables, and on Influences void of Reality.   Yet absurd as it is, and ever
was, it obtained Credit, and the more it spread, the
greater injury was done to the cause of Virtue.   Instead of the exercise of Prudence and wise Precaution
it substituted superstitious forms and childish Practices, it enervated the courage of the brave by appre-
hensions grounded on Puns and Quibbles, and encouraged the Wicked, by making them lay to the charge
of a Planet, those evils which only proceeded from
their own Depravity.

But not content with these absurdities, which destroyed the very idea of Liberty they asserted that
these stars, which had not the least connection with
Mankind, governed all the Parts of the human body [a], and ridiculously affirmed, that the Ram

" lestial Signs have, by little and little, receded from the vernal
" Equinox, and drawn back to the East : Notwithstanding this,
" the point of the Zodiack that cuts the Equator is still called
" the first degree of the Ram, tho' the first Star of the Ram be
" thirty degrees beyond it, and all the other signs in the same
" Proportion. When therefore any one is said to be born under
" the first Degree of the Ram, it was in Reality one of the De-
" grees of Pisces that then came above the Horizon; and when
" another is said to be born with a Royal Soul, and heroic dispo-
" positions, because at his Birth the Planet Jupiter ascended the
" Horizon in Conjunction with the first Star of Sagitary; Jupi-
" ter was indeed at that time in Conjuction with a Star thirty
" Degrees eastward of Sagitary, and in good Truth it was the
" pernicious Scorpion, that presided at the Birth of this happy,
" this incomparable Child.   Abbe Pluche's Hist. of the Heavens
Vol. I. p. 255.

[a] Each hour of the Day had also one ; the Number seven,
being that of the Planets became of mighty consequence. The
en Days in the week, a period of time handed down by Tradi-
on, happened to correspond with the Number of the Pla-
ets; and therefore they gave the Name of a Planet to each
Day

prefided over the Head ; the Bull over the Gullet ; the Twins over the Breaft ; the Scorpion over the Entrails ; the Fifhes over the Feet, &c By this Means they pretended to account for the various Diforders of the Body ; which was fuppofed to be in a good or bad difpofition, according to the different Afpects of thefe Signs. To mention only one Inftance ; they pretended that great Caution ought to be ufed in taking a Medicine under Taurus, or the Bull, becaufe as this Animal chews his Cud, the Perfon would not be able to keep it in his Stomach.

Nay, the Influences of the Planets were extended to the Bowels of the Earth, where they were fuppofed to produce Metals. From hence it appears, that when Superftition and Folly are once on Foot, there is no fetting Bounds to their Progrefs. Gold, to be fure, muft be the Production of the Sun, and the Conformity in Point of Colour, Brighnefs and Value was a fenfible Proof of it. By the fame Way of Reafoning the Moon produced all the Silver, to which it was related by Colour ; Mars all the Iron, which ought to be the favourite Metal of the God of War ; Venus prefided over Copper, which fhe might well be fuppofed to produce, fince it was found in Plenty in the Ifle of Cyprus, which was fuppofed to be the favourite Refidence of this Goddefs. By the fame fine Way of Reafoning, the other Planets prefided over the other Metals. The languid Saturn was fet over Mines of Lead ; and Mercury, on Account of his Activity, had the Superintendency of Quickfilver ; while it was the Province of Jupiter to prefide over Tin, as this was the only Metal that was left him.

Day ; and from thence fome Days in the Week were confidered as more fortunate or unlucky than the reft : And hence feven Times feven, called the climacterical Period of Hours, Days, or Years, were thought extremely dangerous, and to have a furprifing Effect on private Perfons, the Fortunes of Princes, and the Government of States. Thus the Mind of Man became diftreffed by Imaginary Evils, and the Approach of thefe Moments, in themfelves, as Harmlefs as the reft of their Lives, has, by the Strength of Imagination, brought on the moft fatal Effects.

From hence the Metals obtained the names of the Planets; and from this opinion, that each Planet engendered its own peculiar Metal, they at length conceived an opinion, that as one planet was more powerful than another, the metal produced by the weakeſt, was converted into another by the influence of a ſtronger Planet. Lead, though a real metal, and as perfect in its kind as any of the reſt, was conſidered as only a half Metal, which through the languid influences of old Saturn, was left imperfect; and therefore under the aſpect of Jupiter it was converted into tin; under that of Venus into Copper; and at laſt into Gold, under ſome particular aſpects of the Sun. And from hence, at laſt, aroſe the extravagant opinions of the Alchymiſts, who with wonderful ſagacity endeavoured to find out means for haſtening theſe changes or tranſmutations, which, as they conceived, the Planets performed too ſlowly; but, at laſt, the World was convinced, that the Art of the Alchymiſt was as ineffectual as the Influences of the Planets, which, in a long Succeſſion of Ages, had never been known to change a mine of Lead to that of Tin or any other Metal.

II. Of Prodigies.

WHOEVER reads the Roman Hiſtorians[a] muſt be ſurprized at the Number of Prodigies which are conſtantly recorded, and which frequently filled the People with the moſt dreadful Apprehenſions. It muſt be confeſſed, that ſome of theſe ſeem altogether ſupernatural; while much the greater part only conſiſt of ſome of the uncommon productions of Nature, which ſuperſtition always attributed to a ſuperior Cauſe, and repreſented as the Prognoſtications of ſome impending Misfortunes.

Of this claſs may be reckoned the appearance of two Suns, the Nights illuminated by Rays of Light,

(p) Particularly Livy, Dionyſus of Halicarnaſſus, Pliny, and Valerius Maximus.

the

the Views of fighting Armies, Swords and Spears darting thro' the air ; showers of milk, of blood, of stones,
of ashes, or of fire ; and the birth of monsters, of children, or of beasts who had two heads, or of infants
who had some features resembling those of the brute
creation: These were all dreadful prodigies, which
filled the People with inexpressible astonishment, and
the whole Roman Empire with an extreme Perplexity ; and whatever unhappy event followed upon
these, was attributed to be either caused or predicted
by them.

Yet nothing is more easy than to account for these
Productions ; which have no Relation to any Events
that may happen to follow them: The appearance
of two Suns has frequently happened in England, as
well as in other Places, and is only caused by the
Clouds being placed in such a situation, as to reflect
the Image of that Luminary ; nocturnal fires, inflamed
spears, fighting armies, were no more than what we
call the Aurora Borealis, northern Lights, or inflamed
vapours floating in the air ; showers of stones, of ashes, or of fire, were no more than the effects of the e-
ruptions of some Volcano at a considerable distance ;
showers of milk were only caused by some quality in
the air condensing, and giving a whitish colour to the
water ; and those of Blood are now well known to be
only the red spots left upon the earth, on stones, and
the leaves of trees, by the butterflies which hatch in
hot or stormy weather (a).

III. Of Magic.

MAGIC, or the pretended Art of producing
by the assistance of words and ceremonies,
such events as are above the natural Power of Man,
was of several kinds, and chiefly consisted in invoking
the good and benevolent, or the wicked and mischievous Spirits. The first, which was called Theur-

[a] This has been fully proved by M. Reamur, in his History
of Insects.

gia

gia, was adopted by the wifeſt of the Pagan World, who eſteemed this as much as they deſpiſed the latter which they called Goetia. Theurgia was, by the Philoſophers, accounted a divine art; which only ſerved to raiſe the mind to higher perfection, and to exalt the ſoul to a greater Degree of Purity ; and they who by means of this kind of magic, were imagined to arrive at what was called intuition, wherein they enjoyed an intimate intercourſe with the Deity, were believed to be inveſted with their Powers : So that it was imagined, that nothing was impoſſible for them to perform.

All who made profeſſion of this kind of Magic, aſpired to this State of perfection. The Prieſt, who was of this Order, was to be a man of unblemiſhed Morals, and all who joined with him were bound to a ſtrict purity of Life ; they were to abſtain from women, and from animal Food ; and were forbid to defile themſelves by the touch of a dead Body. Nothing was to be forgot in their Rites and Ceremonies ; the leaſt Omiſſion or the leaſt miſtake, rendered all their Art ineffectual. So that this was a conſtant excuſe for their not performing all that was required of them, though as their ſole employment, (after having arrived to a certain degree of perfection, by Faſting, Prayer, and the other methods of purification) was the ſtudy of Univerſal Nature ; they might gain ſuch an inſight into phyſical cauſes, as might enable them to perform Actions, that might very well fill the ignorant Vulgar with Amazement. And it is hardly to be doubted but that this was all the knowledge that many of them ever aſpired after. In this ſort of magic, Hermes Triſmegiſtus and Zoroaſter excelled: And indeed it gained great Reputation amongſt the Egyptians, Chaldeans, Perſians, and Indians. In times of Ignorance, a Piece of Clock-work, or ſome curious Machine, was ſufficient to entitle the Inventor to the Works of Magick : And ſome have even aſſerted, that the Egyptian Magic, that has been rendered ſo famous by the Writings of the Antients, conſiſted only in Diſcoveries drawn from the Mathematicks

maticks and natural Philofophy, fince thofe Greek Philofophers, who travelled into Egypt, in order to obtain a knowledge of their Sciences, returned with only a knowledge of Nature and Religion, and fome rational ideas of their ancient Symbols.

But it can hardly be doubted, but that magic in its groffeft and moft ridiculous fenfe was practifed in Egypt, at leaft amongft fome of the Vulgar, long before Pythagoras or Empedocles travelled into that Country

The Egyptians had been very early accuftomed to vary the fignification of their Symbols, by adding to them feveral plants, ears of Corn, or blades of grafs, to exprefs the different employments of Hufbandry; but underftanding no longer their meaning, nor the words that had been made ufe of on thefe Occafions, which were equally unintelligible, the Vulgar might miftake thefe for fo many myfterious practices obferved by their Fathers; and hence they might conceive the notion, that a conjunction of Plants, even without being made ufe of as a Remedy, might be of Efficacy to preferve or procure health. " Of thefe," fays the Abbe Pluche, " they made a collection, and an " Art by which they pretended to procure the blef- " fings, and provide againft the evils of Life." By the affiftance of thefe, men even attempted to hurt their enemies, and indeed the Knowledge of poifonous or ufeful Simples, might on particular occafions, give fufficient weight to their empty Curfes or Invocations. But thefe magic Incantations, fo contrary to humanity, were detefted and punifhed by almoft all nations, nor could they be tolerated in any.

Pliny after mentioning an Herb, the throwing of which into an army, it was faid, was fufficient to put it to the Rout, afks, where was this Herb when Rome was fo diftreffed by the Cimbri and Teutones? Why did not the Perfians make ufe of it when Lucullus cut their Troops in pieces?

But amongft all the Incantations of Magic, the moft folemn, as well as the moft frequent, was that of calling up the Spirits of the Dead, this indeed

was

was the Quinteſſence of their Art; and the Reader cannot be diſpleaſed to find this Myſtery unravelled.

An Affection for the Body of a perſon, who in his Life time was beloved, induced the firſt nations to inter the Dead in a decent manner; and to add to this melancholy inſtance of their eſteem, thoſe wiſhes which had a particular Regard to their new State of Exiſtence, the place of burial, conformable to the Cuſtom of characterizing all beloved places or thoſe diſtinguiſhed by a memorable Event, was painted out by a large Stone or a Pillar raiſed upon it. To this place Families, and when the Concern was general, multitudes repaired every Year, where, upon this Stone, were made Libations of Wine, Oil, Honey and Flour; and here they ſacrificed and eat in common, having firſt made a Trench in which they burnt the Entrails of the Victim, and into which the Libation and the Blood was made to flow. They began with thanking God for having given them Life, and providing their neceſſary Food; and then praiſed him for the good Examples they had been favoured with. From theſe melancholy Rites were baniſhed all Licentiouſneſs and Levity; and while other cuſtoms changed, theſe continued the ſame. They roaſted the Fleſh of the Victim they had offered, and eat it in common, diſcourſing on the Virtues of him they came to lament.

All other Feaſts were diſtinguiſhed by names ſuitable to the ceremonies that attended them. Theſe Funeral Meetings were ſimply called the Manes, that is the Aſſembly. Thus the Manes and the dead were words that became ſynonymous. In theſe meetings, they imagined that they renewed their Alliance with the deceaſed, who, they ſuppoſed, had ſtill a Regard for the concerns of their Country and Family, and who, as affectionate Spirts, could do no leſs than inform them of whatever was neceſſary for them to know. Thus the Funerals of the Dead were at laſt converted into methods of Divination, and an innocent Inſtitution, into one of the groſſeſt pieces of Folly and Superſtition.

But

But they did not ftop here ; they grew fo extrava-
gntly credulous, as to believe that the Phantom drank
the Libations that had been poured forth, while the
Relations were feafting on the reft of the Sacrifice
round the Pit : And from hence became apprehenfive
left the reft of the Dead fhould promifcuoufly throng
about this fpot to get a fhare in the Repaft they were
fuppofed to be fo fond of, and leave nothing for the
dear Spirit for whom the Feaft was intended. They
then made two pits or ditches, into one of which they
put wine, honey, water and flour, to employ the generality of the dead ; and in the other they poured
the blood of the Victim ; when fitting down on the
brink, they kept off by the fight of their Swords, the
Crowd of Dead who had no concern in their Affairs,
while they called him by Name, whom they had a
mind to chear and confult, and defired him to draw
near (a).

The Queftions made by the Living were very intelligible ; but the Anfwers of the Dead, as they confifted of filence, were not fo eafily underftood, and
therefore the Priefts ard Magicians made it their Bufinefs to explain them. They retired into deep Caves,
where the darknefs and filence refembled the ftate of
death, and there fafted and lay upon the fkins of the
beafts they had facrificed, and then gave for anfwer
the dream which moft affected them; or opened certain Books appointed for this purpofe, and gave the
firft fentence that offered. At other Times the Prieft
or any perfon who came to confult, took Care at
his going out of the Cave, to liften to the firft Words
he fhould hear and thefe were to be his anfwer. And
tho' they had no relation to the bufinefs in hand, they
were turned fo many ways, and their fenfe fo violently wrefted, that they made them fignify almoft any

[a] Homer gives the fame Account of thefe Ceremonies, when
Ulyffes raifes the Soul of Tirefias ; and the fame Ufages are
found in the Poem of Silius Italicus. And to thefe Ceremonies
the Scriptures frequently allude, when the Ifraelites are forbid
to affemble upon high Places.

Thing they pleased.   At other times they had Re-
courſe to a number of Tickets, on which were ſome
Words or Verſes, and theſe being thrown into an
Urn, the firſt that was taken out was delivered to the
Family.

IV. Of Augury.

THE ſuperſtitious Fondneſs of Mankind, for
ſearching into Futurity, has given Riſe to a
vaſt Variety of Follies, all equally weak and extravagant. The Romans, in particular, found out almoſt
innumerable Ways of Divination; all Nature had a
Voice, and the moſt ſenſeleſs Beings, and moſt trifling
accidents, became Preſages of future Events.   This
introduced Ceremonies, founded on a miſtaken knowledge of Antiquity, that were the moſt childiſh and
ridiculous, and which yet were performed with an
Air of Solemnity. The Perſons appointed to unravel
the Decrees of Heaven, were thoſe of the moſt reſ-
pectable Characters, and the higheſt Stations, who received great Honour from the Privilege of exerciſing
this Office.

Cicero, who was perfectly ſenſible of the Folly of
theſe practices, relates a ſaying of Cato, who declared
that one of the moſt ſurprizing Things to him was,
how one Soothſayer could look another in the face
without laughing: and indeed that Prieſt muſt have
a ſurpriſing command of himſelf who could avoid ſmi-
ling whenever he ſaw his Colleagues walking with a
grave and ſtately air, and holding up the augural ſtaff,
to determine the limits beyond which every thing
ceaſed to be prophetical.

Birds, on account of their ſwiftneſs in Flying, were
ſometimes conſidered by the Egyptians as the ſymbols
of the winds; and Figures of particular Species of
Fowl, were ſet up to denote the time when the near
approach of a periodical wind was expected. From
hence, before they undertook any thing of conſe-
quence, as ſowing, planting, or putting out to

fea it was ufual for them to fay [a], Let us confult
the Birds, meaning the Signs fixed up to give them
the neceffary Informations they then ftood in need of.
By doing this they knew how to regulate their conduct; and 'it frequently happened, that when this
precaution was omitted, they had Reafon to reproach
themfelves for their neglect. From hence, Mankind miftaking their meaning, and retaining the
Phrafe, Let us confult the Birds, and perhaps hearing
old Stories repeated of the advantages fuch and fuch
perfons had received, by confulting them in a critical
moment, when the periodical wind would have ruined
their affairs, they began to conceive an opinion, that
the Fowls, which fkim thro' the air, were fo many
Meffengers fent from the Gods, to inform them of future events, and to warn them againft any difaftrous
undertaking. From hence they took notice of their
Flight, and from their different manner of Flying,
prognofticated good or bad Omens. The Birds were
inftantly grown wondrous wife, and an Owl who hates
the Light could not pafs by the Window of a fick
perfon in the night, where he was offended by the
Light of a Lamp or a Candle, but his Hooting muft
be confidered as Prophecying, that the Life of the
poor Man was nearly at an End.

The Place where thefe Auguries were taken, a-
mongft the Romans, was commonly upon an eminence;
they were prohibited after the month of Auguft, becaufe that was the time for the moulting of Birds, nor
were they permitted on the Wane of the Moon, nor
at any time in the afternoon, or when the air was the
leaft difturbed by winds or clouds:

When all the previous Ceremonies were performed
the Augur cloathed in his Robe, and holding his augural ftaff in his Right Hand, fat down at the door
of his tent, looked round him, then marked out the
Divifions of the Heavens with his Staff, drew a Line
from Eaft to Weft, and another from North to South
and then offered up his facrifice. A fhort Prayer, the

[a] Abbe Pluche's Hift. of the Heavens Vol. I. p. 241.

Form

Form of which may be sufficiently seen, in that offered to Jupiter, at the Election of Numa Pompilius, was as follows: " O Father Jupiter, if it be thy will
" that this Numa Pompilius, on whose Head I have
" laid my Hand, should be King of Rome, grant that
" there be clear and unerring signs, within the bounds
" I have described " The Prayer being thus ended, the Priest turned to the Right and Left, and to whatever point the Birds directed their flight, in order to determine from thence, whether the God approved or rejected the Choice

The Veneration which the Romans entertained for this Ceremonial of their Religion, made them attend the Result of the Augury with the most profound silence, and the affair was no sooner determined, than the Augur reported his Decision, by saying, The Birds approve, or the Birds disapprove it. However, notwithstanding the Augury might be favourable, the enterprize was sometimes deferred, till they fancied it confirmed by a new sign.

But of all the signs which happened in the air, the most infallible was that of thunder and lightning, especially if it happened to be fair weather. If it came on the Right Hand it was a bad Omen, but if on the left a good one, because, according to Donatus, all Appearances on that side were supposed to proceed from the Right Hand of the Gods.

Let us now take a view of the sacred Chickens; for an Examination into the Manner of their taking the Corn that was offered them, was the most common method of taking the Augury. And indeed the Romans had such Faith in the Mysteries contained in their manner of feeding, that they hardly ever undertook any important affair, without first advising with them. Generals sent for them to the field, and consulted them before they ventured to engage the Enemy, and if the Omen was unfavourable, they immediately desisted from their enterprize. The sacred Chickens were kept in a Coop or Penn, and entrusted to the care of a person who, on account of his office, was called Pullarius. The Augur, after having commanded

ltanded filence, ordered the Penn to be opened, and threw upon the ground a handful of Corn. If the Chickens inftantly leaped out of the Penn, and pecked up the corn with fuch eagernefs as to let fome of it fall from their Beaks, the Augury was called Tripudium, or Tripudium Soliftimum, from its ftriking the Earth, and was efteemed a moft aufpicious Omen; but if they did not immediately run to the corn, i they flew away, if they walked by it without minding it, or if they fcattered it abroad with their wings, it portended danger and ill fuccefs. Thus the fate of the greateft undertakings, and even the fall of Cities and Kingdoms, was thought to depend on the appetite of a few Chickens.

Obfervations were alfo taken from the chattering, finging, or hooting of Crows, Pies, Owls, &c. and from the running of Beafts, as Heifers, Affes, Rams, Hares, Wolves, Foxes, Weefels and Mice, when thefe appeared in uncommon Places, croffed the way, or run to the Right or Left, &c. They alfo pretended to draw a good or bad Omen from the moft common and trifling Actions or Occurrences of Life, as Sneezing, Stumbling, Starting, the Numbnefs, of the little Finger, the Tingling of the Ear, the fpilling of Salt upon the Table, or Wine upon one's Cloaths, the accidental meeting of a Bitch with Whelp, &c. It was alfo the Bufinefs of the Augurs to interpret Dreams, Oracles, and Prodigies.

The College of Augurs, as firft inftituted at Rome, by Romulus, was only compofed of three perfons taken from the three Tribes, into which all the inhabitants of the City were divided; but feveral others were afterwards added, and at laft, according to a Regulation of Scylla, this College confifted of fifteen perfons, all of the firft diftinction, the eldeft of whom was called the Mafter of the College; " It was a " Priefthood for Life, of a character indelible, which " no crime or forfeiture could efface; it was necef- " fary that every Candidate fhould be nominated to " the people by two Augurs, who gave a fo- " lemn Teftimony upon Oath, of his Dignity and

Z 2

" Fortune

" Fitnefs for that office [a]."   The greateft Precautions were indeed taken in this Election; for as they were invefted with fuch extraordinary Privileges, none were qualified but perfons of a blamelefs Life, and free from all perfonal Defects.   The Senate could affemble in no place but what they had confecrated. They frequently occafioned the difplacing of Magiftrates, and the deferring of publick Affemblies:
" But the Senate, at laft, confidering that fuch an un-
" limitted power was capable of authorifing a number
" of Abufes, decreed that they fhould not have it in
" their power to adjourn any Affembly that had been
" legally convened (b)."

Nothing can be more aftonifhing, than to find fo wife a people as the Romans addicted to fuch childifh Fooleries. Scipio, Auguftus, and many others have, without any fatal confequence, defpifed the chickens and the other Arts of Divination: But when the Generals mifcarried in any enterprize, the people laid the whole blame on the heedleffnefs with which they had been confulted, and if he had entirely neglected eonfulting them, all the blame was thrown upon him who had preferred his own Forecaft to that of the Fowls, while thofe who made thefe kinds of Predictions a fubject of Raillery, were accounted impious and prophane. Thus they conftrued, as a punifhment from the Gods, the defeat of Claudius Pulcher, who when the facred chickens refufed to eat what was fet before them, ordered them to be thrown into the fea; If they won't eat, faid he, they fhall drink.

V.   Of the ARUSPICES.

IN the moft early Ages of the World a Senfe of Piety, and a Regard to Decency, had introduced a cuftom of never facrificing to him, who gave them all their Bleffings, any but the foundeft, the fateft and moft beautiful Victims. They were examined with

[a] Middleton's Life of Cicero.
[b] Banier's Mythology, Vol. I. p. 400.

the clofeft and moft exact attention, that none might be offered but the moft perfect. This Ceremonial, which doubtlefs fprang at firft from Gratitude, and fome natural ideas of fitnefs and propriety, at laft degenerated into trifling Niceties and fuperftitious Ceremonies, which they conceived to be of the utmoft importance, and even commanded by the Deity.. And it having been once imagined, that nothing was to be expected from the Gods, when the Victim was imperfect, the Idea of Perfection was united with abundance of trivial circumftances ; fuch a Deity was fond of white Victims, others of Black, and others of Red.— The Entrails were examined with peculiar Care, and the whole Ceremony was imagined to be entirely ufelefs, if the leaft defect was difcovered ; but on the other Hand, if the whole was without Blemifh, their Duties were fulfilled, and under an affurance that they had engaged the Gods to be on their fide, they engaged in a war, and in the moft hazardous undertakings, with fuch a confidence of Succefs, as had the greateft tendency to procure it.

The Idea of the neceffity of this perfection naturally increafed, as foon as it was believed to be an infallible means of fatisfying the Gods, and procuring their affiftance and protection ; and this introduced their calling in the affiftance of thofe who fhould aid the Prieft in his office, and make it their bufinefs to ftudy all the Rules neceffary to be obferved, to avoid the ill confequences that might attend the flighteft miftake. Thefe introduced all the obfervances that followed ; the Rules were obferved merely for the fake of the Prediction they were to draw from them, they had no longer any connection with the pious motives that had at firft inftituted them ; and it became their grand principle, that the perfection or defects of the outward and inward parts was a mark of the confent or difapprobation of the Gods. All the motions of the Victim that was led to the Altar became fo many Prophecies. If he advanced with an eafy Air in a ftraight Line, and without offering

Resistance, if he made no extraordinary Bellowing when he received the Blow, if he did not get loose from the person that led him to the slaughter, it was a prognostick of an easy and flowing success.

The Victim was knocked down, but before its belly was ripped open, one of the Lobes of the Liver was allotted to those who offered the Sacrifice, and the others to the Enemies of the state, that which was neither blemished nor withered, of a bright Red, and neither larger nor smaller than it ought to be, prognosticated great prosperity to those for whom it was set apart; that which was livid, small, or corrupted, presaged the most fatal mischiefs.

The next thing to be considered was the Heart, which was also examined with the utmost care, as was the spleen, the gall, and the lungs; and if any of these were let fall, if they smelt Rank, or were bloated, livid or withered, it presaged nothing but misfortunes. Lucan has elegantly described almost all these imperfections, as meeting in one Victim.

> The Liver wet with putrid streams he spy'd,
> And Veins that threatened on the hostile side;
> Part of the heaving Lungs is no where found,
> And thinner Films the sever'd Entrails bound;
> No usual motions stirs the parting Heart,
> The chinky Vessels ooze in every Part:
> The cawl, where wrapt the close Intestines lie,
> Betrays its dark Recesses to the Eye.
> One Prodigy superior threaten'd still,
> The never failing Harbenger of Ill:
> Lo! By the fibrous Liver's rising head,
> A second Rival Prominence is spread.
>
> ROWE's Lucan.

After they had finished their Examination of the Entrails, the Fire was kindled, and from this also they drew several Presages. If the Flame was clear, if it mounted up without dividing, and went not out till the Victim was entirely consumed, this was a Proof that the Sacrifice was accepted; but if they found it

difficult

difficult to kindle the Fire, if the flame divided, if it played around inſtead of taking hold of the victim, if it burnt ill, or went out, it was a bad Omen.

At Rome the Aruſpices were always choſen from the beſt Families, and as their employment was of the ſame Nature as the Augurs, they were as much honoured. It was a very common Thing indeed to ſee their Predictions verified by the event, eſpecially in their Wars: Nor is this at all wonderful, the Prediction never lulled them into Security, or prevented their taking every neceſſary precaution; but on the contrary, the aſſurance of victory inſpired that intrepidity and high courage, which in the common Soldiers was the principal thing neceſſary to the attainment of it. But if a'ter the appearance of a complete Favour from the Gods, whom they had addreſſed, their Affairs happened to miſcarry, the blame was laid on ſome other Deity. Juno or Minerva had been neglected. They ſacrificed to them, recovered their ſpirits, and behaved with greater precaution.

However, the Buſineſs of the Aruſpices was not reſtrained to the Altars and Sacrifices, they had an equal Right to explain all other Portents. The Senate frequently conſulted them on the moſt extraordinary Prodigies.

" The College of the Aruſpices (a) as well as
" thoſe of the other religious Orders had their par-
" ticular Regiſters and Records, ſuch as the memo-
" rials of Thunder and Lightnings, the (b) Tuſcan
" Hiſtories, &c.

VI Of

[a] Kennet's Roman Antiq. Lib. II. c. 4.
[b] Romulus, who founded the Inſtitution of the Aruſpices, borrowed it from the Tuſcans, to whom the Senate afterwards ſent twelve of the Sons of the principal Nobility to be inſtructed in theſe Myſteries, and the other Ceremonies of their Religion. The Origin of this Art amongſt the People of Tuſcany, is related by Cicero in the following Manner: " A Peaſant, ſays he,
" ploughing in the Field, his Plowſhare running pretty deep in
" the Earth, turned up a Clod, from whence ſprung a Child,
" who taught him and the other Tuſcans the Art of Divination.'
See Cicero de Div. l. 2. This Fable undoubtedly means no
more,

VI. Of Oracles.

IT is very evident, that whatever were the politic Reasons that induced the wifeſt Nations to continue and encourage the above ſuperſtitions, which were but little regarded by ſome of the moſt learned and ſenſible Men among them, yet they all originally aroſe from the Imperfection of human Nature, the Diſſatisfaction which a Man frequently finds in the enjoyment of the preſent Moment, the Eagerneſs with which his Hopes and Fears ſtretch forwards into Futurity, a poſſibility of regulating his conduct, by knowing what would be the Reſult of particular actions, added to that Curioſity and inquiſitive diſpoſition, which adheres to the Minds of the greateſt part of Mankind. Theſe prepared the way for all the various methods, which ſuperſtition has pointed out for diſcovering future events. This weakneſs paved the way for the ridiculous extravagancies of Aſtrology, Magic, the innumerable little obſervances ranked under the Ideas of Prodigies, good and ill omens, all the whimſies of the Augurs and the Aruſpices, and all the deluſions of the Oracles.

Thus Mankind, by endeavouring to become ſomething more, have in all Ages rendered themſelves unhappy, ſubject to groundleſs Fears, and endleſs Inquietudes. The Knowledge of Futurity was wiſely concealed from mortals: This is a truth that the Heathens themſelves could not but confeſs; and Cicero, though a Roman, though an Augur, gives us his ſentiments on this ſubject, with that affecting elegance of Expreſſion, which ſhews that he ſpoke the naked Sentiments of his Heart. " In what a deep " Melancholy, ſays he, had Priam ſpent the remain " der of his Days, had he been ſenſible of the un-

more, than that this Child ſaid to ſpring from a Clod of Earth, was a Youth of a very mean and obſcure Birth, and that from him the Tuſcans had learned this method of Divination. But it is not known whether he was the Author of it, or whether he learnt it of the Greeks or other Nations.

happy

" happy Fate that awaited him? Would the three
" Confulfhips, the three Triumphs of Pompey, have
" given him the fmalleft Beam of Joy, had he been
" able to forefee what even we cannot mention with-
" out Tears, that on a fatal Day, after the lofs of a
" Battle, and the total Defeat of his Army, he fhould
" fall in the Defarts of Egypt? And oh! What would
" Cæfar have thought, if he too had been fenfible
" that in the midft of that very Senate, which he had
" compofed of his Friends and his Creatures, he
" fhould be ftabbed near the Statue of Pompey, in
" the fight of his Guards, and covered with wounds
" by his beft friends; that his body would be abandon-
" ed, and not a man dare to affift him? It is furely
" then much better to be ignorant of the Evils of Fu-
" turity than to know them."

The Egyptians, one of the moft inquifitive Nations
on Earth, were probably verfed in moft of the above
methods of Divination, at the time when Mofes led
the Ifraelites into the Wildernefs.   They had frequently heard him talk of confulting his God; they
had feen him go out for this purpofe, and at his Return had heard him predict things that were fpeedily
to come to pafs, and the Event always anfwered to
what he had foretold.   They were terrified by miraculous events, which as they were above the Power
of man to perform, they probably confidered them
only as fome Phænomenon in Nature, or in Providence, which he by his knowledge in Aftrology, or
fome of the other Arts of Divination, was enabled to
forefee, and which he was willing to impofe upon them
as a Proof of his acting under the Authority and Influence of Heaven.   Filled with thefe ideas, no fooner was the effect of one Prediction over, than they re-
lapfed into fcepticifm and a fond fecurity; but at laft
wearied out by their fufferings, and in fome meafure
convinced in fpite of themfelves, they relinquifhed
the advantage they reaped from the flavery of the
Ifraelites, and gave them permiffion to retire out of
the Country; but finding that they had efcaped the
Power of a formidable Army, and had miraculoufly

croffed

eroffed the Red Sea in Safety, while the King and all his Forces were drowned, they were probably conquered by the Strength of the Conviction, and convinced that the whole was miraculous, and that God really condefcended to foretel things to come; and that had their Priefts confulted him in the fame manner Mofes had done, all the Evils that had fallen upon them might have been prevented. The Priefts were then doubtlefs reproached for their negligence, when to fatisfy the defires of the people, they might be obliged to confult their Gods upon the mountains, their ufual places of worfhip, and to fupport their credit with the people by pretended Revelations.

It is not improbable but that this might be the firft Rife of Oracles, as the moving Temple or Tabernacle of the Ifraelites, in which God was confulted, might fpread the opinion of Oracles among the neighbouring nations, and give the firft intimation of building a Temple. The Priefts and Magi, who were utterly unacquainted with the methods and ceremonials necef-fary to obtain an anfwer to their Petitions, had Recourfe to feveral Methods, which ferved at once to amufe the People, to infpire them with the Idea of their extraordinary Penetration, and to give the air of Science to the Art of interpreting the will of the Gods; which they almoft always took care to exprefs in fuch ambiguous terms, as to prevent any difhonour falling upon their order, by a contrariety between the Event and the Prediction.

Of all the Nations upon the Earth, Greece was the moft famous for Oracles, and fome of their wifeft Men have endeavoured to vindicate them upon folid Principles, and refined reafonings. Xenophon expatiates on the Neceffity of confulting the Gods by Augurs and Oracles. He reprefents Man as naturally ignorant of what is advantageous or deftructive to him felf: that he is fo far from being able to penetrate into the future, that the prefent itfelf efcapes him; that his defigns may be fruftrated by the flighteft objects; that the Deity alone, to whom all Ages are prefent, can impart to him the infallible Knowledge of Futurity; that no other Being can give Success to his Enterprizes, and that it is highly reasonable to believe that he will guide and protect those who adore him with a pure Affection, who call upon him, and consult him with a sincere and humble Resignation. How surprising it is that such refined and noble Principles should be brought to defend the most puerile and absurd Opinions! For what arguments can vindicate their presuming to interrogate the Most High, and oblige him to give Answers concerning every Idle Imagination and unjust Enterprize

Oracles were thought by the Greeks to proceed in a more immediate manner from God than the other Arts of Divination; and on this account scarce any Peace was concluded, any War engaged in, any new Laws enacted, or any new Form of Government instituted without consulting Oracles. And therefore Minos, to give his Laws a proper Weight with the People, ascribed to them a divine Sanction, and pretended to receive from Jupiter, Instructions how to new model his Government. And Lycurgus made frequent Visits to the Delphian Oracle, that the People might entertain a belief, that he received from Apollo the Platform which he afterwards communicated to the Spartans. These pious Frauds were an effectual means of establishing the Authority of Laws, and engaging the people to a compliance with the Will of the Lawgiver. Persons thus inspired were frequently thought worthy of the highest Trust; so that they were sometimes advanced to regal Power, from a Persuasion, " That as they were admitted to the Councils of the " Gods, they were best able to provide for the Safe- " ty and Welfare of Man (b)."

This high Veneration for the Priests of the Oracles, being the strongest Confirmation, that their Credit was thoroughly established, they suffered none to consult the Gods but those who brought Sacrifices and rich Presents to them; whence few, besides the Great, were admitted. This Proceeding served at

(b) Potter's Antiquities of Greece, Vol. I. p. 263.

once

once to enrich the Priefts, and to raife the Character of the Oracles amongft the Populace, who are always apt to defpife what they are too familiarly acquainted with · Nor were the Rich, or even the greateft Prince admitted, except at thofe particular times when the God was in a Difpofition to be confulted.

One of the moft ancient Oracles, of which we have received any particular Account, was that of Jupiter at Dodona, a City faid to be built by Deucalion, after that famous Deluge which bears his Name, and which deftroyed the greateft Part of Greece. It was fituated in Epirus, and here was the firft Temple that ever was feen in Greece. According to Herodotus, both this and the Oracle of Jupiter Hammon had the fame Original, and both owed their Inftitution to the Egyptians. The Rife of this Oracle is indeed wrapped up in Fable. Two black Pigeons, fay they, flying from Thebes in Egypt, one of them fettled in Lybia, and the other flew as far as the Foreft of Dodona, a Province in Epirus, where fitting in an Oak, fhe informed the inhabitants of the Country, that it was the Will of Jupiter that an Oracle fhould be founded in that place. Herodotus gives two Accounts of the Rife of this Oracle, one of which clears up the Myftery of this Fable. He tells us that he was informed by the Priefts of Jupiter, at Thebes in Egypt, that fome Phœnician Merchants carried off two Prieftefles of Thebes, that one was carried into Greece, and the other into Lybia. She who was carried into Greece took up her Refidence in the Foreft of Dodona, and there, at the Foot of an Oak, erected a fmall Chapel in honour of Jupiter, whofe Prieftefs fhe had been at Thebes (c).

We learn from Servius (d), that the Will of Heaven was here explained by an old Woman, who pre-

(c) The Abbe Sallier takes this Fable to be built upon the double Meaning of the Word Peleiai, which in Attica, and feveral other Parts of Greece, fignifies Pigeons, while in the Dialect of Epirus, it meant old Women. See Mem. Acad. Belle Lettres, Vol V. p. 35.
(d) Servius in 3 Æn 5. 466,

tended to find out a meaning to explain the murmers of a Brook that flowed from the Root of an Oak.— After this, another method was taken, attended with more Formalities; Brazen Kettles were suspended in the Air, with a statue of the same metal, with a whip in his Hand (a); this figure, when moved by the wind, struck against the kettle that was next it, which also causing all the other kettles to strike against each other, raised a clattering Din, which continued for some time, and from these sounds she formed her predictions.

Both these ways were equally absurd, for as in each the answer depended solely on the Invention of the Priestess, she alone was the Oracle. Suidas informs us, that the answer was given by an Oak in this Grove, as Homer also has delivered; and as it was generally believed to proceed from the Trunk, it is easy to conceive how this was performed; for the Priestess had nothing more to do than to hide herself in the hollow of an old Oak, and from thence to give the pretended Sense of the Oracle, which she might the more easily do, as the distance the suppliant was obliged to keep, was an effectual means to prevent the cheat from being discovered.

There is one remarkable circumstance relating to this oracle yet remaining, and that is, that while all the other Nations received their answer from a woman, the Bœotians alone received it from a man, and the Reason given for it is as follows: during the war between the Thracians and Bœotians, the latter sent Deputies to consult this Oracle of Dodona, when the Priestess gave them this Answer, of which she doubtless did not foresee the consequence, If you would meet with success, you must be guilty of some impi-

[a] As this was evidently a Figure of Osiri, which was on particular Occasions represented with a Whip in his Hand, it is an additional Proof, that this Oracle was derived from Egypt.

ous action. The Deputies no doubt surprized, and perhaps exafperated, by imagining that the Prieftefs prevaricated with them in order to pleafe the Pelafgi from whom fhe was defcended, and who were in a ftrict alliance with the Thracians, refolved to fulfil the decree of the Oracle ; and therefore feizing the Prieftefs burnt her alive ; alledging that this action was juftifiable in whatever light it was confidered, that if fhe intended to deceive them, it was fit fhe fhould be punifhed for the deceit; or, if fhe was fincere, they had only literally fulfilled the fenfe of the Oracle. The two remaining Prieftefles (for, according to Strabo, the Oracle at that time had ufually three) highly exafperated at this cruelty, caufed them to be feized, and as they were to be their Judges, the Deputies pleaded the illegality of their being tried by women. The Juftice of this plea was admitted by the people, who allowed two Priefts to try them in conjunction with the Prieftefles, on which being acquitted by the former and condemned by the latter, the votes being equal, they were releafed. For this Reafon the Bœotians, for the future, received their Anfwers from the Priefts.

The Oracle of Jupiter Ammon in Lybia, we have already faid, was derived from Egypt, and is of the fame antiquity as the former of Dodona, and though furrounded by a large tract of burning fands, was extremely famous. This Oracle gave his anfwers not by words but by a fign. What was called the Image of the God, was carried about in a gilded Barge on the fhoulders of his Priefts, who moved whitherfoever they pretended the divine Impulfe directed them. This appears to have been nothing more than the Mariners Compafs (a), the ufe of which was not intirely unknown to that age, tho' fo long kept fecret from the Europeans. It was adorned with precious ftones, and the Barge with many filver Goblets hanging on either fide ; and thefe Proceffions were accompanied with a

---

[a] Umbilico fimilis, fmaragdo & gemmis coagmentatus Hunc navigio aurato geftant facerdotes. Q CURTIUS, l 4, c. 7.

Troop

Troop of Matrons and Virgins singing Hymns in Honour of Jupiter. These Priests refused the Bribes offered them by Lysander, who wanted their Assistance to help him to change the Succession to the Throne of Sparta. However, they were not so scrupulous when Alexander, either to gratify his Vanity, or to screen the Reputation of his Mother, took that painful March through the Deserts of Lybia, in order to obtain the Honour of being called the Son of Jupiter, a Priest stood ready to receive him, and saluted him with the Title of, Son of the King of Gods,

The Oracle of Apollo at Delphos, was one of the most famous in all Antiquity. This City stood upon a Declivity about the Middle of Mount Parnassus; it was built on a small Extent of even Ground, and surrounded with Precipices, that Fortified it without the Help of Art [a]. Diodorus Siculus relates [b] a Tradition of a very whimsical Nature, which was said to give Rise to this Oracle. There was a Hole in one of the Valleys, at the Foot of Parnassus, the Mouth of which was very strait; the Goats that were Feeding at no great distance, coming near it began to frisk about in such a Manner, that the Goat-herd being struck with surprize, came up to the place, and leaning over it, was seized with such an enthusiastic Impulse, or temporary Madness, as prompted him to utter some extravagant Expressions which passed for Prophecies. The Report of this extraordinary Event drew thither the neighbouring People, who on approaching the Hole were seized with the same Transports. Surprized at so astonishing a Prodigy, the Cavity was no longer approached without Reverence. The Exhalation was concluded to have something divine in it: They imagined it proceeded from some Friendly Deity, and from that time bestowed a particular Worship on the Divinity of the Place, and regarded what was delivered in these Fits of Madness as Predictions; and here they afterwards built the City and Temple of Delphos.

[a] Strabo, lib. 14. p, 427, 428.
[b] Diod. 4, 1.

A a 2

This

This Oracle, it was pretended, had been poſſeſſed by ſeveral ſucceſſive Deities, and at laſt by Apollo, who raiſed its Reputation to the greateſt Height. It was reſorted to, by Perſons of all Stations, by which it obtained immenſe Riches, which expoſed it to be frequently plundered. At firſt it is ſaid, the God inſpired all indifferently who approached the Cavern; but ſome having in this fit of Madneſs thrown themſelves into the Gulph, they thought fit to chooſe a Prieſteſs, and to ſet over the Hole a Tripos, or three legged Stool, whence ſhe might without Danger catch the Exhalations; and this Prieſteſs was called Pythia, from the Serpent Python, ſlain by Apollo. For a long Time none but Virgins poſſeſſed this Honour, till a young Theſſalian, called Echecrates, falling in Love with the Prieſteſs, who was at that time very beautiful, raviſhed her; when to prevent any Abuſes of the like kind for the future, the Citizens made a Law to prohibit any Woman being choſen under fifty Years old. At firſt they had one Prieſteſs, but afterwards they had two or three.

The Oracles were not delivered every Day; but the Sacrifices were repeated till the God was pleaſed to deliver them, which frequently happened only one Day in the Year. Alexander coming here in one of theſe Intervals, after many Entreaties to engage the Prieſteſs to mount the Tripod, which were all to no Purpoſe; the Prince growing impatient at her refuſal, drew her by Force from her Cell, and was leading her to the Sanctuary, when ſaying, My Son, thou art invincible, he cried out that he was ſatisfied, and needed no other Anſwer.

Nothing was wanting to keep up the Air of Myſtery, in order to preſerve its Reputation, and to procure it Veneration. The neglecting the ſmalleſt Punctilio was ſufficient to make them renew the Sacrifices that were to precede the Reſponſe of Apollo. The Prieſteſs herſelf was obliged to prepare for the Diſcharge of her Duty, by faſting three Days, bathing in the Fountain of Caſtalia, drinking a certain Quantity of the Water, and chewing ſome Leaves of Laurel

rel gathered near the Fountain. After these Prepa-
rations the Temple was made to shake, which passed
for the signal given by Apollo to inform them of his
Arrival, and then the Priest led her into the Sanctuary and placed her on the Tripod, when beginning to
be agitated by the divine Vapour, her Hair stood an
end, her looks became wild, her mouth began to
foam, and a fit of trembling seized her whole body.
In this condition she seemed to struggle to get loose
from the Priests, who pretended to hold her by force,
while her shrieks and howlings, which resounded thro'
the Temple, filled the deluded By-standers with a
kind of sacred horror. At last being no longer able
to resist the impulses of the God, she submitted, and
at certain intervals uttered some unconnected words,
which were carefully picked up by the Priests, who
put them in connection, and gave them to the Poets
who were also present to put them into a kind of
Verse, which was frequently stiff, unharmonious, and
always obscure; this occasioned that piece of Raillery
that Apollo the Prince of the Muses was the worst of
the Poets. One of the Priestesses who was named
Phemonoe, is said to have pronounced her Oracles in
Verse; in latter times they were contented with delivering them in Prose, and this, in the opinion of Plutarch, was one of the Reasons of the Declension of
this Oracle.

Crœsus intending to make Trial of the several Oracles of Greece, as well as that of Lybia, commanded
the respective Ambassadors to consult them all on a
stated Day, and to bring the Responses in Writing.
The Question proposed was, " What is Crœsus, the
" Son of Allyattes, King of Lydia, now doing?" The
rest of the Oracles failed; but the Delphian answered
truly, that " He was boiling a Lamb and a Tortoise
" together in a brazen Pot." This gained his confidence and a Profusion of the richest Offerings. In
Return, the Oracle on the next enquiry, informed
him that " By making War upon the Persians, he
" should destroy a great Empire." The Event is

well

well known. This vain confidence loft him both his Crown and Liberty [a].

Trophonius, who according to fome Authors, was no more than a Robber, or at moft a Hero, had an Oracle in Bœotia, which acquired great Reputation. Paufanias, who had confulted it, and gone thro' all its Formalities, has given a very particular Defcription of it, and from him we fhall extract a fhort Hiftory of this Oracle.

The facred Grove of Trophonius, fays this Author [b], is at a fmall diftance from Lebadea, one of the fineft Cities in Greece ; and in this Grove is the Temple of Trophonius, with his Statue, the workmanfhip of Praxiteles.   Thofe who apply to this Oracle muft perform certain ceremonies before they are permitted to go down into the Cave where the Refponfe is given.   Some days muft be fpent in a Chapel dedicated to Fortune and the good Genii, where the Purification confifts in Abftinence from all Things unlawful, and in making ufe of the Cold Bath He muft facrifice to Trophonius and all his Family, to Jupiter, to Saturn, and to Ceres, firnamed Europa, who was believed to have been the Nurfe of Trophonius The Diviners confulted the Entrails of every Victim, to difcover if it was agreeable to Trophonius that the perfon fhould defcend into the Cave.   If the Omens were favourable, he was led that night to the River Hercyna, where two Boys anointed his Body with oil. Then he was conducted as far as the fource of the River, where he was obliged to drink two forts of water, that of Lethe, to efface from his mind all profane thoughts, and that of Mnemofyne, to enable him to retain whatever he was to fee in the facred Cave ; he was then prefented to the Statue of Trophonius, to which he was to addrefs a fhort Prayer ; he then was cloathed in a Linen Tunic adorned with facred fillets and at laft was conducted in a folemn manner

[a] Herodot. in. Clio.
[b] Paufan. Lib. 9. p. 602, 604.

to the Oracle, which was inclosed within a stone Wall on the top of a Mountain.

In this inclosure was a Cave formed like an Oven, the Mouth of which was narrow, and the Descent to it not by Steps, but by a short Ladder: on going down there appeared another Cave, the Entrance to which was very strait. The Suppliant, who was obliged to take a certain Composition of Honey in each Hand, without which he could not be admitted, prostrated himself on the Ground, and then putting his Feet into the Mouth of the Cave, his whole Body was forcibly drawn in.

Here some had the Knowledge of Futurity by Vision; and others by an audible Noice. They then got out of the Cave in the same manner as they went in, with their Feet foremost, and prostrate on the Earth. The Suppliant going up the Ladder was conducted to the Chair of Mnemosyne, the Goddess of Memory, in which being seated, he was questioned on what he had heard and seen; and from thence was brought into the Chapel of the good Genii, where having stayed till he had recovered from his Affright and Terror, he was obliged to write in a Book all that he had seen or heard, which the Priests took upon them to interpret. There never was but one Man, says Pausanius, who lost his Life in this Cave, and that was a Spy who had been sent by Demetrius, to see whether in that Holy place there was any thing worth plundering. The Body of this Man was afterwards found at a great distance; and indeed it is not unlikely, that his Design being discovered, he was assassinated by the Priests, who might carry out his Body by some secret passage, at which they went in and out without being perceived.

The Oracle of the Branchidæ, in the Neighbourhood of Miletus, was very ancient, and in great Esteem. Xerxes returning from Greece, prevailed on its Priests to deliver up its Treasures to him, and then burnt the Temple, when to secure them against the Vengeance of the Greeks, he granted them an Establishment in the most distant part of Asia. After the
Defeat

Defeat of Darius by Alexander, this Conqueror deftroyed the City where thefe Priefts had fettled, of which their Defcendents were then in actual Poffeffion ; and thus punifhed the Children for the Perfidty of their Fathers.

The Oracle of Apollo at Claros, a Town of Ionia in Afia Minor, was very famous, and frequently confulted. Claros was faid to be founded by [a] Manto the Daughter of Tirefias, fome years before the taking of Troy. The Anfwers of this Oracle, fays Tacitus [b], were not given by a Woman but by a Man, chofen out of certain Families, and generally from Miletus) It was fufficient to let him know the Number and Names of thofe who came to confult him ; after which he retired into a Cave, and having drank of the Waters of a Spring that ran within it, delivered Anfwers in Verfe upon what the People had in their Thoughts, though he was frequently ignorant, and unacquainted with the Nature and Rules of Poetry. " It is faid, " our Author Adds, that he foretold the fudden " Death of Germanicus, but in dark and ambiguous " Terms."

Paufanias mentions an Oracle of Mercury, in Achaia, of a very fingular kind ; after a variety of Ceremonies, which it is needlefs here to repeat, they whifpered in the Ear of the God, and told him, what they were defirous of knowing ; then ftopping their Ears with their Hands, they left the Temple, and the firft Words they heard after they were out of it, was the Anfwer of the God.

But it would be an endlefs Talk to pretend to enumerate all the Oracles, which were fo numerous, that Van Dale gives a lift of near three Hundred, moft of which were in Greece. Not that all thefe ever fub-

[a] Manto has been greatly extolled for her Prophetic Spirit; and Fabulous Hiftory informs us, that lamenting the Miferies of her Country, fhe diffolved away in Tears, and that thefe formed a Fountain, the water of which communicated the Gift of Prophecy to thofe who drank it ; but being at the fame Time unwholefome, it brought on Difeafes and fhortnefs of Life.

[b] Tacit. Annal. l. 2. c. 54.

fifted

ſisted at the ſame time ; the ancient Ones were frequently neglected, either from a diſcovery of the Im-
poſtures of the Prieſts, or by the Countries in which
they were placed being laid waſte by war, earth-
quakes, or the other Accidents to which Cities and
Kingdoms are expoſed.

But no part of Greece had ſo many Oracles as Bœotia, which were there numerous, from its abounding
in mountains and caverns ; for as Mr. Fontenelle ob-
ſerves, nothing was more convenient for the Prieſts
than theſe Caves, which not only inſpired the people with a ſort of religious Horror, but afforded the
Prieſts an opportunity of forming ſecret paſſages, of
concealing themſelves in hollow ſtatues, and of making Uſe of all the Machines, and all the Arts neceſſary to keep up the Deluſion of the people, and to encreaſe the Reputation of the Oracles.

Nothing is more remarkable than the different
manners by which the ſenſe of the Oracles was conveyed ; beſides the methods already mentioned, in
ſome the Oracle was given from the bottom of the
ſtatue, to which one of the Prieſts might convey himſelf by a ſubterranean Paſſage. In others by Dreams ;
in others again by Lots, in the Manner of Dice ;
containing certain characters or words, which were to
be explained by Tables made for that purpoſe. In
ſome Temples the Enquirer threw them himſelf, and
in others they were dropped from a Box ; and from
hence the proverbial Phraſe, The Lot is fallen.——
Childiſh as this Method of deciding the Succeſs of E-
vents by a Throw of the Dice may appear, yet it
was always preceded by Sacrifices and other Ceremonies.

In others the Queſtion was propoſed by a Letter
ſealed up and given to the Prieſt, or left upon the
altar, while the perſon ſent with it was obliged to lie
all Night in the Temple, and theſe Letters were to be
ſent back unopened with the Anſwer. Here this wonderful Art conſiſted in the Prieſts knowing how to o-
pen a Letter, without injuring the Seal, an Art ſtill
practiſed, on particular occaſions, in all the General-

Poft- Offices in Europe. A Governor of Cilicia, whom the Epicureans endeavoured to infpire with a contempt for the Oracles, fent a Spy to that of Mopfus at Mallos, with a letter well fealed up ; as this man was lying in the Temple, a perfon appeared to him and uttered the word Black. 'This anfwer he carried to the Governor, which filled him with Aftonifhment, though it appeared ridiculous to the Epicureans, to whom he communicated it, when to convince them of the Injuftice of the Raillery on the Oracle, he broke open the Letter, and fhewed that he had wrote thefe Words, Shall I facrifice to thee a White Ox or a Black ? The Emperor Trajan made a like experiment on the God at Heliopolis, by fending him a Letter fealed up, to which he requefted an Anfwer. The Oracle commanded a Blank Paper, well folded and fealed, to be given to the Emperor, who upon his receiving it, was ftruck with Admiration at feeing an Anfwer fo correfpondent to his own Letter, in which he had wrote nothing.

The general Charaƈteriftic of Oracles, fays the juftly admired Rollin (a), were Ambiguity, Obfcurity, and Convertability ; fo that one anfwer would agree with feveral different and even oppofite Events : and this was generally the cafe when the Event was in the leaft dubious. Trajan convinced of the Divinity of the Oracle, by the Blank Letter above mentioned, fent a fecond Note, wherein he defired to know, whether he fhould return to Rome after the conclufi on of the war which he had then in view ; the Oracle anfwered this letter by fending him to a vine broke in pieces. The prediƈtion of the Oracle was certainly fulfilled ; for the Emperor dying in the war, his body, or if you pleafe his bones, reprefented by the broken Vine, were carried to Rome. But it would have been equally accomplifhed had the Romans conquered the Parthians, or the Parthians the Romans, and whatever had been the event, it might have been conftrued into the meaning of the Oracle. Under fuch Ambi-

Ancient Hift. Vol. 5. p. 25.

guities

guities they eluded all Difficulties, and were hardly ever in the wrong. In this all their Art, and all their fuperior knowledge confifted ; for when the queftion was plain, the anfwer was commonly fo too. A man requefting a cure for the Gout, was anfwered by the Oracle, that he fhould drink nothing but cold water, another defiring to know by what means he might become rich, was anfwered by the God, that he had no more to do but to make himfelf Mafter of all between Sicyon and Corinth (a)..

VII. Of ALTARS, open TEMPLES, facred GROVES, and SACRIFICES.

ALTARS and Sacrifices mutually imply each o-ther, and were immediately confequent to the Fall of Man, tho' the original Altars were fimple, being compofed of Earth or Turf, or unhewn Stones. There is great Probability that the cloathing of our firft Parents confifted of the fkins of Beafts facrificed by Adam in the Interval between his offence and ex-pulfion from Paradife. Cain and Abel, Noah and the Patriarchs, purfued the Practife. Even thofe who for-fook the living God, yet continued this early Me-thod of Worfhip. Thefe Idolators at firft imitated the fimple manner in which they had been raifed by Noah. But the form and materials infenfibly changed; there were fome fquare, others long, round, or tri-angular. Each Feaft obtained a peculiar Form. Some-times they were of common ftone, fometimes of Marble, Wood, or Brafs. The Altar was furround-ed with carvings in Bas-relief, and the Corners orna-mented with Heads of various Animals. Some reached no higher than to the knee, others were rear-ed as high as the waift, while others were much high-er. Some again were folid, others hollow, to receive the Libations and the Blood of the Victims. Others were portable, refembling a Trevet, of a magnificent form, to hold the Offering from the Fire, into which

[a] Banier, Vol. 1.

they

they threw Frankincenfe, to over power the difagree-
able fmell of the Blood and burning Fat.   In fhort,
what had been approved on fome important occafion
paffed into a cuftom, and became a law.

Where the Altars were placed, there was faid to be
in the early ages of the World an Houfe or Temple
of JEHOVAH, which was moftly upon Eminencies, and
always uncovered.   Where they could be had, upright ftones were erected near them   This in Scripture is called fetting up a Pillar ; nor was it done
without a particular Form of Confecration.   The behaviour of the Patriarch Jacob, to whom we refer the
Reader [a], will explain the whole.

It is faid of Mofes likewife, That he rofe up early
in the morning, and builded an Altar under a Hill,
and twelve Pillars, &c. [b] The entire Work of
thefe facred Eminences was furrounded at a convenient diftance, by a Mound or Trench thrown up, in
order to prevent the profane Intrufion of the People
[c].

At other Times the Altars were enclofed by Groves
of Oak [d].   Whence this Tree is faid to be facred
to JOVE.   The Heathens, when they left the Object,
yet continued this ufage alfo of the original worfhip ;
which indeed was fo linked to Idolatry, that it became
neceffary for Mofes to forbid the Hebrews planting
Groves about their Altars, to prevent their falling into the Practifes of the Nations round about them.——
Thefe Groves were hung with Garlands and Chap-
lets of Flowers, and with a variety of Offerings in fo
lavifh a mannner, as almoft entirely to exclude the
Light of the Sun.   They were confidered as the peculiar Refidence of the Deity.   No wonder therefore

[a] Gen. xxviii. 18, 19, 20, 21, 22, and xxxv. 7, 14, 15.
[b] Exod. xxiv. 4. Thecketh, inferius, deorfum, on the Declivity of the Hill.
[c] Exod. xix. 12, 23.
[d] Gen. xxi. 33. xii. 6, 7. xxxv. 4. xiii. 18. Deut. xi. 30.
Judges ix, 6, &c.

that

that it was deemed the moſt inexpiable Sacrilege to cut them down [a].

The high Antiquity and Univerſality of Sacrificing beſpeak it a divine Inſtitution. The utter impoſſibility that there ſhould be any Virtue or Efficacy in the Thing itſelf, ſhews plainly that it muſt have been looked upon as vicarious, and having Reſpect to ſomewhat truly meritorious, and which thoſe who brought the Sacrifice were at firſt ſufficiently acquainted with the Nature of. For it is not to be preſumed upon what Grounds Men could be induced to think of expiating their ſins or procuring the divine favour by ſacrifical Oblations. It is much more reaſonable to conclude it a divine appointment. All nations have uſed it. They who were ſo happy as to walk with GOD, were inſtructed in it from age to age. And they, who rejected him, ſtill ſacrificed. But they invented new Rites; and at length, miſtaking and perverting the original intent and meaning, offered even human Victims! It is indeed moſt ſurprizing to obſerve, that almoſt all nations, from the Uſe of beſtial, have advanced to human Sacrifices; and many of them from the ſame miſtake and perverſion, even to the Sacrifice of their own Children!

This moſt cruel cuſtom among the Carthaginians, of offering Children to Saturn (b), occaſioned an embaſſy being ſent to them from the Romans, in order to perſuade them to aboliſh it. And in the Reign of Tiberius, the Prieſts of Saturn were crucified for preſuming to ſacrifice Children to him; and Amaſis,

[a] Lucan mentioning the Trees which Cæſar ordered to be felled, to make his warlike Engines, deſcribes the conſternation of the Soldiers, who refuſed to obey his orders, till taking an Axe he cut down one of them himſelf. Struck with a religious Reverence for the Sanctity of the Grove, they imagined that if they preſumptuouſly attempted to cut down any of its Trees, the Axe would have recoiled upon themſelves. They however believed it lawful to prune and clear them, and to fell thoſe Trees which they imagined attracted the Thunder.

[b] Thoſe Sacrifices were practiſed annually by the Carthaginians, who firſt offered the Sons of the principal Citizens; but afterwards privately brought up Children for that purpoſe.

B b

King

King of Egypt, made a Law, that only the Figures of Men should be sacrificed instead of themselves. Plutarch informs us, that at the Time of a Plague the Spartans were ordered by an Oracle to sacrifice a Virgin; but the Lot having fallen upon a young Maid whose name was Helena, an Eagle carried away the sacrificing Knife, and laying it on the Head of an Heifer it was sacrificed in her stead. The same Author informs us, that Pelopidas the Athenian General dreaming the night before the engagement, that he should sacrifice a Virgin to the Manes of the daughters of Scedasus, who had been ravished and murdered, he was filled with Horror at the inhumanity of such a Sacrifice, which he could not help thinking odious to the Gods, but seeing a Mare, by the advice of Theocritus the Soothsayer, he sacrificed it, and gained the Victory.

The ceremonies used at Sacrifices were extremely different, and to every Deity a distinct Victim was allotted [a]: but whatever Victims were offered, the greatest Care was to be taken in the Choice of them; for the very same blemishes that excluded them from being offered by the Jews, rendered them also imperfect among the Pagans.

The Priest having prepared himself by Continence, during the preceding night, and by Ablution, before the Procession went an Herald crying Hoc age, to give the People notice, that they were to give their sole attention to what they were about; then followed the Players on several instruments, who between the Intervals of Playing, exhorted the People in the same manner. The Priest, and sometimes the Sacrificers went before cloathed in White, and the Priest, besides being dressed in the Vestments belonging to his office, was sure to be crowned with a Chap-

[a] Lucian informs us, that, " The Victims were also different according to the quality and Circumstances of the Persons who offered them. The Husbandman, says he, sacrifices an Ox; the Shepherd, a Lamb; the Goat herd, a Goat. There are some who offer only Cakes, or Incense, and he that has nothing sacrifices by kissing his Right-Hand. De Sacr."

let

let of the leaves of the Tree sacred to the God for whom the Sacrifice was appointed; the Victim had his Horns gilt, and was also crowned with a Chaplet of the same Leaves, and adorned with Ribbons and Fillets. In Greece, when the Prieft approached the Altar, he cryed who is here? To which the Spectators answered, Many good People (a) The Prieft then said, Be gone all ye Profane, which the Romans expreffed by saying. Procul efte Profani. The Victim arriving at the Altar, the Prieft laid one hand upon the Altar, and began with a Prayer to all the Gods, beginning with Janus and ending with Vefta; during which the ftricteft Silence was obferved. Then the Sacrifice began, by throwing upon the Head of the Victim, Corn, Frankincenfe, Flower and Salt, laying upon it Cakes and Fruit [b], and this they called Immolitio, or the Immolition. Then the Prieft took the wine, and having firft tafted, he gave it to the Byftanders to do fo too (c), and then poured it out, or fprinkled the Beaft with it between the Horns. After this, the Prieft plucked off fome of the rough Hairs from the Forehead of the Victim threw them into the Fire, and then turning to the Eaft drew a crooked Line with his Knife along the Back, from the forehead to the Tail, and then ordered the fervants [d], to flay the Victim, which they had no fooner done than he was opened, and the Duty of the Arufpex began, which was no fooner over, than the Carcafs was cut in Quarters, and then into fmaller pieces, and according to Paufanias [e] and Apollonius Rhodius (g), the Thighs were covered with Fat, and facrificed as the part allotted to the God; (a) after which they

[a] Polloi Ka'gathoi.
[b] All thefe were not ufed for every Sacrifice.
[c] This was called Libatio.
[d] Thefe inferior Officers, whofe Bnfinefs it was to kill, to imbowel, to flay and wafh the Victim, were called Victimarii, Popæ, Agones, Cultrarii.
[e] Lib. 5. p. 192.
[g] In Att p. 42.
[h] In the Holocaufts, the whole Victim was burnt, and nothing left for the Feaft.

                    regaled

regaled themselves upon the reſt, and celebrated this religious Feaſt with Dancing, Muſick, and Hymns ſung in honour of the Gods.

Upon ſignal Victories, or in the midſt of ſome publick Calamity, they ſometime offered in one Sacrifice an hundred Bulls, which was called an Hecatomb: But ſometimes the ſame name was given to the Sacrifice of an hundred Sheep, Hogs, or other Animals.— 'Tis ſaid, that Pythagoras offered up an Hecatomb for having found out the Demonſtration of the forty ſeventh propoſition in the firſt Book of Euclid.

VIII. Of the PRIESTS, PRIESTESSES, &c. of the Greeks and Romans.

IN the early Ages of the World the Chiefs of Families compoſed the Prieſthood; and afterwards when publick Prieſts were appointed, Kings, as Fathers and Maſters of that large Family which compoſed the Body-politick, frequently offered Sacrifices; and not only Kings, but Princes and Captains of Armies. Inſtances of this kind, are frequently to be met with in Homer.

When the Ancients choſe a Prieſt, the ſtricteſt Enquiry was made into the Life, the Manners, and even the bodily external Perfections of the Perſons to be choſen. They were generally allowed to marry once, but were not always forbid ſecond Marriages.

The Greeks and Romans had ſeveral Orders of Prieſts; but as Greece was divided into many independent States, there naturally aroſe different Hierarchies. In ſeveral Cities of Greece the Government of Religion was intruſted to Women, in others it was conferred on the Men; while again in other, both in Concert had a Share in the Management of it. The Prieſteſſes of Argos were very famous At Athens a Prieſteſs preſided over the worſhip of Minerva; there was alſo a Prieſteſs for Pallas, at Clazomenæ; for Ceres, at Catanea, &c. The Hierophantæ, were very famous Prieſts of Athens, and both they and their Wives, who were called Hierophantidæ, were ſet apart

apart for the Worship of Ceres and Hecate, as were the Orgionphantæ, and the Women ſtiled Orgiaſtæ, appointed to preſide over the Orgies of Bacchus, &c. Beſides, the Prieſteſs of Apollo, at Delphos, who was by way of Eminence called Pythia (a) ; there belong-ed to thſs Oracle five Princes of the Prieſts and ſeve-ral Prophets, who pronounced the ſenſe of the Oracle. There were alſo chief Prieſts, one of whom preſided over a city, and ſometimes over a whole Province ; ſometimes he was inveſted with this Dignity for Life, and at other Times only for five Years. Beſides theſe, there were chief Prieſteſſes, who were the Su-perintendants of the Prieſteſſes, and were choſen from the nobleſt Families ; but the moſt celebrated of theſe was the Pythia.

The Prieſts of Rome enjoyed ſeveral very conſider-able Privileges, they were exempted from going to war, and excuſed from all burthenſome Offices in the State. They had commonly a Branch of Laurel and a Torch carried before them, and were allowed to ride in a Chariot to the Capitol. Romulus inſtituted ſix-ty Prieſts, who were to be at leaſt fifty Years of Age, free from all perſonal Defects, and diſtinguiſhed both by their Birth and the Rectitude of their Morals.

The Pontifex Maximus, or the High-Prieſt, was eſteemed the Judge and Arbitrator of all divine and human Affairs, and his Authority was ſo great, and his Office ſo much revered, " That all the Emperors, " after the Example of Julius Cæſar and Auguſtus, " either actually took upon them the Office, or at

---

(a) Thus the Prieſteſs of Pallas at Clazomenæ, was called Heſychia, and that of Bacchus, Thyas, and in Crete, that of Cy-bele, Meliſſa. Among the Athenians, the inferio Miniſters were ſtiled Paraſiti, a Word that did not at that Time carry with it any mark of Reproach ; for it is mentioned in an Inſcription at Athens, that of two Bulls offered in Sacrifices, the one ſhould be reſerved for the Games, and the other diſtributed among the Prieſts and Paraſites. Theſe Paraſites had a Place among the chief Magiſtrates, and the principal Part of their Employment was to chooſe the Wheat appointed for their Sacrifices. Banier's Myth. Vol. 1. p. 283.

" leaft ufed the Name, (a)." He was not allowed to go out of Italy tho' this was difpenfed with in Favour of Julius Cæfar; whenever he attended a Funeral, a Veil was put between him and the Funeral Bed; for it was thought a kind of Profanation for him to fee a dead Body.

The Rex Sacrorum (b), according to Dionyfius of Halicarnaffus (c), was inftituted after the Expulfion of the Roman Kings, to perpetuate the Memory of the great fervices fome of them had done the State. On this account the Augurs and Pontifices were directed to choofe out a fit perfon, who fhould devote himfelf to the care of Religious Worfhip, and the Ceremonies of Religion, without ever interfering in civil Affairs: but left the Name of King, which was become odious to the People, fhould raife their Jealoufy, it was at the fame time appointed, that he fhould be fubject to the High Priefts. His Wife had the title of Regina Sacrorum.

The Flamines, according to Livy (d), were appointed by Numa Pompilius, to difcharge thofe religious Offices, which he imagined properly belonged to the Kings. At firft there were but three (e], which were chofen by the People, and their Election confirmed by the High Prieft. They were afterwards increafed to fifteen, three of whom were chofen from amongft the Senators, and were called Flamines Majores; and the other twelve chofen from the Plebians, were ftiled Flamines Minores.

The Feciales were alfo inftituted by Numa, and confifted of twenty perfons, chofen out of the moft

[a] Kennet's Rom. Antiq,
[b] He was alfo ftiled Rex Sacrificulus.
[c] Lib. 1.   [d] Liv. lib. 1.
[e] The Flamen dialis of Jupiter, the Martialis of Mars, and the Quirinalis of Quirinus. The firft facred to Jupiter, was a Perfon of a very high Diftinction, tho' he was obliged to fubmit to fome burthenfome Regulations and fuperftitious Obfervances His Wife was a Prieftefs and had the Title of Flaminica; and alfo enjoyed the fame Privileges, and was under the fame Reftrictions as her Hufband. Aulus Gellius, Noct. Att. l. 10. c. 15.

diftin-

diftinguifhed Families.   Thefe were properly the He-
ralds of the Republick, who, whenever it was injured, were fent to demand fatisfaction, which if they
could not obtain, they called the Gods to witnefs
between them and the Enemy, and denounced War.
They had the Power of ratifying and confirming Al-
liances, and were the Arbitrators of all the Differences between the Republick and other Nations ; fo
that the Romans could not lawfully take up Arms
till the Feciales had declared that War was moft ex-
pedient.

The Pater Patratus derived his name from a circumftance neceffary to his enjoying the Title, and in
order that he might be more ftrongly interefted in the
Fate of his Country, he was to have both a Father
and a fon living at the fame time. He was chofen
by the College of Feciales out of their own Body, to
treat with the Enemy on the fubject of War and
Peace.

The Epulones were Minifters appointed to prepare
the facred Banquets at the folemn Games, and had
the Privilege of wearing a Robe like the Pontiffs, bordered with purple. Thefe Minifters were originally
three in number, to which two were afterwards added, and then two more, till in in the Pontificate of
Julius Cæfar they were encreafed to ten. The moft
confiderable of the Privileges granted to the Epulones
was one which they enjoyed in common with the o-
ther Minifters their not being obliged to make their
Daughters Veftals (a).

Befides thefe were the Salii, or Priefts of Mars:
The Phæbades of Apollo, the Baffarides of Bacchus,
the Luperci of Pan, and feveral others who prefided
over the Worfhip of particular Deities, each of which
had a particular College, and conftituted a diftinct
Community.

[a] Aulus Gellius, lib. 1. c. 12.

Of the TEMPLES of the Pagans.

OAKEN Groves with a circular Opening in the Midſt, or upright Stones placed in the ſame order, incloſing an Altar, were the original Temples — The firſt covered one was that of Babel; and in all Probability it was the only one of the kind, till Moſes by erecting the Tabernacle, might give the Egyptians the firſt thought of building a Houſe for their Gods. Had Temples been built in Egypt at the Time when Moſes reſided there, it can hardly be conceived but that he would have mentioned them; and that this moving Temple might ſerve as a Model for the reſt is the more probable, as there is a near Reſemblance between the Sanctum Sanctorum, and the holy Places in the Pagan Temples. In that of Moſes God was conſulted, and none ſuffered to enter but the Prieſts; this exactly agrees with the holy Places in the Heathen Temples, where the Oracle was delivered.

It was the opinion of Lucian that the firſt Temples were built by the Egyptians, and that from them this cuſtom was conveyed to the People of the neighbouring Countries; and from Egypt and Phænicia it paſſed into Greece, and from Greece to Rome.

They all began with little Chapels, which were generally erected by private perſons, and theſe were ſoon ſucceeded by regular buildings, and the moſt magnificent Structures, when even the Grandeur and Beauty of the buildings heightened the Veneration that was entertained for them. They had often Porticoes, and always an Aſcent of Steps, while ſome of them were ſurrounded by Galleries ſupported by Rows of Pillars. The firſt part in entering theſe Temples was the Porch, in which was placed the holy Water for the Expiation of thoſe that entered into the Temple. The next was the Nave (a) or Body of the Temple, and then the holy Place (b), into

[a] Naos.
[b] Called Penetralis, Sacrarium, Adytum.

which

which none but the Priests were allowed to enter
Sometimes there was behind the Building another part,
called the back-Temple.

The Inside was frequently adorned with Paintings,
Gildings, and the richeſt Offerings, among which
were the Trophies and Spoils of War. But the principal Ornaments were the Statues of the Gods, and
thoſe of Perſons diſtinguiſhed by great and noble Actions, which were ſometimes of Gold, Silver, Ivory,
Ebony, and other precious Materials.

The Veneration for theſe Buildings was carried by
the Romans and other Nations to the moſt ſuperſtitious
Exceſs. Before the erecting one of theſe noble Edi-
fices, the Aruſpices choſe the Place, and fixed the
Time for beginning the Work: for here every Thing
was of Importance. They began when the Air was
ſerene, and the Sky clear and unclouded; on the Limits of the Building were placed Fillets and Garlands,
and the Soldiers whoſe Names were thought auſpicious, entered the Encloſure with Boughs in their
Hands. Then followed the Veſtal Virgins, attended
by ſuch Boys and Girls who had the Happineſs to
have their Fathers and Mothers living, and theſe
aſſiſted the Veſtals in ſprinkling all the Ground with
clear Water; then followed a ſolemn Sacrifice, and
Prayers to the Gods, to proſper the Building they were
going to erect for their Habitation: And this being
over, the Prieſt touched the Stone that was to be firſt
laid, and bound it with a Fillet, after which the Magiſtrates, and Perſons of the greateſt Diſtinction, aſſiſted
by the People, with the utmoſt Joy and Alacrity in
removing the Stone, which was extremely large, fixed
it for a Foundation, throwing in with it ſeveral ſmall
Gold Coins, and other Pieces of Money.

When theſe Buildings were finiſhed, they were conſecrated with Abundance of Ceremony, and ſo great
was the Veneration felt by the People for the Temples,
that they frequently, as a Mark of Humiliation,
clambered to them on their Knees; and ſo holy was
the Place, that it was thought criminal for a Man to
ſpit or blow his Noſe in it. The Women proſtrated
themſelves

themselves in them, and swept the Pavements with their Hair. They became Sanctuaries for Debtors and Criminals; and on all Holidays were constantly decked with Branches of Laurel, Olive and Ivy.

One of the first Temples built in Egypt, was that of Vulcan, at Memphis, erected by Menes: At first it had the primitive Simplicity of all other antient Buildings, and without Statues [a]; but the Succeffors of this Prince strove to excel each other in embellishing this Work with stately Porches and Statues of a monstrous Size. There were indeed a great Number of Temples in Egypt, but the most extraordinary Thing of this Kind was a Chapel hewn out of a single Stone, which by order of Amasis was cut out of the Quarries of upper Egypt, and with incredible Difficulty carried as far as Sais, where it was designed to have been set up in the Temple of Minerva, but was left at the Gate. Herodotus mentions this Work with Marks of Astonishment: " What I admire more, " says he, than at the other Works of Amasis, is his " causing a House to be brought from Eliphantina, a " House hewn out of a single Stone: which two " thousand Men were unable to remove thither in less " than three Years. This House was thirty-one Feet " in Front, twenty-one Feet in Breadth, and twelve " in Height; and on the inside twenty-seven Feet in " Length, and seven Feet and a half high."

The Temple of Diana at Ephesus [b], has been always admired as one of the noblest Pieces of Architecture that the World has ever produced. It was four Hundred and twenty-five Feet long, two Hundred Feet broad, and supported by an Hundred and twenty-seven Columns of Marble sixty Feet High, twenty-seven of which were beautifully carved. This

[a] According to the best Historians, there were no Statues in the ancient Temples of Egypt. But this is not at all strange, since Plutarch, who has his Authority from Varro, says, That the Romans were a hundred and seventy Years without Statues; Numa prohibited them by Law; And Tertullian lets us know, that even in his Time there were several Temples that had no Statues.

[b] This Temple was accounted one of the Wonders of the World. Temple,

Temple, which was two hundred Years in Building, was burnt by Eroftratus with no other View than to perpetuate his Memory: However, it was rebuilt and the laft Temple was not inferior either in Riches or Beauty, to the former, being adorned with the Works of the moft famous Statuaries of Greece.

The Temple of Ceres and Proferpine was built in the Doric Orders, and was of fo wide an extent, as to be able to contain thirty Thoufand Men; for there were frequently that Number at the Celebration of the Myfteries of the two Goddeffes. At firft this Temple had no Columns on the Outfide; but Philo afterwards added to it a magnificent Portico.

The Temple of Jupiter Olympius, as well as the admirable Statue of Jupiter placed in it, were raifed from the Spoils which the Elians took at the Sacking of Pifa [a]. This Temple was of the Doric Order, the moft antient, as well as the moft fuitable to grand Undertakings; and on the Outfide was furrounded with Columns, which formed a noble Periftyle. The Length of the Temple was two hundred and thirty Feet, its Breadth ninety five, and its Height, from the Area to the Roof, two hundred and thirty.——From the Middle of the Roof hung a gilded Victory, under which was a golden Shield, on which was reprefented Medufa's Head; and round the Temple, above the Columns hung twenty-one gilt Bucklers, which Mummius confecrated to Jupiter after the Sacking of Corinth. Upon the Pediment in the Front was reprefented with exquifite Art, the Chariot-Race between Pelops and Oenomaus: And on the back Pediment, the Battle of the Centaurs with the Lapithæ at the Marriage of Pirithous; and the Brafs Gates were adorned with the Labours of Hercules. In the Infide, two Ranges of tall and ftately Columns fupported two Galleries, under which was the Way that led to the Throne of Jupiter.

The Statue of the God and this Throne were the Mafter-pieces of the great Phidias, and the moft magnificent and higheft finifhed in all Antiquity. The

[a] Paufanias in Eliis, p. 303. & feq.

Statue,

Statue, which was of a prodigious Size, was of Gold and Ivory, so artfully blended as to fill all Beholders with Aftonifhment. The God wore upon his Head an Olive Crown, in which the Leaf of the Olive was imitated in the niceft perfection. In his Right Hand he held the Figure of Victory, formed likewife of Gold and Ivory; and in his Left a golden Scepter, on the Top of which was an Eagle. The Shoes and Mantle of the God were of Gold, and on the Mantle were engraven a Variety of Flowers and Animals. The Throne fparkled with Gold and precious Stones, while the different Materials, and the Affemblage of Animals and other Ornaments, formed a delightful Variety. At the four Corners of the Throne, were four Victories that feemed joining Hands for a Dance; and at the Feet of Jupiter were two others. On the Forefide, the Feet of the Throne were adorned with Sphinxes plucking the tender Infants from the Bofoms of the Theban Mothers, and underneath were Apollo and Diana flaying the Children of Niobe with their Arrows, &c. At the Top of the Throne, above the Head of Jupiter, were the Graces and Hours. The Pedeftal which fupported the Pile, was equally adorned with the reft: It was covered with Gold; on the one fide Phidias had engraven Phœbus guiding his Chariot; on the other, Jupiter and Juno, Mercury, Vefta and the Graces. Here Venus appeared as rifing from the Sea, and Cupid receiving her, while Pitho, or the Goddefs of Perfuafion, feemed prefenting her with a Crown: There appeared Apollo and Diana, Minerva and Hercules. At the Foot of the Pedeftal were Neptune and Amphitrite, with Diana, who appeared mounted on Horfeback. In fhort, a woollen Veil died in Purple, and curioufly embroidered, hung down from the Top to the Bottom. A large Balluftrade painted and adorned with Figures encompaffed the whole Work; There with inimitable Art was painted Atlas bearing the Heavens upon his Shoulders, and Hercules ftooping to eafe him of his Load. The Combat of Hercules with the Nemæan Lion, Ajax offering Violence to Caffandra, Promotheus in Chains, and a Variety of other Pieces of Fabulous Hiftory.

Thi

This Temple was paved with the fineſt Marble, a-dorned with a prodigious Number of Statues, and with the Preſents which ſeveral Princes had conſecrated to the God.

Though the Temple of Apollo at Delphos, was greatly inferior in Point of Magnificence to the former, yet the immenſe preſents ſent to it from every quarter, rendered it infinitely more Rich. The principal Value of the former aroſe from its containing the works of Phidias, and his Maſter-piece was really invaluable ; but what this Temple wanted, in not containing the production of ſo curious an Artiſt, was amply made up by a Profuſion of Treaſure, which aroſe from the Offerings of thoſe who went to conſult the Oracle. The firſt Temple which was built being burnt the Am-phictyones, or general Council of Greece, took up-on themſelves the Care of rebuilding it ; and for that Purpoſe agreed with an Architect for three hun-dred Talents, which amounts to Forty-five thouſand pounds, and this ſum was to be raiſed by the Cities of Greece : Collections were alſo made in Foreign Countries. Amaſis, King of Egypt, and the Grecian Inhabitants of that Country, contributed conſiderable Sums for that Service. The Alcmæonedes, one of the moſt powerful Families in Athens, had the charge of conducting the Building, which they rendered more magnificent, by making, at their own Expence, con-ſiderable Additions that had not been propoſed in the Model.

After the Temple of Delphos was finiſhed, Gyges, King of Lydia, and Crœſus, one of his Succeſſors, enriched it with an incredible Number of the moſt valuable preſents, and after their Example, many other Princes, Cities, and private Perſons, beſtowed upon it a vaſt Number of Tripods, Tables, Veſſels, Shields, Crowns, and Statues of Gold and Silver of incon-ceivable Value. Herodotus informs us [a], that the Preſents of Gold made by Crœſus alone to this Tem-ple, amounted to more than two Hundred and Fifty

[a] Her. Lib. 1. c. 50, 51.

C c

Talents

Talents, or 33,500l. Sterling ; and it is probable that thofe of Silver were not of leſs Value. And Diodorus Siculus (a) adding thefe to thofe of the other Princes, computes them at ten Thouſand Talents, or about 1,300,000l. (b).

Plutarch informs us (c), that amongſt the Statues of Gold, which Crœfus placed in the Temple of Delphos, was one of a Female Baker, of which this was the Occaſion : Alyattus, the Father of Crœſus, having married a ſecond Wife, by whom he had Children; ſhe formed the Deſign of ſecuring the Crown to her own Iſſue, by putting a Period to the Life of her Son-in law ; and with this View engaged a Female Baker to put Poiſon into a Loaf, that was to be ſerved up at the Table of the young Prince. The Woman ſtruck with Horror, at the thought of her bearing ſo great a ſhare in the Guilt of the Queen, let Crœſus into the Secret : on which the Loaf was ſerved to the Queen's own Children, and their Death ſecured his Succeſſion to the Throne, which when he aſcended, from a Senſe of Gratitude to his Benefactreſs, he erected this Statue to her Memory in the Temple of Delphos. An Honour that our Author ſays ſhe had a better Title to, than many of the boaſted Conquerors or Heroes, who roſe to Fame only by Murder and Devaſtation.

Italy was no leſs famous for abounding in Temples than Greece ; but none of them were more noble or more remarkable for the ſingularity of their Form, than the Pantheon, commonly called the Rotundo, originally confecrated to all the Gods, as it is now to all the Saints. It is generally believed to have been built at the expence of Agrippa, Son in law to Auguſtus. This noble Fabric is entirely round and with-

<hr>

(a) Diod. Lib. 16. p. 453.
(b) It is impoſſible to form any tolerable Idea of theſe Sums without bringing alſo into the Account the comparative Scarcity of Gold at that Time, which rendered its real Value vaſtly greater than what it bears at preſent. The Mines of Mexico and Peru have deſtroyed all Compariſon.
(c) Plut. de Pyth. orac. p. 401.

out Windows, receiving a sufficient Degree of Light from an opening admirably contrived in the Center of the Dome. It was richly adorned with the Statues of all the Gods and Goddesses set in Niches. But the Portico, composed of sixteen Columns of granate Marble, each of one single Stone, is more beautiful and more surprising than the Temple itself, since these Columns are five Feet in Diameter, and thirty-seven Feet high, without mentioning the Bases and Chapiters. The Emperor Constantius the Third, stripped it of the Plates of gilt Brass that covered the Roof, and of the Beams, which were of the same Metal. Of the Copper Plates of the Portico, Pope Urban, the Eighth, afterwards formed the Canopy of St. Peter; and even of the Nails, which fastened them, cast the great Piece of Artillery, which is still to be seen in the Castle of St. Angelo.

But of the Roman Temples the Capitol was the Principal; with an account of which we shall therefore conclude. In the last Sabine War, Tarquinius Priscus vowed a Temple to Jupiter, Juno and Minerva. The Event of the War corresponded with his Wishes, and the Auspices unanimously fixed upon the Tarpeian Mountain for the destined Structure. But little more seems to have been done towards it, besides this Designation, till the Reign of Tarquinius Superbus, a Prince of Loftiness and Spirit, conforming to his Name, who set about it in Earnest; having laid out the Design with such Amplitude and Magnificence as might suit the King of Gods and Men, the Glory of the rising Empire, and the Majesty of the Situation. The Volscian spoils were dedicated to this Service. An incredible sum was expended upon the Foundations only, which were quadrilateral, and near upon two hundred Feet every way: The Length exceeding the Breadth not quite fifteen Feet. When the Foundations were clearing, a human Head was found, with the Lineaments of the Face entire, and the Blood yet fresh and flowing: Which was interpreted as an Omen of future Empire. This Head was said to have belonged to one Ollus or Tolus;

whence

whence the Structure received its compound Name.
Tho' possibly it might be as well to deduce the Name
from CAPUT only; and that too upon another Account, because it was the commanding Part, the
Head and Citadel of Rome, and the chief place of its
religious Worship. The Edifice was not finished till
after the Expulsion of the Kings; the Completion of
it being a Work, says Livy, reserved for the days of
Liberty. It stood the space of 425 Years to the Con-
sulate of Scipio and Norbanus, when it was consumed
by Fire; but was rebuilt By Sylla, whose Name was
inscribed in Letters of Gold upon the Fastigium or
Pediment of it. In the midst were formed three Cells
or Temples, separated by thin Partitions, in which
stood the golden Images of the Deities, to whom it
had been devoted. Those of Juno and Minerva were
on each side of Jupiter; for it was not usual for him
to be worshipped without the company of his Wife
and Daughter. The three Temples were covered by
one Eagle with his Wings expanded. This wonderful Structure seems to have been of the Doric Order,
in Imitation of those raised to the same Deity in
Greece, and abounded with curious Engravings and
every plastic Ornament, particularly the Fastigium.
The spacious Entrances, or Thresholds, were composed of Brass. The Lofty Folding Doors, which
were of the same Metal, most elegantly embossed,
grated harsh Thunder upon brazen Hinges, and were
afterwards entirely overlaid with Plates of Gold. The
tessellated pavement struck the Eye with an astonishing Assemblage of rich Colours from the variegated
Marble. The Beams were solid Brass; and the Splendor of the fretted Roof was dazzling; where (a).

—The glittering Flame
Play'd on the Temple's Gold and awful Height,
And shed around its trembling Rays of Light.

(a) Flamma nitore suo Templorum verberat Aurum,
　　Et tremulum summa spargit in æde Jubar.
　　　　　　　　　　　　　　OVID Fast. l. 9.
　　　　　　　　　　　　　　　　Without,

Without, the Covering was of Plates of Brafs, fafhioned like Tyles, which being gilt with Gold, reflected the Sun beams with exceffive Luftre. The Front to the South was encompaffed with a triple Row of lofty Marble Columns beautifully polifhed, brought from the Temple of Olympian Jove at Athens, by Order of Sylla : All the other Sides by a double Row.——— The Afcent was by an hundred fteps that gently rofe, which made the Paffage to it extremely grand and ftriking.

But this Capitol was likewife burnt in the Civil War between Vitellius and Vefpafian ; and reftored by the latter, with fome Addition of Height : It quickly after underwent the fame Fate and was raifed again by Domitian with more Strength and Magnificence than before ; who arrogated the whole Honour of the Structure to himfelf. The Poets were miftaken, when they promifed to this laft Fabric an eternal Duration : For not many Years intervened before it was fired by Lightning, and a great Part of it confumed. The Left-Hand of the golden Image of Jupiter was melted. Afterwards, under Arcadius and Honorius, the Plunder of it was begun by Stilicho ; who ftripped the Valves or Folding-Doors of the thick plated Gold which covered them : In one part of which was found a grating Infcription, declaring them RESERVED FOR AN UNFORTUNATE PRINCE. Gizeric, King of the Vandals, carried with him into Africa moft of its remaining Ornaments, among which one Half of the gilded Tyles of Brafs ; and great part of it was deftroyed by Totilas the Goth. Theodoric indeed made fome Attempts to repair the Capitol, the Amphitheatre, and other the more fplendid Buildings of the City, but in vain ; the prevailing Light of Chriftianity left them for the moft part ufelefs and deferted.

INDEX.

A

INDEX.

INDEX.

INDEX.

B.

INDEX.

INDEX.

INDEX.

D.

D d

Diomede.

Fame

INDEX.

F.

G.

        Good

INDEX.

INDEX.

I.

Inferior

L.

N.

O.

Ops,

INDEX.

INDEX.

Q.

R.

S.

D d   Tantalus,

INDEX.

T.

Theia

INDEX.

X.

Z.

FINIS.

www.ingramcontent.com/pod-product-compliance
Lightning Source LLC
Chambersburg PA
CBHW051214120726
47905CB00004B/1117